Knight

Kristen Ashley

Discover other titles by Kristen Ashley:

www.kristenashley.net

Knight

ISBN-10: 0615803830
ISBN-13: 9780615803838

Warning

This book is an ADULT EROTIC romance featuring an anti-hero. This novel contains explicit scenes of pain play, domination (control) and bondage. The hero in this novel lives a life by his own code with no apologies. In an effort not to spoil it for you, I will not explain further about the hero, but he is most definitely not your (or my, in my other books) "normal" hero. Please read the Author's Note, but if you do not enjoy the above, I would suggest that this novel is not for you.

Author's Note and Acknowledgements

Knight is a departure from my usual novels insofar as it is shorter as well as more erotic, exploring the building of trust and connection between two people falling in love. Heads up: there are heavy elements of control and erotic punishment in this novel.

It is my goal as a female writer to send a message through my novels that no matter how wacky zany, shy or wounded you may be, you need to stop listening to that demon that sits in your head and start to pay attention to those around you who love you.

Embrace yourself, even your faults, and understand you have something to contribute, and more, people want it, love it, crave it.

Further, baby can have back, an awesome rack and a Buddha belly and still find a wonderful man who makes her melt because she has all she has and is all she is. The media bombards us with images that we take in as desirable; our inner demon absorbs these and tells us that is what we should strive to be.

And it is impossible.

This is damaging.

And I don't like that. Because my inner demon tells me the same thing and I fight it all the time. And my work is one of the ways I do that.

My books won't change the world, I know. But if they inject just a little bit of steel in your spine that lets you go forth into the world as you, only you, and expect what you should expect, that you are beautiful and worthwhile and people see that, my job is done.

Further, if you've read any of my books, you'll know I feel that a healthy sex life with a compatible partner is crucial to a relationship. In this book, I explore this further.

All of it.

Just as every woman should feel beautiful and worthwhile, she should feel desirable and explore her sexuality with a partner who makes this safe and protects her and their relationship along the way. This, too, is a theme in all my books, but especially this one.

Kristen Ashley

Writing is my passion. It is also my livelihood. So I was understandably anxious about making my already racy books even racier. In an effort not to offend my readers, I reached out to a posse of women, readers and friends, to read this with me as I wrote it. The pouring forth of support, encouragement, excitement, friendship and love was un-be-freaking-leivable. They gave me the strength to tell Knight and Anya's story to its fullest. It is not erotica, it is a love story. But it is an erotic one.

So I would like to thank these women who took my back. They know how much it meant to me but you should too. So Jenny Aspinall, Sali Benbow-Powers, Gitte Doherty, Shelley Egerton, Lori Francis and Nikki Griffiths, thank you, my Secret Project Action Team. You made this fun and *beautiful*. Love you, my girlies, straight to the bottom of my heart.

And lastly, to Chasity Jenkins-Patrick who was my first cheerleader in this project and who always takes my back, if you don't know already, God shined his light on me when you hit send on those emails. Know it.

To everyone else, I give you *Knight*. I hope you love it as much as me and my girlies.

Chapter 1

Pointless but It's Somethin'

I was standing in the corner.

I didn't want to be there. I hadn't wanted to be there for a while, and I was considering making a move not to be there anymore when he walked in.

But these thoughts flew from my head. In fact, every thought flew from my head as I caught sight of him and blinked.

Then I stared.

He was tall. I had no idea how to describe how tall he was, but the only word I could think of was "very". Very tall. He was wearing a nice, tailored, black wool overcoat. With the lighting, all I could see was that he had on trousers. Not their color or style, just that they weren't jeans or cords. I could also see he had on nice shoes. Those could also be described as the "very" variety of nice. They were shiny and clearly expensive. Other than that, with his side to me, I couldn't take anything else in.

And I really didn't try.

I was fascinated by it all, but my attention was taken by his face. His features, even mostly in profile, were striking. Not perfection, but so intensely masculine I'd never seen anything like it. It was almost unreal.

But his hair surprised me. He had on an expensive overcoat, expensive shoes, and he was here, at this party, in this lavish apartment in a way that I knew, unlike me, he belonged here. But his very dark, thick, slightly wavy hair needed a cut. It wasn't long and unkempt. It was simply longish and unruly. Like he had better things to do than to get regular haircuts, and those things weren't clubbing, hanging with his crew and taking fastidious care of his body, clothing and all other parts of his physical being so that he could play and then nail every female who threw herself at him.

Then again, if he did that, he'd never come up for air.

His height, his clothes, his looks, his hair were not all that fascinated me.

He was angry. It was not only etched in the hard line of his strong jaw, his lips pressed together in unconcealed annoyance or his gaze sharp on the scene that lay before him.

It was physical. A swell of vibrating heat that filled the room.

I wasn't the only one who noticed. With some effort, tearing my eyes away from him, I saw those closest to him had turned to look at him. Some were even taking a few steps away to retreat.

I didn't blame them. I was all the way across the room in the corner and I still felt it. But if I was close, I, too, would shift away.

It was terrifying. Utterly.

I wondered if Nick had a roommate, and my guess was he did. My other guess was he had no idea Nick was having a party.

My eyes swept the space. The sunken living room and the elevated areas surrounding it were cluttered with bodies. There was a bottle of champagne that had overturned on the coffee table, and it clearly had been at least half full considering the wet stain on the carpet and the puddle on the table. I knew two people had broken glasses. I heard them. One, some girl cleaned up. The other, the pieces had been kicked around and likely smushed into the kickass furry carpet or ground into the dark wood floors, luckily not causing any injuries (yet). There were beer bottles, liquor bottles and glasses everywhere, even sitting on the floor or having rolled under tables. There were overfull ashtrays, ashes on the floor, even butts. The music wasn't ear-splitting loud, but considering it was after one in the morning, it was still too loud. The neighbors in this swank building definitely could hear it, not to mention the noisy buzz of conversation, and they probably wouldn't like it.

I knew I wouldn't, and I didn't.

And neither did Nick's roommate.

My eyes went back to where he was standing and they did this hesitantly. Part of me wanted to see him again. I was a woman and he was the kind of man a woman would look at. Any woman. No matter what their tastes ran to. He just attracted female attention and any woman would want a second look. Part of me was scared to look, mostly because he was pretty scary. This was because a man who could walk into a room wearing an overcoat, be there a moment and fill the room with a searing, angry vibe *was* pretty scary.

But when I looked back, he was gone.

And I took this as my cue to be gone.

I didn't want to come anyway, but Sandrine had had her sights set on Nick for a while now. Viv and I had told her time and again he was a player, and we knew this because we knew a number of girls he'd played. But Sandrine saw him as the golden goose. She spent a goodly amount of time on the hunt for the golden goose, and the minute she laid eyes on the handsome Nick Sebring she decided he was The One.

The minute I laid eyes on him my stomach turned. He was good-looking, this was fact. He was also a jerk. This was impossible to miss. And he was something else. Something I couldn't put my finger on, something I didn't like. Not at all.

But to Sandrine, he had it all. Flash, dash, beauty...

And money.

Yes, my friend was a gold digger.

Still, call me crazy (and I called myself that more than once over my years of knowing her) I loved her. She was a pain in the behind a lot of the time, and I had to say her single-minded pursuit of The One (just as long as The One was gorgeous, built and loaded) kind of freaked me out sometimes, alarmed me others and flat out scared me on occasion. But at least she knew who she was and what she wanted.

And this, I thought, surveying the scene, was what she wanted. She wanted to reign as queen at exactly this kind of scene. Free-flowing booze and champagne. Well-dressed lackeys. Sumptuous apartments with sunken living rooms, state-of-the-art kitchens and wraparound balconies. And we'd put our coats in Nick's bedroom so I'd had a quick look. Seriously, one look at Nick's bedroom and even I nearly reconsidered his jerk status. It was that gorgeous.

Then, approximately a half a second later, I remembered nothing was worth putting up with a jerk. Not even a beyond gorgeous bedroom. Especially not a jerk like Nick.

I put my mostly unconsumed drink on the black marble countertop that adorned the long bar that separated the kitchen from the living room and started to make my way to the balcony.

I didn't want to do this and this was the reason why I was hiding in a dark corner. I'd tried mingling, but this wasn't my scene and the people there knew it just as well as me. Sandrine told me I should buy a dress and keep the tags on, just tuck them in to hide them. She also told me to buy a pair of shoes and she'd go with me to make a scene if they wouldn't accept the return because they were scuffed. But I thought this was uncool, so I refused like I did all the other times Sandrine suggested this.

She didn't mind doing this and did it all the time. Sweat stains, martini stains; it didn't matter. Once she'd even returned a pair of shoes whose strap broke while she was dancing. And it was the fourth time she'd worn them.

Not me.

So I was wearing a pair of high-heeled sandals I bought two years ago. They were cute, even, I thought, sexy but they were cheap, not even real leather. I'd taken care of them, but still, they looked what they were. Same with my dress. TJ Maxx, and not even a way out of season designer. Just a no name. I thought it was pretty. It showed just enough skin, not too much, it fit like a glove and it was the perfect color for me, But it wasn't silk, satin or labeled. It was polyester, and even at TJ Maxx I bought it on sale.

And the eyes came to me, moving up and down, lips curling, noses scrunching, eyes rolling.

This was the girls.

The guys, eyes right to my breasts, hips or legs. At this point of the evening, they didn't care if they banged class or someone who thought they could buy it. They just wanted to bang anything and would take what they could get.

Sandrine had headed out to the balcony about half an hour ago with Nick. She'd not returned so this was my destination. Therefore, my journey was a long one, weaving through bodies, avoiding crossed legs or stepping over straightened ones of those sitting on couches, feeling gazes following me the entire way.

It seemed to last an hour but probably lasted around two minutes.

Then I was through the glass door and outside.

It felt good out there; cold but good. No smoke, the stuffiness of too many bodies in a space gone. I allowed myself a moment to drink it in.

Then I looked around.

A couple to the right in a clinch. Not Sandrine.

I turned my head left, and nearly at the corner of the balcony I saw Nick had Sandrine against the floor to ceiling window. They were also in a clinch.

Ugh.

I clicked over in my inexpensive (but cute) sandals, and when I got somewhat close called, "Uh... sorry to disturb."

Nick's head came up and both of their eyes came to me. Otherwise, they didn't move a muscle.

Nick's eyes dropped to my breasts.

Sandrine's eyes widened in a clear but nonverbal, "What the fuck are you *doing* here?" She finally had him where she'd wanted him for a long while and she wasn't happy to be disturbed.

"Again, sorry," I said quietly when I got close and looked to Sandrine. "Honey, I need to go home."

"Okay," she replied immediately. "Text you tomorrow."

I blinked.

We had a pact: never leave a man behind. Not to mention we'd shared a taxi, and since we were sharing one back and she'd driven to my house that meant such a treat was affordable.

"Um... but—" I started.

"I'm good," she cut me off. "Nick can take me home when I go home." Her head turned to Nick. "Right, Nick?"

He didn't move his eyes from my breasts for a moment before they drifted lazily to my face.

"Why are you leaving?" he asked and I stared at him.

What did he care?

"Well, it's getting late and—" I began to explain.

He interrupted with, "Stay."

"Pardon?" I asked.

"Stay," he repeated. Then a grin spread on his face that I did not like. Not that I liked much about Nick, as in nothing. His head turned to Sandrine, who he still had pinned to the windows, then back to me, and in a low voice with unmistakable meaning, he said softly, "The three of us, we'll have a party."

I blinked again, even as I stiffened and saw Sandrine doing the same.

Then I stated firmly, "No, actually, I need to go home, which is where I'm going." I looked to my friend. "Sandrine?"

She looked miffed, not a little, a lot.

At me.

God, Sandrine.

Then she looked at Nick and announced, "I don't do three-ways. It's just me or nothing."

He looked at me. "You uptight like that?" he asked.

See? Jerk!

"Absolutely," I answered.

"Shame," he muttered. Then, still looking at me, "Though, figure, just you'd be enough."

Seriously?

"Seriously?" This came sharp and from Sandrine.

Told you Nick was a jerk. And something else. And whatever that something else was was not good.

"Right, if that's the gig then whoever's stayin' stays and whoever's leavin' leaves," Nick went on, and he did this eyes on Sandrine, who he had pinned to the windows, but somehow, and it wasn't lost on Sandrine or me, he was insinuating it was her he wanted to leave.

God, I hoped this opened her eyes to this dirtbag.

I should have known better. Those eyes came to me and she said, "I'll text you tomorrow."

Somehow, some way I needed to get her to snap out of it. I wished Viv was here with me. She'd lay it out. Then again, she had, more often and with less gentleness than me, and Sandrine never listened to her either.

"Sandrine—"

"Anya, honey, *I'll text you tomorrow.*"

She was getting impatient. She was also living firm in the mistaken knowledge that her beauty (and she *was* beautiful), her style (ditto with the style, she had it in spades) and her abilities between the sheets (I had no idea about that one, though, according to her, she was fabulous) would twine Nick Sebring close and he wouldn't want to break free.

"Sandrine, I'm not comfort—" I started yet again.

"Anya," she cut me off again. "I'll... text... you... *tomorrow.*"

She gave big eyes to Nick who was looking at me and didn't notice. These eyes indicated that I was missing the fact she had her golden goose in her snare and I needed to vamoose, and pronto, so she could work her magic.

I didn't like this. You didn't leave a man behind, but you *really* didn't leave a man behind with Nick Sebring.

But other than drag her kicking and screaming out of the apartment, down fifteen floors and into a taxi, I didn't know what to do.

So I muttered, "Tomorrow."

She grinned at me.

I frowned at her and tried to communicate seven thousand words about Nick being a jerk with my eyes. But she just turned back to him, lifted her hand to his cheek and turned his face to her.

Really, Vivica was right. Sandrine was living in a fantasy world. She'd had a daddy who treated her like she was precious, told her she was beyond beautiful and spoiled her rotten. Then she'd had a high school boyfriend who did the same. Then in college, another boyfriend, the same. From birth to twenty-two, she'd had the golden life, gliding on her beauty and feminine wiles. She hadn't cottoned on to the fact that, after leaving college five years ago, she'd entered the jungle. And further, the particular jungle she chose to hunt in had bigger, more ferocious predators, even after a number of them had already chewed her up and spit her out.

With no choice, I called a soft, "Goodnight," and turned away.

I received no farewells.

I didn't look back.

I headed to my coat, and luckily I had something to do while I did it so I didn't have to feel the eyes on me or see the looks. As I wended my way through bodies and muttered vague "excuse me's", I was pulling my little (cheap but cute) purse open to pull out my cell.

By the time I got to the mouth of the hall, I had it out.

The apartment was strange. I thought this because it was huge. I'd never been in an apartment that large before. I didn't even know they came that large. But it also had a bizarre layout.

Bizarre or not, it was cool, and even if it wasn't my thing and it didn't look all that great now stuffed full of bodies and the detritus of a party, I couldn't say it wasn't stunning. It was.

You walked into a wide hall, at the side of which one wall had two doors (closed). The other was just a wall that delineated the hall from the kitchen. This hall led to the living room, which was mostly sunken; three steps down to the seating area. But around its perimeter was an elevated, wide, dark wood-floored area, and two sides of the living room were surrounded by floor to ceiling windows.

Another hall led off this just as you hit the living room area. It was L-shaped. This had two doors down one side; one at the end, and then you turned down the L and another door at the end of that hall.

Nick's gorgeous bedroom. Where my coat was.

I wandered down the hall toward my coat, head bent, activating my phone. I got to the bend in the L when my phone went blank in my hand and my feet stopped as I stared at it.

"Crap," I whispered, hitting the on button to no avail. I tried again. Still no go. "Crap," I repeated my whisper.

I needed a new phone. I knew this. I was saving for it and was only two paychecks away from buying it. My phone lost its charge in an hour and had been doing so for the last month and a half. My next phone was going to be a good one, not a cheapie. This was not because I wanted to keep up with the gadgets. This was because I'd been through three cheap phones in as many years and I felt this investment was sound. If I had a phone that cost three times as much as the ones I'd been buying but lasted for three years with zero headaches, I'd be ahead of the game.

I looked to the end of the hall where Nick's bedroom was and was about to start walking again but my body froze solid.

This was because on the floor in the hall was a huge pile of coats.

I stared, shocked. I, myself, had put my coat on a pile on Nick's bed. Now they were on the floor in the hall.

I looked from the coats to the end of the hall.

The bedroom door was open, the lights on and blazing, unlike before when I put my coat there and the lights were dim, romantic. An indication of a promise of what was to come for the girl who would be lucky enough (gag) to join Nick there later.

Jeez, some drunk idiot tossed all the coats in the hall. I hadn't seen anyone acting like an idiot, but there were people who were careening beyond inebriated to sloshed. This happened at an open bar where the booze was plentiful and flowed freely, seeing as it was free.

I pulled in breath and walked to the coats. Doing a knees closed squat, I held my cell and purse in one hand and pawed through the coats with my other one. Finding mine, I yanked it out and straightened. I did this with my eyes aimed down the hall but unfocused. They focused when I spied the shiny silver, thin, curving, unbelievably cool cordless phone in a black dome base sitting on the nightstand in the bedroom.

That phone was the means to a taxi. One without having to ask someone in the living room if I could use their phone, interrupting Sandrine and Nick again, or hoofing it on the sidewalk in hopes I'd find a payphone, then standing outside in the cold to wait.

Excellent.

I carefully skirted the coats, having to step on some as it was impossible to move around them without doing this, and walked into the bedroom to the phone. I didn't look around, even though I wanted to take a closer look. I wanted more to get the heck out of there.

I picked up the phone from its base thinking the same thing I thought the first time I walked into that room. The room smelled odd. An attractive blend of some heady masculine aftershave or cologne and cigarette smoke. Yes, cigarette smoke. But it blended strangely well together, making the room seem wicked, but in a good way. Now, the cigarette smoke was the stronger of the two, when before it was the aftershave/cologne smell. This was less attractive but more wicked.

I thanked the powers that be that taxis, something I rarely took because I could rarely afford them, had their numbers emblazoned on all their cars. I had dialed in the four and one of the four, one, two, four, one, two, four number when I heard a low, smooth, very deep, definitely annoyed man's voice asking, "What the fuck?"

My head swiveled and I froze in mid-dial.

The tall man with dark, disheveled, longish hair and freakishly masculine, markedly attractive features was standing in one of the two sets the arched French doors that led to the balcony across the room. He was smoking. He'd lost his overcoat and I saw he was wearing a deep lilac, slim-fit tailored shirt that showed he not only was tall, but broad, lean and had a torso unmistakably packed with power,

Oh, and he was pissed.

Oh my.

And.

Oh crap.

"Uh…" I mumbled then mumbled no more as he swiftly knifed sideways, clearly to stub out his cigarette. His angry, dark gaze sliced back to me as his long legs started bringing him to me.

Crap!

"You got a cell in your hand," he informed me. "You need to hit my room and my phone?" he asked.

Yes.

Pissed.

"Uh…"

He was moving across the room so I again shut up.

This room too had a sunken level. The large bed was on the normal level and it was covered with a black satin comforter (yes, *satin*) with black satin cases on the pillows (satin!) which meant satin sheets. The black lacquered headboard was very tall, as tall as me. The footboard was at least half a person high. The head of the bed was flanked with two black lacquered nightstands that were elegantly shaped and topped with lamps with slim, glossy black bottoms and wide but squat ivory shades. The bed was sitting on an ivory rug that had a slender black border edged in a thicker ivory.

The same rug was in the sunken area that also held an ivory, sweep-lined couch tumbled with black toss pillows and an equally sweep-lined black armchair with ivory toss pillows that had a matching ottoman. There was also an oval, black lacquered coffee table down there, and tall, now-illuminated floor lamps flanking the couch that coordinated with the lamps on the nightstands.

Up three steps was another area with a matching-but-narrow rug that looked made to fit the space. On either end were identical tall, black lacquered chests of drawers topped with bigger lamps with wider bases. But, like the floor lamps, they somewhat matched the ones on the nightstands.

All the lights were turned on, including the three overhead ones, which had stunning arrays of pinned but dangling crystals covering them.

And last, there were three doors along the wall. Two closed. One opened though not lit, but I could still see it was a bathroom.

I took all this in distractedly because he was making his way to me and I was paralyzed.

He was moving up the steps closest to me as he called, his eyes slightly narrowing, "Hello? Are you breathing?"

"I thought this was Nick's room," I blurted, and he stopped suddenly by the footboard of the bed.

"It's not," he ground out.

Yep. Totally. *Pissed.*

And yep.

Totally.

Scary.

Terrifying.

Utterly.

"I need to go home," I whispered. "I came in a taxi and I need to call one to take me home. My cell, it's acting up. It doesn't hold a charge for more than an hour. It's dead. I should have known. I didn't think. But I came here with my girlfriend, so I guess I thought she could call. She's staying, though. And I put my coat in here and I thought it was Nick's room, seeing as he told us to put our coats in here. I just thought I'd use your phone real quick and get a taxi. I'm so sorry. I had no idea this wasn't Nick's room and I was intruding. Truly. I'm very sorry."

I stopped talking and he stared at me.

It was then I saw his eyes were blue. A strange, startling, dark, vibrant, *Prussian* blue.

And they were beautiful; the color, the shape, the long, curving lashes.

My breath stuck in my throat.

His eyes dropped, but not to my breasts, my hips or my legs.

To my arm, which was attached to my hand that was clutching my purse, my cell and had my coat draped over it.

They cut back to my face and in his smooth, deep voice, he declared, "I'll take you home."

I blinked.

He moved.

I braced, but before I could do a thing about it or say a word he slid his phone from my fingers. He leaned deep into me and I smelled that the after-shave or cologne was his.

I was right. It was attractive. So attractive all I could do was stand still and take in that glorious scent.

He put the phone in its charger then leaned back and took my coat from my arm.

At that, I came out of my freeze.

"Um… I don't——" I started, but clamped my mouth shut when his fingers curled around my upper arm, and suddenly I found my body turned so my back was to him.

"Arm," he ordered.

I twisted my neck to look at him at the same time I tried to force myself to breathe.

"What?" I whispered.

He was standing behind me with my coat held up for me to slide into.

"Arm," he repeated, sounding a lot less patient. And considering he didn't sound patient at all before, this was even *more* terrifying.

"I think—" I started, but said no more when his hand shot out, grabbed my wrist and pulled it back. It wasn't rough. It didn't hurt. But I was shocked all the same.

He dipped my coat and slid it up my arm.

"Other arm," he commanded, and without delay, I awkwardly switched my purse and cell to my other hand and reached behind me to find the sleeve of my coat.

In no time I felt his hands settling it on my shoulders. One moved, wrapped around my bicep and suddenly I was facing him. Then I was moving with him to the door, his hand still on my arm.

I struggled but I found my voice.

"I'm really okay with a taxi," I told him as he pulled me out of the room. He slightly tugged my arm and brought me to a stop.

Totally ignoring me, he curved his torso around the door and did something around the knob. He came out, his hand going the other way, and the lights were extinguished, making the room go black. He closed the door, locked it, pocketed the key and turned us to the hall.

He did all of this with his hand still holding my arm.

It was at this point I realized my heart was racing and I was finding it difficult to breathe.

Then I stopped breathing altogether when he shifted quickly, bending into me. I had time enough to sway an inch away from him before I was up in his arms.

My legs flying through the air, reflexively, I slid one arm around his hard-muscled shoulders, the other one swinging out in front of him to grab my hand at his neck and hold on as he strode *over* the coats, walking right on the pile.

Holy crap!

Once free of the coats, he bent and dropped me to my feet. It again wasn't rough, but it wasn't gentle, and my body jolted when my feet hit floor. I had no time to recover, not from being on my feet again, not even from being *off* them, not from the easy way he swung me into his arms like I weighed as much as a body pillow.

Not from *any* of it.

Not before his fingers curled around my upper arm again and he propelled me down the hall and around the bend in it.

Okay, I had to get control of this situation and do it *now*.

I opened my mouth to do just that at the same time I was about to tug my arm from his hold when he stopped abruptly, stopping me with him. His head slightly cocked before his angry, blue eyes cut to me, and I forgot I had to get control of the situation and do it *now*. I forgot everything.

For some reason he adjusted me, not gently, not cruelly, but definitely firmly to the side of one of the doors in the hall.

He let me go, and without knocking he opened the door, but where I was situated, I couldn't see inside.

I heard a woman's horrified gasp and a man starting, "What the——?"

"I gotta take someone home," my unwelcome ride told the couple. "You got that time to turn off the fuckin' music, empty this fuckin' place of bodies and clean up as much as you can. She wants to finish that ride you're meanin' to give her, she helps you clear out this place. She doesn't help, get her ass outta here, too. You don't want me to come home to see you not takin' me seriously and I hope you get me 'cause I'm not fuckin' with you, Nick, and I am not happy."

Then he stepped out and closed the door. He grabbed my arm again and pulled me down the hall.

My first thought was that he'd just walked in on Sandrine and Nick.

My second thought was obviously Nick had a less spectacular room.

My third thought was that he'd positioned me to the side of the door. I found this surprising and intriguing because he'd heard them in there. They couldn't have gotten far, but they definitely were moving things on. Still, he'd shielded me from whatever was behind that closed door, and I didn't know what to make of that.

We'd rounded the other hall on our way to the front door when I cleared these thoughts and came back to the matter at hand.

"Um… listen, uh…" Damn! "Um, I don't know your name but——"

"Knight," he stated, cutting me off.

"Right, Mr. Knight——"

"No, Knight," he interrupted me again. He stopped me by one of the doors in the hall, let me go and opened the door.

"That's what I said, Knight," I told him. "Now, Mr. Knight—"

He came out of that door with his overcoat and turned his eyes to me.

I interrupted myself then when they hit me and I clamped my mouth closed.

"No, not Mr. Knight. *Knight.* My name is Knight."

I stared up at him as he shrugged on his overcoat and then asked, "Your Christian name is Knight?"

"If that means first name, yeah," he answered. He grabbed my arm and pulled me down the hall to the front door.

As he did, curious at this information even though I should be seeing to other business, I asked, "With a 'K'?"

He looked down at me as he opened the door, "Yeah, babe, with a 'K'."

Then he pulled me out the door.

"That's an unusual name," I muttered.

"Yeah," he agreed, dragging me down the luxuriant hall toward the elevators.

"I kind of like it," I blurted, because I did. But after I blurted that I kind of wished I didn't.

"I can die happy," he murmured.

I pulled in breath at his murmured, mild sarcasm, which was kind of funny instead of being rude, and this man did not strike me as a guy who could be funny, kind of or otherwise.

He pulled me to a stop at the elevator and I watched him lean in and tag the button. This was when I saw he had hands that matched his body. Attractive. Long fingers. Well-veined. They weren't professionally manicured, but his nails were well-kept, even if his hands looked like the hands of a man who didn't have a lavish bedroom in an opulent apartment and wore expensive shoes, tailored shirts in a color that suited him so well a stylist had to pick them for him, and pricey overcoats.

Time to stop thinking about his hands and sort this.

"Knight, I appreciate the offer, really. Thank you, but truly, I can get a taxi home."

"Yeah, you can but you aren't."

"I—"

His eyes sliced to me and I braced.

"Listen, babe, I take you home, I'm doin' something. Something that requires my attention. Like driving, getting a woman home safe, then driving back here. This will give me time maybe to calm down. And this will take my mind off the fact I wanna rip Nick's dick off, shove it up his ass and send that motherfucker over my balcony."

Without my brain telling me to do so, I yanked my arm free of his hold. My feet took me one step away from him and my hand came up to press against the gleaming, wood-paneled wall by the elevator as I stared up at him.

I didn't know if he meant this. I didn't think he did. It would be bad form to toss your roommate over a balcony, even if he did have a party you obviously weren't invited to that happened to occur in your own home. Not to mention, it was highly illegal.

I did know he was angry.

And last, I knew he didn't mind sharing just how angry he was, and doing it with a woman he did not know in any way. He'd dragged me through an apartment, didn't let me finish hardly any sentences and *picked me up* to carry me over a pile of coats that *he* obviously threw in the hallway.

I had my hand on the wall because my legs were shaking and I needed it there to help hold me up. And my legs were shaking because I remembered he terrified me. And there was reason. He was terrifying.

As I stood there wondering if I should scream at the top of my lungs or turn on my cheap (but cute) high-heeled sandal and run as fast as I could, something happened.

He started paying attention to me.

Although it was sheer lunacy that I considered it unflattering, I did, and what I considered unflattering was the fact that suddenly he seemed to be looking at me and actually *seeing* me. Until I shifted away from him, I didn't exist. I was just an excuse to get him away from his apartment and Nick before he let loose his fury. Now he was looking at me, his eyes moving over me, taking me in. My face. My hair. My hand pressed against the wood paneling. Down the length of me to my shoes and up.

And when his eyes caught mine again, his face was no different. Hard jaw, angry eyes. Pissed, but not at me.

But his voice was soft when he said, "I won't hurt you."

"I'd really like to take a taxi," I whispered.

Swiftly and almost imperceptibly (but I caught it, and he meant me to) his eyes dropped to my feet then came back to mine.

"Taxi won't be a hit?" he asked, still soft, and I knew that he knew from what he saw of me that paying for a taxi would be a hit for me.

I straightened my spine, dropped my hand and assured him, "I'll be fine."

The elevator doors opened. Without taking his eyes from me he lifted his hand to catch one so it wouldn't close as he spoke. "I'll take you home. Safe. You'll have no problems from me. Just a ride. And you're doin' me a favor, givin' me a chance to calm my shit. But swear to Christ, you can trust me."

"I don't—"

"Babe, swear to Christ, I'm just a ride. Take advantage. And do me a favor and give me an excuse to get outta here."

I saw his anger now. I remembered what I felt when he walked into the apartment earlier. And it was fresh in my mind, all that had just happened to me at his hand. None of it hurt me, but all of it was bizarre in a dangerous, scary way that demonstrated irrefutably that I should know better than to court further time and attention from this man.

And still, I found my head tipping down so I could look at my feet. Feet that were walking me toward the elevator.

Knight shifted his arm high. I ducked under it to enter, and he entered after me.

The doors started closing as he tagged the button B2.

I stared at the doors.

Yes. Sheer lunacy.

"You're called?"

My neck twisted and my eyes moved up to his to see his looking at down me.

"What?" I asked.

"Name, babe."

"Anya."

He stared at me.

Then he asked, "Anya?"

"Anya," I confirmed.

"Anya," he repeated and I nodded. "And you think my name's unusual?"

"Yes, I've never met anyone named Knight," I informed him.

"And I've never met anyone named Anya," he informed me. "What is that?"

"What is what?"

"Your name."

"It's a family name. As in my grandmother's."

"Before that," he stated.

"It was her grandmother's," I shared.

"And before *that*," he pushed then explained, "Origins."

"Russian," I told him.

"You're Russian?" he asked.

"My grandmother was," I answered.

"She grow up here?" he asked.

"No, she grew up in St. Petersburg when it was called Leningrad. But she died here."

His head cocked slightly to the side but his face remained impassive. "Died?"

I nodded. "Seventeen years ago."

"Babe, what are you? Twenty-three? Four?"

"Seven."

His head righted. "Twenty-seven?" He sounded like he didn't believe me.

"Yes, twenty-seven."

He studied me but didn't give anything away.

Then he stated, "Still, she had to be young."

"Liver failure. She was Russian, as in from Russia. She drank vodka like it was water and that's not a stereotype. That's very real."

And it was. And she passed it down to my aunt, unfortunately.

He looked to the doors, muttering, "That's the fuckin' truth."

I kept my eyes to his profile and asked, "Are you Russian?"

The doors opened and his hand came to me. Not to my upper arm this time, but to my elbow, and he propelled me out, answering, "Fuck no."

His answer was emphatic and therefore insulting since I *was* half Russian, but I didn't call him on this. I also wondered at his knowledge of the Russian vodka drinking habit, but I didn't ask about it. I simply walked with him through the brightly lit, cement underground parking garage.

He took me to a sleek, shining, low-slung, gunmetal gray sports car, the likes I'd never seen. It was so clean it was gleaming, and it looked like it had been driven there direct from the showroom floor. I had no idea what it was, and the only clue was on the back it had the word "Vantage". I'd never heard of a make or model named "Vantage". All I knew was, like his bedroom, apartment and clothes, it was fabulous.

He moved me to the passenger side door and opened it for me.

"What kind of car is this?" I asked, aiming my behind to the seat.

"Aston Martin," he muttered, eyes to my feet that I was swinging in. That was all he said before I cleared the door and he threw it to.

Aston Martin. I wasn't sure, but I thought some James Bond or another (or several of them) drove Aston Martins.

Wow.

I buckled up and looked around, experiencing the feel that, like everything that had anything to do with Knight, was pure opulence.

He got in. He didn't buckle up but started the car, and it purred all around us.

Yep, pure opulence.

He wrapped an arm around my seat, twisted around and looked back to reverse. Once out, he straightened. He put the car in gear and away we went.

Fast.

Crap.

We were at the second level of parking under the building and I was reminded of one of my few (but I had them) irrational fears. That was the fact that I didn't like underground parking. Sure, there were huge cement pillars I knew someone with a great deal of schooling designed to hold up the weight of the big building. But all I could think was if that dude was drunk one day at work, screwed up and the building came tumbling down; there was no hope for me. It didn't help that Knight had a high performance vehicle and that he clearly liked to explore the boundaries of its functionality, so now he was scaring me in a different way.

He hit a button as we were speeding up the ramp that would take us to freedom. He luckily slowed for the gridded gate (that kept the riffraff out) to slide up, then we were out of the danger zone and idling at the entrance to the street.

I took a breath.

Knight called, "Babe."

I looked at him to see he was looking at me. Or, more accurately, looking at my hand that had a death grip on the armrest of the door.

His eyes came to me and he declared, "One, been drivin' since I was twelve. I know what I'm doin', so you can quit tryin' to fuse with the car, relax and enjoy it. Two, I kinda gotta know where I'm goin'."

"You've been driving since you were twelve?" I asked.

He didn't answer. Instead, he asked back, "Where am I goin'?"

"Capital Hill."

He looked away, turned left and I gave him my full address.

Conversation was non-existent as he negotiated the streets like he was attempting to set the land speed record from downtown Denver to Capital Hill. I tried to "relax and enjoy it". I failed spectacularly at this effort, but didn't fail at prying my hand from the armrest, though I did knot both in my lap while praying.

We hit my block and he found an unusual nighttime, daytime or anytime parking spot on the street two houses down from my building. However, it wasn't a spot, as such. More like an opening. Still, in one go, with a speed that made my heart slide in my throat, parallel parking, he whipped that expensive car into a space that I was certain wouldn't fit it, but somehow did.

I closed my eyes, sucked in a breath and turned to him to thank him, grateful the night was over and relieved my time with him was too.

But my view was of his back as he was angling out of the car.

"Crap," I whispered, uncertain I liked his peculiar demonstrations of gentlemanliness. Giving me a ride. In a not-offensive way noting I needed one. Shielding me from whatever I'd see in the bedroom. Gentleman and Knight didn't go together somehow. I found it perplexing in a way I knew I shouldn't give any headspace, seeing as this was the one and only time I'd be in his presence, but I also knew I'd give headspace way beyond this night.

I unbuckled. My door was opened, his long fingers were wrapped around my elbow and I was out. He slammed the door and guided me to the sidewalk but stopped us both.

I looked up at him, preparing to tell him I was grateful for the ride and his attention and he didn't have to walk me to my building, but the words didn't come out. This was because his eyes were aimed down the block, and my eyes went where his were.

My street had, back in the day when the economy was booming, flourished. The houses had been renovated, repainted and landscaped beautifully. Two crappy apartment buildings had fallen so smart, trendy condos could be built on their lots. The cars on the street were new to new-ish. Maybe not luxury, but not economy and the vibe was quiet. Families or double-income couples lived in these homes and condos. They cared about them and this was reflected on the entire block.

Except my apartment building, which was where Knight was looking. It was old. No attention had been put into what it would look like when it was built. No attention was put into how it was now maintained. It was a blight on the neighborhood. The good thing was rent was low and it came with a parking spot. The bad thing was the neighbors hated it, hated the landlord, and sometimes, by association, hated the tenants, which included me.

Now, weirdly, Knight was staring at it, again his face giving nothing away, but his contemplation of it was deep.

"Knight," I called softly. His head jerked very slightly and his eyes tipped down to me. "You don't have to walk me to my building. I'm good. Thank you for bringing me home."

He didn't answer and again totally ignored me as, hand still curled around my elbow, he moved us toward my building.

"Really," I went on as we were walking, "this is a good neighborhood."

It was like I didn't speak. Eyes to my apartment building, he kept moving, his fingers firm around my flesh.

I sighed and gave up. It wasn't that far and soon this would be over.

We walked up the steps to the door and Knight stopped us.

I looked up at him to thank him again but he spoke before me.

"Punch in the code, babe."

I stared up at him and asked, "The code?"

He jerked his head to the keypad by the door.

I looked at it, knowing it didn't work because it hadn't for six months. Then I lifted a hand and pushed open the unlocked door. As I did this, I could swear I heard the quiet hiss of an indrawn, pissed-off breath, but when my head quickly turned to him at the sound he simply drew us through.

Once inside he stopped us. He looked down at me and declared, "Babe, please tell me you don't live on the first floor."

This was a strange thing to say, and I looked into the hall at the doors of the apartments on the first floor.

Then I looked up at him and replied, "No, top floor."

"Thank Christ," he muttered.

He moved us, eyeing the first staircase that had a rope across it with a sloppily hand-printed notice tacked to it that said "Not in use." Then Knight was moving us to the elevators, but his step faltered when he saw the sloppily hand-printed sign on it that said "Out of Order." I definitely heard his sigh when he moved us to the other set of stairs and up them.

I didn't know what to make of this, but it kind of irritated me. I mean, he'd made it clear he knew where I was coming from, and that wasn't the land of sunken living rooms and Aston Martins. My building might be crap and the rent relatively cheap, but it was also in a relatively safe neighborhood, so the rent wasn't *that* cheap and thus the tenants were pretty awesome. For instance, we were walking up the stairs, there were no loud parties (unlike at *his* building) and all was quiet and peaceful.

We got to the third floor and he guided me down the hall, even though it was me who was leading us to my door. I chanced a glance up at him and noted his head was tipped back. Mine did too, and I saw that down the corridor, three of the five overhead lights were out. The hall was thus understandably murky. I'd called about this situation four times (as I had about the elevator, security system and stairs), but nothing had been done. So I stopped calling and decided to change the light bulbs myself, eventually, when I had a free second.

My body swayed toward my door and Knight took us there and halted us. I dug in my purse, coming out with my keys and my lips parted when his fingers closed around them. He slid them out of my hand and, like he had a sixth sense, he picked the right one. He inserted it, opened the door, swung inside and hit the light switch so my overhead light went on.

He grabbed my upper arm, pulled me in and closed the door but positioned me at the side of it.

Then, again weirdly, he looked me in the eye and ordered, "Do not move."

I blinked.

He moved.

I stared as he walked through my one-bedroom apartment into the kitchen that was open like his and delineated by a short breakfast bar. He switched on the light and looked around even though he could see everything (nearly) from the living room. Leaving the light on, he moved out. He opened the door to the bathroom, turned the light on, swung his torso in and looked inside.

What on earth was he doing?

Again, light left on, he swung out and moved to my bedroom.

My body jolted and I called, "Um... Knight?", but he didn't hesitate. The light went on and he disappeared behind the door.

Seriously, what on *earth?*

"Knight?" I called, taking two steps into my apartment, but he reappeared and prowled with his long-legged strides to me, face still impassive but eyes on me.

He stopped in front of me and held my keys out to me.

"You're good," he declared as I took them. "Nice to meet you, Anya."

Uh... what?

His eyes went to the door. They narrowed on it strangely, like the sight of my door pissed him off in a not at all vague way. He looked back at me and his eyes unnarrowed, but the pissed-off look didn't go away.

Then he muttered, "Jesus."

I stared at him, confused. Or, I should say, profoundly confused.

Before I could ask, though I was uncertain I would, he went out the door. He stopped in it and turned back, his eyes leveled on me, and he commanded, "Lock this after me, babe. Pointless but it's somethin'.

Then he was gone.

Chapter 2

We Slid over the Edge, Together, Holding Tight, into Nothing

I was sitting on the wraparound balcony. The cushions on the wrought iron furniture were comfy. The view of the Front Range was awesome. The sun was warm. I had a piece of toast in my hand and was about to take a bite when I stopped and twisted my neck to look over my shoulder.

Knight was walking to me; dark gray, drawstring pajama bottoms on, long-ish hair sexy messy from sleep, chest with its enticing array of dark hair bared, eyes on me.

I felt my lips curve.

"Hey," I whispered.

He didn't reply.

He walked to me, his hand gathering my hair then twisting it around. He tugged my head back. It wasn't gentle. It was rough, a hint of pain spiking through my scalp and shooting pleasure straight between my legs. So much, I felt my lips part as I watched his strikingly handsome face coming toward me.

I closed my eyes slowly and waited impatiently for his lips to hit mine.

I opened my eyes and I was in Mrs. Herndon's room. Second grade. I was sitting at my desk but I was an adult so the desk didn't fit me. There was a knock at the door. All the kids' eyes went to it and I felt my heart clutch, my stomach drop.

I remembered this. I'd never forget it. Not ever. Not ever.

Not ever.

Mrs. Herndon got up from her desk at the front of the room and walked to the door.

Don't go there! Don't open that door! My mind screamed, but I sat at that desk that was too small for me and just watched, not able to move, not able to do anything, just sit there, powerless, about to be cast adrift, lost in a way that felt like forever.

She disappeared behind the door and I kept my eyes glued to it, waiting... waiting...

She came back in and her gaze came right to me. I remembered that, too. I'd never forget. Not ever. Not ever.

Not ever.

Her face was gentle and kind, tender, embattled, pained.

No! No, no, no, no!

Then he walked through. Knight. His eyes on me too, his face blank, giving nothing away. But relief washed through me.

This wasn't how it happened. This was different. Better. Out there in the world a child had no control over, everything was torn from me but I had him. I had him.

Knight was there. Tall, broad, strong, dangerous. I could lean on him. He'd be there for me.

And he was. Without hesitation he walked to my desk, bent and grabbed my hand. His fingers closing warm and firm around mine, he pulled me away from the desk.

Right. Good. This was good. I could face this. I could face the pain. The loss. I could face this with Knight at my side.

My fingers curled deeper into his and his hand gave me a squeeze as he walked me through the room. All my classmates' eyes on me, Mrs. Herndon's head tipped slightly to the side, her eyes bright, tears shimmering.

We moved to pass her and I whispered, "I have Knight. It's all gonna be okay."

Her head jerked slightly. Her face became confused and her eyes lifted to Knight.

He walked me through the door, taking me toward unbearable pain.

Unbearable pain that this time I knew Knight would ease.

We walked out the door of my second grade classroom, Knight was gone and I was swept in a flood of water that flowed though the corridor. I tried to strike out toward a door knob, anything to grab onto, but I was moving uncontrollably toward the wall at the end of the corridor. The water and I broke through the wall, the bricks exploding, and I was in a swelled, rushing river. Nature all around. Me careening down the river, powerless. Huge boulders rising from the water came at me, but the current swept me to the side before I could crash into one and be broken to bits.

I fought. I moved my arms, my legs, trying to direct myself to the shore, but nothing I did changed the direction the flow was taking me.

I looked to the shore and saw Vivica running along it, her mouth open, her eyes terrified, shouting but no sound coming out. She tripped and fell to her hands and knees and disappeared.

Then there was Sandrine, running like Vivica, eyes on me, fear etched in her face. But suddenly Nick was there. She stopped, looked up at him, smiled and threw herself in his arms. His head bent, her hands went into his hair and they started kissing.

Figured.

Then, weirdly, since I hadn't seen him in years, there was my high school boyfriend, Sean. He was running along the shore too, his arms moving in a breast stroke, calling out instructions, I knew, even though no sound came out. I did what he said but nothing helped. I kept whirling and gliding violently with the stream.

"*Anya!*" he shouted, his voice tortured, he ran into a tree and vanished.

And then there was my aunt. She didn't move. Just stood on the shore, arms crossed on her chest, mouth smirking.

That figured too.

I lost sight of her and kept moving. Fighting. Exhausted. Terrified out of my mind. I was going to smash into one of those boulders. I knew it. I knew.

No, no. Fear pulsed through me as I saw up ahead the river falling away to nothing.

And there I was, alone, lost in a current I couldn't fight, careening headlong into nothing.

I felt him and my head jerked to the shore.

Knight.

He wasn't running along the side. Without hesitation, he dove in, his long body slicing through the air and into the water. Then he was cutting through it, his powerful arms bringing him straight to me.

Thank God, Knight.

Thank God, I wasn't going to face nothing alone.

I'd have Knight.

He made it to me, his arms wrapping around me, one hand sliding up my neck, into my wet hair, cupping the back of my head. My legs fought through the water to wrap around his hips as our bodies met. My arms wrapped tight around him and I held on.

"You're here," I whispered.

He didn't respond. He just held my eyes and held on.

And we slid over the edge, together, holding tight, into nothing.

My eyes blinked open as my body jolted, still in freefall from my dream.

I was breathing slightly heavily, trying to shake away the dream.

I dreamed a lot. It started in second grade. I remembered them when I woke up. They were clear, vivid, powerful. It didn't happen every night, but it happened frequently. Sometimes they were good. Sometimes they were horrifying.

I steadied my breath and shook off my dream.

Then I got up to an elbow, lifting my other hand to pull my hair away from my face and looked to the window with my misty, pretty (but cheap) curtains over the slightly battered Venetian blinds that came with the apartment. I felt under me the abrasive, worn pills of the cheap sheets I'd had too long, but I knew, after I bought my new cell phone, new, nicer sheets were on the schedule.

And I tried not to think about the fact that I could still feel Knight's arms tight around me.

Chapter 3
Filled with Knight

After I parked, I hurried to the trunk. I opened it up and grabbed my canvas bags filled with groceries, swinging one over my shoulder with my purse and snatching up the other two. I put one to the cement of the parking lot, slammed the trunk, nabbed it and hurried.

It was the Wednesday after the Saturday night party at Knight-slash-Nick's. Saturday night (or, really, Sunday morning), I'd dreamed of Knight. I'd also dreamed of him Monday night. And last night.

And I couldn't get him out of my head.

I knew why and there were several reasons.

One, he was hot. He might be scary, but scary never eradicated hot. Or, at least, not his kind of hot.

Two, he'd given me nothing. Well, he'd given me his anger, a hint he had a sense of humor and a tendency toward throwaway chivalrous gestures. But other than that, nothing. He didn't laugh, smile or talk very much. I knew he didn't like Russians. I knew he didn't like loud parties, people and mess in his apartment. I knew he had money and good taste, or sense enough (and the finances) to hire someone who did. But other than that, I knew nothing. Not even his last name. And, not knowing much, I didn't want him to, but he intrigued me.

Three, he'd picked me up and I'd felt his hard-muscled shoulders and the power of his body. It was affecting. I wasn't heavy, but I certainly wasn't slight. This, too, intrigued me, but in a very different way.

And last, after contemplating it for some time, (too much of it; like, nearly always), his reaction to my building irked me. He didn't shield me from his anger or his personality, such as it was, but his clear contempt of my living arrangements (and I was certain that was it), was offensive. It was also, though I couldn't know this but I felt it, out of character. No one who could show signs of courtesy and take care to be sensitive to the differences in our financial circumstances at the same time pointing them out should behave the way he did when he saw my humble abode. It didn't fit but it *did* annoy me.

As I rounded the building and walked up the front steps all of this was on my mind as it had been for days. Along with this I wondered *why* it was on my mind since I'd never see the guy again. And along with *this,* what was on my mind was that I couldn't deny the fact that this was upsetting. Like I knew at a glance Nick Sebring was a jerk, I knew at a glance Knight Whoever was dangerous. I should steer clear. I knew this and the fact of the matter was I had no choice. Knight Whoever and I would not cross paths. Still, I couldn't help but wish we did.

Which was crazy.

I put my hand holding the handles of one of my totes to the front door of my building and pushed in, my body moving with my push, and I slammed right into it. Mostly because it didn't move.

I blinked.

Then I pushed again.

It didn't budge.

What on earth?

I noticed movement inside. A man wearing gray pants and a matching gray shirt with a patch over his heart declaring his name was "Terry" and he worked for "Avionics Elevators" was coming my way and smiling. Automatically, I smiled back as his hand came to the inside handle and he opened the door.

"Everyone's doin' that," he told me as he held the door open for me.

I stared at him as I walked in and he kept smiling at me.

"Got a notice in your place that has the codes," he informed me as he let go of the door and it closed behind me.

I looked back, hearing it latch in a way it hadn't latched in months, then I looked back at Elevator Man Terry.

"The door is fixed?" I asked and he nodded.

"Yup, dude left when I got here. Keypad and call system, all a go."

Whoa.

Belatedly, I took him in and my eyes drifted to the elevators that had plastic barricades around with signs on them that said "Elevator out of order. Men working." The doors were opened and the naked elevator shaft was in view with work lights dangling inside.

I looked back at Terry. "You're fixing the elevator?"

"Nope." He shook his head. "Fixed. Needed a doohickey. Doohickey replaced, all's good." He tipped his head down to my totes and grinned again. "You live on one of the upper floors, you just got help."

"Cool," I whispered, even though I never used the elevator. This was another irrational fear I had. Buildings crushing me in underground parking lots and elevators plummeting me to my death. I avoided them if I could, and since I was capable of walking up two flights of steps at my apartment building, I did. I noticed his grin got bigger then I took in his patch and looked back at him. "Aren't avionics about airplanes?"

He shrugged, still grinning. "Boss is a good guy but he ain't too bright. Knows elevators, though. Just doesn't have much of a vocabulary. I think he thinks he made up the word. He might not be bright, but he's a decent dude so no one has enlightened him."

"Ah," I mumbled and he kept grinning.

I started moving toward the stairs, calling, "Well, thanks for fixing it."

"My job, darlin'," he called to my back.

I threw a smile over my shoulder and headed to the stairs.

Jeez, wonder if the jerk Landlord Steve won the lottery.

I made it to the third floor, turned into the hall and stopped dead.

Charlie, our rarely seen maintenance man, was on a stepladder switching out a light bulb.

"Yo, Anya," Charlie called when he spotted me.

"Hey, Charlie," I called back, moving toward him. "I see you've been activated too."

"Sho' 'nuff," he confirmed the obvious.

I stopped at the side of the stepladder and looked up to watch him screwing in a light bulb. "What lit a fire under Steve? Did someone call the building inspector or something?"

Charlie climbed down and grinned at me. "No idea. Doubtful though. Do know the man got roughed up. Split lip so fat it's a wonder he can talk. Eye purple and swollen shut. Holdin' his body funny so whoever it was took some shots at his ribs. Totally fucked up. That one plus his one of callin' on me made two, so I'm thinkin' Gearson in apartment 2C. His woman had a baby. Does shit to a man, especially when his bitch or him has gotta drag that stroller down a flight of stairs anytime they wanna take that kid somewhere."

I could see this. I knew Wash Gearson. He was quick to smile. If he saw you carrying stuff into the building, he'd help you with it. He always opened the door and let you go through first, and he loved his partner and new, adorable baby. They had a two bedroom on the second floor and I knew Wash got in Steve the landlord's face regularly. And seeing as Wash was a big, somewhat soft (but definitely not-a-guy-you-messed-with) black dude and Steve had messed with him, Wash had messed back.

I didn't condone violence, but I wasn't going to say no to a security system, an elevator that worked (even though I never used the latter, others did) and lighting in the halls that didn't make the place look ripe to become a location for a slasher flick.

"I don't think I'd let Wash hear you call his woman a bitch," I advised quietly, but still grinning.

"He calls her his bitch and we share the same lingo." This was true enough. Wash's mouth was even fouler than Charlie's, which was going to make child rearing interesting in the Gearson household. "Think he'd be cool," Charlie went on. "Especially when I fixed his fridge last week after he called me direct 'cause Steve didn't do shit for three days. This could be what tipped him. Though, call Bertha "Bertha" to her face."

Bertha, Wash's woman, had an unfortunate name. Luckily, her parents gave her glamorous beauty and life gave her a good man who might not make a mint, but he loved her, so that counteracted her name. I knew this because her smile was as easy as her man's and she laughed a lot.

"And, get this," Charlie went on, "monthly schedule. Even if the bulbs don't need changin' out, I come in first of the month and change the whole lot."

I stared at him and whispered, "Really?"

"Really, sweetheart, no fuckin' joke. Thought I was in an alternate universe when Steve came to see me today. Then again, I saw the results of the visit whoever gave him, so I'm also not surprised. You fuck folks around, eventually they'll fuck back. And since no one likes to be fucked unless they wanna be, when they're moved to do it, they fuck harder."

Charlie Philosophy. In the five years I'd lived there, he'd delivered it often. It was always liberally sprinkled in curse words. And it was always usually right.

"Words to live by," I muttered.

"Damn straight, Anya. Fuck only when they wanna be fucked. You never know what's gonna tip someone and you also never know who you're fuckin' knows."

"I'm not a fuck-with-people person," I shared and he smiled.

"Well, just in case you consider a turn to the dark side," Charlie advised.

"Right. Heard, cataloged, filed. Consider your wisdom processed, Charlie," I assured him and his smile got bigger. I moved as I said, "See you later, honey."

"Later, sweetheart," he replied. He grabbed his ladder and moved down the hall.

I did the juggling bit at the door to open it, walked through and saw the paper on the floor that had been slid under the door. I closed the door, ignored the paper and walked to the kitchen to dump my totes. Then I walked back, bent to retrieve the paper and turned it to face me. On it was a badly photocopied message.

Dear Tenant,

The building call system has been repaired as well as the security keypad. The new code is 7849. This code will be changed monthly and you will be notified by memorandum as well as emailed with the new codes one week prior to the code changing. If we do not have your email on file, please contact us immediately.

In the next two weeks, Charlie will be installing deadbolts and chains on all the doors. We will attempt to do this at your convenience but would prefer to do this during normal working weekday hours. Please complete and detach the slip at the bottom of this memo and return it to the management office with a time within the next two weeks that would be convenient for you.

As this work takes place, we thank you in advance for your patience.

-Management

I stared at the memo, the first of its kind in my tenure there, and definitely more polite than I'd ever expect in a million years coming from "Management", otherwise known as "Steve".

My eyes drifted to my door. There was one lock; it turned on the knob. I'd never thought anything of it, but as I stared at the door, a tingle slid up my spine, the back of my neck and radiated over my scalp.

Knight had stared at that door and what he saw pissed him off.

And now, out-of-the-blue, when I'd never complained about it, though I didn't know if anyone else did, we were getting deadbolts *and* chains.

"Babe, please tell me you don't live on the first floor."

He'd looked at the elevator. He'd noted the lights.

"Pointless but it's somethin'."

That tingle rushed back down and infused my entire body.

"Oh my God," I whispered.

"I got this." I heard Charlie say from outside the door.

"I got it." I heard another voice I recognized as my out-of-work, moron, slightly creepy, didn't-know-how-he-managed-to-pay-his-rent neighbor Dick, whose name said it all.

"No, I said... I got it," Charlie returned firmly, then there was banging at my door.

I moved to it and looked out the peephole. I saw Charlie and Dick standing out there and opened it because, although Dick was standing out there, so was Charlie.

"Hey," I greeted and Charlie stuck out a large, bubble wrap lined envelope at me.

"This came for you. Dick accepted receipt," Charlie announced. "Now Dick's goin' to his place, closing the doors, sittin' his ass down and thinkin' of baby bunnies."

I avoided Dick's eyes and pressed my lips together. I understood Charlie's meaning, but considered that if Dick's thoughts turned to bunnies they would be thoughts of boiling them or torturing them.

I took the envelope. The front had a label that was typed and said only "Anya, 3D"

"Thanks, uh..." my eyes slid through Dick, "guys."

"Later, Anya," Charlie said meaningfully. I looked at him and his face told me to close my damned door because Dick was a dick and Charlie didn't want him around me.

"Right, later," I replied, and I did as I wasn't told (but still was).

I locked the door that would soon have a deadbolt and chain, but my mind wasn't on Dick or Charlie or deadbolts or sudden activity making my apartment building safer at what had to be a serious cost. My mind was on the bubble wrap envelope that had no address, no last name, and I hadn't ordered anything.

I took it to the kitchen and ripped it open. I upended it and a shiny, black box slid out, as did a small, business card-sized card.

I stared at the box. I pulled out the cardboard tag that held it secure, opened the side and slid out the innards.

Then I froze and stared.

In my hand, wrapped up shiny and new, nestled in protective foam packaging, was a cell phone the likes I'd never seen. Glossy black on its curved shield-shaped outside, the entire front was a screen. I looked at the box and saw the brand. I'd never heard of it. I looked back at the phone and its accoutrement. Then I realized my heart was beating and doing it hard.

I put the box and phone down and tagged the card. It had fallen face down on the counter so I flipped it and stared at the black slashes that formed words.

Anya,

No woman should be without a functioning cell.

K

The tingle came back and it didn't start at my spine. It just straight out covered my entire body.

I knew no "K's". No friend. Definitely no family. No workmates. No one.

Except Knight Whoever.

"Oh my God," I whispered.

My home phone rang and I jumped.

I dropped the card and dashed to the phone in the kitchen.

"Hello," I greeted when I put it to my ear.

"Get this, day four almost done, no... fucking... call."

Sandrine.

I pulled in a breath and tried to shake off what was happening all around me, who I figured was responsible for it and what that might mean, and started, "Honey—"

"I helped him clean up for... like, *three hours,* in, like, the wee *morning* hours," she reminded me of something she'd already shared several times. Then she told me something that made my breath catch. Something she hadn't yet shared in her two days of bitching about Nick Sebring. "His brother came back, was a total, freaking asshole *to both of us,* and I took that. I cleaned, and after that I gave him all my good moves, which means he got off *twice,* plus *twice more* on Sunday. He promised he'd call and he hasn't. Player zone I get, it could take two days. Even three. *But four?*"

I powered through the knowledge that Knight was Nick's brother and reminded her, "Sandrine, this guy has jerk written all over him."

"*I gave him my best moves and four orgasms!*" she shouted and I winced.

Then I settled in and I did it silently. She had to work this out and I had to let her, even though I didn't have time. I had groceries to put away. I had a freak out about the possibility that Knight had roughed up my landlord and sent me an extortionately expensive cell phone to recommence and figure out my next move. I had to make a sandwich and get on the road so I didn't miss class. I had things to do.

"Now, I know, *I know,* no one gave him that," Sandrine informed me. "No way. And no way he was faking it. I know that, too."

Men, for obvious reasons, couldn't fake it, so I didn't know why she felt the need to point this out. And I didn't ask. I kept silent.

Sandrine didn't.

"And he doesn't come back for seconds? He doesn't ask me out? He doesn't do *anything?*" she asked and kept ranting. "I've called him four times, and, as you know, this breaks my golden rule of one call only. *Four times! Four voicemails!* And, I will add, two texts. And *nothing.*"

She shut up. I gave her a beat.

Then I told her, "Honey, I'm sorry. He's a jerk. They're all jerks. And we'll gab about this, but you know I have to get to class."

"Anya, this guy is The One," she told me.

"No, Sandrine, he's an asshole. And I'll point out one of his obvious asshole traits, and that was he suggested a *three-way* with you and your *best friend.*"

"Guys are into that shit," she dismissed.

"Yeah, definitely, but guys who could be The One most certainly aren't."

She had no reply and never did when I was right.

So I said yet again, "I have to get to class."

"Fuck me," she muttered, and I recognized she was sliding into self-absorbed, poor me zone. I had to take evasive maneuvers and fast or I'd miss class or be seriously late.

"Sandrine, this weekend. Your appointment. We'll talk," I promised.

"Right, and maybe we should hit it Saturday night, see if he's out."

God, seriously?

"We'll talk about it while I do your nails on Saturday. Now I gotta go."

"Four days, Anya," she whispered, sliding straight into the zone and holding on tight to take me with her.

I pulled in a steadying breath.

Then I said firmly, "Saturday, Sandrine."

Pause then, "Right, I'll call Viv. Laters."

Then she was gone.

God, Sandrine.

As I beeped off my phone, I reminded myself that there *were* things to love about her.

For instance, when Viv had that bad breakup that she didn't want to talk about, I was too busy with class and work to give her my attention like I'd want to. But Sandrine called her every day and went over to her house nearly every night to check in, keep her company and she didn't pry. And when I sprained my ankle badly, it was Sandrine who dropped everything and came to get me at the doctor then made everything easy for me to negotiate at my apartment. And Sandrine not only was a client of mine; she also talked me up to all her friends and co-workers in an attempt to help me build my clientele. And when Viv's Mom got that terrible, weird pneumonia that didn't seem to want to let her go, both Sandrine and I were at Viv's side when it looked like it was going to go south. And we both celebrated with her when it didn't.

Right, so Sandrine was a pain in the ass. But there were times that pain eased.

I put the phone in its charger and immediately began multitasking. Freaking out about Knight's possible activities at the same time putting away groceries. Then I freaked out at the same time I made a sandwich. I also freaked out at the same time I ate my sandwich and changed clothes. I further freaked out as I walked out to my car and continued to freak out as I drove to class.

And luckily I'd freaked out enough that by the time I hit class I could set it aside and concentrate.

Unfortunately, by the time I got home from class, I was back to freaking out. Which meant I found it hard to sleep.

And it further meant when I finally slept, my dreams were filled with Knight.

The next evening I had little time. I had a client. She was showing at my house at her six thirty slot and I had to be home and set up in time. But I also had to do what I had to do.

And I was going to do it.

It was after work. I had a full-time job as a file clerk in a medical office that had six doctors and four nurse practitioners. I made shit money, but the job wasn't taxing. The office ladies were funny and they had excellent benefits. These included kick-butt insurance, and if you worked there for two years, partial payment on any further education you wanted to take, even if it was beauty school.

And beauty school was where I decided to go so, three years ago, I went. I'd already completed my nail technician certification and was building a clientele whose appointments I had to take in the evenings and on weekends. The goal was to have enough to go full-time and therefore be able to rent a station in a decent salon. This was difficult, what with a job and school, but I was doing it.

Since, I'd finished classes in applying makeup and now I was close to completing a course to be a certified skin technician. I liked nails and I liked chattering to my clients. It was cool, seriously low stress and it actually paid pretty well. But I knew that I'd lose my mind sitting around doing nails forty hours a week so I had to diversify.

That was why I took classes to be a makeup artist and was close to completing my course as a skin technician. I liked doing facials the best. It was the quiet. It wasn't only relaxing to the client but also me. And I liked the bright-but-tranquil look my test subjects gave me when I was done. Not only was I making their skin look great, I was making them feel good. And that was cool.

But this wasn't my life's dream. In fact, I didn't have a life's dream. I'd learned that living a dream, finding a dream, or having a dream find me was not in my future, and I'd learned this early.

That said, I was ambitious.

I didn't want to rule the world.

I wanted to own my own spa.

A good one that was all about relaxation, pampering and beautification in a peaceful, safe, gorgeous setting. Maybe up in the mountains somewhere. It would look good. It would smell good. And it would be a treat for anyone who opened the doors and walked in.

Including me.

So I had a plan. Nails, makeup and facials down (nearly), building up a clientele as I went along and finding a salon or spa that would rent me space or take me on as an employee in the meantime. Then move onto the whopper deluxe: massage therapy. I was doing all this while saving to open my own place. Living frugal. Being smart. Getting educated. Building a clientele and providing excellent service to keep them so whenever I moved and when I settled, they'd follow me.

Then be my own boss, and that boss was the boss of indulgence.

How freaking awesome would that be?

Perfect. With my life, facing the rest of it filled with offering tranquility and indulgence was perfect for me.

This was on my mind instead of what I didn't want to be on my mind as I found a spot somewhat close to the front doors to the high-rise complex. It took me three attempts before I did a terrible job at parallel parking my car. It didn't matter; I wouldn't be there long. I got out, fed a nickel into the meter which gave me a nanosecond (not really) but enough time to do what I needed to do.

I dashed into the building and went to the doorman's desk.

When we were there on Saturday there was no doorman on duty, which meant day and evening hours. But the door had been locked (as it now wasn't) and we'd had to buzz up. However, I'd seen the desk so I'd hoped it had someone behind it sometime, and luckily I was right.

I smiled at him and he smiled at me as I walked up to him.

I stopped at the desk, put the taped down, bubble wrap envelope on it and asked, "Can I leave that and you'll give it to Knight, I think his last name is Sebring, in apartment 15A?"

His brows went up. "Mr. Sebring? Unit 15A? Sure," he replied. "But you want, I can call up. See if he's here."

His hand was drifting to the phone so I lifted mine swiftly and shook my head. "No, thanks. I'm in a rush and he needs that but I have to dash. Can you just make sure he gets it?"

He nodded again. "Sure."

I smiled. "Thanks."

He smiled back.

I skedaddled.

Right, that down, point made, note written, *Thanks, Knight. That's very kind and generous but I can't accept. Be well, Anya.*

And that was it. The end.

The end.

I drove home thinking of the end of Knight Sebring, at the same time wishing, with what I knew was sheer lunacy and I didn't get it at all, was that it was the beginning.

The next night it was late and I was coming home from class thinking about my weekend. Four clients on Saturday, including Sandrine who I knew would stay through the client after her and bitch about Nick (who *still* hadn't called, not surprisingly to anyone but Sandrine), and stay even after that trying to convince me to go out with her to the clubs that evening in search of him.

Because this wasn't an eventuality but a certainty, Viv and I had already formed a plan of attack. Viv was making her world famous (not really, but it should be) chicken, lemon and asparagus risotto. I was bringing a bottle of wine, my facial gear and my copy of *Thor*. We were going to eat. I was going to give Vivica and Sandrine (if she was smart enough to bag on the Nick hunt) a facial, then we were going to perv on Chris Hemsworth.

The perfect evening.

Don't get me wrong, there was a time when I liked to go out, mostly because I liked music, but I *loved* dancing. And even though I didn't have the greatest clothes, I chose selectively, liked what I chose and they suited me. I liked to get all dressed up, made up, hair out to there, heels even higher, go out, have a few drinks, loosen up, flirt a little, maybe get asked out on a date, but especially dance.

But now I was twenty-seven, not twenty-two (or three or four), and this happening every weekend with a wild party thrown in here and there was wearing. I was never out to be part of the scene. And I wasn't on the hunt for a man. I dated. A couple of times I dated a guy for a while before I broke it off. So I was open to meeting men and exploring things. But I hadn't found anyone who struck me. I wasn't desperate. If it happened, it happened. If it didn't, I could take care of myself. But if it happened, it had to be right.

"Anya?"

I knew that smooth, deep voice like I'd heard it every day, hundreds of times a day, since birth. So I stopped mid-punching-in of new security code and woodenly twisted to see Knight Sebring striding up the steps of my apartment building toward me.

Okay, um...

Crap!

I pulled it together and greeted, "Hey," then added, "What are you doing here?"

I didn't need to ask. I was taking in his face and his well-cut, dark suit. His shirt that was the color of moss, and it suited him, even with blue eyes, to perfection, and the fact that he seemed mildly annoyed. But I didn't miss the glossy black box he held in one long-fingered hand.

He made it to me and held up the box. "Take it," he ordered. No greeting, no smile, nothing but those two words.

I looked down at the box then up to his eyes.

"Knight, I can't," I said softly.

His head tipped slightly to the side and his brows drew together as he asked, "Why the fuck not?"

"Because I looked it up at work and I know it costs nine hundred and eighty-nine dollars."

"So?" he returned instantly.

I stared at him.

Then I repeated his, "So?"

"Yeah, babe. So?"

I turned fully to him. "So, I don't know you."

"So?"

"So?" I again repeated his repeat.

"Jesus, fuck, babe," he jerked the box to me sounding impatient, "got shit to do. Take it."

"Knight, *I can't,*" I reiterated.

"Anya, babe," he leaned in and reiterated back with some scary emphasis, "*why the fuck not?*"

I stared into his eyes. He was impatient. He was annoyed. I did not know this man and he was trying to give me a nearly one thousand dollar phone like it was nothing.

"Why are you pressing this phone on me?" I asked quietly, and he leaned back.

"Told you in the note. You read?" he asked. This sarcasm was not amusing, but I didn't call him on that. I nodded. "Then you know. A woman needs a functioning phone."

"I'm saving," I shared. "I'll have one in a couple of weeks."

His eyes held mine.

Then he whispered, "Saving?"

Crap. *Crap!*

I ignored that and all it exposed and assured him, "Anyway, I'm fine. Good. Or I will be on the phone front in a couple of weeks."

He didn't say anything for a few beats then, softly, he ordered, "Anya, take the phone."

"Knight—"

"Take the phone."

"I don't—"

"Babe, take the fucking phone."

"Did you beat up Steve?"

I blurted that and I didn't know why. If he didn't, it was a rude thing to assume. If he did, I didn't want to know.

But he didn't hesitate to reply, "No."

I felt relief sweep through me.

"But I sent the boys who did," he finished.

My entire body got tight, but I forced through stiff lips my, "What?"

"Though," he amended, "it wasn't me taking shots at that motherfucker only because I had other shit to do."

I said nothing and stared.

Knight got more impatient. "Anya, got shit to do now, too. Take the fuckin' phone."

"Why'd you have boys beat up Steve?" I asked, and again didn't know why. I didn't want to know. But I asked anyway and he answered.

"Babe, your building, a fire hazard. One flight of steps for a building that size? Fuck no," he bit out, now not sounding impatient but pissed. "A fire could cut off from your escape route, you only got one. And the door open for any motherfucker to walk through? They see you, trail you, you're fucked. Totally. Not only because you only got one set of stairs, and it's the one furthest away from the front door, but also, once you get up to your hall, it's dark and your door's got a lock, one boot to it, it'll pop right open. That's bullshit. Your rent isn't steep, but it isn't shit either. You pay for a workin' fuckin' elevator and a secured door. I sent my boys to have a word. The words your landlord returned they didn't like much. They gave me a call, I gave them the go-ahead. You got a secured door, lighting and a fucking lock that might give you enough time to at least dial 911 before some motherfucker is on you."

Okay, that explained that.

At the same time it absolutely did *not*.

"Why?" I whispered.

"What?" Knight didn't whisper.

"Why? Why did you take that trouble, or, I mean, send boys to do it? You barely know me."

And that was when Knight Sebring laid it out. And when he did, I didn't feel tingles. I felt shivers. I just didn't know what the shivers meant.

"Babe, your clothes. Shit. But you work 'em, and you do because you've got one serious fantastic body. Your hair is even better and your face is a face that launches a thousand hard-ons. Trust me, any man you've looked at probably since you were thirteen has jacked off thinkin' of you. All this is a recipe for disaster if you live alone in an unsecured building with a lock like the one you got. Someone had to step up. Seein' as you aren't the only one who lives here, and my guess, at least one person in that building bitched and nothin' got done, so I stepped up. It took my boys an hour. Your landlord was a dick so it was an hour they enjoyed. Not a big deal. Now take the fuckin' phone."

Trust me, any man you've looked at probably since you were thirteen has jacked off thinkin' of you.

Did this mean him too?

Oh my *God!*

"Anya," he growled, it was a scary growl so I lifted my hand immediately and took the box.

"Jesus," he muttered.

"I don't know what to do to thank you," I muttered back.

"I ask for gratitude?" he asked. I shook my head so he went on, "Then I will now. Use that phone. Don't sell it. Don't set it aside. Take it upstairs. Charge it. Use the piece a' shit you got, if it works long enough, to tell your people your new number which is written in the shit in the box. Then use the phone. That's how you can thank me."

"Okay," I whispered.

"Fuck," he whispered back and turned to leave.

To leave!

Was that it?

All this effort, money and a vulgar compliment that still managed to be a whopper and he just leaves?

I turned to watch him go and found my voice calling, "Knight?"

One step from the sidewalk, he halted, twisting his torso to look up at me.

I didn't know what to say. He laid the terms out for his "gratitude", but I got more out of them than he did, so I felt some other gesture was in order. I doubted he'd want a manicure or facial so I was at a loss.

"Anya, told you, got shit to do," he prompted, and I shook myself to get it together.

Then I said softly, "Thank you," not believing I was thanking a man I barely knew for having my landlord beat up and giving me a new phone the money it cost could buy a used car (a crappy one, but still), but doing it anyway.

His eyes held mine. Then he shook his head while turning away.

Then he was gone.

I walked up to my apartment. I plugged in my new phone to charge, found the new number and used my old phone to text it to everyone in my phonebook. In the middle of this, my old phone died.

Not long after, I went to bed.

I tossed. I turned.

And when I finally slept, I dreamt of Knight.

Chapter 4
Only for Me

Mission accomplished last Saturday: we got our night with risotto, facials and Chris Hemsworth, and Sandrine participated in the festivities. She did it bitching about Nick, though not through the movie. Not even Sandrine could bitch about a hot guy jerk while Chris Hemsworth was on screen.

Now it was a week later and Viv, Sandrine and I were dolled up and on the town because Sandrine was on a tear. Nick still hadn't called, and Sandrine, being Sandrine, still hadn't given up.

Viv was out because she was in the mood to be out. The reason she hadn't been at Nick's party was because she knew, like I knew, he was a jerk, and she had no desire to spend time with him or his crew. So she didn't.

I was either a pushover or too exhausted from my busy life to bear up against a Sandrine Onslaught so I went.

Tonight, though, I was in Viv's mood.

It had been just over a week and nothing from Knight. No more chivalrous gestures, no matter how scary, scarily generous or criminal. Nothing.

I wanted to let it go and be relieved. I had a phone. It was awesome and did *way* more than taking calls. It did email, internet, apps, the whole shebang. All of this looking cool as hell and like something NASA designed, but fifty years from now... it was *the bomb*. I had a safer apartment building and so did all my neighbors. He told me in no uncertain terms he found me attractive, but he didn't stop by and before he left didn't say he would contact me, nor did he ask for a date. So the only thing I could assume was that although he was scary, he still was a man who saw that something needed to be done and he did it. It was a lot more than him hearing I needed a ride and him giving it to me, but, bottom line, it seemed simply that was who he was and the kind of thing he did.

So he did his thing and onward.

For a guy like him, I was probably a memory.

I didn't like this and yet I did. I was relieved and upset. It was odd. And these feelings weren't fading. Not even a little.

Which sucked. Not just because they weren't fading, but because they were confusing as all get out.

I still wondered if he thought about me when he was doing a certain deed. After a few days of trying to convince myself I didn't (as well as trying not to think about it at all, and failing at both) I admitted to myself that I liked this idea, even as it freaked me out just how much I did (which was a lot). However, it was highly unlikely a man like him ever needed his fist, as in ever, so it was also highly doubtful.

So I decided to go out. Have a few drinks, dance and celebrate new sheets, a new comforter and new pillows. Without having to buy the phone, bed linens had been stepped up on my schedule of things I could buy. I got the good kind of those too, going way beyond what I would normally allow myself, and doing it because I not only had the money, but because Viv brought me a new client. An extra fifteen dollars every two weeks for a steady, Sunday manicure appointment. And for me, thirty dollars a month was *awesome*.

So celebration it was.

"You know, asking around, that Knight Sebring guy owns this club."

This was Viv shouting in my ear as we walked into Slade, the trendiest nightclub in downtown Denver. It was trendy in a bizarre way where it wasn't trendy just for a year or two, but had been since I started clubbing when I was twenty-one. The cover charge was high, but it was *the* place to see and be seen.

It was uncanny since clubs went in and out, but Slade stayed popular. So popular, when celebrities hit town they hit Slade. This was because Slade had small, medium and large VIP seating that was cordoned off from the commoners. Movie stars went there. Rap stars. R&B stars. Broncos. Nuggets. They took their posses to their VIP sections, had their own cocktail waitresses and bouncers. They didn't see, but were up on daises so they could be seen.

This was so rare, I had actually given headspace to this phenomenon and came up with the fact that Slade stayed the hotspot because every year it was closed down for a month and the entire inside was gutted and renovated. It was like getting a whole new club and yet it wasn't. And it was always the best, the coolest, the hippest. A costly but clever ploy, I thought, and it worked.

Not to mention the cocktail waitresses were always gorgeous with amazing bodies, the bartenders were hot, and the bouncers and security were huge; scary, but all attractive. So if you hit Slade there were other treats for both sexes. Not just hot music in a hip atmosphere with well-poured drinks in fan-tastic glasses but eye candy.

Further, there was a line to get in, every night, even weekdays. And whether you agreed or not it was the right thing to do, the bouncers picked and chose who got in. It wasn't just about clothes and money. If you were gorgeous, you went to the front of the line. Then, if you looked like you had serious cake, you got in. All others could stand out there for hours and never get in so they'd learned over the years not even to bother.

We got in because Sandrine had her sheet of strawberry blonde hair, fake breasts an ex-boyfriend bought her and her ability to say no to desserts *all the time,* and therefore her body was slim and perfectly toned. Not to mention there was Vivica, with her tall, slender frame, dark, flawless midnight skin, unusual tawny eyes, graceful giraffe neckline and perfect skull with her short cropped afro. And, lastly, apparently the new intel was me, who had a face that could launch a thousand hard-ons. Not a flowery compliment, but still, it said it all even if it pulled no punches.

Once I noticed this (not, obviously, the bit about me, since I didn't know that until a week and a day ago), this had made me, for a six month stretch, swear off Slade. Sandrine, of course, wore me down and I lifted my ban.

So now I was back, and had been back for a couple of years, though with decreasing regularity.

Further, last Saturday I'd told both Viv and Sandrine all about Knight.

Sandrine's comment was, "Hope he leaves you alone. He's totally hot but he's also a total asshole."

Vivica just stared at me and said nothing. This was her way. She tended to cast judgment only when she had all the facts, even if, I found, one of those facts included the knowledge that some guy had sent "his boys" out to beat someone up for me. Still, it was one of the three million, twenty-two thousand, six hun-dred and eleven things I loved about her. That said, once she cast judgment, whether it was right or wrong (or whether I thought it was right or wrong), it would take torture to make her change her mind. This could get a tad bit irritat-ing. But it was, as far as I could see, Viv's only flaw. And since we put up with enough of them from Sandrine, it all balanced out.

Until I mentioned him, neither of them knew Knight Sebring.

But obviously, Viv had asked around. I wasn't surprised. This was also Viv's way. She tended to be curious, and that curiosity would go into overdrive once a man gave me a thousand dollar phone and had my landlord beaten up to make me safe(ish).

"Really?" I shouted back.

She nodded. "Yep. Since it opened eight years go."

Wow. Interesting.

Suddenly, I was happy that I'd pulled out my best going out dress. It *was* designer, but I bought it at a secondhand shop. Black, skintight, two inches above the knee, one shoulder bare, other arm sleeveless. Across the side it gathered to a big, opened hole that exposed the skin of my other side under the sleeveless arm from ribs to the top of my hip. It wasn't hot. It was *scorching* hot. And part of that scorching was the obvious fact that, to wear it, there was no way I could wear underwear. I loved it. I'd paired it with spike-heeled, strappy sandals that were black, but looked like they were coated with silver glitter. They didn't cost the bomb—I got them on sale at a mid-scale shoe store—but they were sexy as all heck.

"Did you, uh…" I was still shouting in her ear as we pressed through the bodies on our way to the bar, "learn anything else about him?"

Her eyes caught mine and she shook her head. "Nope. No one knows much about him except he's Nick's older brother. I think he's thirty-four, thirty-five. Got different ages on him, but only those two. He's not Nick's biggest fan, which means I'm leaning toward liking him. He's also got a serious, kickass name. And he owns this club."

Not a lot of information. Some of it I already knew, but still interesting.

"*Ohmigod!*" We both heard Sandrine shriek and our eyes went forward to where she was powering through the club, cutting a swath for Viv's and my passage, to see she'd turned back to us. "That asshole is *here!*"

Before my eyes could move to where her finger was pointing, Sandrine was again powering through toward a VIP dais that was medium-sized, across the club from us, but had a spectacular elevated view of the room since it had at least five steps up. But this time she was practically throwing people out of the way to do it.

This was because Nick Sebring was clearly visible up there. This was not a surprise. We met Nick here, and Nick was almost exclusively and always here in his own VIP section.

My first thought, and I acted on it, was to scan the dais for Knight.

He was not there.

My second thought was that this was a bummer.

My third thought was to remind myself it wasn't. He had someone beat up and lamented the fact he couldn't do it himself. Sure, he did it for me, and Landlord Steve was a jerk, but he did it and that was scary.

My last thought was that I better get my booty in gear because Sandrine was riled, and when Sandrine was riled this usually caused a scene.

Vivica had my last thought first and was hurrying behind Sandrine in the futile hope of heading her off.

And it was futile.

Before I was even close and Vivica was twenty feet behind, Sandrine was up the steps to the dais and pushing past a bouncer who was looking behind him toward Nick to see if he had the all-clear for her entry. Sandrine, with years of experience, was adept at getting anywhere she wanted to go; past bouncers, security, to the front of lines, backstage, her ass at choice window tables in trendy eateries. You name it, she found her way to get it, even if she had to use her toned muscles to do it.

Which she did now.

I watched Vivica follow, and the bouncer didn't turn back to see if he had the all-clear for Viv. He caught one look at Vivica's rounded behind in her tight, turquoise dress and didn't stop looking.

Seeing as he was distracted, this made it easy for me to get by him too.

Vivica was too late, and I was woefully too late. I knew this the instant I hit the scene.

And I say woefully because Nick Sebring was not just a mammoth jerk.

Nick Sebring was scarier than his brother.

And I knew this because I interrupted Knight Sebring having a calming cigarette by intruding in his very personal space and helping myself to his phone. Even though he made his irritation clear, he ended up giving me a ride.

Nick, on the other hand, was done with Sandrine, her texts, her phone calls and her storming into his VIP section intent on making a scene, and he'd chosen a terrifying way to communicate this to her.

And I knew *this* when I got to their side, opposite Vivica. I got close and saw Nick had Sandrine by both upper arms. He'd jerked her so her body was against his, his face in hers, and I knew his hold hurt because Sandrine's beautiful face was twisted in pain.

"Nick, let me go," she whispered, "you're hurting me."

"Am I gonna hear from you again?" he asked in a way I knew he was repeating himself.

"No," she said quietly.

"Had you, don't want more, don't want your shit," he growled, still in her face and still clamped onto her. "Get me?"

"I get you."

"Willin' to make my point clearer, you even think you'll have second thoughts." He kept at it, pissed-off in a way I didn't think it would calm for a while, and he had his hands on my friend so I got closer.

"Nick, please, let her go. She'll be cool. I promise. Just let her go and we'll be out of here," I said loudly to be heard over the music, but also softly in order to let him know I meant what I said.

Nick's head turned to me, and it took a lot but I didn't quail.

Yep, definitely scarier than his brother. Knight Sebring had control. Nick Sebring absolutely did *not*.

"Nick, please, I promise, no more. Let me go. You're *hurting me*." That was Sandrine in a tortured plea, but Nick's eyes were on me and he didn't let her go. He held on and held my eyes.

"You want me to let this bitch go?" he asked me.

"Yes," I answered immediately.

"Then make sure this bitch gets the fuck outta here, but you stay and have a drink with me," Nick replied and my stomach clenched.

"No, let her go and we're all outta here." Vivica entered the conversation, but Nick didn't tear his eyes from me even as he gave Sandrine a shake. I heard her whimper so I knew either the shake had scared her or his hold had tightened.

"You gonna let me buy you a drink?" he asked.

"Yes," I replied. "Absolutely."

"Anya," Vivica said low.

"Let her go," I said to Nick.

Nick looked back at Sandrine, pulling her up to her toes so she was nose to nose with him and visibly wincing.

"Bitch, I don't see you. I don't hear from you. I don't even fuckin' *smell* you," he growled. He then pushed her off, hard.

She staggered back on her four and a half inch sandals (that I knew she'd return in the next week because they cost six hundred dollars, something she couldn't afford). Vivica shot to her to catch her from falling.

I did too, but I came up short when a hand clamped around the inside of my elbow.

My neck twisted so I could look at Nick who now had a hold of me.

"Drink," he clipped.

My stomach in knots, my heart beating wildly, I nodded.

"Anya!" Vivica yelled, and I looked to her even as Nick started to turn me to the back of the dais where there was a long, plush, raspberry colored booth seat.

"I'm good!" I yelled back. "Go! Just a drink and I'll text you when I'm out."

Vivica's eyes went from me to Nick to another bouncer who was hovering that I hadn't noticed until then, and finally her eyes came back to me.

"We'll be at the bar!" she shouted.

"You're with that bitch, you'll be in the fuckin' street!" Nick shouted back, still dragging me. "You lose her, you stay up here."

No. I didn't want Vivica anywhere near there.

"Go!" I yelled.

Vivica held my eyes as she held Sandrine in the curve of her arm, a Sandrine who was now crying and staring at me, fear in her face. I lost sight of them when Nick let go of my elbow, slid an arm along my waist and turned me to face the direction he was taking me.

Crap. Crap. *CRAP!*

God, *Sandrine*.

Seriously, some day that girl was going to be the death of me.

Right. A drink. I could have a drink with Nick.

Crap.

He sat us down, him too close to me, and immediately his eyes went across the dais and his mouth opened up to clip a loud, "Yo!"

The cocktail waitress came scurrying. It was then I saw the bouncer who had been hovering was now at the end of the dais. Another black-suited bouncer was standing on the floor under him. He had his hands up to cup around his mouth and he was yelling something.

"What are you drinking?"

I tore my eyes from the bouncer, sucked in breath and looked at Nick.

"Sparkling water," I ordered.

"Fuck, you fuckin kidding me?" he bit out.

Okay, that was the wrong answer.

He looked at the waitress. "Get her a cosmo. Me, Hennessy, Paradis."

Her eyes bugged out a second before she pulled it together, obviously having witnessed the scene or just knowing Nick, and she scurried away.

Nick looked at me and announced, "Your friend's a pain in my ass."

She was a pain in mine too. Then again, at that moment, so was he.

I decided not to answer.

"Fuck, she thinks she can make me come and she owns me?" he asked.

I had no answer for that either. Though, I had to admit, he was a screaming jerk, but he was kind of right.

"You're also a pain in my ass," he declared.

What did I do?

I didn't ask. First, I didn't want to know. Second, I was trying not to throw up and/or have a heart attack, and I thought both were priorities.

"Only way I know your honey isn't locked up in ironclad panties is I'd see 'em through that fuckin' dress. Jesus, do you fuck anybody?" he asked.

"Um…" I mumbled, but said no more. Mostly because this was none of his business. Partly because I had, indeed, hit a long, dry spell. And lastly because he was scaring the heck out of me.

I watched him pull a hand through his hair and it hit me that he slightly resembled his brother, but not much. They both had black hair with a bit of wave in it, but Nick kept his perfectly cut and styled with product. Nick also had blue eyes, but they were nowhere near as vibrant as Knight's. He was at least two inches shorter but still tall. And although Nick was built, he was slighter of frame.

Their facial features, however, were not the same. Not at all. Nick was handsome, but he didn't pack the punch of Knight's pure, aggressive, masculine beauty. Not even close.

He dropped his hand and looked at me.

"Fucked up," he muttered.

"What?" I whispered. He watched my mouth move, which was uncomfortable, but considering the fact I was whispering in a club, if he didn't lip read he'd have no idea what I said.

He leaned in and repeated, "I fucked up." Then he went on, "With you. That scene. Fucked up."

Yeah he did.

"Don't worry about it," I said back, this time louder so he could hear me. "Let's just have this drink then I'll, uh... go and, uh... check on things."

His eyes held mine and I noticed the anger had leaked out of his. "What's it take with you?"

I felt my eyebrows draw together. "Pardon?"

He leaned further in and I tried not to lean back because he seemed not to be angry anymore, but I didn't want to test it.

"What's it take with you? Dinner?" he asked.

Oh God, please, do not ask me out. Please, please, please.

I was considering the option of informing him I was a lipstick lesbian, concerned about the fact this might turn him on more, when I felt it.

That swell of frightening, searing, vibrating heat.

I knew the feel of that so I knew he was coming.

Nick did too, because his body jerked, his head whipped around and mine did as well, to see Knight stalking up to us, face a mask of unadulterated fury, eyes on his brother.

He stopped in front of Nick, chin tipped down, eyes scorching, and I froze.

"Knight—" Nick started.

"You put your hands on a woman in my club?" Knight asked, his voice vibrating with that same heat he was radiating.

I debated the merits of inching away when Nick started again, "Knight—"

That was all he got out because suddenly, Nick wasn't sitting next to me. Suddenly, Nick was out of his seat and flying across the dais. He slammed into the back of a couple of guys and some girls who all went down with him.

I jumped from the seat.

Knight's head snapped around so his eyes could pin me to the spot, which they absolutely did.

"Do not move," he growled.

I stopped moving.

He looked back at Nick, and so did I, to see him getting up, three bouncers closing in. The people he took down with him also slowly coming to their feet, and Nick's entire VIP dais posse beating a hasty retreat.

"Lesson," Knight clipped to one of the bouncers. The bouncer nodded and put hands on a now pale-faced Nick and instantly dragged him to the steps as another of the bouncers followed. Knight kept talking. "Find Anya's friends.

They don't have a car, escort them home. They do, escort them to their car. And VIP vouchers. Now."

Wow, that was nice. VIP vouchers at Slade. Everyone knew what that meant. Your own dais for you and your friends, your own cocktail waitress, your own bouncer, and if you carried the voucher card, you drank for free.

I was thinking this, therefore when Knight's hand closed around mine hard, scrunching my fingers together somewhat painfully, it came as a shock.

I had no time to respond to this mostly because now *I* was being dragged to the steps. He didn't release the pressure on my hand and I was working hard not to fall as well as keep up with him, so I didn't make a peep as he prowled down the steps with me in tow. He then prowled through the crowd around the dais, shoving them aside without hesitation. Then he prowled to the back of the club toward a door. A bouncer standing beside it opened it before we arrived and I saw it led to some lit stairs. Suddenly, we were through it and I was climbing the stairs, clamoring after a very swiftly moving Knight.

"Knight!" I snapped. "Slow down! I can't keep up."

Mistake.

He jerked my hand as he turned and I started falling. He caught me, swinging me up in his arms as I cried out in shock and grabbed on like I did the night he carried me over the coats. Then we were up the stairs. He dipped down, opened a door and walked through. He slammed me down on my feet, hard, the movement jarring me, and he closed the door. The music that was muted when we walked into the stairs disappeared completely when the door closed and I found myself facing down a seriously angry, seriously terrifying Knight Sebring in a private office to the strains of what sounded to my uncultured ears like Beethoven.

"What… the fuck… is the matter with you?" he asked slowly, his voice still vibrating, the fury still radiating and I blinked.

What?

I didn't do anything.

And I thought he should know that and not mistake it.

So I yelled it, leaning toward him and everything.

"I didn't do anything!"

He came at me fast. I retreated, not as fast. I hit something and went into freefall. My bottom landed sideways in a chair, my back to a cushioned armrest, legs over the other one. Knight leaned over me, one hand to the top back of the chair, one hand in the seat beside me, face an inch from mine.

God, God, God, he was scaring *the hell* out of me.

Why was he angry? At me!

"You put on that dress, didn't you?" he whispered, and it was sinister.

"What?" I whispered back.

"You... do not... leave your house... dressed like that... without being on the arm of a man like me," he ground out on a terrifying staccato with scary pauses.

"A man like you?" I whispered.

"A man who'd shoot another man in the face he even looked at you. Yeah, Anya, a man... like... *me.*"

He meant that. He meant it. Every word. God, he meant *every word of that.*

"Knight, you're scaring me."

Yep, still whispering.

"Good," he bit out. His eyes moved over my face for a while then he growled, "Fuck me. Fuck me. Fuck... *me.*"

What now?

No, no. I didn't want to know. I didn't want VIP vouchers either, even though I could possibly sell them on the internet for half the cost of opening up a mountain retreat spa.

I just wanted to go.

Now.

"Can you move up so I can get up and get out of here?" I requested cautiously.

"Tomorrow, I'm giving you breakfast. I'll pick you up at nine."

I blinked.

Then, yes, *still* whispering, "Pardon?"

"You heard me."

I shook my head. "I can't."

"Bullshit. Nine. You say no again I'm givin' you breakfast anyway, but only because tonight, all night, until morning, you're tied to my bed."

There it was. The whole body shiver I wasn't sure was good, as in very, *very* good or bad, as in very, *very* bad.

"Knight," I breathed.

"Nine."

"I have a client at eleven," I blurted, and his head jerked as his brows shot together.

"A client?"

"Acrylics. Um… fake nails. Standing appointment every two weeks. Her name is Shirley," I explained, though went overboard on the information because I was *freaking out*.

He stared at me and I felt my entire body heat from the infuriated blaze coming from his eyes.

Then he said, "Lunch, one."

Oh God.

"Knight—" I repeated.

"Lunch, Anya, one. You come to me. My place. I don't get a call up at one, the boys find you and bring you to me."

He meant that too. God, he meant every word.

"You're scaring me," I told him quietly and honestly.

"Good, then you'll do what the fuck I say," he bit back. "Now, I'm gonna go, send up a drink and you're gonna drink it while you wait for me to find a man I trust to take you out back so no man's eyes are on you as you walk through my club. He's gonna put your ass in a car and take you home. He's walkin' you to your door. He's also doin' a walkthrough of your place. You give him shit, he'll tell me and I'll punish *you*. Are you with me?"

"Not really," I whispered.

"You will be," he whispered back, pushed off and stalked to the door.

By the time he got there, I'd pushed myself up in the chair but had not been able to scramble out of it before he pinned me to the spot with his eyes.

"That dress, babe. You wear it again, it's only for me."

Then he disappeared through the door. I heard it lock from the other side and he was gone.

Chapter 5
Wars Fought Over a Face Like This

Call me crazy. Heck, even I thought I was crazy, but the next day, at quarter 'til one, I was in my car heading to Knight's high-rise.

I did not call the police.

No, not me.

But I did call Vivica and Sandrine and gave them the lowdown, because if I disappeared I figured someone should know where to begin to search for my body.

Last night, shortly after Knight left, a waitress came in, accompanied by a bouncer who was there, I knew, so I wouldn't try to escape.

I tried ordering a sparkling water again, hoping that if Knight got that pissed because Nick put his hands on Sandrine, he wouldn't order a bouncer to wail on me for ordering water.

He didn't. They retreated, and in order to attempt to calm my terror I looked around.

The walls were a rich, warm red; not blood, bordering on wine. A huge, dark wood desk covered in stuff. Knight worked, that was obvious. Laptop, multi-line phone, papers and folders strewn, two (that I could see) expensive-looking pens lying on top of papers, big manila envelopes, etc. There was a high-back black, swish-looking swivel chair behind the desk; in front of it, two supple, burgundy leather chairs. There was a matching sofa against the wall, in front of it a dark wood coffee table. In a corner, another dark wood table, this round with five, burgundy leather chairs surrounding it. A long, low chest against the wall opposite the couch; on it were bottles of booze. No fancy decanters. Just a bottle of Jack Daniels, one of Grey Goose, one of Tanqueray, one of Patrón tequila. A variety of heavy, cut, crystal glasses.

Down from the booze and glasses, a smooth piece of warm-colored wood intricately, artistically and interestingly carved into the shape of a voluptuous female's torso from neck to top thigh, arms wound behind her back, the wood and curves of her figure all waves, undulating with the grain. It was fantastic, though I didn't want it to be because that would say Knight had good taste (or even better than I already expected), and I didn't want to think anything good about him.

But there was further proof of it in the prints on the wall. Enormous panoramas of black framed, cream matted, black and white shots of Denver skylines.

There was a credenza behind Knight's desk, also covered with work detritus. On one side there were two narrow cases with glass fronts that held a whopping huge collection of CDs. Mounted on the wall was a slim but tall CD player that held ten CDs. It was a work of art. I'd seen it on the website of where he bought me my phone, and although I didn't check the price, I knew it had to cost *way* more than my phone. To top that, there were awesome speakers set on curved wood stands in each corner of the room.

After I was served my water, I sipped it and waited. I did this as I stared at the heaving club through the big, what I knew was one-way window that started at my waist and took nearly the rest of the wall. And I did this watching the dancing bodies, the lights, the flirting, the laughing, all bizarrely incongruous as the strains of soothing classical music drifted around me.

I would not guess Knight was a classical man. I would guess he was an unbelievably good-looking psychopath, but not one who listened to Beethoven (or whoever).

But there it was.

I had about ten minutes to sip my water before I was whisked away by a bouncer who didn't introduce himself. He didn't speak and looked somewhat like the Incredible Hulk but without green skin. But even though I didn't know his name, he walked me up to my apartment, walked through it then, luckily, walked out of it.

I did not dream of Knight last night mostly because I did not sleep a wink.

What I did do was get up, prepare carefully for my confrontation with him, call my friends to share my story and organize my stuff to take my client.

Incidentally, neither Vivica nor Sandrine were hip on me confronting Knight Sebring on my own. Vivica because she was smart enough to be terrified and equally smart enough to do the right thing, like call the cops. Sandrine because she had a taste of the Sebrings last night and she didn't like it much. It pierced the Daddy's Little Princess fortress she wandered through life behind and she was terrified for me. I was pleased this fortress was pierced and hoping that maybe she'd wake up a bit, but I was absolutely *not* pleased by how this happened.

We would see.

Now I was wearing my best pair of jeans. And also my best pair of high-heeled, brown boots (yes, crazy, but I wanted height, and the toe was pointed so if I had to kick him in the shin, that would sting). I paired this with my best sweater; cashmere, a pale pink, another secondhand store purchase. It had a super-low dip in the back. But I covered up the expanse of skin it would show with a creamy, pointelle racerback tank. Sure, you could see my pink bra straps and often the sweater drooped off a shoulder, but I also had on my smart, blazer-style brown leather jacket (bought two seasons out at a discount designer warehouse at the outlet stores in Castle Rock). I didn't intend to take off the blazer so the sweater didn't matter anyway.

Smoothed out hair. Enough makeup to hide I had no sleep, but subtle. A spritz of perfume, mostly out of habit. Silver hoops in my ears, also mostly out of habit. And the rest, just me.

Unfortunately, the only parking spot I could find was around the corner and half a block up from his place. This meant (after I fed the meter enough to give me fifteen minutes, wondering why in this 'hood they didn't give Sundays free) when I hit the lobby of his place to see the doorman worked Sundays, I was seven minutes late.

If Knight was livid, screw him.

This was going to stop, now. Both him *and* his brother. And I was going to make that point. Personally.

If it didn't, next stop: the police.

"Miss Gage," the doorman greeted, smiling at me, freaking me out that he knew my last name and picking up the phone, "Mr. Sebring said you'd be arriving. I'll ring up."

Before I could say word one, he had the phone to his ear.

I took in a breath and smiled back because he wasn't a jerk. Just one—no, two—of his tenants were, and I settled in to wait, mentally girding for battle.

He put the phone in the receiver, smiled again and invited, "Mr. Sebring says to go right up."

Apparently, after he exposes the full psychopath, he forgets how to be a gentleman.

Whatever.

I tossed another smile at the doorman and stomped to the elevators, trying not to look like I was stomping. Though I did stub my finger with the strength I used to jab the elevator button.

Doors to one of the two sets opened. I walked in and they closed on me.

And as they did, where I was, the confrontation imminent, belatedly, I considered this might not be the best idea.

Before I could rethink, the doors opened and I was nearly bowled over by two men wearing navy pants, matching navy shirts and carrying boxes.

"God! Sorry!" one of them exclaimed.

Movers. On a Sunday. Weird.

"No problems," I muttered.

I skirted them, sucked in breath and headed to Knight's door.

Right, go in, say what I had to say and *get out*.

When I got there, the door was wedged open with a triangle of wood.

There was music coming from inside. It was soft. It was also classical, it was all piano and I didn't even have a guess as to what it was.

I reached in, knocked on the door and called, "Knight?"

"Kitchen." I heard his deep voice call back.

Yep, psychopath out, gentleman gone.

I walked down the hall and nearly bumped into two more men in navy pants and matching shirts who were carrying a mattress.

Was it Knight who was moving?

"Sorry, sorry," I muttered, squeezing back against the wall to the kitchen and sucking in my stomach (like this would help; still, I did it) as they lumbered by me.

They passed. I righted myself and saw the living room in all its grandeur without bodies, empties and ashtrays, and decided it sucked he wasn't awesome and into me but psychotic and into me, and turned the corner to the kitchen.

Then I stopped and stared.

No suit. Black tee, worn, fitting him way, way, *way* too well across the muscles of his back with, from what I could see with just his torso partially twisted to me, a faded out Metallica insignia. Faded jeans that also fit him way, way, *way* too well, and since I had his back I could see his ass in them, so I knew this for certain. Bare feet. Thick, black hair now definitely needing a cut, tousled and messy. Hands engaged in unwrapping something in white butcher paper. Face expressionless but no less gorgeous. Vibrant blue eyes on me.

Holy crap.

Metallica?

"Babe, come here."

An order.

I instantly jolted out of my Knight's a hot guy reverie.

Jerk!

I didn't go there.

Instead, I asked, "Are you moving?"

"Fuck no," he answered. "Kickin' Nick out. You're late. Come here."

I crossed my arms on my chest. "Actually, no. I don't have time to go there. I've only got fifteen minutes on the meter, but it won't take that long to say what I have to say to you."

His eyes never left me as I spoke and they stayed on me when I was done. They did this a while. Then they stayed on me as he moved to the phone, pulled it out of its charger, hit a button and put it to his ear.

"Spin? Yeah, Knight. Listen, there's a blue Corolla parked somewhere on the street, rosary beads and St. Christopher medallion hanging from the rearview. Meter's gonna run out. Feed it. I'll get the keys to you to move it into the garage in ten, maybe fifteen. Yeah?" Pause then, "Great. Later."

Then he put the phone down and went back to his butcher wrapped meat.

I stared.

Knight looked down at meat, declaring, "Shit car, babe. Gotta get you something decent."

"There's nothing wrong with my car," I snapped.

His neck twisted and his eyes came back to me. "Boring."

"It gets me from point A to point B," I replied.

"Yeah, but it does it with absolutely zero style."

Why were we talking about my car?

"You sent Spin or… whoever on a wasted journey. I'm just here to tell you it would make me very happy if I never saw you or your brother again. And if I do, it would make me very *un*happy in the sense that I would feel the need to phone the police. If you would like to avoid that hassle, I'll avoid your club and you make sure you and Nick avoid me."

"Babe, come here."

Was he high?

"No, I'm leaving," I fired back.

"You don't wanna walk away from me."

My brows shot up. "I don't?"

"No."

"Wrong," I retorted. "I do. Sorry," I went on then finished, "Good-bye Knight."

As I heard movers coming back, I turned to round the wall of the kitchen.

I got one step in. Then I was not only *in* the kitchen but across it, my back pressed to the counter and Knight pressed into me.

I had my hands clenched in the sides of his tee at his waist, my head tipped back. My chest was rising and falling rapidly and I was freaked.

He had movers, right there *in the house* and he manhandled me.

"Move away," I whispered, mainly because I couldn't make my voice get louder.

"No," he whispered back and moved.

His hands came up toward my face and I flinched, preparing for anything, but they settled, cupping my jaws. My squinted eyes opened wide. This was because his touch was gentle, and, even freaked out, it could not be denied it was sweet.

And his face was different. Not expressionless. As those vibrant blue eyes moved over my face, there was something working at the backs of them. Something I didn't know him enough to get, but something that I knew instinctively boded bad things for me.

"Wars fought over a face like this," he murmured like he was talking to himself. My heart stopped beating and his thumbs moved lightly across my cheeks. "A man would work himself into the ground for it, go down to his knees to beg to keep it, endure torture to protect it, take a bullet for it," his eyes came to mine, "poison his brother to possess a face like this."

Oh.

My.

God.

"Knight," I breathed.

"You are not walkin' away from me."

"Okay." I found myself agreeing.

"He made his play for you last night. Shoulda known, you on the scene, you'd catch his eye. I heard. I lost it. Was pissed at him, took it out on you. Babe, I get pissed, I do it a lot, that'll happen."

"Okay," I repeated.

"I'll try to stop it, but I know me. There are times I'll fail. You gotta get it and roll with it."

"Okay," I whispered again.

"Now, movers're almost done. I'm gonna cook. You're gonna take your coat off and give me your keys so Spinolli can move your car. And you're gonna drink a glass of wine, eat and spend the afternoon with me."

"Okay," I said softly.

He held my face in his hands as he held my eyes.

Then he whispered, "Okay."

My breath left me. My heart, which had finally started beating again, tripped as his hands tipped my face up, his head dipped down and he slid his nose along the side of mine as he continued to hold my eyes captive.

"I'll kill him, he touches you again," he murmured.

Oh boy.

"Knight," I breathed, my fingers clenching tighter in his tee.

"Kill anyone, they touch you."

Oh God.

I closed my eyes and felt his nose slide back up as a tingle slid up my spine into my scalp. I felt his forehead touch mine right before he released me.

Since he was moving away, I had no choice but to let his shirt go, so I did and opened my eyes.

"Yo!" he called as he walked to the opening to the kitchen. "One of you boys go downstairs, can you take a set of keys to the doorman?"

"No worries," one of them called back.

Knight turned to me.

I stared at him a beat then took my bag off my shoulder, dug in it and pulled out my keys. I walked to him and he lifted his hand palm up. I dropped them in and his eyes caught mine a second before he turned and disappeared around the wall.

I stood in his kitchen holding my purse, wondering what on earth was wrong with me.

Then it came to me.

Wars fought over a face like this.

I was trembling, scared now for a different reason, a far more terrifying reason, but I didn't move. I just stood in his kitchen trembling.

He reappeared and looked at me.

"Jacket, Anya," he stated. "Throw it wherever. I gotta see to the steaks then I'll get you a glass of wine. Make yourself at home."

He went to his meat.

I shakily shrugged off my jacket while walking out of the kitchen.

Okay, all right.

What the heck was I doing?

Okay, all right.

Oh boy.

Shit!

I wandered down to the sunken living room and tossed my jacket and purse on one of the two identical black leather couches that faced each other. Then I wandered across it and up to the area on the other side that was all windows. I stood there looking through the clear day to the uninterrupted vista of the Front Range thinking spring was coming. Soon, I could wear flip-flops.

"Where's Nick gonna go?"

Yep, that was me asking the window.

"Don't know, don't care." Pause then, "Do you?"

"Not really," I mumbled, and considering I was across the grand expanse of his apartment he probably didn't hear me.

"Out of my place, out of my business," Knight muttered to himself and I rethought him not hearing me mumbling since I heard him just fine.

I looked from the Front Range to him.

"He works with you?"

His neck twisted and his eyes came to me. "For me, and not anymore."

Oh brother.

As in literally.

I turned to face him fully. "Knight, if this is about me—"

"Anya, it isn't," he cut me off. I lost him as he bent to shove the meat in the oven but his voice kept sounding. "It is and it isn't. That party?"

He stopped and I prompted, "Yeah?"

He reappeared and moved around the kitchen. "Not the first time. Not even the fuckin' second. This is not his place. It's mine. He was crashin' here.

Then he moved a bunch of shit in here. I don't care, never around anyway, but he knows I don't want or like attention. He's always gettin' it for me."

He moved to the counter that delineated the kitchen from the living room and set two, wide-bowled wineglasses on it, then shifted back through the kitchen as I watched.

"So he's out," I called to his back.

"Yeah. Out. Done comin' home to him fuckin' bitches on my couch. My food gone. My booze gone. My wine gone. Blow residue on mirrors my cleaners find because he leaves them out everywhere. Them complainin' to me about used condoms in the fuckin' trash bins. Jesus. I don't need that shit." He came back to the counter with a bottle of wine and a corkscrew and his eyes came to me. "Last night, he touched your girl. My boys told me it was not a good scene. Then he touched you and made his play the way only Nick can make a fuckin' play with a woman like you, which was also not a good scene. I'm done."

"Right," I whispered thinking with all that and all I knew of Nick Sebring, I would be done too.

I turned back to the windows.

I heard the movers reappear, but I didn't look as I heard them speak.

"Done, Mr. Sebring."

"Good. Invoice or pay now?" That was Knight.

"Invoice."

"Right." Again Knight.

There was nothing for a while, then, "Whoa, thanks, Mr. Sebring."

That, obviously, was not Knight. But apparently, Knight tipped well.

Not surprising.

"Don't mention it." That was Knight, in a mutter.

Then nothing as I stared at the Front Range and did everything in my power to stop my mind from moving to why I was still there. Yes, the wars fought over a face like this comment was epic. That didn't make me any less crazy, because evidence was suggesting Knight Sebring was a whole lot crazier than me.

Tingles slid up my spine into my scalp radiating out when I felt a finger lightly tracing the edge of my racerback tank.

I turned and Knight was there, eyes down, hands both holding wineglasses, index finger on one out clearly to touch me.

God.

Seriously.

I was totally crazy.

And I should never, never, *ever* have worn this sweater. It was my best, but it was also my coolest *and* sexiest.

His eyes came to mine and he held out a glass.

"Red," I whispered, taking it.

"You don't like red?" he asked, and I looked from my glass to him.

"Yeah, I like it," I answered softly.

"Good," he replied just as softly.

"I'm a vegetarian though," I blurted, mostly because I liked his light touch, I liked his soft voice, I was losing myself in both, and I had to keep my wits about me.

He blinked.

Blinked!

I made Knight Sebring blink!

"Not really," I let him off the hook.

His eyes held mine, then he threw back his head and burst out laughing.

I stared.

I'd never seen him anything but impassive, irritated and angry. He was gorgeous even through those.

Now, laughing, it wasn't to be believed.

Oh God.

Seriously.

I wasn't crazy.

I was in trouble.

Still laughing, his arm swept out, catching me at the waist and pulling me into his shaking, hard, warm body.

Yep, totally in trouble.

His chin dipped and his dancing, vivid, blue eyes caught mine.

Oh so totally, completely *in trouble*.

Still smiling a hell on wheels beautiful smile, he muttered, "My baby's funny."

Oh God.

Oh God.

Oh no.

Oh *crap.*

My baby.

I liked that.

Seriously, totally, completely, *absolutely in trouble.*

With effort, I pulled it together again.

"How do you know what I drive?" I asked.

"Watched you pull into your place that Friday," he answered.

"And you saw the rosary and St. Christopher?" I pressed, knowing this was impossible unless he had Superman vision.

"Had a look before I took off. Seriously, you need another car."

"I don't. There's nothing wrong with it. I get it serviced yearly. Tires rotated. Regular oil changes. Toyotas last forever."

"It's ordinary."

"So?"

"Anya," his arm gave me a squeeze, "babe, you are *not* ordinary."

That tingle came back.

"You need a class ride," he kept talking. "No flash. You need no more attention than you already get. Just class."

I studied him.

Then I informed him, "Knight, I'm not sure the world sees what you see in me."

He shook his head. "No, babe, *you* do not see what the world sees. Totally fuckin' clueless."

"I'm not," I returned.

"How many men smile at you?" he asked immediately, and my head jerked.

"Pardon?"

"Men," he stated. "How many men whose eyes you catch smile at you?"

I thought about this and answered, "All of them."

He stared at me but murmured, "Right."

"They're just being friendly."

"Uh... no. They want in your pants, even if they're walkin' by you on the street."

"That isn't true," I retorted. "Women smile at me, too."

"All of them?"

I thought about this too and muttered, "No."

"Good-lookin' ones?"

My eyes slid away.

"Anya, eyes to me."

My eyes slid back.

"Good-lookin' bitches, they don't smile at you, do they?"

"Uh…" I mumbled but didn't say more.

"Competition," he decreed.

I studied him again.

Then, quietly, I declared, "Knight, seriously, honestly, all this is crazy."

"Anya, babe," another arm squeeze with a head dip and I held my breath, "seriously, honestly, you're absolutely fuckin' right. This is fuckin' whacked. It's also fucking happening."

"What *is* this?" I ventured.

"The start of you and me."

My body went still. That tingle came back, my eyes stared into his and my heart again stopped beating.

Then I whispered, "What?"

"Babe, you're standing in my arm, in my house, drinking my wine after agreeing in the kitchen."

"I haven't even sipped the wine," I pointed out.

His lips twitched.

Twitched!

I made Knight Sebring's lips twitch!

"Right, well, you will," he muttered.

"And I didn't agree to anything," I went on.

Another lip twitch.

Then a repeated, "Right, well, you will."

"Knight," I lifted a hand and hesitantly placed it on his chest (which was rock-hard by the way… seriously *in trouble*). I powered through how good his chest felt under my hand and pressed ever onward, informing him cautiously, "You kind of scare me."

"Yeah. I'm that guy 'cause I need to be that guy," he stated mysteriously. Then his face dipped to mine again and he talked quieter when he continued, "Straight up, baby, I'm also that guy 'cause I just *am* that guy. But you'll learn you got nothin' to fear from me."

"You drag me around," I whispered.

"Yeah, and you follow me."

"I kind of have no choice," I pointed out.

His head went back and all traces of amusement left his face when he informed me, "You always have a choice. You didn't take it. Except once, when you pulled away from me at the elevator."

This was, casting my mind back, kind of true.

"There were two times that you carried me," I reminded him.

"And both times you held on."

Damn. This was true too, and not kind of at all.

"I need to ponder this."

His arm tightened and a gorgeous smile spread on his equally gorgeous face. It was at both that I realized I said that out loud.

A buzzer sounded in the kitchen.

"Right, then do it eatin' a steak. I'm hungry," he ordered. He let me go and sauntered toward the kitchen.

I stood, watched him move and took a sip of my wine.

Then I found my feet following him.

When I arrived, he was pulling out the grill pan in order to flip the meat.

"Can I help?" I offered.

"Yeah, grab some placemats. Drawers this side of the bar." He took me up on my offer as he slid the grill pan back in the oven.

"You have placemats?"

He straightened and looked at me.

"Yeah. Why?"

"A man who wears a Metallica tee doesn't have placemats," I informed him and his lips twitched again.

"Yeah, you're right, unless he's also a man who hired a bossy bitch who seriously likes to spend money to kit out his new condo. *That* man owns placemats."

My eyes swept the kitchen with its black KitchenAid appliances, counter appliances and the hooks under the counter where the shiny, expensive-looking cooking utensils hung. It had a black-on-black theme with black marble countertops, shiny black cupboards and even black tiles on the floor.

My eyes kept moving through the living room with its stream-lined couches, low, glass-topped coffee table and large, tall, chrome, curved lamps at kitty-corners with their domed, white shades drooping over the area. All this sitting on a charcoal gray rug that looked like a huge, square piece of fluffy fur.

My eyes continued moving over the low chest at the top, situated against the wall that had three black, huge, glossy bowls on top that were wicked cool but held nothing. Then my eyes took in the heavily-framed print on the wall above it that looked like a lot of gray and black splotches and strokes that depicted nothing and made me feel less. And last, there was another state-of-the art, expensively-designed CD player mounted on the wall.

It was all spare, colorless but dead cool.

I looked back at Knight. "So this woman bought everything?"

He was pulling down glossy black plates from a cupboard as he answered, "Asked my favorite color, that was it. Then she bought everything."

"Let me guess, you told her your favorite color was black."

His eyes came to me and his lips twitched.

Again!

"No, I said it was red."

I stared at him.

Then it was *me* who burst out laughing.

Through my laughter I asked, "Seriously?"

"No fuckin' joke." He put the plates on the bar and opened a drawer as I moved to open and close two before I found and grabbed two black, cloth place-mats. "Jacked. I was away on business, came back, this is what I got. Not a hint of red in the place. Not a hint of *anything*."

I set the placemats by the stools on the other side of the bar and asked, "Did she do your bedroom?"

"Yeah."

"So you don't like satin sheets?"

His eyes came to me. There was something in them that made me go still, but he answered, "Took one look at them, nearly lost my mind. Luckily, she wasn't around. Slept on 'em one night, would never sleep on anything else. Not at home."

"So they're nice," I whispered.

"Fuck yeah," he whispered back.

We stared at each other a beat as I felt his two words hit me in a very secret place.

Then Knight's eyes moved over my face before they caught mine and he said quietly, "Think it's a good idea we quit talkin' about my sheets."

I nodded because I agreed.

Definitely.

He put cutlery on the counter and ordered, "Arrange that shit and park your ass on a stool, babe. I'll serve this up."

I grabbed the cutlery, shifted around the other side and arranged it on the placemats as Knight worked in the kitchen. Then I parked my ass on a stool, sipped wine and watched.

He was cutting open steaming baked potatoes when I noted, "You explained the car. How do you know my last name?"

"What?" he asked, buttering the potatoes.

"The doorman knew my last name. I can only assume you told him."

His glanced at me then went back to the potatoes, now grinding pepper over them. "Nick told me."

I felt my brow furrow. "Nick knows my last name?"

He put the pepper aside and grabbed some maldon salt out of a small black bowl and tossed it on the spuds. "Day after I ripped him a new asshole about the party, he asked who I took home. I told him your first name then he said, 'Anya Gage?' and since you're probably the only Anya in Denver, and definitely the only Anya at that party, I guessed. So, yeah, Nick told me."

"How did Nick know?" I asked.

"No clue," he muttered, moving to the fridge.

I didn't like that.

"I don't know if I like that. I never told him my name."

Carrying a tub of sour cream, Knight's eyes cut to me. "Your girl?"

That could be.

"Maybe," I muttered.

"Speakin' of her," he started, reaching into a drawer to grab a spoon, "she needs to tone it down."

"What?"

He glopped big spoonfuls of sour cream on the potatoes and his eyes came to me. "You gotta advise her to tone it down. Seen her at my club more than once, though never with you. She's on the hunt. Makes men edgy. Makes her vulnerable. She'll do what she's gotta do to get what she wants and they know it. They also know what she wants. She opens it up right off the bat, they take what they want, throw the rest back. And they throw the rest back because she gives the vibe they let her in even a little bit, she'll suck 'em dry. She needs to watch you, make your moves."

"My moves?" I asked as he set the sour cream aside and went for the oven door.

"Yeah," he answered, sliding out the grill pan.

"What are my moves?"

He answered as he put the thick, fillet steaks on the plates.

"The girl in the corner, surveying the scene, playing it cool. You don't go to them. They come to you, if they got the balls to do it, which, my guess, they rarely do because they can't hack not cuttin' it and losin' the promise of you. You're the girl you take out to dinner. Get the good champagne. You pay her attention. Buy her some shit that softens her up and makes her happy. Then you hope all that sweet turns wild when you get her in bed."

He saw me in the corner?

And he thought all that other stuff about me?

My throat felt clogged but I forced out, "Excuse me?"

His eyes came to me, brows raised. "Am I wrong?"

"Yes," I answered immediately.

"Bullshit," he muttered then went back to the fridge.

"Uh... Knight, I would know and you are."

He didn't answer. He just came back with a bowl of salad.

Then it hit me.

"Is this you paying me attention, softening me up in order to get me to bed?" I asked.

"You'll be in my bed, Anya," he told the plates as he mounded salad on them.

After the brief satin sheets discussion, I wanted to be.

Now.

Not so much.

"Sure of yourself," I muttered. He turned with both plates and dropped them on the placemats.

Then he put both hands out wide, palms flat on the counter and leveled his eyes to me.

"One thing we got left that we gotta know is covered is that you suit me in bed. That happens, babe, you know there's gonna be a you and me. Where that goes, anyone's guess, but however it goes, there'll be a you and me."

Right. Now he was a gorgeous, scary, psychopath who was genius at throwing out compliments however they came and unbelievably arrogant.

"What I know is I'm going to set a record for the fastest steak consumption in history and then I'm gonna get out of here."

One side of his mouth curved up, his eyes warmed and he turned back to the fridge.

He came back with a couple bottles of salad dressing, dropped them on the counter in front of me then rounded it and took the stool beside me.

I grabbed the ranch and started pouring.

"Babe, you need to take my point," Knight said quietly.

"Which one?" I asked cuttingly, spearing into my salad with my fork.

"Call down your girl. She needs to cool it. She doesn't, she'll get hurt and that hurt can come a lot of different ways."

"I think last night your brother taught her that lesson," I informed him and shoved salad in my mouth.

Knight didn't reply.

I chewed, swallowed and speared more salad as I went on, "And right now, you're teaching me a different one."

Suddenly, his hand was wrapped around the back of my neck and my eyes weren't on my plate. They were on his because he'd pulled me to him twisting.

"Don't fight this," he warned.

"I've decided there's no *this* to fight," I returned.

"You're terrified of me and you walked in here yourself. No one dragged you here. You brought no one to take your back. No one made you stay. Don't try to bullshit me or yourself about the fact that you don't wanna explore this with me. You want it or you wouldn't be here. I get you fighting it. I'm just tellin' you, you are not gonna win."

"You don't know that," I told him.

"Yeah, I do, because you're sittin' right here with me."

"And I can walk away."

"Yeah, you can do that, but you're not going to, and I know this because you came in the first place. And I also know this because when we were talkin' about my sheets, your face told me you wanted to know what I could do to you on them. And no matter what your head tries to fuck you with, you're not gonna be able to stop until you find out."

"I'm not certain I like you."

"You don't need to like me to let me fuck you, but since I like you, I'd prefer it that way."

I stared at him, feeling my belly curl despite being pissed at him.

Then I whispered, "You like me?"

His eyes again moved over my face before locking on mine and he whispered back, "Babe, you apologized for bein' in my bedroom and you meant it. In one day, you returned a phone that cost a G and you did it with all its packaging. You thanked me for roughin' up your landlord. And you made me laugh. And this doesn't get into how much I like lookin' at you. So, yeah, I fuckin' like you, and I do because you are the only woman I've met in over a decade who'd do any of that shit."

I liked that. I liked a lot of things about him. I also disliked a lot of things about him. And there was so much coming at me, I couldn't keep track of which was winning out.

"I find all of this very confusing," I admitted cautiously.

"You get in my bed, I'll sort you out."

Seriously?

Something for the dislike side.

"You're that good?" I asked with mild sarcasm, but he pulled me closer so my face was an inch from his.

"Yeah, I am, baby. I will take care of you there in all the ways you need me to do it. That I can guarantee."

I could feel my heart beating in my neck as I looked into his super serious eyes.

Call me crazy, but his confidence and the words that went with it which pretty much promised he'd look out for my needs was definitely on the like side.

Time to shut this down.

So I blurted, "I've decided I'm hungry."

His eyes went from serious to warm again. When they did that last time I wasn't up close to get the full impact, and having it, I wished I didn't at the same time I memorized that look and the feeling it gave me.

Then he said gently, "Then I better let my baby eat."

"That'd be good," I replied quietly. "But can we do it without talking? Most the time you talk, it freaks me out."

It was then his eyes lit with humor close up and that was even better.

"Works for me," he muttered then, "You cut into that steak and taste it, you won't be talkin' anyway. You'll be shoveling more in."

"Can't wait," I whispered. His eyes dropped to my mouth and darkened.

Okay, that was the best.

Then his eyes came back. His hand gave my neck a squeeze and he released me.

He turned back to his plate. I followed suit. He started eating. After a gulp of wine that almost choked me, I resumed.

About five seconds later I found he was right about the steak.

Melt in your mouth.

Perfect.

Chapter 6

Something Calm
and Nourishing

My eyes opened slowly and I had no clue where I was. I just knew I was supremely comfortable and warm.

Then I saw them. Floor to ceiling windows and the lights of Denver twinkling.

I was on the slouchy, comfortable, gray suede couch in Knight's whatever room, the one at the end of the hall where he kept his TV and clearly where he did his normal, average, everyday living (if he did that). It was decorated in shades of gray from dove to charcoal, but it was far less stylized. Decked out for comfort not visual impact. And it was where he led me to wait it out when he got called away for some business he didn't exactly explain to me.

I saw the enormous plasma TV mounted on the wall was blue screen which meant the DVD Knight loaded for me was done. I'd missed it. With a sleepless night, I'd zonked out.

But I'd done it without the soft, woolen throw on me.

Knight was home and he'd thrown a soft, woolen blanket over me to keep me warm.

Okay, right.

Um…

Crap.

I took in a deep breath, stayed stretched out warm and comfortable on his couch and allowed my mind to sift through our post-lunch activities, which were what led me to agree to hang while he saw to what he needed to see to in order for me to be there when he returned.

He had, as agreed, not talked while we ate. He had also provided me with an amazing lunch. It wasn't just the steak which was, incidentally, by far and away the best piece of meat I'd ever tasted. The baked potato was delicious too. The skin was crunchy and somehow flavored in spices, garlic, Italian herbs, and the inside was fluffy with just the right amount of seasoning, butter and sour cream. It was simple, filling and yummy.

When we'd finished, he'd broken the seal on speaking to tell me to "keep your ass on the stool". I did this while he picked up our plates, carried them to the sink and casually dropped the cool-as-heck crockery in with a clatter. He left them there without rinsing and moved to refill my wineglass.

Then he'd sauntered out of the kitchen, disappearing around the wall only to return within moments with a pack of cigarettes and a Zippo lighter in his hand. He came direct to me. He tagged my wineglass, handed it to me then took my other hand. Gently, he tugged me off my stool and moved toward the doors to the balcony, not going down the steps to the sunken portion but guiding me around the edge.

Even in bare feet and just a tee in the mid-March Colorado chilly air, he walked out, taking me with him. He let me go to shake out a cigarette and light it with flicks and twists of his Zippo. I was not a smoker, but call me crazy, I'd always thought Zippos were cool. Then he dropped the pack and the lighter on the wrought iron table, wrapped his fingers around my elbow and positioned me at the balcony railing.

I held my breath as he positioned himself behind me and wrapped an arm around my chest, pulling me back into his front side.

He lifted his cigarette and took a drag. I lifted my wine and took a sip.

"You shouldn't smoke," I advised after I swallowed.

"Heard that before," he muttered.

"I bet you have," I muttered back.

"It bother you?" he asked, and I thought about this.

Even though I was a lifelong non-smoker, it didn't. It was whacked, but it reminded me of home. My Dad smoked. So did my aunt. I was used to the smell. As far as my Dad was concerned, it made me nostalgic. As far as my aunt was concerned, it was just the way it was. It was home. Both of them that I had growing up.

"No," I answered softly but honestly. "It reminds me of home."

"Your folks smoke?"

"Yeah, my Dad. Then my aunt. She was a chimney. Pack and a half a day."

I felt his body tense and he asked, "Your aunt?"

"She raised me after my parents died."

He was silent a moment, the tenseness increasing, then his arm loosened around my chest only for his hand to shift me. He shifted too, resting a hip against the railing. Then his arm around my waist pulled me close to his front, almost touching, as he looked down at me.

"Your folks passed?" he asked quietly, his eyes intent but his face back to blank.

"Yeah, when I was in second grade."

His eyes slightly narrowed. "Both of them?"

"Carjacking."

No blankness then. A flash lit his eyes and I heard him draw in a sharp breath.

Then he whispered, "What the fuck?"

"They worked together. No..." I shook my head. "They *went* to work together. They worked in buildings across from each other so they drove in together. They drove me to school, dropped me off, then drove into work together. Witnesses said they were sitting at a red light and some guy with a gun opened Dad's door. He shot him three times, yanked him out to the street, got in and took off with Mom in the car. Fifteen miles from there, they found my Mom, in the road, also shot. Dad survived the trip to the hospital but died in surgery. Mom took a bullet to the temple. She was gone before he shoved her out of the car."

His arm left me, his eyes did not. His hand came to the side of my neck and slid up into my hair as he muttered, "Jesus, fuck, baby."

I shook my head. "Knight, it's okay. I know it sounds dramatic, but it isn't. Shit happens all the time to a lot of people. Obviously, they had no idea that they were going to die at the same time so they didn't make arrangements for what to do with me. My aunt, Mom's sister, got me and control of their estate, such as it was, and life insurance policies. My uncle, Dad's brother, lives in Alaska. He went through the motions of trying to get me to take care of me, but he worked on a pipeline, wasn't married and lived in a barracks with a bunch of other guys. Judges didn't go for that. And my grandmother, Mom's Mom, was already sick so she was out. She left my grandfather and he went back to Russia because apparently he was a jerk, but also he missed home. But he didn't miss his daughters and had nothing to do with them after he left. Dad wasn't close to his parents. They'd already raised two sons and weren't hot on having a seven year old to raise so they didn't try for custody. Still, they were relatively cool and still are, though they live in Arizona now. So my aunt raised me and she, um... smoked. And also, uh... she drank a lot of vodka."

Knight's eyes kept mine captive and he asked, "Drank? She gone too?"

"No, she's very alive. Apparently, if you become one of Satan's Minions, as a reward, he makes you immune to cancer, heart and liver disease."

At "Satan's Minions", I felt his fingers flex tightly against my scalp but he waited until I was done speaking before he asked, "She didn't do right by you?"

As an answer, I explained, "I had a job at Arby's and moved in with three girls. Paid rent, slept on a couch for eight months until one of them moved out, and I did this two days after I turned eighteen. I still went to high school until I graduated, but at eighteen I was g... o... n... e... *gone.*"

"She didn't do right by you," he murmured then twisted his neck and I watched him take a drag from his cigarette and exhale an angry stream of smoke. He then contemplated the Front Range with an expression on his face that made him look like he was plotting to annihilate it.

"Years ago, Knight," I said quietly, and his eyes again tipped down to me.

"She beat you?" he clipped out.

I shook my head. "No, she's just not very nice."

"In Anya Speak what, *exactly,* does not very nice mean?"

"Anya Speak?"

"You're playin' it down, I know that. But I don't know you enough to know how you're doin' it. So I want to know and I want to know it *exactly.*"

"Knight—" I started, and his face dipped to mine even as his hand in my hair pulled me up to him.

"Exactly, babe," he ordered.

I sighed.

Then I started talking because I didn't know him very well either. But I was getting to know the fact that he tended to find ways to get what he wanted, and most of these ways involved extreme levels of bossiness mixed with tenacity.

When I started talking he shifted away, let me inch back, and he smoked while I did it.

"She was just not nice. And her not-nice got bitchy-not-nice when she drank a lot, which unfortunately was often. We didn't have a lot and she didn't have a lot before she took me on, and I'm not certain she was smart because she didn't count on the life insurance policies and the rest of what she got selling our house and stuff running out so fast. But since she blew all that on vodka, smokes, clothes, new furniture, a stereo, a TV, dumping me with my sick Gram and going to Vegas or on a cruise and stuff like that, it was bound to."

Knight kept smoking as I was speaking, but his hand in my hair slid down to my neck and his thumb stroked the skin there.

It felt nice. So nice it was a distraction, and to keep my mind off how nice his thumb felt lightly stroking my skin, I kept talking.

"But she wasn't even nice before the money ran out. I knew I was a drain on her because she told me. I knew she felt she deserved compensation for taking me on because she pretty much made me her slave. I cooked. I cleaned. The minute I could drive I did the grocery shopping. She didn't do any of that, and when I say that I mean never. She sat on her butt and if she wanted a drink, she told me to get it for her. Iced tea, occasionally. Vodka, mostly. She didn't help me with my homework, though she probably wasn't smart enough to help. Didn't care about my grades. She constantly made remarks about my clothes, my hair. Just being nasty. The minute I could get a job she made me, then she made me buy my own stuff and stopped giving me money. Only a roof over my head and feeding me. She was in a bad mood perpetually. Life wasn't good for her, never was. But if life isn't good, she's not the kind of person to find a way to make it that good, or at least make it better. Just expected it to be, and as time wore on and it didn't get better, even if she didn't do anything to improve it, she got more and more pissed."

Knight kept smoking, watching me, stroking me, and I pulled in a breath and continued.

"She had no man, or no man who hung around a lazy woman for very long, though she blamed that on me, too. She said the men in her life dumped her because she had me hanging on her neck. But really, it was just her. And worse, she really loved my Mom. Like, *really*. It's jacked, but I think the only person in her life she really loved was my Mom. I look like my Mom. She told me that all the time. I reminded my aunt of my Mom and she said more often than not that it sucked I was there and my Mom was not. I've thought about it, and I always wondered if it was that that made her such a bitch. That she missed my Mom, didn't know how to deal, had an overabundance of feelings she had to get rid of and didn't know how, and was the kind of person to take that out on me. Whatever. Bottom line, it was no fun. So the minute I could, I got out. I never see her anymore. Now she's just a memory."

Finished, I stopped talking.

Knight didn't move, not his body or his eyes away from me.

Then his hand left my neck and he shifted around me to go to the table to put his cigarette out in a clean, cut glass ashtray that was sitting on the wrought iron table. Once done with this errand, his eyes went back to the mountains.

He did all this and did not speak.

I didn't either, but I turned to watch him and kept watching him as he surveyed the Range.

Finally, thinking this was weird, I called, "Knight?"

His eyes instantly came to me.

"I'm taking you to dinner tomorrow night," he declared and I blinked.

I'd done what he asked, explaining about my aunt *exactly* and he had no comment.

Jeez, this guy was weird. Hot, but weird.

"I can't," I told him. "I have class."

"Class?" he asked.

"School. Beauty school. I'm getting certification in skin technology."

"Tuesday," he stated immediately, and I shook my head.

"Clients. Two of them. One at six thirty. One at eight."

"Clients?"

"I'm already a certified nail technician. Both are acrylics."

He turned to face me fully and asked, "Why do you take clients on evenings and weekends?"

"Because I work as a file clerk full-time during the day."

He studied me.

Then he murmured, "Life isn't good, find a way to make it that way, or at least make it better."

"What?" I asked quietly, but I knew what. Those were my own words coming back to me.

"Don't know shit about this," he announced. "Do women who do nails need to have a full-time job to cover their asses?"

"Um... no. But I only have a part-time clientele. To rent a station in a salon or whatever and make a living at it, I need a full-time clientele. I'm working to that."

"Babe, full-time work with school, just pointing out, that's an impossible feat."

"I only have a few weeks left on my skin technology certification so I can start taking clients on Mondays, Wednesdays and Friday nights. That'll make it easier. And I can diversify and pick up facial clients, too."

His mouth got tight. Then his eyes went back to the Range.

"Knight?" I called.

His eyes cut back to me. "Schedule you keep, babe, no time for me. Not likin' that."

I pressed my lips together because this was kind of true.

"I don't work Saturday nights and most of Sundays," I said softly.

"I *do* work Saturday nights which leaves only Sundays," he replied then repeated, "So, not likin' that."

Jeez. He said he liked me, but evidence was suggesting he *liked* me.

And I liked that.

"You come to the club on Saturday," he declared. "Bring your girls. I'll give you a VIP and send a car for you and them. Any friends you got that you want there, I'll give you Kathleen's number, she'll get you the passes you need for them to join you in your section. I'll spend time with you in the club if I got it. But rest up. You'll be spending time with me after I'm done. I also claim Sunday."

"I have clients on Sunday morning," I told him.

"I'll take you home to take them and I'll pick you up to spend the rest of Sunday with me."

Take me home?

This meant he assumed I'd be spending the night with him.

And I liked his assumption.

My heart squeezed.

The cell in Knight's back pocket rang.

"Give me a second, babe," he muttered, pulling it out, looking at the display then hitting a button and putting it to his ear. "Yo," he greeted, paused then there was a semi-growled, "Tell me you're shittin' me." Another pause then an annoyed, "What time is it?" Pause then, "Why the fuck did she wait until nearly two fuckin' thirty to drag her ass to you?" Silence then, "Jesus, fuck, this bitch is gonna do my fuckin' head in. Shit for brains. She report he's a regular?" Pause then, more annoyed, as in *far* more annoyed, "He's done it before?" Another pause then, sinisterly quietly, "Oh no. This is a message I'm gonna relay. Got

Anya with me. Gonna get her settled and I'll meet you at the club." Pause then, "Right. Twenty, maybe thirty. Later."

He hit a button and his eyes came to me.

"I gotta go do something and I want you to wait here for me."

"Maybe I should—" I began, but he shook his head.

"I want you to wait here for me."

"Knight—"

"Anya, you aren't gettin' this, but two weeks ago when you walked into my bedroom to use my phone, the life you been livin', which isn't all that good, got better. A fuckuva lot better. Because I'm gonna make it that way. And in return, I'm gonna ask very little of you. And right now, all I'm askin' is for you to hang here until I come home so I can spend more time with you since I'm probably not gonna see you again for another week."

He was going to make my life better.

Oh God.

Oh my.

Oh crap.

He was right. He already had. Expensive phones. Safe apartment. Saved costs of a taxi. Succulent steaks. My girls enduring a scene and getting VIP vouchers and escorts to their car to try to make it better.

Shit car, babe. Gotta get you something decent.

Oh God.

He was thinking of buying me a car!

"Anya?"

My body jolted and my eyes focused on him.

"Knight, I don't know."

He was three feet away.

Then he wasn't. His hands were cupping my jaw again and his face was all I could see.

"Babe, eat what you want, drink what you want, watch TV or a movie and just wait for me. All I'm askin' is for your time, and when I get back, your company. And I'm tellin' you I really want you to give it to me," he said gently.

God, seriously, he liked me.

And I liked how much he liked me.

Because, call me crazy, I liked him.

"Okay," I agreed.

I watched from close as his eyes smiled.

My heart squeezed and my lips parted.

Then I watched from close as his eyes dropped to my mouth. Then I watched them darken.

At that, my breasts swelled, my knees got weak and my one free hand came up to grab onto the side of his tee at his waist.

"Fuck, wanna take that mouth," he muttered like he was talking to himself, but I heard him since he was right there with me, looking at my mouth, eyes now dark *and* hungry, and that tingle slid up my spine, my neck, radiating over my scalp as another tingle hit a secret place deep inside me.

Okay, right.

Okay, God.

I wanted him to "take" my mouth. I wanted that with every part of me.

My body swayed into his, but his hands tensed on my jaw and his eyes moved to mine.

"Not now, baby," he whispered. "I take your mouth, I wanna give it time and attention, and I don't have the first. And I give it the last, I won't do what I gotta do."

That was disappointing. Seriously disappointing.

Even so, I whispered back, "Okay."

He didn't let me go, just looked in my eyes.

Then, the pads of his fingers tensing into my skin, in a rough, sexy-as-heck voice that also tingled in a secret place in me, he growled, "Fuck, I cannot fuckin' *wait* to have you under me and lookin' up at me like you're right now fuckin' lookin' at me."

Okay, right.

Okay, *God.*

I liked that, too.

"Knight—" I breathed.

"Jesus, I'm gonna possess that beauty."

Oh God.

Another secret tingle.

"Honey," I whispered as I swayed closer.

"Step away from me, Anya," he ordered.

"Pardon?"

"Step away from me, baby. Now."

I looked into his eyes. Then I did what I was told.

His hands fell away but one grabbed mine. He took me to his shades of gray, comfy whatever room and loaded up a movie for me. Then he ran a finger across the hip of my jeans, promised me he'd be back soon and he left me.

When he did, I sipped my wine and freaked out. I stretched out on his comfy couch while still freaking out and sipping wine. Then I put my wine on the square coffee table in front of me and tried to focus on the movie.

Then, obviously, I fell asleep.

And while I was sleeping, Knight came home and covered me with a soft, warm, woolen throw.

Two weeks ago when you walked into my bedroom to use my phone, the life you been livin', which isn't all that good, got better. A fuckuva lot better. Because I'm gonna make it that way.

I closed my eyes and sighed.

Then I threw off the blanket, pulled myself up and walked across the room to the windows. No sunken portion to this room, all one level. Still, it was awesome.

I stared at the view, noting what I'd already noted vaguely. No time, day or night, was Knight's view bad. Sunshine, Denver and mountains during the day. Moonlight, city lights and midnight-purple mountain shadows at night.

As my eyes unfocused, the twinkling lights of Denver went hazy and I saw me reflected in the windows.

I had good hair. Even Sandrine said she wished she had my hair and her hair was amazing. I also had a lot of it. It was long, past my bra strap at the back. It was shiny even when I didn't use shine-inducing products. A deep, rich, glossy brunette.

I also lucked out in the skin department. When I was younger, around that time of month I might get a blemish or two, but this stopped in my early twenties. My skin also had the uncanny ability to look good in a rosy, creamy pale way in the winter, but I tanned relatively easily in the summer.

And even I liked my eyes. This was because they were my Dad's and my Mom always used to look in my eyes, smile her sweet smile, and whisper to me in her sing-song way, "When Irish eyes are smiling…" My Dad was Irish and even though neither of them had been to Ireland, both declared with grave authority that the Irish had the most beautiful eyes in the world. And Mom put Dad and my eyes forward as proof, and she did this repeatedly.

I couldn't see them very well in my reflection in the window, but I knew they were a light gray with a very thin ring of midnight blue at the edge of the iris. They were set well in my face and with Mom giving me her dark, long lashes and dark, arched brows, even I had to admit my eyes were striking.

I was five seven. I had tits and ass and a slightly rounded tummy. And even though I tried to run as often as I could, did ab crunches and stability ball crunches, not to mention regular pushups and other stuff, that roundness didn't go away. My midriff was lean, my waist tiny. I had decent arms; not as toned as Sandrine, but they weren't flabby. But that round in my belly always got to me. Vivica told me I worked it, it looked good on me, men totally dug it, especially as it came with my little waist, big ass and breasts. She also told me I'd learn that as time went on and get over hating it.

But that had yet to happen.

Other than that, looking at my reflection and knowing it by heart in my mind's eye, still, I was seeing me differently.

I was seeing what Knight saw in me.

People were people and everyone was different. There were as many different tastes and opinions as there were people. And it wasn't lost on me there were men who liked tits and ass and hair far, far more than they liked super lean and cut.

And, clearly, Knight was one of those.

But it was my face he talked about, and standing there, I remembered how Dad used to stop Mom for no reason but to cup her cheek and run his thumb over it as his eyes moved over her face. He did this like he was mesmerized, like he was seeing her for the first time, even though he'd had her for years. And he did it always smiling.

And I also remembered how my aunt would get drunk on occasion and wax on and on about my mother's extreme beauty.

"Coulda had anybody," she'd slur. "*Anybody*. A movie star. A millionaire. With one look. That was how beautiful was my Ekateirna."

It didn't hit me until right then that even though she talked trash to me often about what I wore, my makeup, my hair, she also told me often I looked just like my Mom. So her giving Mom that compliment meant she was also, even though she didn't get it, giving it to me.

I had a face that launched a thousand hard-ons. A face men would fight wars for. A face that a man as aggressively masculine and beautiful as Knight wanted to possess. So much, he barely knew me but knew he had little time with me and intended to make ways to get as much as he could get.

I watched my hazy reflection in the glass smile a secret smile that was just for me as I felt something calm and nourishing settle deep inside me.

Then I moved out of the room in search of Knight.

The minute I opened the door, I heard Billie Holliday. It was super quiet and I knew that was because he wanted music, but he didn't want it to disturb me.

I smiled my secret smile again but it didn't curve my lips. It curved in that tranquil, sated place inside me.

I hit the living room-kitchen area and saw the under the counter lights on in the kitchen and one domed light softly illuminating the sunken living room. There was also a tall floor lamp I hadn't noticed in the corner of the windows on the upper level that was casting a soft glow on the space.

Knight was not to be seen until my scan of the area took in the outside of the balcony, and I saw his shadowy frame and the glowing tip of a cigarette.

I moved there and out and saw him turn to me.

He'd put on boots and a black turtleneck. I wondered if it covered Metallica or if Metallica was gone and totally casual, personality-showing Knight was a memory, and I had somewhat casual, hot guy club owner in an expensive turtleneck Knight.

"Hey," I called as I moved across the balcony to him. "Sorry I fell asleep."

"Here, baby," he called back softly even as I was going there, but when his arm came out I knew he meant he wanted me *there* as in, in his arm.

I thought about it as I moved the two feet I had left.

Then I did it and his arm curled around my waist. He pulled my lower body into his.

"Business done?" I asked, tipping my head back to look at his face softly illuminated partly by moon and city lights and partly by the lights coming from his apartment.

"Yeah," he answered then asked, "You sleep last night?"

"Not even a little bit."

"Fuck," he muttered then got half the reason right, "Nick."

He was the other half of the reason, but I didn't share this. I didn't say anything.

He shifted and crushed his cigarette in the ashtray he had resting on the edge of the railing.

Then he came back to me, curving his other arm around me so he held me loosely in both and asked, "What happened to him?"

This question was confusing so I asked back, "Who?"

"Guy who did your parents."

I sucked in an unexpected breath like he'd struck me with a surprise body blow.

He either didn't hear it or was focused because he repeated, "What happened to him?"

"He got life," I whispered.

"No shot at parole?"

I shook my head. Two murdered people who were doing nothing but driving to work. They were the parents of a seven year old and killed by a man who took their car because he was literally on the run from cops. Cops who finally caught up with him because he was wanted for putting his pregnant girlfriend in the hospital because he was pissed she was pregnant. A problem he solved since she lost the baby.

No. No parole.

Knight kept at it. "He livin' a long one?"

I shook my head. "I don't know."

"He died in prison, it's likely cops would let you know."

"Would they tell my aunt?"

"If he bought it when you were a minor, maybe, expecting her to tell you. Now, no. They did it, they'd find you."

"Well, I haven't heard anything."

He was quiet a moment before he muttered, "No shot at parole, nothin' to inform you about."

I suspected this was true, but I had no idea. I didn't think about him. Ever.

And I didn't want to now either.

"Why are you asking about him?" I asked quietly, and his arms gave me a light squeeze.

"Nothin'. Just curious, baby. I'll shut up about it, yeah?"

I nodded.

Knight asked, "Hungry?"

For some reason I giggled then explained, "Uh... lunch was kinda big."

"Yeah, babe, but lunch was also six and a half hours ago."

I blinked up at him.

"Is it that late?"

"Uh… yeah."

Whoa.

"Maybe I should go home," I mumbled to his throat and I got another light squeeze.

"No, maybe you should answer my question if you're hungry."

Thinking about it and knowing the time, suddenly I was.

"Yeah. But if you make me steaks, I'll explode."

I heard his soft, deep chuckle. I also felt it. I'd never done either and I liked both immensely.

Then he told me, "Got a quota, baby. I cook once a week. You got that thrill. I'll take you out for something."

A date. In fact, that day had been the longest, weirdest, strangely most comprehensive date in history, even though I'd showed at his place to tell him I never wanted to see him again. We'd shared. We'd touched. We'd had profound moments of intensity. He'd cooked for me. I'd napped in his house. And now we were going out to eat together for the first time.

As I thought this, I got another light squeeze and a simple order. "Jacket, Anya."

I didn't move, but looked into his shadowed face. "Can I drive your car?"

"No," he denied immediately.

"I'm a good driver."

"Your ass is next to me, I drive. You wanna borrow it sometime, it's yours."

"Knight, I only had one experience, but I think I'm actually a better driver than you."

"This is doubtful, babe, seein' as I drove drags, sprints and raced streets. My Dad was a fuckin' race freak. Lived it, breathed it, put me behind the wheel of a cart when I was eight and never looked back."

This explained the "driving since I was twelve" comment, though he'd semi-lied since I thought go-carts counted so he'd been driving since he was eight.

I didn't quibble this fact. Instead I pointed out, "Those race people get in wrecks all the time."

"When's the last time you heard of a driver getting in one on a city street?"

He, unfortunately, had a point.

I decided not to tell him that and concede through silence.

He accepted then declared, "I drive. You ride. Not a rule, that's a law. Get me?"

"What if you've had a freak accident and you've broken your arm and ankle?" I asked for specifics.

"If that shit happens, I hope to God you're smart enough to pick up a phone and call an ambulance rather than draggin' my ass to my car, which would be agony, shoving it in, which would be more agony, and taking me to the hospital."

Another valid point.

Again I conceded through silence.

Knight's body started shaking and his voice was too when he asked, "Are we done with this fuckin' stupid conversation?"

"I guess," I muttered, still wanting to drive his car.

I got another light squeeze and he dipped his smiling face in mine. "Whenever you want, baby, you can take my ride out. Just say the word. I'll arrange it. I'm just not gonna be in it with you."

"Why?" I asked.

"Because I'm a man," he answered.

"So?"

"I'll clarify," he offered. "I'm a man who does not let my woman or any woman drive when my ass is in the car."

"That teeters over the edge of macho crazy, Knight," I informed him.

"Yeah," he was completely not offended, "Heads up, babe, get used to that."

It was then it occurred to me he was pointing out the obvious.

So I conceded not with silence, but instead by sharing, "Now, I'm even more hungry."

I got more of his hard body shaking against mine. I liked it and he reiterated, "Then *jacket*, babe."

"Right," I whispered.

I pulled away and moved into his apartment to get my jacket and purse.

I met him where he was waiting for me at the top of the three steps in front of the mouth of the hall.

He took my hand.

He took me to his car.

Then he drove like the ex-speed-racer he was and took me to dinner.

I was lying in bed, feeling my new soft sheets, thinking Knight's satin ones were probably way softer. I was also staring at my ceiling and thinking that Knight Sebring had claimed me, no doubt about it, but he had yet to kiss me.

Dinner wasn't good; it was great. He took me to Wynkoop's and suddenly, somehow, after the day, the nap, me coming to my understanding and our lighthearted, safe and amusing bickering, I was at ease. Knight always seemed at ease even when he was pissed or annoyed. He was just Knight. And I settled into that.

He told me about his race-freak Dad. He told me about his race-widow Mom. He told me they both were still alive and lived in Hawaii. He told me I was right, Slade stayed popular because he closed it down for a month every year after he put out bids to designers to offer their visions of a shit-hot new look, he picked one and went with it. He told me his business that day had to do with a side business that also vaguely linked with the club (though he didn't fully explain). He told me Nick had always been a pain-in-the-ass fuck-up, but he'd also, obviously, always been a brother. So Knight put up with it and covered a lot so his parents wouldn't take any hits from Nick's asshole behavior and fuck ups, but that didn't make him any less done with it.

I told him about Vivica and Sandrine. I shared detailed specifics of my schedule. I hesitantly and shyly told him about my goal of opening my spa, during which he watched me weirdly intently the whole time I talked about it rather than just with his usual deep interest. I told him next up in the buying schedule was not a sweet ride, but an excellent quality table where I could do my facials. And I shared that the Wynkoop and its beer were one of my top five favorites in Denver on both the restaurant and beer counts.

This was easy conversation with a number of smiles, a few deep chuckles (Knight), a few soft giggles (me). Since we sat on the same side of the booth, more than once, when my sweater drooped down to expose my shoulder, Knight's finger came up to trail my skin lightly. It was at these times I congratulated myself for my heretofore unknown clairvoyance that wearing that sweater was the very right idea. I did this after he quit touching me and before I pulled the sweater back up. And I pulled it back up because I knew it would drop down again, catching Knight's attention (because he never missed it, not once) and I'd get his touch back.

It was a game. We both knew it but it was debatable which one of us liked it better.

He'd driven me back to his place, parked beside my Corolla that was in his second parking spot, and informed me the remote to operate the gate to his garage was on my visor. He handed me my keys that he collected from Spinolli while I was sleeping.

Then one of his hands cupped my jaw, his face dipped close and I stopped breathing because I thought he was going to kiss me, and I really, really wanted him to.

Instead, he slid his nose along mine in that sweet way he did earlier, holding my eyes locked to the warm intensity of his the entire time. But then, to my disappointment that was so extreme it was almost despair, he lifted his head up half an inch.

Then he whispered, "Call you soon, baby. See you Saturday."

He dropped his hand and moved away.

With no choice but to throw myself at him, which I was not going to do, I just smiled, got in my car and drove off.

He stood with his arms crossed on his chest, the side of thigh resting against the back of his car and watched. I knew this because I saw him in my rearview until I had to take the turning ramp up to the next level.

Now I was in bed wondering why he didn't kiss me and wishing I'd thrown myself at him.

And also thinking that Saturday was a long, long way away.

Chapter 7

Cornucopia of Feminine Delights

Tuesday afternoon, I was in the file room at work when my kickass, space age phone rang and I saw the display said "Knight".

He'd called the day before (he obviously had my number since he bought my phone). I programmed him in after he called, and he'd done it late, ten thirty. I was already in bed reading, or trying to read, and trying not to be disappointed he hadn't called (or alternately, pissed he hadn't). I answered thinking I shouldn't, since it seemed he was playing me because I figured he called that late because he was, well… playing me.

But he wasn't. I knew this instantly when I heard the club sounds in the background so loud I could barely hear him. And his first words were a short but succinct description of the fact he'd had "shit come up all day", and he had little time to talk right then but wanted to "connect" with me. The growly factor of his voice was at the upper levels in my limited experience so I knew this was frustrating, as was the fact our conversation had to be short, hurried and, on his part, growled very loudly.

Now it was an hour and half until quitting time, not even twenty-four hours since his last call, which, in the Jerk Player Handbook, garnered severe penalties unless you weren't a Jerk Player.

I took the call, put it to my ear and said softly, "Hey."

"Hey, baby," he said softly back, and that tingle hit my spine and spread north again. Then it stopped when he asked bizarrely, "Who's Dick?"

"Pardon?"

"Dick. Who is he?"

"Uh…" I mumbled, thrown by a question I didn't understand and thus not knowing the answer.

"Neighbor, babe," he clarified.

"Oh," light dawned, "Dick."

"Yeah. Dick. Who is he?"

Suddenly I thought our conversation was not only strange but funny.

I didn't share this. I just asked, "How do you know Dick?"

"I don't know Dick, but that isn't what we're talkin' about. We're talkin' about how you do."

"He's my neighbor. He lives across the hall from me," I explained.

"A friend?"

What was this about?

"Uh... no. And now I know you don't know Dick because if you did, you wouldn't ask that. Now, why are you asking about Dick?"

"Sent some shit to your house. Last time with the phone, sent Kathleen. She's got it goin' on, but she's got so much goin' on, sometimes she doesn't pay attention to outside shit. She said the call system was reactivated and she just kept hitting directory buttons until someone picked up and would accept delivery. Since she was busy, she didn't pay a lot of attention to who accepted it. The boy I sent with the shit today did the same, but he's a guy, and for certain things, guys get unbusy. He got Dick so he got unbusy, seein' as he did not like Dick. He also did not like how excited Dick got about accepting a delivery for you. Luckily, some guy called Charlie came up while my boy was gettin' acquainted with Dick. Said he was the maintenance guy, had a passkey and would put the shit in your place. He told Dick to take a hike and after Dick took off, Charlie told my boy that if he had more stuff for you that he should not, under any circumstances, hand it off to Dick. Then he gave him his contact details as well as a list of people in your building who he would trust to take deliveries. My boy reported this to me, so I'd like to know about Dick."

God, I loved Charlie.

And I also wondered what "shit" Knight was delivering.

I wondered too long, clearly, and I knew this when Knight's voice came at me impatiently, "Anya. Clue me in on Dick."

"Dick is that burden every single girl living on her own in a slightly seedy apartment complex endures. He's the creepy, out of work neighbor who lives across the way."

"He make you uncomfortable?"

"Uh... yeah. He's Dick."

"Then it's time Dick moved."

My body went completely still, but somehow I managed to get my mouth to force out, "What?"

"It's time… Dick… *moved.*"

His smooth deep voice was not firm.

It was steel.

"Knight—" I whispered.

Knight cut me off, "I'll send a boy today to share with Dick his new relocation plans. I'll also call you later. When's your last client leave?"

I blinked repeatedly at the tall, square counter where I did my filing and didn't speak.

"Anya, babe, someone needs me. When's your last client leave?"

"Nine, she doesn't feel chatty," I said breathily. "Nine thirty more regularly, after she shares a glass of wine with me."

"I'll call you after nine thirty. Later, baby."

Then he was gone.

I dropped my hand with the phone to the counter I was still staring at.

Dick had relocation plans because Knight didn't like me living across the hall from someone creepy.

"Holy crap," I whispered.

"What?" Beth, one of the front desk ladies asked, walking in.

I looked to her and whispered, "Nothing."

She stared at me then moved to me and peered closer. "Jeez, Anya. Is everything okay?"

And to that, in the throes of understandable temporary insanity, I blurted, "I have a new boyfriend. He's awesome. Protective. And scary. And he regularly freaks me out by being all of those at once."

Her face spread in a huge grin. "You have a new boyfriend?"

"A new boyfriend who's awesome, protective and scary. A lot of the time mostly the last."

"Cool," she said like she didn't hear me. Or, I should say, she selectively heard me.

"Beth, I said he's scary," I reminded her.

"Girlfriend," she said, flipping her hand in the air, "count your blessings. Any dude hooked to you has got to have more than his fair share of scary. He doesn't, new scary, awesome, protective guy will steal you right out from under his nose. So, my advice, ride the awesome and protective and ignore the scary." Her eyes narrowed. "Unless... does he do scary shit to you?"

I decided to quit sharing and start lying. "No."

Her smile came back. "Right on. Tell him he needs to come and take you to lunch. Give me a heads up. That way, I can amass all the girls up front to give him a once-over and when you get back, we'll deliver our verdict."

Unfortunately, my mouth decided to start sharing again so it said, "He's sheer, raw, aggressive masculine beauty from head to toe."

She blinked. Then she smiled big again.

Then she announced, "I am not surprised. And now, knowing that, his behind better be here soon so you better get on that since I'm walking out, passing this juicy morsel around. Therefore peer pressure is about to go extreme."

Me and my big mouth.

Beth dumped some papers in my in tray with a farewell of, "Later, gorgeous."

Then she hurried out to share the juicy morsel I volunteered very, very stupidly.

I stared at the papers thinking that filing was getting old. It was boring. It was mindless. And it was never ending.

Then I thought about how nice it would be to live without the constant possible disquiet of running into Dick somewhere in the building and having to find a way politely to get the heck out of his presence.

Then I wondered how Knight's "boy" would convince Dick to go.

I decided not to think about it.

After I did that, I wondered about myself that I wouldn't think about it when I knew I should. And not only that, I should wonder about a man who could and would do the stuff Knight clearly had no problem doing.

Then someone else came in and dumped a bunch of stuff in my in tray, so I quit thinking about all of that since I had to get to work.

After work, I successfully made it to my apartment without a run-in with Dick. This didn't happen often. Not even regularly, since Dick was dedicated to whatever creepy shit he did in his apartment and less dedicated to creeping out his neighbors by lurking in the halls or creeping out the general population of Denver by joining their numbers. But still, I counted myself lucky and again buried the urge to turn over in my head the fact that my new boyfriend was going to remove him from my life. How he was going to do that. How that was morally probably not okay. And the fact my new boyfriend was clearly my new boyfriend and he hadn't even kissed me.

All these thoughts flew from my head after I locked all three (two new) locks on my door and wandered into my apartment looking for the "shit" Charlie put in there that Knight's boy delivered.

I froze as I got abreast to my couch and saw the plethora of glossy bags on it.

Incidentally, my couch was awesome. It was flower print, girlie, but it was a cool print, and since it was the only thing in the room that was flowery, it worked (even though the rest was pretty girlie). As usual, I bought it on sale and since it had a small rip in one of the cushions, the price was seriously reduced. But I just flipped it over and, *voila!* Perfect couch.

And right then, it was even more perfect when I saw the names on the bags that were on my couch.

My shoulder slumped so deep my bag fell right to the floor. Then I hustled to the couch, dropped my keys on my vintage, oval, white, awesomely chipped, quirky coffee table (that, yes, was totally girlie) that I bought for three dollars at a yard sale and I reached into the first bag.

I pulled out an expertly tissue wrapped parcel, carefully tore the tissue away and shook out a black dress, it's fabric so far away from polyester or any synthetic fiber it was... *not...* funny.

It felt like what I thought heaven would feel like.

When I held it up I saw it looked like what an angel would wear too, if she had her own personal Italian designer, showed serious skin, wore black and not white and had whopping, mega style.

Holding it to me, I smoothed it down my front as I felt my nose start to sting.

I'd never seen anything so exquisite; never touched it, held it and certainly never, ever *owned* it.

I carefully laid it out across the back of the couch and went back to the bag.

Dress two, a metallic platinum. Sublime.

Dress three, red. Flawless. Awe-inspiring.

After smoothing the red out on the couch, I went to the next bag.

Shoes. Three pairs. All high heels. All sandals. One pair black. One platinum. One red. The prices on the labels on the sides were not torn off or marked out and the least expensive pair was seven hundred and fifty dollars.

My heart, beating hard, started racing.

Next bag, three exquisite evening clutches. Red sequins. Black jet beads. Champagne satin.

Next bag, this one smaller: a bunch of little boxes. One, a collection of thin bangles, all set with tiny red beads. Another, earrings that matched the bangles, long threads of red beads mixed with long threads of thin silver links. Another, a twisting choker of strings and strings of jet beads. Another, matching earrings that were a burst of the same. Yet another, a wide bracelet with an intricate, heavy, complicated clasp that was part of the adornment off of which were strung dozens upon dozens of tangled champagne, seed pearls. The last, earrings of the same, so long, when I held them up to my ear, they brushed my shoulders.

And finally, at the bottom of the dress bag, a business card-sized card with Knight's black slashes, ordering:

A, Saturday, pick one. K

Pick one.

Pick one.

Nose still stinging, I stared at my couch and coffee table over which was strewn a cornucopia of feminine delights as delivered by my awesome, protective, scary new boyfriend who hadn't even kissed me yet.

Stiltedly, I walked to my purse on the floor. I bent, grabbed it and equally stiltedly walked back to my couch as I dug out my phone. Once my fingers curled around my extortionately expensive phone, I dumped my cheap (but cute) purse next to the expensive new "shit" Knight had delivered to me. Then I bent my head and hit buttons.

I put the phone to my ear.

Knight's smooth, deep voice said in my ear, "Sebring, leave a message."

And the message I left was a soft, trembling, "Honey, you haven't even kissed me yet."

Then, feeling stupid, scared, elated, mystified and anxious—not only that this felt so good, often times right, many times terrifying, sometimes confusing—but also anxious that he'd given me so much, no matter what it was, that I wouldn't live up to the promise he saw in me. I beeped the button to disconnect and stared at my booty.

I sucked in breath and carefully, reverently put my stash away in my bedroom before I made a quick sandwich, ate it and set up for my client at my cute, chipped, white-painted, quirky dinette that a friend gave me when she moved in with her man and he declared he would not sit his ass at that dinette.

I was riding an elephant. It was white, its trunk up and trumpeting.
I was in my new red dress, shoes and bangles and I was giggling.
And somewhere my cell phone was ringing.

My eyes opened and I saw dark. I heard my cell stop ringing and I blinked at my alarm clock.

It was twelve thirteen.

I heard the call up buzzer sound in my living room.

What on earth?

I threw back my new, down comforter with its subtle, soft, flowery pattern (okay, so I had more flowers, but they were in another room so that was acceptable). Part sleepy, definitely groggy, I dashed in my baby blue with tiny pink polka dots drawstring, pajama short-shorts and my baby pink shelf bra camisole into the living room.

I flipped on the overhead light, grabbed the phone off the wall by the side of the door and muttered, "'Lo."

"Anya, babe, been out here five fuckin' minutes. You gotta sleep like the dead. Buzz me up."

My breath left me.

Knight.

I blinked. Then I shook myself and depressed the button that buzzed him up.

I heard the door outside open through the receiver then nothing.

I put the phone back in its cradle and stared at it.

He hadn't called after my client. He hadn't called between clients. He hadn't called at all, not even after I left a message. This was disappointing and a little scary. But I got to sleep telling myself that when my day ended his started, so I had to get over it because clearly his demonstration that day was not about game playing.

And now it was after midnight and he was here.

Here.

Right now.

Taking the elevator (maybe).

And I had bed head, no makeup and was in my pajamas.

Oh God!

Panic instantly froze me as a million thoughts coursed through my head. None of which I had time to do anything about—like changing, swiping on mascara, brushing my hair and/or teeth or spritzing with perfume—and I knew this because there was a knock at the door.

I shifted to it since I was standing at it, looked through the peephole and saw Knight's handsome head tipped down staring at what I figured was my doorknob.

Suit, dark again. This time a shirt the exact color of his eyes.

God, God, he was beautiful.

Another knock. Impatient.

I jumped, unlocked the deadbolt, the twist lock on the knob and slid off and dropped the chain. I put my hand to the knob to turn it but it was turning in my hand already.

I jumped back when the door opened and Knight surged through.

I looked up at his face, seeing instant and extreme intensity and whispered, "Honey, is everything oh—?"

I got no further. This was because his hands were cupping my jaws and pulling me firmly up until I was on my toes at the same time his head was descending.

Then his mouth slammed down on mine.

I made a noise at the back of my throat, lifted my hands and curled my fingers into the lapel of his jacket.

His tongue darted out against my lips.

My mouth opened and it swept inside.

Oh my, he tasted *good*.

I whimpered, held his lapels tight as my legs got weak and my body swayed into him.

His tongue plundered my mouth, and there was no other word for it. That was it, *plundered.* And he did this delicious activity in a kiss that was very wet, very hard, very long, very demanding and very, very *amazing.*

So much so, I whimpered into his mouth, one hand detaching from his lapel to slide swiftly up and around the warm, sleek skin of his neck and into the soft, thick mess of his hair. I pressed my torso deep into his as best as I could, still holding onto his jacket with his hands at my jaw.

And I gave myself to the kiss. To Knight. All of me cupped in his hands. All of me plundered by his talented tongue.

He tore his mouth from mine and I made a mew of protest because I didn't want to lose it. It had become the reason for my being. It was existence. At the same time my fingers spasmed in his hair and I pushed even closer in a nonverbal effort to share this message.

I felt his warm breath on my lips, it was coming fast and my eyes slowly opened to look into Knight's dark, hungry ones.

"Now I've kissed you, babe. Feel better?" he asked, his voice rough and so... *fucking...* beautiful.

I wanted to laugh because it was funny. It was also sweet.

But I couldn't.

I could only hold on and breathe, "Yes."

His eyes moved over my face and darkened, that intensity corresponding with the intensity of the wetness gathering between my legs, and he asked, "Like the dresses?"

"Yes," I repeated breathily.

"Good," he whispered then, still in a whisper, "Gotta get back, babe."

I blinked and my hand spasmed in his hair again.

"What?"

"Work, Anya. I got shit to do. Didn't have time. Took it to get your gratitude now I gotta get back."

I didn't move. I held on and held his eyes.

He let me for a long, happy moment before muttering, "My baby doesn't want me to leave."

No. I didn't.

I didn't share that. I let my body do the talking and it did this by continuing to hold on and not move.

"Told you, baby," he said softly, "when I took your mouth, we'd need time so I could give it attention. Your sweet message, couldn't wait so I didn't. But, fuckin' sucks, now, I gotta go."

He'd taken time out to come all the way to me.

God.

God.

I liked that.

And he needed to go.

So I pushed away, my hand sliding out of his hair as I whispered, "Okay, honey."

The thumbs of his hands still at my jaw swept my cheeks. Then he leaned in, slid his nose along mine, lifted up as he pulled my face down and kissed my forehead.

He tipped my face to him again.

"Later, baby."

"Later, Knight."

His fingers gave my face a gentle squeeze then he let me go and he was gone.

I followed him, locked the locks, turned off the light, turned my back to the door and stared into my dark living room.

I wrapped my arms around my middle and smiled.

Huge.

Chapter 8

Hold the Fuck On

I walked into the nearly summer-like air of the late March night.

It was Saturday, just after ten. Less than five minutes ago, I got a buzz up with the announcement, "Yo. Ride to Slade at the curb."

And that was it.

No greeting, no introduction, and I knew by the electronic click he was gone.

So I got my bag, dashed to the bathroom to give myself one last look, opened my bag to make sure everything was there and I ran down.

The car was long, big, black and gleaming. It was also double-parked. And Hulk was standing outside it wearing a black shirt, black trousers, black blazer and a scowl.

"Back's full, woman, you take front," he declared when I got close then he opened the passenger-side door.

I smiled into his scowl because first, I was wearing a killer outfit. Second, I had a killer night with my friends ahead of me. And third, after three days of quick phone calls, nothing at all that day and the rest of the time Knight was sight unseen, I was going to see him that night.

I slid in and twisted immediately to look into the backseat where Viv and Sandrine where sitting, decked out, eyes on me, smiles huge.

"That… dress… is… *hot!* Ohmi*god!*" Sandrine shrieked.

"No joke, fuckin' shit, she is not lying," Viv concurred.

I grinned and whispered, "I know."

Their huge smiles beamed. They knew about the dresses because I'd told them. In fact, I told them everything, so they had both done an understandable about-face about Knight Sebring.

Hulk slid in, twisted his tree trunk neck and aimed his scowl at me.

"Woman. Buckle," he grunted.

I looked back at the girls then turned to face forward and followed Hulk's orders.

The minute he heard the click, Hulk put the car in gear and we started rolling. Then he reached into his inside jacket pocket, pulled out a phone, flipped it open and hit buttons. He did all this with his eyes to the road.

He was taking a right when he said, "Yo." Pause, "Yeah. She's here." Pause then, "Red." Pause, "Later."

He flipped his phone shut and shoved it back into his pocket.

But me...

I had stopped breathing.

Red.

He was reporting in.

Knight wanted to know which dress I was wearing.

I twisted my neck and looked back at the girls.

They had big eyes and still wore their huge smiles.

They knew what I knew.

I giggled.

They giggled too.

Hulk muttered, "Shit."

I giggled harder.

They giggled harder too.

Hulk drove us to Slade.

I was standing in our VIP section, holding a martini glass with the dregs of my lemon drop in my hand, when the three friends I was talking to of the twenty-five I invited that night looked beyond me.

But I knew.

It was late. I'd been there hours. It had to be well past midnight. I'd had four lemon drops.

And finally he was there.

I turned my head and saw an aubergine shirt and black suit jacket, then my eyes tipped up in time to see Knight's head dip down right before his lips skimmed the skin of my bare shoulder.

That tingle came back, but it slid up to my scalp and down to the small of my back, radiating out across my waist, hips and bottom.

God, lovely.

He lifted his head barely an inch, but his eyes came to mine.

"Hey," I whispered and I could, even in the loud club. He was that close.

"It fits," he whispered back.

"Yeah," I confirmed the obvious. The dress fit perfectly. Like it was made for me.

His eyes shifted over my shoulder and unfortunately he straightened, but I felt the heat of his body hit my back as he got close.

"Ladies," he greeted, his smooth voice pitched loud to be heard over the music.

I looked from Knight to them to see my girls were all staring in various degrees of shock and wonder.

"Knight," my voice was pitched higher too and I indicated them in turn with their names, "this is Monica, Helen and Christie."

He tipped his chin up.

Monica swallowed.

Helen peeped, "Hey."

Christie flashed a quick wave and her lips moved but no sound came out.

I stifled a giggle.

"Right. You're hot, my girl's dress is scorching and I'm in the VIP section drinking free so, just FYI, you've elevated yourself above that dickface douche-bag of a brother. Now, I get he's your brother, and our skin isn't the same, neither is our blood, but I'm sister to Anya and Sandrine so I think you also get me."

This was Viv perpetrating a sneak attack from the side, and to make certain her important message was received over the music, she was shouting at Knight.

His head had turned to her. My heart had stopped beating. And Christie, Helen and Monica wisely affected a hasty retreat.

"I get you," Knight replied.

"And there may be some universe where my girl Anya wears cheap shoes and saves for a fucking cell phone, but this one isn't it. Therefore she's been living a travesty. I'm glad you're sorting that shit out," she went on, again loudly.

I felt Knight's arm slide around my waist as I watched his lips twitch, but he did not reply.

I, however, did.

"Viv, now's a good time to *shut up*."

"Men understand direct communication. It's bitches who speak in code," she returned.

Knight's arm got tight, pulling my side into his.

I liked this, it felt nice. I wanted to enjoy it.

But since my friend was crawling up my nose being as she could be, direct, protective and crazy, instead of doing that, I retorted to Viv, "Right, well you communicated pretty directly. Now shut... *up*."

"He bought you that dress, those shoes, so he's way into you in a way nothing I can do would make him less into you," Vivica shot back.

"Let's not test that, shall we?" I suggested loudly.

"As entertaining as this is," Knight broke in, "if you wouldn't mind, I wanna steal her a second."

"Be my guest," Vivica agreed magnanimously, sweeping her arm out and everything.

The good news was Knight immediately moved me to a darkish corner where there was privacy, a booth seat lining the wall and no one around. And the no one I wanted to be around at that moment was freaking *Viv*. The other good news was Sandrine was tipsy and therefore on the dance floor dancing by herself, which was her way. This wouldn't last long since one, two, five or twelve guys would join her eventually. But it meant she wasn't there, so she could not also embarrass me. And the last good news was that Knight *was* there. Finally.

And there was no bad news.

We got to the corner and Knight shifted me in a way I knew he wanted me to plant my bottom in the seat so I did. He moved in beside me, close beside me. He slid an arm along the back of the booth seat, but his eyes went across the platform, locked on something and he jerked up his chin.

I followed his eyes and saw the cocktail waitress rushing our way.

I felt my glass sliding out of my hand. I looked down to see it was now in Knight's, then I followed it to watch him hand it off to the cocktail waitress.

"Anya gets San Pellegrino the rest of the night starting now," he ordered, she nodded and dashed away.

I looked at Knight.

"What? Why? I have a VIP card. Kathleen dropped it off for me. I've never been a VIP. I need to live it up."

"Babe, you're mine. Anytime you're in Slade you're a VIP and drink free."

Oh.

Cool.

"Really?" I asked.

He stared at me then shook his head and one side of his mouth curved up.

I guessed that was my answer since he said nothing further, and although his head shake was negative my guess was his answer was positive.

Since he didn't say anything, I did.

"Why water, Knight? I'm not drunk. I'm not even tipsy."

"And you're not gonna get that way. I'll fuck you drunk, baby, but not the first time."

My breath left me in a hard whoosh.

Knight kept talking. "So water, the rest of the night. You get me?"

I nodded.

His eyes moved over my face.

Then he asked, "You got anything for me?"

I stared. Then I panicked.

He gave me a driver, a VIP section and four free drinks (as well as unlimited San Pellegrino, not to mention the dress I was wearing, etc.). Was I supposed to bring a thank you gift?

"Uh…" I mumbled then stopped.

"Anya, I haven't seen you since Tuesday."

This was true.

"I know," I somewhat yelled over the music.

"And you got nothin' for me?"

"Um…" I began, stopped then bit my lip.

His twitched, he dipped his face close and ordered, "Baby, fuckin' kiss me."

Oh.

God.

Oh God!

I'd never kissed him and he'd only kissed me once. And when he did, I didn't really kiss him back. I just went along for the ride.

Oh God.

God!

Well, fuck it. If I sucked it would only mean my world coming to an end. No pressure.

Damn.

I lifted a hand to his neck, tipped my face back, held his eyes and pressed my lips to his.

Then I closed my eyes as I smelled his cologne.

God. Amazing.

I ran my tongue along the crease of his lips.

Then suddenly his arm was locked around me. My torso was tight to his, my body twisted so I was angled across his and partially in his lap and his other hand drove into my hair as his tongue thrust into my mouth and *he* kissed *me*.

Plunder.

I had it once.

I missed it desperately.

My arms circled his shoulders, one hand in his hair. I held on and enjoyed the heck out of the ride.

He broke the kiss but pressed my head in, his shifting so my lips were at his ear and his were at mine.

"You see me, four days, fourteen, four hours, Anya, you kiss me," he growled in my ear.

"Okay," I whispered in his.

His hand at my waist slid up my side then down as he murmured in my ear, "My baby and lemon drops."

I shivered.

"When I fuck you drunk, you drink lemon drops."

I shivered again and whispered, "Okay."

"Okay," he whispered back then, "Fuck. So fuckin' sweet."

I turned my head slightly so I could smell his neck.

I didn't know what that was, but whoever created his cologne should be given a medal, an island or their very own small country.

Knight, who didn't miss much, didn't miss me taking him in.

"You like that?" he asked.

"Yes," I whispered.

"Good," he whispered back on an arm squeeze. Then I got another one that didn't relax in a way that felt different, and I pulled my head back to look at his profile.

He was focused on something that was not me and I twisted my head to see Hulk gesturing to him.

I felt Knight move and saw the end of a chin jerk then his eyes came to me.

"You gotta go," I said softly.

His eyes moved over my face and back to mine.

"Yeah," he replied softly.

I tipped my head to the side. "See you later?"

"Definitely."

I smiled.

His eyes moved to my mouth. He leaned in and brushed his lips against mine.

Then he pulled back and locked our eyes.

"Did you wear the red for me?"

For some reason I felt timid suddenly, but still I answered, "It's your favorite color."

I was rewarded immediately. His face got soft, his eyes got dark and his beautiful lips whispered, "Baby."

And I instantly decided I was adding a lot more red to my wardrobe.

Before I knew it, I was on my feet, my hand in his and he led me to Vivica.

"You're on duty," he informed her.

She smiled huge and he trailed his fingertips across my hip as his eyes held mine a second.

Then he was gone.

"I… fucking… *love him,*" Viv announced and my eyes went from where I last saw Knight to her.

Quick judgment.

Shocker.

"All the intel isn't in yet," I reminded her. "And you've been in his presence, like, a second."

"Girl, this is what I know. That guy would have to be a freakin' terrorist for me not to… *love him.*"

"Why?" I asked.

"Uh… that dress?" she answered.

Point well made.

"The look on your face right now," she went on.

Another good point.

"The fact that he walked through a club that's filled with beautiful people, most of them women, and from the instant I spotted him to the instant he left he only had eyes for you."

My stomach melted.

"Really?" I whispered, my word swept away by the music, but she watched my mouth move and nodded.

Game, set, match to Knight.

My eyes shifted to the floor and I grinned a secret grin that wasn't really secret, but it felt that way.

Vivica kept going.

"Nick, one look, douchebag motherfucker. Knight, one look, yeah, the guy is a guy you do not fuck with, but other than that, class, command, confidence and cash. And that last in a way that he just has it because he earns it, and he's not in your face about it because he's got so much of the other three he doesn't need to be."

"I already decided I'm going to explore this, Viv." I shared something she knew loud enough for her to hear, but hopefully not loud enough for the others around us. They were my friends, but this kind of stuff was only for the close posse.

"Yeah, and what I'm saying is as you do, that man, you'll find out shit that will freak *your* shit right out. You power through, girl, and get to the other side. Because if he stays the way he is with you right now—and I am not talking about dresses and space age phones, I'm talking about him making the world melt away while he sits with you on a booth seat in the busiest club in Denver—it will be worth it."

"What do you mean I'll find out shit that will freak me out?"

She glanced around then pulled me to the side away from some friends.

Then she started talking.

"He went from a drag racer to a club owner in a hop, skip and a jump. Club success at age twenty-six. He's the master of all you survey and as far as I know answers to nobody. So that means no investors, so that means he dumped his own money into this place. I have no clue, but just the glasses cost a whack so the rest of this place, my guess, millions. I also have no clue about drag racing, but, my guess, that doesn't make a millionaire. He drives an Aston Martin. He owns seriously exclusive real estate and sends a driver to pick up his woman and her friends. He keeps his shit so tight *nobody* knows a thing about him, and trust me, I've been asking around. He owns Slade. He's got a motherfucker for a brother. He drives a sweet ride. He does not date, but he gets wild amounts of pussy by picking and choosing from his dance floor. And none of those bitches talk, but if you bring him up, they sure do smile. No one, but no one, who has all that, does all that and no one knows fuck all about all that doesn't have secrets. Big ones. So he freaks your shit out, Anya, his secrets come out, you hold on and roll with it. Are you getting me?"

I stared at her.

Then I asked, "Wild amounts of pussy?"

She stared at me and stated emphatically, "*Wild.*"

Oh my God.

"Babe, girl, babe, listen to me," she said quickly, her hand grabbing mine and I knew I must have been freaking out visibly as well as internally. I focused on her and she continued, "You know me. I do my homework. And that shit dried up two weeks ago."

"You're sure?" I asked.

"No. I'm no PI and I don't follow him home. But I know folks who practically live here. They see him, know who he is and know he gets himself some, and he hasn't been checking out his regular smorgasbord in a while."

My head tipped to the side. "He doesn't date?"

"That's the word."

"What does that mean?"

"He likes you, he'll cook for you at his house. He wants to get off, he does and you go home."

Cooks for you at his house?

Oh God.

Vivica's hand gave mine a squeeze. "Babe, he took you to Wynkoop's. And I don't have to remind you that he cooked for you but he didn't *do* you."

"Oh God."

Her hand now gave mine a shake. "Babe, listen to me. The dresses, the phone, the car, the VIP section, *not* his MO. Wynkoop's, *definitely* not. Intel is still comin' in, but it's slow and there's not much to be had. But if he was a man on the town, it wouldn't be. People would see him and report back. They haven't. His life is this club and his condo. The girls go there then the girls leave there, and more often than not, don't come back. And they don't go there for a steak, heart to heart conversation about their dead parents, a nap, then he takes them out to eat and sends them home without a kiss. Nor, to my knowledge, does he show at their house in the middle of a night finally to get that kiss. He's into you. If he was a big spender, his fuck buddies would be reigning supreme in one of these sections and doing it regularly. From what I heard, *you* are the first."

I was rethinking having shared such detail about my Knight Encounters but, alas, too late.

"Why didn't you tell me all this before we went out?" I asked.

"Because I wanted to see him with you to know what all the rest meant. Now I know. He's into you, and not for a fuck. He's just *into you*."

My eyes shifted over her shoulder and I muttered loudly, "Cocktail waitress, two o'clock."

Viv let my hand go and turned to my side. I smiled as the waitress arrived and I accepted my San Pellegrino.

Viv turned to the cocktail waitress and asked baldly, "You know if Sebring set up any of his other women in their own VIP section?"

Oh God, Viv and her curiosity. She was an assistant catering and banquet manager at a swank hotel. She should have been an investigative journalist.

The waitress got pale, I could tell even by the club lights.

She swayed away but answered politely, "Mr. Sebring doesn't allow gossip."

"We won't tell," Viv assured.

"I can't take that chance," she replied. "I'm sorry, but when I say Mr. Sebring doesn't allow gossip, I mean, if he found out, I'd lose my job."

Wow. Interesting.

Viv looked at me. "See what I mean?"

I gave her wide eyes and looked back to the waitress. "Sorry, she didn't mean to put you on the spot."

"If he asks, tell him I didn't say anything," she stated and I felt my brows draw together.

But I answered, "Okay."

"It was a big thing, me getting a VIP section. He only picks the right girls for that. This is my first. He gives you a bonus if you get a section like this because sometimes the drinks are free or go on a tab and they forget to tip. Rich people, they do that a lot. Even celebrities, they get so much free stuff, they can be not-such-hot tippers. Or that's what the girls say who've worked these sections. So Mr. Sebring gives a good bonus. Way beyond any tips you can make, and he gives it even if you make tips, like your friends are giving tonight. I want to do it again. I have a kid. I can use a bonus, regular-like. So, you know, his woman, her friends curious, he might get that you'd ask me then ask if I spilled. You'll tell him I didn't, right?"

"Right," I said quietly, but she still heard me. I knew this from the relief on her face and I figured she was a dab hand at hearing stuff through loud music since she had practice.

"You need another water," she tipped her head to my water then looked at Viv with her half-full martini, "or a Grey Goose martini," she smiled gamely, showing she remembered Viv's order, "you just call me. Yeah?"

"Yeah," Viv replied.

"And I'll tell him you did a good job," I added, but she shook her head.

"You don't have to. He'll know. He watches. From his window. He sees everything, or one of his boys does. That's why I think he might ask you if I spilled, in case he sees me right now or one his boys does and reports it to him because they tell him everything."

"Well, if you're nervous, you don't have to stick close, honey," I told her.

She nodded. "No offense, but Mr. Sebring's rules are no matter who the celebrity, everyone in the section gets attention so I should do a walkthrough."

"Go right ahead," I offered.

She nodded again, smiled then took off.

I looked at Viv to see she was looking after the waitress.

Then her head turned to me and she grinned.

"You're a celebrity."

"Uh, Viv, didn't you think that was weird?"

"Uh, Anya," she leaned in, "*yeah*. What did I tell you? The man keeps his shit *tight*."

I didn't like this.

"You don't like that."

I blinked, my head jerking and I stared at Viv.

"Get out of my head," I ordered.

"Girl, I've known you eight years and you've been my best friend seven and three quarters of those eight years. It's impossible for me not to be in your head. So I'll repeat and use an example this time. Sandrine. We both have been watching for six years that girl trying to land the golden goose. You landed yours. No matter how bumpy the ride gets, listen to your Auntie Vivica: hold the fuck on."

My back straightened. "Knight's not a golden goose."

She leaned in and her face was serious. So serious, I held my breath.

"He is. He absolutely, one hundred percent is… the… golden… goose. And that's dresses, phones, shit-hot apartments, Aston Martins and a beautiful man who only has eyes for you and makes the world melt away when you two are together, even if that together lasts five minutes. There are very few women who meet men like that in their lifetime because there are very few men like that alive. And there are fewer women still who recognize it, take care of it and move heaven and earth to keep it. Now, listen to me. Hold. The. Fuck. *On*."

"Okay, Auntie Vivica," I whispered.

She leaned back, grinned and ordered, "You waver, you call me."

I sucked in breath.

Then I agreed, "Okay."

Her eyes dropped to my hand then back to me.

"San Pellegrino?" she asked.

"Knight doesn't want me drunk," I answered.

She grinned again. It was slower. It was knowing. And her eyes got warm.

"You do the nasty, you also call me."

I rolled my eyes.

"I don't care if he makes you sign a contract and sues your ass for telling me. I wanna know how that man is in bed."

"How about this," I started to suggest. "We set up a scoring system right now and that way I can just give you a number, it says it all and I avoid being sued."

"One, he's shit, not worth discussing and you're dumping his ass but keeping the phone, shoes, bags, dresses, and etc." She said instantly and went on, "Two, he's shit but not such bad shit it's worth losing the apartment, the ride and the VIP section. Three, he's still shit but there were moments. Four, he's somewhat shit, but only because you think it's new, worth another go and it'll get better. Five, average and workable. Six, slightly above average and promising. Seven, he got you off in a happy way, but there's room for improvement. Eight, all good and possibility of getting better. Nine, he rocked your world. Ten, he created all new ones and you never wanna come up for air. Work for you?"

"I'm not sure I'll remember that."

"Well, I will so don't worry. I'll give you a refresher when the time comes."

She *so* would.

I burst out laughing.

Viv slid her arm around my waist, pulled me close and she burst out laughing too.

I slid mine around her waist and once I quit laughing I took a sip of my San Pellegrino with lemon in it.

Then I turned my head, tipped it back the inch it had to go to catch my girl's eyes, leaned close and whispered, "I so love you."

"And I so love you, too. And, babe, let me tell you, this guy is real, doesn't play you and fulfills the promise everything about him shouts straight out, I will get on my knees and thank God. Because since you were born, you deserved great. And since you were seven years old, you got shit and then worked your ass off for every little scrap of good you could earn. And if he's the sun finally on your horizon, I'm naming my first boy after him. Which, admittedly, is not a hardship since his name is badass and not Herbert. But, still."

I smiled into her tawny eyes.

She smiled into my gray ones.

Then she sucked back martini.

I sucked back water.

Then I asked, "Wanna dance?"

To which Vivica answered, "Absolutely."

We set our drinks aside and hit the dance floor.

***

Fifteen minutes later, on the dance floor I felt a hand on the small of my back that didn't move.

I twisted my neck and blinked at Hulk.

He leaned in and shouted in my ear, "Knight wants you off the dance floor."

I couldn't have possibly heard him right.

So I leaned into him, still swaying to the music and shouted back, "What?"

He kept his mouth to my ear, hand to the small of my back and repeated, "Woman, Knight wants you off the dance floor."

I pulled back, caught his eyes and asked, "Off?"

He nodded. "Yup."

"The dance floor?"

Another nod. "Yup."

What on earth?

"Why?" I asked.

"I don't question. I just do. And Knight wants you off *the dance floor.*"

I leaned into him and shouted, "What if I don't go?"

"Then I carry you to his office, lock you in, tell him you declined and leave you to explain to him why you did."

Oh God.

I looked up toward the window to Knight's office.

I didn't know what to do. I liked to dance. I didn't like to be told I couldn't. Not at all. But this was his party and he'd paid for it in a lot of ways, which was something at that moment I did not like.

Crap.

I looked at Hulk.

He'd carry me to Knight's office. Totally.

Crap!

I turned to Vivica who was moving but watching, and I put my hands to my mouth.

"Gonna go back to the section," I shouted.

Her eyes shifted from me, to Hulk, to me.

Then her hands went to her mouth and she shouted back, "Like I said. Hold the fuck on."

She swayed away and started to bust a move, which was also Viv's way. She could dance alone and get into it and she didn't even have to be tipsy.

Hulk escorted me to the VIP section.

I went back to my San Pellegrino and looked up to Knight's window. I also took several deep breaths.

Right, okay.

Talk to him. Ask what gives. Listen.

Then decide.

A couple of my friends wandered over to me and I went back to having a different kind of fun that didn't involve booze or dancing.

The club was emptying out and I was standing at Knight's window watching it.

Hulk had escorted me up to Knight's empty office before he had escorted a shitfaced Sandrine and not-shitfaced (but definitely happy) Vivica out the back way to the waiting car so he could take them home.

My friends were all gone. It was after three in the morning and my night with Knight was finally starting.

As I watched out his window, even though the lights were up and the music was off, stragglers were gathering their stuff and moseying out and the staff was beginning clean up, I was fascinated. And since I'd been standing there for the last half an hour before the lights went up and the music was off, I'd been fascinated awhile. In fact, there was so much happening, so much to see, so many people and it was so easy to see it all from this vantage point, I figured I could watch it for hours and never get bored.

The one thing that bothered me was that you could see everything. Absolutely everything. And if you were a handsome, wealthy club owner who could pick and choose, you could stand there and select from your smorgasbord of pussy.

You could also see your new girlfriend dancing and send your lackey to make her stop on a whim.

On this thought, the door opened. I twisted my neck and watched Knight walk in.

It really kind of sucked that he looked just as good in a suit as he did in a faded Metallica t-shirt and jeans. And it sucked because I couldn't decide which Knight I liked better.

"Hey, baby," he said while closing the door behind him.

"I like to dance," I blurted, and his head tipped to the side.

He held my eyes, and he did this for some time while I waited.

Then he said, "Right. It's time to talk about this anyway."

He walked to his desk.

I watched thinking, *Talk about what?*

He sat behind his desk and ordered, "Come here, Anya."

I turned from the window, walked to his desk and stopped at the opposite side but remained standing.

Leaned back in his chair looking up at me, he stated quietly, "Baby, I said, come here."

"I'm here," I replied.

"You're there," he returned with a tip of his head to me then he gestured to his lap with a hand. "I want you here."

Oh boy.

I pressed my lips together. Then I moved around his desk.

When I was within reaching distance, he reached. Hooking his arm around my waist, slowly and gently, he guided me in. He turned me then pulled me into his lap so I had my legs over one arm of chair, my back resting against the other, my behind in his lap and both his arms around me.

"Okay, Anya, babe, before I take you home to my bed, it's important you get me," he said quietly.

I stared at him and when he didn't go on, I nodded.

"I think you get from the times you've been with me that I like control," he went on.

Well, I got that all right.

I nodded again.

"Right." His arms gave me a squeeze then one hand slid lightly up my arm, causing goose bumps the entire way until it went over my shoulder and finally stopped at my neck, where he curled his fingers around. He dipped his face close to mine. "What you need to get is I... like... *control*. In all things."

"Okay," I whispered.

"So, I tell my woman not to drink, she doesn't drink. I tell her not to dance, she doesn't dance. I do these for my own reasons and you comply. You don't, you answer to me. You put one of my boys out, you again answer to me. And, baby, you don't want to answer to me."

Right, okay.

This I did not like.

"Knight—"

His hand at my neck clenched gently and his face dipped closer. "I won't hurt you. I would never hurt you. Not the way you're thinking. But I would make you pay, and how you'd pay might involve pain."

Oh my God.

"What?" I breathed.

"An example: you got this, you knew it before now, you told Kurt you were gonna dance anyway, right now you'd be over my knees a different way. Do you get me?"

Oh. My. *God!*

My body went still.

Knight pulled it closer. "The punishment will fit the crime, Anya. Not lasting, no marks and it won't go on for hours. And after, always, I'll take care of you. Tonight, you look good, that dress looks good on you and men's eyes were on you. I didn't like that. In your section, they can look, they can see, they cannot get close. On the dance floor, they see more, you movin' the way you do when you dance, you give them more to see and they can get close. You're mine. No one touches what's mine, gets close to what's mine, they don't even think about it. You on that dance floor, I saw them watching you and I knew they were thinking about it. That bothered me. I stopped it. If you don't get it now, you will that I won't ask you to do something you don't like or that makes you uncomfortable. I'll only ask you to do shit or not do shit that's important to me. If I'm important to you, you'll do it. And all this is the same when we're in bed."

I didn't say anything, couldn't think of what to say. I just stared at him.

Knight kept talking.

"You please me, I'll please you. You do what I tell you to do, I'll take care of you. You disobey me or act out, I'll punish you *then* I'll take care of you." His thumb swept my jaw and he whispered, "And if you like your punishments, act out all you want, baby, then I'll give them to you, but I'll always take care of you."

Was he crazy?

Or just kinky?

"Are you into S&M?" I whispered.

He moved back an inch. "What I'm not into is labels. What I am into is control. You do not drive my ride. You do not get drunk when I want to fuck you sober. You do not dance if I tell you not to. I am not into kink, animals, candle wax, toys, knives, blood, needles, clamps, strangulation and definitely not any shit that goes beyond all that. It's not a chosen lifestyle, playrooms and gear. It's not an inclination. It's life. I told you I'd ask very little of you, baby and this is what I'm asking. That you get this about me, you give it to me and if you fuck up, you take your punishment and we move on. You like it, wanna make it a game, you'll get my limits. You'll understand how I hand out punishment, you'll know what you're buying. You buy it, I give it to you. I don't need it but I like it, and if you want that game, I'll say, straight up, I'll be happy to play it."

"And what if I don't want that game?" I asked hesitantly.

"That would be disappointing," he answered unhesitantly.

I studied him, my heart beating wildly, and I whispered, "Is this what dresses, shoes and cell phones buys you?"

I froze solid at the change in his face and the fury in his eyes as he whispered back, "That, Anya, you confirmed you got me, would right now have your ass bared to me."

Oh God.

I pushed away.

His arm and hand got tighter.

I stopped pushing and breathed deep.

"You stick by me," he ground out, "you, and only you, will learn why I am how I am. No one knows. No one. But you, Anya, you stick with me, I'll share. And right now, bonus. I'll tell you what you already know but you don't understand. I like control and I have a temper. I see the world a certain way. I want *my* world a certain way. And I set about getting it. If I don't, if I can't control that, harness it, things can get ugly. So I do. When I do, say when I'm punishing you, I *never* lose control because what I'm doing is a release. And the only time I'll lose control is when I'm finally inside you and you'll like that, I promise you."

God, now he was turning me on, putting me off and making me curious all at the same time!

He drew in breath and the anger slid out of his eyes.

Then his thumb glided over my jaw, his hand shifted up to cup it and his thumb slid across my cheek and then my lips as his eyes held mine and he whispered, "I can do gentle. I can do normal. I can and will do you a lot of ways, baby. And you got a preference, all you gotta do is ask, and if I'm in the mood, I'll give it to you. But you're in my bed, my home, my ride, my club, you gotta get that I'm the man. Yield to that and trust that I'll always take care of you."

Do me a lot of ways?

I sought clarification.

"Are you into, like, um… tying me up?" I asked.

"Bondage? Restraints? Gags?" he asked back.

I nodded.

He answered, "Absolutely."

Wow.

That just turned me on and made me curious.

Crap.

"This is…" I paused, "a little," I searched for a word, "unusual."

One side of his mouth curled up. "Yeah. It's also me."

"Can I be me?" I asked, and his brows drew together.

"What?"

"If I'm, um… *yielding* to you, I don't know if… I mean, can I be me?"

"Uh… yeah."

"How?"

"You'll get the boundaries."

"Without any explanation?"

"Babe, I bought you that phone because you needed one. I bought you those dresses because, the way you dress, I know you like clothes but can't afford the good shit, so I got you the good shit you'd like that would make you happy. I did not do any of that shit to buy anything from you. And me doin' something nice and you implying I'm buyin' you was not cool. So that, *that* would get punishment in a way you'd have trouble sittin' down for a couple of days. I told you I drive my ride when you're in it. You kept pushin' that, knowin' I laid that out, that would get you punishment. I already explained the dance floor. Are you not seein' the pattern of boundaries here?"

"But I like to dance," I whispered.

"Then put on music at my place and dance all the fuck you want. Have a party and ask all your friends over and dance. Go out with your girls not at my club and dance. But you're in your section in my club, you don't dance."

This didn't seem that bad.

"So you don't mind guys looking and getting close at other clubs?"

"Babe, they might look, but they won't get close. I told you go out and dance with your girls at another club, but that doesn't mean I won't put a man on you. I will and I'll do that for three reasons. One, not only you, but both your girls are beautiful, and I already explained the recipe for disaster you are on your own. The three of you is a triple threat and makes me all kinds of uneasy. It's a miracle your girl's scene with Nick was the first you three had. You *need* a man on you and you do the town not in your section at my club, you got one. Two, I don't want some asshole touching you or getting near you. *You.* And I got a man on you, that won't happen. And three, he's your ride. No taxi fares. You can all get hammered and still get home safe."

Seriously, how could one man be so awesome and so crazy all at the same time?

"I think I need to think about this, Knight," I said quietly.

"Then do it, but don't think you're fuckin' doin' it alone in your bed. I've waited a week for your body to be under mine between my sheets and I'm not waiting any longer."

"I'm not sure—" I started.

"You don't want me to fuck you tonight, I'll wait until the morning when you've slept on it and you agree. But as you're sleepin' on it, you'll be doin' it beside me."

I blinked.

Then I stiffened.

Then I snapped, "Seriously?"

He leaned in, grinning.

Grinning!

"Anya, babe, clue the fuck in. The first time I met you and onward, I have been the man I explained tonight. And you have held on, followed me, come to me, kissed me and didn't want to let me go. Tonight, I said no booze. You said okay. Tonight, I sent Kurt to get you off the dance floor. I watched, babe, and you left the fuckin' dance floor. Not ten fuckin' minutes ago, I told you to come here, you didn't get close enough, I made it clear I wanted your ass in my lap. And babe, right now, without a word of protest, you are sittin' with your sweet ass in my lap. I get this shit is intense because *I'm* intense, that's the whole fuckin' deal. I get it'll take you a while to get used to it. But you want it. Fuck, you even like it. You just don't understand it yet. But you will."

Knight Sebring had scared me often. He'd confused me maybe more. He'd totally freaked me out. He'd also been very sweet. And now he was being all of them. Except maybe the sweet part, but kind of that too, since he was being open with me, laying it out honestly and taking the time to explain. Though he did think the end was a foregone conclusion, his arrogance didn't come as a surprise since he'd been that way before. Further, I couldn't blame him for that because what he said was absolutely right.

I wanted to know his secrets. I wanted just to know more about him. I liked spending time with him.

But he still freaked me out.

"What's workin' in that head of yours?" he asked softly, and I realized I'd gone unfocused so I focused on him.

"You scare me, confuse me, freak me out and you're also sweet, so I don't know what to do with you."

He was honest, I could be too.

"Okay, babe," he whispered, his thumb gliding back across my lips, my cheek then his fingers clenched gently into my jaw as he went on, "Another bonus. You take me how I am, I take the burden of you having to wonder all the time what to do."

There it was. Confusion again.

"Pardon?" I whispered back.

"You've carried a heavy load for a long fuckin' time, Anya. You trust me, I take that burden. Don't look into this shit, ask around and make assumptions. You are not wearin' that dress because I'm what's considered a classic Dominant. You dress yourself. You eat what you want. You live your life. But you trust me, you keep lettin' me in, I share your load. And you give me you, we work out, in it for the long haul, I swear, baby, I'll be happy to take it all and let you live free."

And there it was. Sweet.

My tension ebbed away as my belly melted and I whispered, "Knight—"

"Anya, baby, I wanna take you home, but I still got shit to do. And I want you to sit right where you are while I do it. Then I'll take you home. Then I'll take you to bed. You'll sleep with me. We're done talking. I laid it out. You get me. I'm givin' you time. Tomorrow, you decide."

I licked my lips.

Knight's thumb stroked my cheek.

Then, it wasn't lost on me all it said about me, about him, about how I was with him already, when I whispered, "Okay."

One side of his lips curved up and I knew it wasn't lost on him, either.

Then he sat back, pulled his phone out of his inside jacket pocket and hit some buttons.

And like I agreed, I sat in his lap while he did the shit he had to do.

Chapter 9
Whatever You Want

I walked into the huge garage, cars all around. Some nothing but shells, some elevated on those greasy pole thingies with lights hanging from their undercarriages, some with hoods up.

But I was moving toward the middle where there was a large, elegant rug, graceful furniture and soft lighting.

All around there were homeys wearing jeans that hung so low, you could see their underwear and baseball caps that peaked high and the bills were off to the side.

Reclined on the couch was Vivica in an evening gown that looked like it was made of crystal.

Her tawny eyes came to me.

"Hold the fuck on," she whispered.

I blinked.

Then I woke up and felt the unexplainably soft, sleek, cool silkiness of satin sheets surrounding me.

I opened my eyes and saw black satin and beyond, ivory walls, the sun shining through French windows I couldn't see.

Last night Knight made calls, took calls, did shit at his desk, all with me in his lap, all without explaining any of it to me.

Then he took me out back where his Aston Martin was waiting and took me to his place, leading me directly to his room.

"Couple more calls, babe," he muttered. "Bed for you."

Then he kissed my forehead and sauntered out.

I examined the room, my head full, fear clashing with curiosity then I moved across it to the chests of drawers and opened some until I found Knight's tees. I took the one off the top, went to his bathroom and found it was as opulent as the bedroom and decorated entirely in ivory. No color, not even black. Nothing. But every tile, gleaming fixture, light and accessory was fit for a king.

I had nothing to clean my face or moisturize and I didn't know if I should. Then I thought it would be uncool to get makeup on Knight's sheets. So I undressed, pulled on his tee and used his handwash to clean off my makeup.

I left the bedroom and smoothed my dress out on the back of his couch. I lined my shoes up perfectly at the side, walked up the steps and slid into his bed.

The sheets. Divine.

Seriously.

Surprisingly, with all that was happening and all Knight said, and not surprisingly considering it was way late, my mind unjumbled and I fell almost immediately to sleep.

Now it was morning and I had a decision to make.

Before I could put my thoughts in order to do just that, an arm curled around my belly and I was pulled to my back.

Then Knight was on top of me.

On top of me!

I blinked up at him and before I could get out even a, "Good morning," his mouth was on mine where he growled, "Open for me."

My stomach dropped but my mouth opened.

Knight kissed me.

It was not a sweet good morning kiss. It was hungry, hard and his usual marauding. He ended it with my arms around him holding on tight like I was about to fall and I needed him to catch me.

His head moved back an inch and his eyes captured mine.

"You agree?" he asked, his voice thick, at the same time still rough with sleep.

Amazing.

Oh God.

I needed to think and not with his hard, heavy, warm body crushing me to the bed, his hard, demanding kiss boggling my mind and his thick, rough, sexy voice doing a number on me.

"Anya, you agree?" he pushed.

"Knight, I need—"

"Gonna take you now," he cut me off. "Right now, Anya, not waiting. Do you agree?"

"Please," I whispered.

"You either get that you want it or you don't. Do you agree?"

"Knight."

"Do... you... agree?"

Oh God.

"Yes," I breathed.

His eyes darkened immediately, pupils dilating so fast I was mesmerized, and his face dipped so it was a breath away.

"That's what I wanna hear, baby."

Then his hands were in his tee starting to pull up.

I froze in panic and my arms went from around him so my fingers could curl around his wrists tight.

"I need to tell you something," I stated quickly.

His eyes focused on me. "What?"

I didn't tell him what. I wasn't thinking. I was freaking out. I wanted him and was scared how much I did. I was scared of what having him meant, and lastly I was scared about what I'd just agreed to.

"It's important you're warned," I whispered.

"What?"

"With the way you think you see me, you need to know before you find out."

His head jerked slightly, his eyes held mine intently, and one of his hands twisted my fingers free and came up to curl around my neck.

Then he whispered, "Baby, *what?*"

"My tummy's round," I whispered back and he blinked.

Then he repeated, "What?"

"I, um... I'm not perfect. I have a little Buddha belly."

He stared at me.

Stupidly, I kept talking. "I run, do crunches, you know... stuff like that. I do it regularly, I mean, as regularly as I can, which kinda isn't *regularly* regularly it's just um... somewhat regularly. But it doesn't go away. And, um... I don't want you to be disappointed when you see because I think you see something in me and you need to know I'm just me. I'm not how you see me. I'm not perfect."

He stared at me some more then he slid off to my side. Once there he slid the covers down to my thighs.

Holding my eyes, he ordered quietly, "Show me."

Oh God!

"Uh... you won't see. I'm lying on my back and it—"

His hand still at my neck tensed and he repeated, "Show me."

I pulled my lips between my teeth. Then I watched as his head dropped because my hands were at his tee pulling it up my belly and his eyes were trained there.

When the shirt was up to under my breasts, his hand left my neck and went to rest warm and flat on my stomach, but his eyes came back to me.

"You get I picked those dresses," he stated.

"Pardon?" I asked.

"Your dresses. I picked them."

"Oh," I whispered.

"Guessed the size," he went on.

"Oh," I breathed.

"Baby," his hand pressed lightly into my belly, "I haven't missed this."

Okay, all right.

Oh God.

Was this embarrassing? With the warm way he was looking at me, I couldn't tell.

"Right," I said softly.

"You *are* perfect. I wanted to fuck cut, first, I'd wonder if I lost my fuckin' mind, not havin' sweet and soft and all woman. Then, I'd fuck cut. But I don't want cut. I want my cock in a woman who's sweet, soft and..." his face got close, "*all woman.*"

Oh my.

I liked that, as in *really*.

And I liked it even better that Knight made it not embarrassing.

He wasn't done.

"You run, you do your crunches, I don't give a fuck. But you lose *any* of that ass, those tits, those hips or your Buddha belly, just sayin', babe, you lose me."

Oh.

My.

Yes, I liked that. *Really.*

"Knight," I whispered, but said no more. Not because he interrupted me, just because what he said meant so much to me and I didn't know what to say.

"Now, you got anything else you wanna talk about before I fuck you?"

"No," I said softly.

"Fuckin' great," he muttered, then his head dropped and he kissed me.

And he kissed me like he always kissed me. Hard, demanding, but this time better because it kept going as his hand moved over my belly. Then his fingertips skimmed the top edge of my underwear. His hand flattened again, slid to my waist and feather-light up my side.

I trembled as he did this and held on as best I could since he was still lying beside me.

Then his lips released mine and slid down my cheek to my ear.

"Hands off me, babe. Palms flat on the bed and open your legs for me."

My belly curled, then knotted, and heat rushed to a secret place in me.

He lifted his head and caught my eyes. I bit my bottom lip then slid my hands away from him and did as he asked.

"Keep them there, baby, no matter what I make you feel," he ordered gently and I nodded. "Now spread," he whispered.

Slowly, I opened my legs and Knight's neck twisted to watch.

Then he murmured, "My baby's bein' good."

Oh God.

Why was that such a turn on?

His hand slid back and in, just the very tips of his fingers skimming the legs of my panties at the core of me. Then down the inside of my thigh.

"Cock your knees, Anya, and open wider for me."

My breathing was erratic, my entire body hot, my breasts swelled and I felt wet gather between my legs as I did what I was told.

Knight's fingertips slid to the back of my thigh and up, skimming the back of my knee. He shifted, leaning in so they could go down the back of my calf to my ankle.

Okay, that felt good. Sweet, light, amazing.

Then his hand moved to the other leg and he retraced the same path to the heart of me and again his fingers glided feather-soft along the inside edges of my panties between my legs.

My hips shifted impatiently.

God, I needed more.

"Honey," I whispered and Knight's hand went away but his eyes came to me.

"You take what I give, baby, you do what I say and you hush."

Hush.

Oh God.

Why did that turn me on, too?

I wanted his hand back so I nodded.

He watched me nod and his face got lazy.

"Good, baby."

I licked my lips. He watched that too and his face got hungry.

Okay, all right.

God, just watching that look take over his beautiful features turned me on, too.

His neck twisted again to watch as I felt his hand come back, and this time it skimmed me over my panties.

My hips jerked.

"Still," he whispered.

His fingers skimmed back over my panties and it took everything to keep still, my fingers clenching into his sheets, and when I accomplished this, I got my reward instantly. His finger hooked into the gusset and pulled it away. Simple, a bare touch, my panties tugging at my hips but it was effective. "Soaked," he growled then moved.

Shifting between my legs, I felt his nose glide against me in a barely-there touch that sent trills shooting over every inch of my skin. Then he opened his mouth, covering me over my panties, and I felt his tongue press in.

Oh God. Oh God.

My neck arched, my hands clenched the sheets and I whimpered.

"Jesus, fuck, baby," Knight growled. "I like that. Gonna eat that. Gonna eat it clean."

He rolled away, my legs jerked straight as my panties were yanked off and his voice came at me.

"Knees bent, legs up, wide, offer that pussy to me."

I instantly complied and his mouth was on me.

Oh God. Oh God.

God.

Yes, he was hungry. I knew it because he licked. He sucked. He engaged his fingers and they pressed, rolled, spread me open, thrust inside. He finger fucked me. He tongue fucked me. And when his mouth was sucking hard at my clit while two fingers were plunged deep inside, my back left the bed, my head pushed into the pillows, my fingers pulled at the sheets, my mouth opened and a low, deep, long moan tore out as it consumed me. Totally. Head to toe. The world melted away and there was nothing but Knight's mouth on me and the intense, body-shattering orgasm he gave me.

It seemed to last forever, and when I came down, my back settling into the satin, my chin dipping down, my eyes opening, I saw Knight kneeling between my legs. His ass was to his calves and he'd pulled my hips partially up his thighs. His eyes were hot on me, one of his hands cupping my sex, his other hand holding my leg wrapped around his waist. I hadn't even noticed him move and position.

"Beautiful," he murmured, and I felt his thumb slide inside me as the rest of his hand stayed cupped to me. Then he ordered, "Lose the tee."

He held my leg wrapped around him, his thumb inside, his hand cupping me as he watched me pull off the tee and toss it aside.

His dark eyes got darker and I trembled.

His thumb slid out. Both hands moved to span my hips and he instructed, "Nightstand. Protection. You move but you don't lose me."

I licked my lips and rolled them together as I carefully twisted at the waist, reached to the nightstand, opened it and saw a mess of condoms resting in it. I grabbed one, left the drawer open and dropped to my back.

He reached out. I handed it to him then I stared in fascinated wonder as he tore it open with his teeth, slid it out and I watched in panting fascinated wonder as he rolled it on his long, thick, large, beautiful (of course), perfect (completely, from tip to root) cock.

Oh God.

I could swear my breaths were moving the bed as I felt him move. My eyes went from his hard cock to see him bending over me. He gathered me in his arms and lifted me off the bed.

"Both legs around me," he growled.

I acquiesced. He positioned me then slid me down and impaled me, filling me full. So full. So, so *full*.

Oh God.

My head dropped back.

"Look at me."

My head came forward and I focused on him.

"I fuck hard, baby," he whispered.

"Okay," I breathed.

"In a second, you're gonna lose all but my cock. I wanna watch you take me. You keep those legs tight around me as I take that pussy."

"Okay."

"You just gave yourself to me, that includes your pussy, your clit. It's mine, Anya, you don't touch it unless I tell you to. Even if you're close and want it, you let me give it to you unless I wanna watch you helpin' me. Clear?"

"Clear," I agreed immediately.

His hand slid up my back and into my hair, tilting my face down so my lips were resting against his.

Then he whispered, "Prepare, baby."

I didn't need to prepare. I was already prepared. Totally.

Then he bent forward and put my back to the bed. He moved away from me up to his hands on either side of me, arms straight, and he did exactly what he said he was going to do.

As he watched, his eyes hot, hungry, greedy, moving over my face, my torso and dipped down to watch his cock driving inside me, he gave me nothing but that. My legs stayed wrapped tight around his hips as I took him and I clenched my fingers back in the sheets.

He was strong, he had stamina, but it wasn't hard. It was rough, brutal. Brilliant.

Watching him watching me, watching him fuck me, I liked it. A lot. So much, it overwhelmed me. My legs tensed tight, my fingers pulled at the sheets and I felt the walls of my pussy clutch tight as it swept through me. God, so deep, so strong, so unbelievably sweet.

It also lasted a while and during it I felt his body cover me, and his thrusts, already savage, bucked harder, deeper, jolting me even more under him.

"Fuck, that cunt," he grunted in my ear. "That sweet, fuckin' cunt. *My* cunt, so fuckin' beautiful."

Oh God.

"Arms around me, Anya."

I wrapped my arms around him.

"My baby's cunt, so fuckin' sweet," he growled. "Eyes, Anya, I want you lookin' at me when I come in that cunt."

My head turned, his came slightly up and his eyes locked on mine.

"So," he thrust in hard, "fuckin'," he thrust in harder, "*beautiful*," he groaned, driving deep and staying planted, his head slanting, his teeth sinking into my lower lip and my entire body went into spasm.

I knew he was coming down when his teeth released my lip. His tongue glided over it soothingly and some of his weight left me as he planted a forearm in the bed beside me.

I closed my eyes as a tingle slid up my spine, my neck, then radiated along my scalp as he slid his nose along mine then down my cheek to flick my ear with it before he murmured there, "Yeah, my baby suits me."

I felt sheer happiness sweep through me as my arms held him close and tight.

"You did good, baby," he whispered.

"Yeah?" I whispered back and he lifted his head and looked at me.

"Oh yeah."

I smiled.

His hand came up to cup my face and his thumb moved out to trace my smile as his eyes watched.

I melted further into the sheets.

"That's mine," he whispered, his eyes on my mouth as his thumb slid back. Then he watched it slide over the apple of my cheek. "That's mine," he repeated on a whisper. His hand glided into my hair at the side, his eyes still watching, and as his fingers curled around the back his eyes finally came back to mine and his hips pressed into mine. "Now, I possess that beauty."

I stared at him, lips parted, weirdly moved, and when I say that I mean profoundly.

"Say it," he ordered.

"What?" I whispered.

"Who owns you, baby?"

Oh God!

"Knight—"

"Say it, Anya."

My breath started to come heavy.

"Anya, who owns that cunt, that body, that beauty?"

I stared into *his* beauty, feeling his cock still buried deep, smelling him, hints of his cologne, feeling his hard body pressing into me.

"Baby," his face dipped closer and he warned, "I'm feelin' good right now. Don't test me. Who... owns... you?"

"You do, Knight," I whispered.

"Yeah," he whispered back instantly. "I fuckin' do. Every inch, Anya. Every fuckin' inch."

I held his eyes and deep breathed.

Knight watched then his face gentled and he asked softly, "Scared?"

I nodded.

"Don't be," he whispered. He then bent close, his lips brushed mine and he pulled back. "You're scared, worried, confused and still, you gave what you just gave to me, how you did it, trusting me, I'll take care of you, babe. You're with me, one thing you never have to be again is scared. You with me?"

"I'll, um... try to be," I replied quietly.

"I'll get you there," he muttered.

Then he shifted, pulling out unexpectedly. A mew slid out of my throat, equally unexpectedly, as my lips parted and my limbs tensed. His eyes dropped to my mouth as I watched them go gloriously lazy.

"My baby doesn't like losing me."

He was right. I didn't. He felt good. All of him.

And what we'd done felt great but between my legs felt oversensitive, tender, almost raw, but in a weirdly good way.

His hand went to my side, gliding up from waist to ribs and his eyes held mine.

"I gotta go deal with this condom. While I'm gone, you're gonna stay here, on your back, feet to the mattress, legs open, waiting for me."

Okay, all right. I could do that.

Maybe.

Shit!

He dipped his head, brushed his nose along my jaw then he moved off me.

Standing beside the bed looking down at me, he prompted, "Anya."

I blinked.

This was because I was riveted by his lean, sculpted body, his powerful thighs, his cut, arms, his chest hair, the planes of his defined abs and, well, *everything*.

Slowly, my eyes drifted to his face.

"What?" I asked.

"What'd I say?" he asked back quietly.

Oh. Right.

Shit!

I did what he said.

One side of his lips curled up.

Then he sauntered to the bathroom.

Okay, right.

The back view, arguably better.

I thought lying there like that, exposed, legs open, no covers, would be hard. It wasn't. I'd just had two unbelievable orgasms. Knight's body had just then been seared into my memory and I could still see it, back and front. And, incidentally, he didn't take an age before he was coming back to me.

It got super easy when he was back, entering the bed from the bottom side and moving up it between my legs but stopping to kiss me just above the triangle of hair between my legs. Then up and he kissed my belly. Then up and he kissed me between my breasts. Up and another kiss at my throat.

Then he settled back on me, both forearms in the bed at my sides with another order, this one, "Wrap me tight again, babe."

Again, I did as I was told.

His head dropped down and to the side and I felt his nose then lips nuzzling my neck.

That was nice.

He was bossy, freakishly controlling, but still, a nuzzling cuddler after sex.

I could work with this. Definitely.

All of it.

I turned my head slightly and in his ear asked quietly, "Can I touch you?"

His head came up and he looked at me, his face mildly perplexed. "Uh, you are, babe."

"No, I mean..." I whispered, trailing off and also trailing a hand along the smooth skin and hard muscle of his back to demonstrate.

I watched Knight's face clear. His eyes get soft and his voice was softer when he said, "Yeah, baby, unless I tell you what to do or not to do, do whatever the fuck you wanna do."

"Okay," I said on a smile and both my hands went on a voyage a discovery. With what they discovered, I decided instantly to become a dedicated explorer, spending hours, days, weeks, years, if Knight gave that to me, to discover ever centimeter.

"And speakin' of what not to do," Knight started, and I didn't stop exploring but I stopped focusing on the sensations his skin under my hands caused in me and focused on his face. "My tees, no. You crawl into my bed, you do it naked or you bring over some of your cute short-shorts and camis and I'll get you shit I like that you can wear. You can wear my tees around the house after I take you, my shirts if you want, but you do that, you do it without underwear. But you don't sleep in them. And if you're not in your short-shorts, you don't sleep with underwear either. You with me?"

That wouldn't be hard so I nodded.

Knight kept commanding.

"And that cunt you gave me, I'm gonna want it regularly. Not just Saturday nights and when you can fit me in Sundays. What you're doin' means somethin' to you so we'll work around it. But you got the remote for the gate, I'll give you a set of keys. I'll be at work but you'll be in my bed. Come prepared and you tell me what's better for you. The nights after class or the nights after clients?"

"Either," I answered. "I'm used to my schedule, honey. So whatever you want."

His eyes changed in a way I liked and more of his weight settled into me as he murmured, "Whatever I want."

Oh boy.

What did I do?

"Knight—" I started, but his eyes locked on mine.

"Whatever I want includes you givin' me your security code and a set of your keys. I want you in satin, I text you, you get your ass here. I want a switch up, when I'm done, I come to you. Yeah?"

I thought about this and I did it quickly since Knight seemed to like decisiveness.

Then I thought, *Yeah.*

So I said, "Yeah."

"Good," he muttered then asked, "You hungry?"

I grinned. "Yeah."

"Can you cook?"

Cooking for Knight in his kickass black kitchen.

Okay, I liked that.

My grin became a smile and I repeated, "Yeah."

Knight grinned back, right there, my body wrapped around his and he ordered, "Then get your ass out of my bed, back in my tee, no panties and make me breakfast."

Right, call me crazy. You could even call me a freak, I didn't care.

Evidence was suggesting I liked bossy.

So I whispered, "Okay."

Knight liked it that I liked bossy. I knew that when, at my word, I saw his grin become a gorgeous smile and he dipped his head and kissed me. It was wet, it was long, but it was not demanding.

It was all sweet.

And boy, I liked that too.

He lifted his head, slid his nose along mine and whispered, "Right, baby, feed me."

Then he rolled off me.

I rolled the other way, pulled on his shirt, tossed him and the long length of his hard body a smile over my shoulder and I walked to his kitchen.

❧

I was walking out of my bathroom after putting away the last bits and bobs of my nail stuff when I heard a key in the door.

I had made Knight breakfast, and this unfortunately alerted me to the time since it was displayed on his oven *and* microwave, and that alerted me to the fact I didn't have much of it. When he wandered out in jeans and no tee, I informed him of this, even though Knight Sebring in jeans and no tee was worth losing two clients. Definitely.

So I didn't get to go whole hog with something splendiferous that showed my culinary flair (not to be conceited, but I was a really good cook). It was toast and jelly (for me) and a toasted bagel and cream cheese (for Knight). Then he put on a tee and boots, I put on my dress and shoes and he put me in his kickass car and took me home.

He followed me up and did a walkthrough. Once he'd walked through the kitchen, I went to it and got him a set of keys. I gave them to him with the code, he kissed me (a sweet one again) and asked me when I would be done.

I told him, he kissed me again (this one a short one, unfortunately) and he left.

I jumped in the shower and took a quick one. I set up my nail stuff at the same time getting dressed and doing as much hair and makeup as I could in the time I had since Knight was coming back. Then my client came, the next one came close to the end of when the first was done, the first one left, the second one left and now was, well... now.

Knight's key in the lock.

The door opened and he came through, the handles of a paper Wild Oats bag in one hand.

I liked that, him walking into my space.

I liked it a lot.

"Hey," I called on a smile.

"Three hours, five hours, five days, babe," he answered, standing just inside the door he closed.

I blinked at his words. Then I remembered and walked to him.

Putting a hand to his abs, curling the other around his neck and getting up on my bare toes, I pressed my mouth to his.

This time, he didn't take over. This time, he made me do the work.

So I did it and it was *my* tongue sweeping into *his* mouth, exploring, discovering, *plundering*.

Oh my.

He tasted good.

Lovely.

I got into it, both my arms sliding around to hold on tight. One at his neck, one at his back, so I could press my body deep into his. Then Knight got into it. The bag fell to the floor and one of his arms locked hard around me, the other hand drove into my hair, fisted and he took over.

Even I knew my kiss was good.

Knight's was better.

When he let my mouth go, he whispered, "Mark this: that's how I like it, Anya. *Exactly.*"

I got an A and I didn't even study.

I grinned and whispered back, "Consider it marked, Knight."

He grinned back and gave me a squeeze. Then he let me go, retrieved the bag and walked to my kitchen.

"And in the bag is...?" I asked, trailing off my words as I trailed him to the kitchen.

"A guarantee you'll keep that ass, those tits and that Buddha belly," he answered, dumping it on my counter.

God, how on *earth* did I find a man like this man who was so darned *into me?* Just me. Exactly me.

I didn't give it too much headspace. I just smiled a smile that said precisely how happy this made me and his head turned from the bag to me. I watched as his body went completely still and he stared at me.

I noticed as it was impossible to miss, my smile faded and I asked, "Are you okay?"

"Fuck," he muttered.

My brows drew together.

"Knight? Are you okay?"

He was staring at me, but I realized he wasn't seeing me. He was miles away. Then he focused on me and his focus was so extreme it was a physical thing, enveloping me.

No, *ensnaring* me.

"You like how I did you this morning?" he asked, and it was rapped out, abrupt, sharp and all that after the easy we were sharing was shocking.

"Yes," I whispered.

And just when I thought I had him figured out, I was back to confused at all things Knight Sebring.

"You want more?" he asked, and I felt my body start trembling.

"Yes," I answered hesitantly.

"You gonna give it up, take what I give, however I give it, however you get it?"

My hand went out and curled around the edge of the counter but my head nodded.

"You earn it, you prepared to accept punishment?"

"Knight," I whispered.

"Answer me."

Oh God.

"Yes," I said softly.

"The clothes, the shoes, the phone, my place, a car comin' to get you, my club, you into that?"

"Yes," I repeated softly.

"That goes away, you still into me?"

"Knight, what's this about?"

"I asked you a question, Anya."

Okay, now I was getting angry.

So it was snapped when I replied, "I've got clothes and I almost had the money for a phone, and I'm not destitute so I can pay the cover charge, even at your club, which, by the way, is definitely the coolest club in Denver, but still the cover charge is extortionate. So yes, Knight. That goes away, I'm still into you."

He stared at me.

I kept getting angry and I did it fast until I just plain was.

So I told him, "And by the way, what I said last night that you thought was uncool, you're right. It was. But in my defense I said it as you were laying some pretty heavy stuff on me. And just so you know, what you just said to me was *just* as uncool. I *returned* the phone, Knight. And if you want it all back, except the phone which I've used, but that too, and the stuff I wore last night, it's all got its tags still. You can take it. Return it. Give it to someone in your smorgasbord. Whatever. Just don't tell me and I'll make it easy for you to do that because if you think I'm using you, I'll be happy to stop making you think I'm doing that by going away."

"My smorgasbord?" he asked, brows rising.

"Your smorgasbord of pussy at your club," I explained, my face set so hard I could feel it.

He studied me.

Then he murmured, "My smorgasbord of pussy."

"Yeah."

"My smorgasbord of pussy," he repeated, still murmuring.

"Yeah!" I snapped somewhat loudly.

Knight burst out laughing.

I watched, thinking he really looked good doing that. I was also thinking I wanted to find one of my frying pans and clock him with it. I was also thinking I just might cry. And, lastly, I was wishing my apartment was bigger so I could go somewhere, lock the door and throw a tantrum, scream, sob or all of the above.

His laughter died down to a chuckle and he ordered, "Come here, babe."

"If I don't, will you spank me?" I shot back.

His face got serious and he replied shortly, "Yes."

Damn.

I stomped to him.

He turned to me, pulled me in his arms and held me close.

Then he dipped his face close and asked quietly, "You been lookin' into me?"

"No," I answered sharply. "Vivica has. And beware, Knight, she's protective, crazy and as tenacious as you. She loves me. She knows everything about me. She wants me to have a good life and she does that in a way where I could swear she wants that more for me than she does for her own damned self. So her normal extreme curiosity, when it comes to my future happiness and those who might or might not be giving it to me, ratchets up to ludicrous. Though, that said, she's already given you her seal of approval and since that seal isn't a seal so much as a brand burned in so the scar never heals, I think you're good. Unless you're a terrorist, which, she's informed me, is the only reason why she'd stop loving you for me."

That was a lot. Too much, but I still didn't shut up, I was that angry.

"Oh, and, if you don't play me, she's naming her first son after you."

That was when I shut up only to see Knight smiling white and blinding at me.

Then he asked, "You done?"

"Yes," I clipped.

"You wanna tell me why you're so pissed?" he asked.

"No, but you won't let me not do it so I will in order to avoid Knight Hassle. No way, in my life, would I be able to afford a phone like you gave me. The dresses either. The shoes, any of it. I came home to those bags, Knight, and I didn't think of returning it like the phone because I let you in. All I thought was never, never in my life would I ever imagine myself standing in my living room with my couch I got for a steal because it was on sale and had a rip in the cushion, my yard sale coffee table, my dinette a friend gave me, and see strewn across it luxurious beauty that someone thought enough about me to give to me. My parents died when I was seven, but they weren't millionaires. Our life was good. It was loving. It was happy, but I'd never been spoiled. You spoiled me and if it happened once or a hundred thousand times, I know I'd never get used to it because I never in my life expected it. Each time would be a treasure and that treasure would not be the stuff you gave me. It would be that you gave it to me. And, Knight, that's because since my parents died, I learned not to expect *anything*. Life was going to be what I made it, what I worked for it to be, what

I earned. So that moment was beautiful to me and you sullied it by intimating that I was using you, and I'm pissed because feeling pissed is better than feeling hurt, which is really what I feel."

His arm left my back so his hand could cup my jaw and his face came close as he whispered, "Baby."

Without delay, I snapped, "I don't understand what's between us or how I can behave or if I can even be mad, but just so you know, right now, I don't want you to be nice to me and I don't want you touching me."

"Not gonna give you that, Anya," he said gently.

Figured.

I looked away and blew out a sigh.

"Babe, look at me."

I looked back, rethinking this situation because when I was pissed or hurt or whatever, I wanted to be able just to be me.

"You, Anya, are a woman who needs a dog, a house with a white picket fence, one boy, one girl, and a man who worships the ground you walk on, thanks God every night he was fuckin' lucky enough to con you into lyin' your head on the pillow beside his, but still watches football on Sundays. You and me stay the course, you are never gonna get that from me."

I stared at him, again... freaking... *confused.*

"Pardon?"

"I tried to walk away, did it twice, so I could leave you to that destiny. Then you walk in my club in that fuckin' dress. I knew you had no underwear on. I knew without seein' that you walked in my club and every dick on every guy who caught sight of you started gettin' hard seein' you in that dress because you're you, but also because you had no fuckin' underwear on. Then you were with Nick. And seein' you sittin' with him, lookin' beautiful but scared outta your fuckin' mind, I knew two things. One, I had to claim you and look after you before someone or a shitload of someones fucked you in their rabid pursuit of all that is you. And two, I had to claim you because I could not deny any longer how fuckin' much I wanted you. You deserve that life with the dog and the white fence, babe. You deserve good and normal and clean. So when you walked into this kitchen and smiled at me bright like you'd never been so fuckin' happy, I had to know if I gave you that, or what I gave you gave you that. So I set about findin' out. And knowin' it's me that gave you that, knowin' you might be happy without the dog or that white fence, baby, that makes *me* happy."

"You're not good and normal and clean?" I whispered.

"No, Anya, I am not any of that. Someone fucks you, I got no problem drawin' his blood, givin' him pain, makin' absolutely fuckin' certain he'll never do it again. I've already done it and I will not hesitate to do it again. I lay my head down at night, you might be tied to my bed spread-eagled next to me so if I get a taste for you in the middle of the night, I can put my mouth to you without waiting. I am not good. I am not normal. I am not clean. I fuckin' love my life. But I got off way more than normally, tellin' you what I want and watchin' you mind me. You taste fuckin' great. That cunt of yours feels even better. And lookin' in your face when I come is even fuckin' better. And all that made my life a whole lot better. So you gotta know, you gave that to me, I own it but I never intend to be any of those things, good or normal or clean."

I was silent.

I was also more than mildly turned on.

Knight was silent too. Then he wasn't anymore.

"So, Anya, babe, I had to know it was *me* makin' you happy. I asked. You shared. And that's good. Because down the line I don't want it sittin' in my gut that I should have left you to good and normal and clean. I'm pleased as fuck you like what's growin' between us because, babe, seriously, I do, too. And another thing, expect to be spoiled, because I'm gonna work on that, too. You and yard sale coffee tables are a thing of the fuckin' past."

Suddenly, I wasn't breathing.

I was also trembling.

His thumb slid across my lips but stopped in the middle, pressed lightly, and his face got so close, his vibrant eyes were all I could see.

"And last, you call your girl off. I get what she's doin' for you. But I'll let you know what you need to know about me when I'm ready for you to know it. I don't like people lookin' into me. I don't like people askin' about me. And I don't like people knowin' about me unless it's me who puts them in the know. She's your girl, but I'll warn you, I do not like all this enough that if she doesn't stand down, it will be me makin' it clear she's gonna do that. First time, I'll go gently. There has to be a second time, you mean somethin' to me, she means somethin' to you, but still I make no promises. You get me?"

Oh boy. Time to have a serious sit down with Vivica.

I didn't say that.

I didn't say anything.

I just nodded.

"Do you understand to be with me you're givin' up good, normal and clean?"

"I think so," I whispered against his thumb, and in the middle of me speaking, he swept it away.

When I was done, he swept it back and his eyes watched as it pressed in then pulled down taking my lip with it. Then the pad of his thumb glided along my teeth. Automatically, they separated. His thumb slid between them and the pad touched my tongue. Again automatically, my lips closed around his thumb and my tongue stroked it.

I watched his pupils dilate and his thumb pressed down on my tongue as he growled, "Fuck yeah, my baby gets me."

The area between my legs contracted so powerfully, it was almost like a mini-orgasm.

Or maybe it just was.

His thumb slid out and caressed my lower lip again. Then his hand slid back into my hair, but through this I never lost his eyes.

"I was wrong, layin' it out about your girl was not last," he said quietly. "Last is, I like pussy and I will not deny I've enjoyed as much of it as I could get. But that smorgasbord you mentioned, babe, that has dried up. You gave me you, I give you me. You want tests, we'll take them. You're not on the pill or something else, you need to get on it immediately because I want nothing between my cock and you. But you trust me to take care of what you give to me, you can trust that you're the only one gettin' it for as long as you're with me."

Okay, this was good. Very good. Excellent.

"Okay," I whispered.

"The pussy I've had, *all* of it, was just pussy. You are not just pussy. They know they don't talk about what I gave them. But you gotta know they know because they got it. For them, it was a session. For you, it's now part of your life. I get you're gonna share with your girls about me. But I'll ask you to keep that to your crew of three and make them understand I do not like people sharin' wide about me. And be firm about that, baby. I live quiet. I don't like attention. And I won't like you gettin' it for me. That won't mean punishment. That'll mean the end of you and me. You with me?"

I nodded.

"You still pissed?" he asked.

I shook my head.

"You wanna eat or you wanna fuck?"

I blinked.

Then I asked back, "I get a choice?"

"You do right now."

I stared up at him and his words drifted through my head, specific ones.

Then I asked, softly and carefully, something I'd wanted to know for a while and never thought I'd get a chance to ask, and even if I did, I wouldn't.

But I did.

"Did you jack off, thinking of me?"

"Absolutely."

My womb convulsed again.

I knew this sensation showed on my face because I heard him whisper, "Baby wants her Daddy."

Oh.

My.

God.

Definite mini-orgasm.

"Fuck yeah, my baby wants her Daddy," he growled. Then I was up, his hand on my ass, my legs wrapped around his hips, his other hand in my hair, cupping and tilting my head forcing my lips to his as his mouth took mine. Then he walked us to my bedroom.

He took us down together on my bed.

Then baby got her Daddy.

Delightfully.

"Open," Knight commanded.

I opened my mouth and he slid the broken off chunk of carrot cake inside. I made sure I got all the frosting by closing my lips and gently sucking his thumb as he slid it out.

"Fuck me, baby," he whispered.

My eyes lifted to him, I liked what I saw and even still chewing, I grinned.

His eyes instantly got dark, his other hand went to the covers and slid them over my behind.

My chest seized.

He'd done me bossy then he'd gone into the kitchen to get the food. He came back still in the mood to be bossy and I knew this because he told me to stay on my belly and he fed me.

So I was on my belly in my bed, naked, Knight naked beside me. The covers were up to his waist, but now down over my bottom. My arms were crossed on the pillow in front of me, and I knew by the dark, hungry look on Knight's face that Daddy had essentially never left, but he was definitely home.

His hand glided light over my behind as he ordered, "Spread."

I started breathing again but I did it heavy.

Then I spread.

Knight's eyes watched his hand dive in.

I sucked in breath.

He leaned down a bit to get better access.

I started panting.

"Love my pussy, baby," Knight muttered. I knew he did because two fingers were stroking deep, rolling, separating, stretching me, and my hips started jerking. "Be good, Anya."

I bit my lip and stilled

With one of his hands between my legs, the other one went to the plate sitting on the bed between us, his thumb scored through the thick layer of frosting on the cake, scraping it off then it came to my mouth. Knight slid it inside and I sucked it deeper.

His fingers between my legs stroked faster.

He pulled his thumb out of my mouth. He grabbed the plate, shifted it out of the way and did all this as he kept at me between my legs.

Then he shifted close. On a forearm, my eyes lifted to his. His eyes were at my backside and his attention was all on me.

"Lift your ass."

I came up a little on my knees.

"Higher."

I came up higher.

He shifted again so his hand could position, his fingers gliding out and one came to my clit.

Oh God. Oh yes. *Yes.*

My hips bucked.

"My baby likes that," he growled. "Higher."

I went higher.

"There it is, Anya, keep your ass up high for me and find it, baby."

I closed my eyes. His finger worked.

"Look at me."

I opened my eyes and looked at him hazily. His finger kept working.

"You come, still, you climb on my dick and you ride your Daddy through it, you hear me?"

Oh God. Yes. Oh. *Yes.*

I nodded.

"Then you ride me until you give it to me."

I nodded again.

His finger pressed deeper. Nice, so damned nice.

God.

I whimpered.

"Fuck, Anya, you gotta find it. I'm gonna come just watchin' and listenin' to you. Move your hips, find it."

I ground into him desperately, bucking, rocking, jerking.

"Fuck, my baby's so fuckin' hot," he growled, and at his words, the workings of his finger, my desperate hips, I came. I did it hard, but even coming, I minded.

So, still coming, I shifted, moving just as desperately, searching, seeking, and my hand wrapped around his hard, thick cock. He'd helpfully rolled to his back so I threw a leg over to straddle him and drove down.

God. He felt so damned good. My back arched, I threw my head back, my arms flew back to catch myself and my hands curled around his solid thighs.

"That's it, just like that. Stay arched like that and ride me," Knight ordered. His voice was thick, hoarse, abrasive, his hands at my belly, one going up to cup my beast, the other heading down.

I did as I was told and kept coming, one climax rolled into the other then his thumb hit my clit and on its heels came the third. Arched deep, exposed, I rode him hard, fast, oh God, oh God, I was going to split in two.

His thumb left my clit, his hands found my hips and he yanked down as he surged up and I kept riding him.

"Give me that beauty," he growled.

I righted, falling forward to my hands on either side of him, my eyes focusing with difficulty on his face.

He pulled me down tight, surging up, and I watched as I gave it to him.

I knew he was coming down when one hand slid from my hip to my bottom, fingers clenching in, pads pressed deep, possessive and claiming. His other hand glided up my side, in over my ribs then cupped my breast.

His finger and thumb closed on my hard, sensitive nipple and his eyes watched as they squeezed tight then pulled sharply.

Fire shot through me, I gasped and my hips bucked into his.

"Baby likes it rough," he whispered.

"Yes," I breathed.

"Yes, what?"

My hooded eyes found his and I whispered, "Yes, Daddy."

A sexy, rough, hot, amazing, unintelligible growl rolled up his throat. I heard it even as I felt it rumble through the heart of me and his fingers at my nipple tugged again, hard. So I gave it to him again *exactly* as I knew he wanted it.

After I bucked, gasped and moaned, Knight's arms closed around me, he rolled me to my back with him on me, not disconnecting. His mouth crushed mine in a hard, deep, thorough kiss that took what was left of me.

Then he broke the kiss, lifted his head, and his still heated, beautiful eyes roamed my face.

"Wrap me up, Anya," he muttered and I did.

His hand came up and he used the tips of his fingers to slide tendrils of my hair away from my face. Then they moved over my cheek, my jaw, my lips as he watched. His hand glided into the side of my hair as his eyes found mine.

"You full?" he asked quietly, and I was. Full of food, still full of him.

"Yeah."

His eyes held mine and they did this a long time.

Then he asked gently, "Did I make my baby happy?" and my limbs all automatically squeezed.

He wanted that, to give that to me. He wanted it badly.

I gave him this and I liked it.

No, call me crazy. I fucking *loved* it.

And in return, he wanted to give everything to me.

"Yeah," I whispered as his eyes dropped to watch my mouth move.

They came back to mine. I watched one side of his lips curl up and he murmured, "Good."

Chapter 10

Being Bad

"What?"

That was Viv.

"You need to stop asking around about Knight."

That was me and I went on.

"He, uh… knows, or figured it out because we were having words, and I kinda let it slip, then I kinda gave him the full story and you're right. He's private, as in *really* private. He doesn't like attention. He doesn't like people to know shit about him, and he doesn't like it a lot. So, he asked me to ask you to stand down so I'm asking you to stand down."

"Told you this guy's shit is tied up tight," she replied.

She could say that again.

It was Tuesday night, late. I was at Knight's. He came to my place last night, woke me at nearly four in the morning, did me hard and controlling. Then I passed out for about an hour and a half before I woke up to get ready for work. I left him in my bed after I came to him dressed, he yanked me in, rolled me to my back and laid a hot, plundering one on me.

Tonight, my turn in his bed.

Which was where I was, lying across the satin comforter, already in my PJs, talking to my friend.

Or warning her off.

"You had words?" she asked, as was her way, nosily.

"He makes me happy. I was making that clear. He flipped out. Said some stuff to make sure it was him making me happy, not his generosity. That pissed me off. I got in his face about it. We talked it out. All is cool."

"He makes you happy," she whispered, and my heart skipped at the tone in her voice.

"Very," I whispered back.

"Really?" She was still whispering and it was still hopefully.

"Really." I kept whispering too, and shared, "He likes my Buddha belly. He even brought me all sorts of cheese and crackers and bread and pâté, chasing that with carrot cake in order to assist me in maintaining it." My voice dipped low. "Viv, he likes me for me."

"Told you that Buddha belly of yours was hot," she reminded me.

"I don't know about hot. I just know Knight likes soft and sweet and womanly and that's what he's got in me."

"In other words, hot guy Knight thinks that Buddha belly is hot."

"Whatever," I muttered, and she giggled.

Then she stated, "So I take it you fucked him, and that was hot too."

That was when I giggled and through it said, "Uh... you don't fuck Knight. No way. Knight fucks you."

Silence then, "Come again?"

I blinked at the comforter.

After she got my silence in return, she stated, "Right. You signed a contract. First, babe, he doesn't want me asking or gabbing, assure him that's done. I'm not doing dick to fuck this for you. Second, just give me a one to ten."

"Twenty-five," I whispered.

"What?" she breathed.

"Maybe thirty," I amended.

"Uh... no, babe, no. Please tell me you didn't sign a contract."

"I didn't, but, Viv, we talk about this, it's between you and me. I'm not even going to talk to Sandrine about this. She gets drunk, she's not dancing, she gets chatty. You're Fort Knox if you wanna be, and with this, I want you to be. For Knight."

"Lips are sealed, babe," she assured. "Really? A thirty?"

"He's... different."

"He'd have to be," she muttered, and I giggled again.

"It's, Viv... um, he has a gig."

"A gig?"

"A gig."

"What kind of gig?"

"He's bossy."

"Right, well, that's not a surprise."

"Right, well, that kind of thing is who he is. It leaks everywhere. He likes control."

"Control?"

"He tells me what to do, I do it. In pretty much all things at least, um… sexually, but other times too. But only if it's important to him and so far he's taken the time to explain." I paused then said softly, "And if I don't, he'll punish me." I finished on a hurry, "But that hasn't happened."

She was silent. My stomach clenched.

"It's not as kinky as it sounds." I promised quickly. "It's really kind of—"

"Anya, babe, I'm a submissive," she said quietly and I blinked.

My nosy, ballsy, bold, take-no-prisoners, tell-it-like-it-is Vivica was a submissive?

"What?" I breathed.

"Thought about it, get it, like it, do it. To get out of that 'hood and not live my life as a 'ho', or the bitch of some homey who gets a cap busted in his ass or a prison sentence leaving me with three kids, all of whom will grow up to be gangsters, 'ho's or stupid bitches tied to dead guys, I'm like Knight. I have to keep my shit tight. I don't want to be the assistant manager of anything. I want to be manager. Then I want to be director. I want to own my own home. I want a nice place, nice car, nice clothes, nice shoes, nice furniture and a decent guy who takes out the trash at least by the second time I ask, gives it to me regular in a way that I like and whips my ass, literally, when I've been bad."

Oh my God.

She kept talking.

"I gotta work so hard, keep my shit so tight, control my life so much to keep on the right track and get what I want out of life, it's a relief to give all that up and put myself in someone's hands. I trust them to take care of me, and in most cases, they do. I've had two long-term Doms. One I lost and I won't explain because if I do, you'll figure it out and he doesn't want anyone to know, so that's his secret and not for me to share. The other, because he got off on the pain more than the trust or the relationship and sometimes failed to get *me* off, so I got shot of his ass. Some women are into that. I'm not. But I'm looking. Just hard to find one who gets that's bedroom, not life, or not *all* of life."

"Why didn't you tell me?" I asked quietly.

"Because some people think it's jacked, Anya, when it… is… *not*. But I sometimes get shit for the color of my skin. I'm not adding to that with sharing this. No fucking way."

"You don't get shit from me," I reminded her, stung.

"No, and I didn't wanna get it another way," she replied gently, easing the sting.

"You can tell me anything," I whispered.

"Well, now I know that since you shared with me."

We both fell silent.

Vivica broke it.

"So, obviously, if he's a thirty, you like it too."

"Yeah," I said softly.

"And you jack up, he'll punish you?"

"Yeah."

"He's shared that with you?"

"Unh-hunh."

"And you know his limits? He's been open with you? What you can do, what you can't? What he can do, where he won't go with you?"

"Yeah. I mean, he's given me boundaries, which I may or may not explore, but they are far from vague. And he's also been somewhat comprehensively forthcoming about what he's not into. It's not about wax or clamps or any of that. It's about control."

"Covered his bases," she muttered.

Seemed like it.

"Good," she whispered.

"Yeah," I repeated.

"Advice, babe, jack up."

I blinked again.

Then I breathed, "What?"

"No joke. I know it sounds scary crazy but it isn't. It's scary, crazy, *hot*."

My legs started trembling.

"Really?" I whispered.

"Oh yeah. *Hell* yeah. I know he's yours, babe, but just the thought of Knight Sebring taking a crop to me, hun… *nee*. I'm thinking of stopping my gig of trying to talk in code to every guy in Denver to see if they're a Dom and just putting a personal ad in so I can get my ass slapped."

I burst out laughing.

"I'm not kidding," she said into my laughter.

"Right, okay," I said, still giggling.

"Listen to me," she said, deadly serious, and my giggles faded. "Straight up, what you've already done, is he cool with you? You like it?"

"Yes," I whispered.

"To a thirty?"

"Yes, Viv."

"Then jack up. Because if you like him bossing you then you're into it. If you give him reason to take it to the next level then that thirty will become a fifty, I kid you not. Scary. Crazy. *Hot.*"

My trembling legs started shaking as did my hands and my eyes slid to Knight's space age alarm clock on his nightstand.

Ten fifteen. Knight wouldn't be home for hours.

Damn.

"You know something, babe?" Viv asked in my ear.

"I know a lot of things, honey. What do you want to know?" I replied.

Her voice held a smile when she said, "I already loved him for you. Now I love that he's giving this to you and you like it. One of the things about that life, sex will never be boring. There's a trust that's built that's a-freaking-mazing. Closeness comes from that. He builds that for you, I'll love him forever. But it's more. I never had anyone to talk to about this shit except my partners, and that isn't the same thing as having your girls. So he gave this to us, too. So I'm thinking I'll already love him forever."

I had the scary, crazy thought that I might, too.

"Yeah," I whispered.

"You wanna talk to me about anything, I'm here. But more advice, you talk to him. He's already laid this shit out so clearly he intends to be open and honest with you, you tell him where you're at. What you liked, what you didn't. Give him cues when you're ready to go further. Then, I swear, babe, *he'll* love *you* forever. A gorgeous bitch to class his act on his arm that makes him laugh, knows how to cook, understands the meaning of loyalty and who can get his rocks off just the way he likes it. Nothing better. And he'll know it too."

I giggled again then stopped suddenly and whispered, "I'm glad he gave us this too, even though he didn't know he was. I'm glad because you shared with me something about you and now you know no matter what, you can share anything with me, honey."

It was her turn to say, "Yeah."

I grinned.

Then I heard a faraway, indistinct sound echoing in Knight's vast apartment like someone was coming in the front door.

My body jerked and my head went back to the clock.

Ten eighteen.

I listened to the noises.

Knight was home early. Or maybe he just came home to get something.

I listened for footsteps on the floor, didn't hear them and wondered why he didn't come see me as I pushed off the bed and said, "Knight's home. Maybe he's picking something up."

"As you walk your round white ass to wherever he is in that crib, wrack your brain about how you can be a bad girl then call me tomorrow and thank me."

I smiled at the phone so I knew she heard it when I hit the hall and whispered, "Later, honey."

"Bad girl, baby."

"Right," I muttered.

"Right," she stated firmly then softly, "Later."

Then she was gone and I was rounding the L of the hall.

The living room was dark as I left it, since after talking with Viv I was going to bed. But I saw a faint light coming from the hall to the front door.

I rounded the corner and saw the door in the hall that I'd never seen open, opened and light was pouring out.

"Honey, you needed something, I don't usually go to sleep until eleven," I called down the hall, still walking. "You could have phoned me. The club is a ten minute drive. I could have dropped it—"

I stopped in the door and stopped talking. I saw it was an unsurprisingly very big, well-appointed, kickass study, though not in any way like the rest of the kickass, but spare, colorless, stylized apartment but warm, masculine and lived in.

And last, Nick Sebring was squatting next to what looked like a safe set in a golden wood cabinet. The safe was unopened and his furious gaze was aimed at me.

"Take one step to me, Nick, I run to Knight's room, lock myself in and I don't call 911. I call Knight," I warned as he straightened.

"Now I fuckin' get it," he whispered irately, his eyes on me burning with barely controlled fury.

"What are you doing here?" I asked, looking at the safe.

"Not dinner, not you," he hissed. "That pussy's for sale."

My eyes shot to him.

"Um... *excuse me?*"

He crossed his arms on his chest. "Disappointing. Thought you were a sweet piece. Worth it. Worth the work. The trouble. The kind that would make you wanna fix. Permanently. Shoulda known when you showed at that party here. Not your scene. But you wanted Knight, hoped he'd be here. And, congratulations, babe," his eyes swept me in my PJs, "seems you got him."

I sucked in breath and asked, "Nick, how did you get in here?"

His gaze swept me again and it was working. Then something shifted in his face, his eyes. Something ugly, calculating, but I wasn't certain I got it.

Then he spoke, but not to answer my question.

"Heads up: you don't deserve it, but you're not the first."

I sucked in another breath and informed him, "I know that."

His head tipped to the side, he smiled a nasty smile and he asked, "So, you're okay with the charity?" My body got tight. "'Course you are, baby." He took a step toward me, I took a step into the hall, bracing for flight and he stopped. "Comes with the good shit. The apartment. He buy you clothes yet? A car?"

I stared at him as my heart started beating faster.

"No car," he muttered, watching me closely. "Knight, he likes it like that. Sees the pretty ones with the cheap shoes and twenty dollar haircuts. Wantin' more. Got a streak in him, acts on it. Shows 'em good. Shows 'em sweet. Steaks. Nice clothes. Satin sheets. Gets off on it. Advice? Hang on tight for the car, baby. He'll let you keep it."

I ignored this, for now, and stated, "You obviously have keys. It's likely Knight would want you to return those to me right before you leave, which would be about now."

"Don't get lost," he whispered, leaning into me, watching me closely. "Don't think he'll keep you. He gets bored with his charity cases, and he does it easy. Could be days. Could be weeks. Could be longer. Anya, with you, I bet he keeps you around a while. But he'll get tired of you. He'll scrape you off. And you'll have the car, the clothes, but you'll be precisely where you started and Knight won't look back. He never looks back. He just waits for the next pretty one to show at Slade in a dress someone else wore before her and shoes she hopes no one notices and then he'll give it to her sweet. Until he's done with her, too."

I tried to calm my breathing, lifted my hand, palm up and demanded, "Keys."

He walked to me.

I stepped back to give him plenty of room then braced as he stopped in the hall with me.

"Just sayin', I know it's sloppy seconds to my fuckin' brother, but he gets done with you, find me. I'll give you sweet too, and it'll also last a while."

"Keys," I hissed.

He lifted his hand and dropped the keys, but did it purposefully so they missed my palm and hit the floor. I kept my eyes to his, not about to go for them with him still there.

Then I jumped to the side as his leg went back and he kicked the keys. I didn't watch them, but I listened to them sail across the floor and bump down the stairs into the sunken living room.

"Fuck him good, Anya, and when you come to me, you can show me how my brother likes it," he whispered to me.

"Now's your time to leave," I whispered back

He glared at me.

Then he turned and took his time walking to the door.

Knight's door locked automatically. I heard it catch then I ran to it and turned the deadbolt.

I stood at the door.

Charity case.

Clothes.

Steaks.

Car.

Car.

Shit car, babe. Gotta get you something decent.

He said that, not straight out saying he'd buy me one but hinting at it, and he barely fucking knew me.

Nick knew.

The steaks.

The *stupid* steaks.

Nick knew.

Knight Sebring looked at my shoes, fifteen minutes later walked through my apartment and he got himself a live one.

Nick knew.

Knight hadn't even fucked me and he spent thousands of dollars on me.

I should have known in his luxury condo with his Aston Martin and his shit-hot club that Knight Sebring, who could have anybody, would not chose me unless there was some jacked reason why.

Wars fought over a face like this.

Bullshit.

I wondered how many women he'd said that to.

I closed my eyes tight.

Then I turned. Moving stiffly, I reached in and flipped the switch on the light in the study and the windowless room went black. Then, like I'd be graded for the endeavor, I carefully closed the door.

I walked slowly down the hall to the bedroom.

I got dressed and shoved my PJs in my overnight bag. I went to the kitchen, grabbed my purse from the counter and dug out the keys to Knight's apartment. I dropped them on the counter, pulled on my jacket and grabbed my bag and purse.

Then I got the heck out of there.

The covers were yanked off, my eyes flew open and my first thought was that he busted through the chain.

I knew it was him.

And I knew this because the room was filled with vibrating, searing heat.

"Knight—" I whispered, but that was all I got out before I was out of bed, moved, tugged and positioned until I was straddling him as he sat on the side. His arm locked around my hips, his other hand fisted in my hair holding my face an inch from his

"It's fuckin' three thirty in the morning and I drove here from my place where I found my bed empty. Then I got here and the chain was fuckin' on. One word answer," he bit out. "Yes or no. You forget where you were supposed to sleep and who was gonna be sleepin' beside you? And, babe, warning, the answer better be yes."

I stared into his shadowed face.

Then I said, "No."

He instantly started to swing me out.

But I clamped on and snapped, "Knight! No. You don't get to punish me. We're over."

He stilled.

Completely.

"What the fuck?" he whispered.

"Nick came over tonight." His body, already still, went solid under me. "He had a key. We had a chat. I know."

"You know," he clipped then, "You know what?"

"I know about your charity cases."

Silence.

Scary silence.

Terrifying silence.

Then, in a sinister, soft whisper, "My *what?*"

"The girls you find. The pretty ones that you take care of, you spoil then you get tired of and scrape off," I reminded him. "Girls like me."

More silence, and it was more terrifying, the room stifling such was his fury.

I kept going. He might be pissed, really pissed, but I couldn't imagine he'd hurt me.

"So we're over."

"Nick told you that," he stated.

My arms, clamped around his shoulders, loosened and I tried to push away, but his hold got tight so I stopped.

"Yes," I answered belatedly.

"Nick came to my house, saw you, told you that, and you believed it and left me."

It was my turn to still.

And I did it at his tone, which was scathing.

Then I whispered, "Yes."

"Left without callin'. Left without callin' at the very least to tell my motherfucking dickhead of a brother was in my house when he shouldn't be. He shouldn't even have a key, which is obviously somethin' he hid from me and lied to me when I took his other key. Then he talks shit to you about me and you don't call me about that either. You don't wait for me to come home and tell it to me. You just leave."

Uh-oh.

"Knight."

"I'm gonna let you off me, Anya, then you're gonna crawl into bed on your own, cheek to the mattress, ass in the air, and feel lucky we are not at my place. You need a cane, at least a strap, but all I got is my belt, and that might mark you so you're gonna take my hand."

A cane?

I didn't ask that.

"He lied to me?" I asked, and it was the wrong thing to do. His arm got so tight, I couldn't breathe. His fist twisted in my hair and pain spiked across my scalp.

Both these went on for no more than a second before his hold loosened and he spoke.

"Yeah. He lied to you. You know who hasn't lied to you?"

Oh God.

"Knight—"

"Me," he growled.

"Honey."

His arm and hand left me as he ordered, "Crawl in bed, Anya."

"Knight—"

"Do it or I swear to Christ you won't sit easy for a week."

My pulse spiked but my limbs moved. I crawled into bed, my breath stopping and starting until I got to the middle. Then I put my cheek to the mattress, my ass in the air, my arms cocked at my sides.

The bed moved with Knight moving, but I could only see his frame shadowed in the dark room.

"Yank the drawstring," he ordered.

My hand moved and I yanked.

I no sooner did this when my pajama shorts and panties were yanked down to my thighs.

"Spread your legs, Anya, wide. Keep those tight."

I spread my legs until I couldn't spread them further as they caught taut on my shorts and undies.

Surprising me, his hand slid between my legs and my thighs quivered.

159

"My baby is very lucky," he whispered, pressing in and rubbing and my fingers curled into the comforter. "I love her pussy, love this sweet ass. Tonight I'll make that ass throb, but I love that pussy so much, I won't wanna take it tomorrow with pain getting in my way."

I closed my eyes tight and put everything into keeping perfectly still.

His hand left me and the bed moved some more. Then nothing, but I heard the swish and whoosh of clothes hitting the floor. And when the bed moved again I knew he was coming back to me naked.

Oh God.

Viv was right.

I'd jacked up.

Big time.

And this was scary, crazy, *hot*.

My thighs kept quivering.

I felt him above me, then I felt his fingers curl into my camisole and pull it up. My head and arms went with it as he yanked it off and it was gone. But he caught my hair, gave it a rough, gentle tug and I came up to my forearms.

"I wanna be hard and aching when I beat that ass red, baby. Take my cock, make it ache," he ordered, then another tug on my hair until I was on my hands. I felt his hand guiding his cock to my mouth. The tip against my lips, he slid it light against them until I opened them and he surged inside, already hard.

Oh God. I liked that.

Scary, crazy, *hot*.

My neck arched back and I moaned against his cock.

"No," he growled. "Gonna fuck your face, baby."

Oh God!

He held my head back by my hair and he did just that.

And, God, oh my God, I loved every stroke.

He gave it to me and I took it. Slow, faster, harder, Knight using my hair to pull me to him as he thrust into me. When I was moaning, using everything I had to suck as he thrust and keep my fingers from moving between my legs, he slid out.

"Cheek to the mattress," he commanded and I went down.

The bed moved.

Then Knight punished me.

Sharp, hard, stinging, I winced and flinched and gasped and only vaguely noticed his hand never came down in the same place twice.

Then he stopped and rubbed between my legs, hard, deep.

Back to my bottom, again, again. The pain radiating down my thighs, tingling between my legs. My mouth was open but no sound came out because I'd lifted my fist to press it to it. My other hand clenched the comforter.

Then back between my legs, finger hitting my clit, rolling, working me until I whimpered. It slid away and he was at my ass, the sound of his palm striking against my skin filling the room.

His fingers curled into my shorts and panties and yanked them down sharply. They rounded my knees and were whisked away.

"Up on just your knees, Anya," he ordered and I pushed up, breathing heavily and felt his hand at my belly, sliding down, curling in, cupping me as I felt his lips move to my ear. His middle finger sliding through the wet, he whispered, "Baby's soaked. Dripping. Daddy's gonna eat you now. You're gonna come on my face. You gotta grind down, baby, you do it. Take all you can get from my mouth. Right?"

"Right," I breathed.

"Right?" he repeated, his hand cupping my sex drawing up slightly.

Oh *God*.

Scary.

Crazy.

Hot.

"Right, Daddy."

"That's it, baby. Stay still, Daddy'll take you."

Then he did, positioning under me, his hands came to my hips and he pulled me down to his face.

He started eating me.

I was so ready, I instantly ground into him, rocking.

One of his hands left my hip and wrapped around his cock. I knew it, partially watched it through the dark, heard it and felt his groans and growls between my legs as the pads of the fingers of his other hand dug into me.

I kept grinding down into his mouth, moving, shifting, rocking, and it took no time at all before I came. Not hard. *Excruciating*. It rocked me so deep, I cried out and couldn't hold myself up. I went forward, hands in the bed by Knight's waist.

His hand at my hip kept yanking me down as he kept at me and himself. I panted, still rocking, still coming, my eyes glued to his shadowed fist working his cock then I came again. He kept at me and I watched the shadow of his hand moving on his cock and I came *again*.

Oh God, had anyone died from too many orgasms?

"Honey," I rasped.

His hand yanked me down hard and he sucked deep, God, so deep. Then he growled and I came again as he did, too.

He lapped at me and stroked himself lazily as we both came down, then his head turned. He kissed the inside of my thigh and he muttered, "Climb off me, baby. Go get me a wet cloth."

I did as I was told, reaching for my pajamas when my feet hit the floor at the side of the bed and his voice came back at me.

"No clothes, Anya."

I looked to his shadowy form lounging on a forearm in the bed. I nodded then did as I was told, but did it naked.

When I came back, Knight was sitting with shoulders to the headboard, knees up. My sex spasmed at the sight, he was so damned sexy, even in shadow.

"Crawl up from the bottom, baby. I want you between my legs as you clean me."

Again, I moved as instructed and did what I was told.

When I was done, I got, "Take that to the bathroom then come back to me."

I nodded and carried out my order, coming back to a Knight who hadn't moved.

"Crawl up from the bottom again, Anya."

I crawled up the bed and as I did it, the thought came to me. I didn't know if I should, if I was even allowed. But I did it anyway.

So when I got to him, I moved between his legs but stopped, bent and kissed his flat abs. Then I moved up and stopped to kiss his chest. Then up his body until my face was to his neck and I kissed him there, smelling his cologne.

I knew my decision was right when his arms closed around me and his thighs pressed in, imprisoning me.

"My baby, so fuckin' sweet," he muttered.

I rested my head on his shoulder.

One of his arms shifted down and his hand cupped one of the cheeks of my behind gently.

"It hurt?" he whispered.

"Tender," I whispered back.

"First time, I went gentle."

Oh God. *That* was gentle?

"You fuck up that big again, Anya, you'll be callin' off work and spendin' a week in my bed to recover."

"Knight—"

His arms gave me a squeeze.

"Came hard, feel good. Do not piss me off."

I fell silent.

"You learn your lesson?"

I hoped so.

I nodded against his shoulder.

His arms gave me a squeeze as his fingers at my behind dug in gently.

Then he said quietly, "I believe you but I wanna make it clear. Shit might go down between us that'll make this go bad. You don't leave until we both know there's nothin' we can do to retrieve what we had. And if you believe that and I disagree, then you *talk to me* before you leave me. You might hear fucked up shit about me from a variety of sources. But you *talk to me* before you react. I will confirm or deny, I will be honest, and last, I will explain. If it's shit I don't want you to know yet, I'll explain that too, and you'll wait until I'm ready. You feel you can't, then, babe, you still fuckin' *talk... to... me* before you leave me."

I nodded against his shoulder again.

Knight kept talking.

"You can believe about ten percent of anything that comes outta Nick's mouth. This will not be somethin' you need to concern yourself with because you will never see him again. If the impossible happens and you do, I don't care if you're walkin' down the street, he's across the street from you and a half block up, you fuckin' call me. Get me?"

Another nod.

More from Knight.

"I do not give charity fucks. I don't know what he said to you, but honest to Christ, I don't even know what that *is*. Bottom line, no one, Anya and when I say that," his arm and hand gave me another squeeze, "I mean *no one* has had

163

my time, my attention and my cock the way you do. And you don't have those because you're the most beautiful woman I've ever laid eyes on. You have that because you're everything that's you. Somethin' in you made it easy to believe the bullshit Nick fed you. We gotta work that out, babe, and with that project, I'm all in. But there is no... fuckin'... *way* a woman like you, not just one who looks like you, but a *woman like you* should ever think in a million fuckin' years she's a charity case. You need to understand, baby, that in this scenario right here in this bed, no matter whose ass is tender, I'm the lucky one. You with me?"

At the word "lucky" my head jerked up and I stared at his shadowed face.

"What?" I breathed.

"You aren't with me," he muttered.

"Are you serious?"

"Are you comfortable with the fact that my boys roughed up your land-lord?"

My body stilled and I whispered, "Honey——"

"Answer me, babe, are you comfortable with that?"

"Can we——?"

His hand came to my jaw and his arm around me got tight, pulling me closer and he whispered, "Anya, babe, answer me."

"No," I blurted.

"But you're settin' it aside because you're drawn to me and I'm makin' you happy," he surmised.

"Yes."

"Then babe, I'm the lucky one, because with you, I'm not settin' shit aside. And with me, I think you already get without really knowin' that you always will."

My hand slid up his chest and I whispered, "Honey, let's not talk about this."

"Bury your head, baby, please, God, do it. But straight up, you give me good, normal and clean and you do it knowin' you'll never get that back. I'll take that. Fuck, yeah, I'll take that. But I'll only take it knowin' somewhere inside you, you get what you're givin' to me and you understand it'll never be returned."

"You're scaring me again, Knight."

"Enough to ask me to leave?"

"No," I whispered, and his hand clenched my jaw.

"Christ, my baby," he whispered.

I didn't want to talk about this anymore so I changed the subject.

"I'm sorry I believed Nick," I said softly.

"You believin' him didn't say shit about me. It said shit about how you feel about you. We'll work on that."

God, he was scary. Scary sweet, and I was thinking scary smart, too.

"Bet I bought myself a bad girl," he muttered and I blinked.

"Pardon?"

"Baby, how many times did you come on my face?"

I bit my lip.

Then I shared quietly, "I lost track."

Knight burst out laughing, both his arms closing tight around me as he shifted us down in bed and rolled me to my back, him at my side.

When he stopped laughing, his hand slid up to curl around my neck, palm at my throat.

"You gonna be a bad girl?" he whispered.

"I haven't decided," I whispered back, and his hand spasmed.

Then he asked, sounding appalled, "I hurt you?"

"Uh… yeah, Knight. You spanked me."

"Too hard?"

"Um…"

"That you couldn't stand the pain, Anya, that it didn't feel good even as it felt bad. That kinda too hard, babe. I didn't get that from you, not even close. When I was done, you were soaked."

"Well that's because, um… the answer's no. If that's too hard then it wasn't. Not even close."

His hand relaxed as did his body.

God, how could this guy have just spanked me, my bottom still felt warm and tender, and yet at the same time he was unbelievably sweet?

"We need a safe word," he muttered.

"Probably," I muttered back.

"No, babe, we do. We should have worked that out before but I've been goin' easy on you, payin' attention, not pushin' too hard. Didn't think we'd be here this quick. I'll think about it, give it to you before I take you again."

Easy on me.

Something, maybe, to look forward to.

"Okay," I said softly.

At my word, he gave me a squeeze before he shifted, yanking the covers out from under us, flicking them over us then settling onto his back. He rolled me and tucked me into his side.

Then he ordered, "Sleep, baby."

"Okay, Knight."

I settled in. Knight's arm around me drew me closer, then relaxed. My arm snaked across his flat belly, curled around and I held on.

Then I called, "Knight?"

"Yeah, babe."

I bit my lip.

"Babe?"

I stopped biting my lip.

Then I whispered, "Uh… you should probably prepare for me being bad, um… occasionally."

Knight went still for a moment before both his arms locked around me tight and he burst out laughing.

I turned the corner to Knight's study.

Nick was crouched at the safe. It was open. He was rifling through it.

I opened my mouth to say something when his head turned to me.

Then he surged out of his crouch, flying through the air toward me. His entire head had changed from Nick to a wide, gaping mouth filled with rows and rows of sharp, lethal teeth.

I jerked awake, and still held close to Knight's side but still half asleep, feeling his arm around me as a prison, I yanked away from it on a roll.

"What the fuck, babe?" His drowsy, deep, rough voice came at me and I froze.

Torso up and on my ass in the bed, I lifted my knees, soles of my feet to the bed. I put my elbows to them, head to my hands and took in a deep breath.

Knight's hand curled around my wrist.

"Anya?" he called softly.

"Bad dream," I whispered.

"Jesus, it'd have to be," he muttered, pulling gently at my wrist, but my head came up. My hand dropped to the bed, taking his with it, and I looked to his shadowy head.

"Nick was trying to get in your safe," I announced, and I felt as well as saw his body go rock-solid.

"What?" he whispered, that vibrating, angry heat starting to emanate.

"He didn't open it, or not that I know of. I heard him come in and got to him pretty quickly because I thought he was you. I turned the corner to your study and he was crouched at your safe. It wasn't opened. He moved away from it and shared his tale of treachery. I got his keys then he took off. With, um... everything that happened when you got here, I forgot to tell you." I twisted my wrist, dislodging his hand but finding it and curling mine around. "I'm sorry, honey. I totally forgot."

His hand squeezed mine and tugged as he said, "Don't worry about it, baby. I'll deal with Nick."

I nodded and felt the vibrations had stopped, the blaze retreating. I let him pull me down to him and arrange me pressed to his side again, held close.

I drew in a deep breath then snaked my arm around his gut. Then I drew in another one and forced my body to relax against his.

His hand at my hip gave me a gentle squeeze and he murmured, "That dream, was it about Nick?"

"He was crouched by your safe," I whispered. "Then he came at me, flying through the air and his entire head had become a mouth full of teeth."

"Fuckin' hell," Knight muttered.

"Yeah," I agreed quietly.

I pressed deeper into his side and his arm got tight around me.

"When was he there?" he asked.

"Around ten fifteen."

"Doorman gets off at ten. Fuckin' motherfucker, Nick," he muttered. Then, "I'll change the locks. He came when no doorman was on. They haven't changed the door code since he left. I'll tell Spin. He'll deal with the code change. Nick won't be able to get into my place starting tomorrow. He won't be able to access the building in a few days. Yeah?"

"Yeah, honey."

"Shits me he got to you at all, much less when I wasn't there."

"He didn't expect to see me."

"I'll bet he didn't, fuckin' motherfucker." Knight was muttering again.

"I dream a lot, Knight. They're not all good. I'm used to it. It's okay. Nick's not a fun guy to be around but, really, I'm okay."

"Shits me he got to you at all, much less when I wasn't there, Anya, no matter if you're okay or not. It's fuckin' five thirty in the morning. You had a crazy-ass dream. You're freaked. He filled your head with garbage. And you're not with me to have any of that shit happen to you."

"You can't cushion me from the entire world, Knight."

"I can try."

My stomach dropped.

"I'll take measures," he went on like he didn't just rock my world. "You feel safer here, we do your bed for a while. Go back to mine this weekend when the code's changed. Yeah?"

"Okay, honey," I agreed quietly.

"Now you got an hour to sleep. You gonna be able to do that?"

"Yeah."

"Then do it."

I smiled against his shoulder.

Then I whispered, "Okay."

Knight's arm gave me a squeeze.

I felt my belly warm, that tingle gliding up and down my spine, over my scalp, all along my skin until it felt like it was going to consume me.

And I didn't mind.

Not even a little bit.

It felt *great*.

Chapter 11
The Real You

"Tight, Anya."

After his soft words sounded against the skin of my neck, my limbs around Knight squeezed and I stared at the ceiling of his bedroom, nose stinging, heart beating hard.

It was Sunday morning and Knight just made love to me.

Made.

Love.

To.

Me.

Not bossy, not dirty, not an exercise in control. I got to touch, taste, lick, do what I wanted to do and so did he (as usual). It was slow, lazy, gentle.

And beautiful.

Honestly, I didn't know he had that in him. He told me he could do normal, gentle. But after a week of what we'd had, I didn't really think about it. I expected since I was giving it to him the way he liked, he'd take advantage of it.

And he did.

But he woke up in a different mood that morning and gave it to me sweet, letting me give it back. I loved it, and from what I could tell, he did, too.

This meant I had it all from Knight, at least in bed. Scary, crazy, hot. Adventurous. Consuming. Excruciating. Exciting. Unexpected. Slow. Lazy. Gentle. Sweet.

Never in my life, any aspect of it, had I had it all or even expected to.

Now I did, and to say it moved me was an understatement.

Knight quit nuzzling my neck with his nose and lips and his head came up.

My eyes went to his.

His looked into mine a quarter of a second and he whispered, "Baby, what?"

"You want a surprise?" I whispered back, not about to tell him what. Not then. Maybe later.

Hopefully it would be later after it stayed good in a way I knew it always would be.

He held my eyes for long moments and I knew he did it coming to a decision.

Then he came to it.

"Yeah," he answered, thankfully, and it had to be said thoughtfully, letting it slide.

"I called my Sunday clients, all of them. Moved them. Now my Sundays are free."

His eyes went hooded and, seriously, that was a good look.

"So you're mine all day," he said softly.

"Every Sunday," I replied just as softly.

One side of his lips curved up and he kept talking softly when he said, "Thank you, baby."

He wanted that. Me. All day Sunday.

God.

"You're welcome, honey."

His hand came up and his fingertips trailed along the apple of my cheek as he muttered, "Fuck, my baby's sweet."

So was my Daddy.

"I have another surprise," I announced, and his eyes went from his fingers now at my temple to mine.

"Yeah?"

"Anya Gage's World Famous Toasted Almond Pancakes with Almond Infused Maple Syrup. I brought all the stuff over last night."

That got me a full grin. "World famous?"

I grinned back. "Totally."

His eyes went to my mouth, his pupils dilated then they came back to mine.

"My shirt, no underwear while you make them."

Back to bossy.

My womb convulsed.

"Okay, Daddy," I whispered, and his hips between mine pressed in.

"Fuck, how did this happen?" he muttered like he was talking to himself, his eyes moving over my face.

"What?"

He looked back into my eyes. "You're perfect, baby."

I blinked.

Then I whispered, "Knight—"

"No, Anya, no fucked up shit outta that sweet mouth. I'm not gonna listen to it and I'll work my balls off, I don't care if it takes decades, to make you stop even thinkin' it. Instead, you gotta know that every second I spend with you it becomes more and more clear you were made for me. A gift I don't deserve, didn't earn, but I'm not giving it back."

My nose started stinging again and I demanded quietly, "Stop it."

"Not gonna do that, Anya. Not ever. Not until you get it, baby."

"Girls, we're like this," I explained quickly in an effort to move us off this topic. "Except for girls like Sandrine, who, from her Dad on up, had men spoiling her rotten and convincing her she's precious. Which, as you know, causes its own issues. We spend hours convincing ourselves we're faulty. Even Vivica, who's totally awesome and mostly knows that, she's also totally ambitious and driven to be perfect and create the perfect life. You just have to roll with it."

"Bullshit," he replied instantly and I blinked.

"Pardon?"

"Sandrine's Dad knew what he was doin'. It's Sandrine now who's fucking up. You got a girl who's worth it, you're her Dad or you're her Daddy, you spoil her rotten. You let her know she's precious, not convince her of that shit, because it's not about convincing. It's about understanding it's just fuckin' true."

Now I was blinking for a different reason. Rapidly.

"Seriously, Knight, stop it," I whispered.

"Deep breathe. Control those tears. And I'll let it go after I say this. We haven't had the time to get into what Nick did to you and how you believed it so easily. Your aunt, she was negligent, which has the power to create wounds, and on top of that she was a cunt, which scores those wounds deep. You're right, everyone should work to make a better life for themselves however they gotta do it. But that doesn't mean they shouldn't hope and expect good things to come their way. Random and unexpected. Regularly or infrequently. It doesn't matter, good things happen just like bad. And it's fucked up not to think you'll get your share of those, babe. And even more fucked up that when you do you feel you don't deserve them or they're jacked in some way that reflects on you."

He took in a breath as I continued to breathe deep and he continued.

"Nick is an asshole, but that doesn't mean he isn't smart. The way he's smart is he's observant. He notices shit. It's a trait that could be put to good use, and sometimes, he's in the mood, he can use it that way. He's also got a deep, fuckin' mean streak and that's what he works at. He saw you, he read you. He was pissed you were walkin' to him from my bed when he wants you in his and he cut you, went straight in for the kill usin' exactly what he knew would make you bleed. What you gotta get is, that's his shit. You gotta turn that shit back on him and see he's actin' on spite. And he's doin' it because he wants the gift of you, cannot have it and it pisses him off. So what he did was a jacked up, nasty, twisted compliment. And you should have just smiled to yourself, crawled in my bed and waited for me to come home and show you the real you."

My voice was throaty when I warned, "If you want me not to cry, Knight, you seriously need to shut up."

He studied me. Then he smiled at me.

Then he said quietly, "For now, I'll give you that, baby. Now get your ass outta my bed and make me pancakes."

"Okay," I whispered.

He dipped his head and brushed his lips against mine. Then he slid his tongue across my lower lip and my arms and legs automatically gave him a squeeze. My tongue slid out and reciprocated the gesture.

He growled, slanted his head and *kissed me.*

Only after that did I get out of bed, and I felt his eyes on me while I shrugged on his midnight blue, tailored, slim-fit shirt. I continued to feel his eyes while I buttoned the buttons from mid-breast to navel. I continued to feel his eyes while I walked to the bathroom to clean up (by the by, we dispensed with condoms because I was on the pill; this I shared with Knight prior to him giving it to me the second time), brush my teeth and wash my face. And I continued to feel his eyes as I walked out of the bathroom, grinned at him as he lounged on his side in bed, head in his hand, as I walked to the door and even as I wandered down his hall.

And I loved every second of it.

That day was going to be a golden day, I could feel it.

And I knew this because I was standing at Knight's restaurant quality range, smelling his cologne coming from his shirt, my pancakes bubbling on the griddle and they were perfect. I had to admit, there were days (not the golden kind) when even my World Famous Toasted Almond Pancakes could go south.

Today was not one of those days.

I heard the murmur of Knight's voice coming toward me and I knew he was on the phone. As it got closer and closer, I twisted my neck and watched him appear in the living room-kitchen area and I smiled a secret smile that didn't curve my lips but curved deep inside me.

Faded jeans. Bare feet. Beat-up Motörhead tee.

Yummy. I had Jeans and Heavy Metal Tee Knight Sunday.

Totally a golden day.

He spoke into the phone at his ear as he walked, but his eyes were on me.

I gave him a smile and turned back to the pancakes.

"Yeah." I heard him say. Then, "No. Not likin' that."

I felt him come up behind me.

"Right," he said into the phone.

I felt his hand at my belly, his front warm against my back.

I grinned at the pancakes as I flipped them.

"No, we'll do it tomorrow," he told whoever he was talking to.

My legs trembled when his hand found the opening to his shirt and I felt it, skin against skin at my belly.

Another secret inside smile.

"He wants to be there, he's there. But Kurt's on stand-by," Knight stated, and my belly dropped as my eyes went unfocused when his hand slid down and in, cupping me.

"Hang on," I said into the phone and at my ear he whispered, "Open your legs a little, baby."

My hand came out, wrapped around the edge of the marble countertop by the stove, feeling the cool, hard stone and I did as Knight told me to do.

I felt him press into my back as he leaned deeper to get better access, his middle finger slid tight over my clit then it glided inside.

I sucked in an audible breath.

"Back," I heard him mutter into the phone. "Right. Set it up. We'll talk tomorrow. I got Anya all day, keep everyone off me. Yeah?" Pause then, "Later."

I saw his phone hit the counter, felt his lips come to my ear as his free arm slid around my midriff, but I was holding on and deep breathing.

"Those look good, babe," he whispered in my ear.

"Yeah," I breathed.

I felt his chuckle against my skin and I shivered.

Then he asked, "Now do you get my rule of no underwear?"

Oh, I got it all right. I got it so much I was considering throwing all my underwear in the trash.

"Yeah," I breathed again.

He explained it anyway as his finger inside me did a lazy circle. "Instant access, I want even a hint of the thrill of you."

My legs trembled and I held the counter tighter.

"Jesus, can fuckin' feel you gettin' wet."

I pressed my lips together.

"You always ready for me?"

"Yes," I whispered.

"Yes?"

"Yes, Daddy."

His lips moved to the skin of my neck as his finger slid out, over my clit and he whispered, "That's my baby."

I bit my lip.

His hand flattened, coming up and gliding across my belly so he was just holding me.

"Hungry, Anya, so pull it together, babe, and concentrate on pancakes."

"Right," I whispered, and Knight held me as I took in a couple of shaky breaths and pulled it together. As if he sensed it, once my concentration returned and I had my legs firm under me, he kissed my neck and let me go.

He moved to the coffee. I lifted the griddle from the burner and moved to the plates set on placemats that I'd already put out.

I scooped out pancakes as Knight asked, "You got coffee?"

"Yeah, honey."

"Need it warmed?"

I looked at him and grinned. "I'm good. Breakfast is ready."

His face got soft and he took his mug to the bar. I put the griddle on the burner, made sure everything was off and joined him there.

Buttering and syruping commenced.

It wasn't until I was swallowing my third bite that I got the courage to go for it.

"Can I ask you something?"

"Anything," he muttered through pancakes and I looked at him.

I was on the stool next to him, my legs crossed. His legs were splayed wide and he didn't have to tell me he liked my World Famous Toasted Almond Pancakes because the bites he was taking were huge.

"You like the pancakes?" I asked and his eyes slid to me.

"Uh... yeah." Then he forked more into his mouth.

I giggled.

He chewed, swallowed and his brows went up. "That's what you wanted to ask?"

I shook my head.

Then I blurted, "You have a cane?"

His head tipped slightly to the side and he asked, "What?"

"You, um... the other night, you said I needed a, uh... strap or cane. So, um... do you have one? Of, uh... either of those."

He studied me and then a slow, lazy, wicked smile spread across his face.

My toes curled.

"Doin' your homework?" he asked quietly.

"Just curious," I somewhat lied.

He kept smiling his wicked smile as he answered, "Both, baby. No whips, no paddles, no crops. You want me to branch out, we'll go shopping."

I blinked.

"Shopping?"

"Shopping."

Oh my.

Knight kept explaining. "Strap, the edges are smooth. You'll feel the sting, Anya, but no marks. And just to ease that curiosity, you fuck up a little, you get my hand. More, you get the strap. Huge, you get the cane."

I tried not to squirm on my stool and failed, but congratulated myself anyway because it was just a little squirm.

Knight, however, didn't miss it and I knew this when his arm came out, his hand hooked around the back of my neck and he pulled me to him twisting me and leaning in until our faces were close.

"You know, but I'll tell you anyway. I'm fuckin' thrilled you liked takin' that so much, babe. But that shit doesn't happen unless you earn it. You wanna experiment, after pancakes, I'll get inspired. But I tan your ass when you jack up and only then. You like it, you earn it. And I'll tell you this too, even though I already told you, you want that game, I'll be fuckin' thrilled to play it with you. But that's how it is. We got our safe word, we're good to play the game whenever you want. And if you don't get this, I'm controlling, that's what this is about. But baby, you enter that game, that's your way to control me. You with me?"

Controlling Knight.

I liked that.

I nodded.

"Don't be nervous or shy about this shit, Anya. I'll take you as far as you wanna go as long as I'm comfortable with it. You do not sit on anything you're uncomfortable with either. I go too far, you say the safe word. You do not hesitate and I'll stand down immediately. No repercussions, baby, and I won't be disappointed. I promise. We have only what we got right now, I'm way good. And it goes the other way, you like something and want more, you also tell me. And I'll give it to you. Yeah?"

I nodded.

His eyes held mine.

Then he asked gently, "Now, while I'm eatin' pancakes, am I looking for inspiration?"

I nodded again.

He grinned again, slow, lazy and wicked.

My legs started trembling.

"Eat," he whispered then he let me go.

I pulled in a steadying breath and turned my attention to my pancakes.

I got two bites in before my purse sitting close to Knight's place setting rang. He reached out, dragged it across the countertop to him, dug in and pulled out the phone.

He looked at the display, looked at me and offered it to me, muttering, "Sandrine."

I took it from him, swallowed, took the call and put the phone to my ear.

"Hey, honey."

"Anya?"

At her trembling, terrified voice, my back shot straight before I froze.

"Sandrine, where are you? What's the matter?" I asked and I felt Knight come alert beside me.

"Oh God… Anya," she whispered, the words broken then she burst into tears.

My eyes shot to Knight who was studying me, face blank, eyes watchful and working, but I spoke into the phone.

"Sandrine, honey, talk to me. What's going on? Where—?"

Then my phone wasn't at my ear. It was in Knight's hand at his.

"Sandrine. This is Knight. Pull it together. Two minutes. Are you in trouble?" Pause while I stared at him, eyes glued to his impassive face. "Right. You know where you are?" Another pause while I started shivering. Knight looked to me, lifted his other hand and snapped his fingers once then pointed to his phone. "He still there?" Knight asked as I jumped off the stool and rushed toward his phone.

Oh God.

Oh *God*.

"This needs to be straight, Sandrine, so give it to me straight. He force you to do it or did you just do it?"

Oh God!

Oh God!

I grabbed Knight's phone and raced back to him.

"Good, Sandrine. Straight is good. Hang tight. You remember the guy who gave you the ride last weekend?" I held his phone out to him, he took it and I stood close, listening hard. "Good. Either him or me will be there soon. We're both coming. We'll deal with the guy and we'll get you out of there. Hang tight. Don't do anything stupid. Avoid this guy while you're waiting if you can. Are you with me?" Another pause then, "Good. You gonna hang tight?" He waited. I waited. Then, "Good, Sandrine. Someone's coming. I'm letting you go now. Okay?" Pause then, "Be there soon."

He beeped my phone off and handed it to me but immediately started beeping buttons on his.

"I know you're freaked, babe, but I gotta get Kurt in play," he muttered.

"Okay," I whispered.

I could even hear the fear in my voice so I knew why his eyes sliced to me. I also knew why his hand lifted and curled, firm, warm and tight around the side of my neck as he lifted his phone to his ear.

"Kurt? Yeah, Knight. Got a situation. Need you in play." He gave an address and a succinct rundown of the situation that gave me nothing then, "I'll either be there when you get there or I'll meet you there. Don't wait to go in. She's expecting one or both of us. You're there first, get her out and get her here. Whoever's out last deals with the guy. Guess? Piss-ant but be smart. Yeah?" He was silent then, "Later."

He hit a button and looked at me.

I pulled in breath.

Knight gave it to me.

"It's not as bad as you think, but it's fucked. She went out last night, got shitfaced, hooked up. From his address, dude's got money. She went home with him. He offered her something that was mood-enhancing. She was not enthusiastic but she was determined so she took it. He gave her too much. Trip was bad. She doesn't remember much. She's still fucked up, probably high, definitely drunk. But she's not enough of both not to realize she's freaked. He isn't letting her leave. Don't know why, could just be she's tripping bad and drunk and he's concerned so he's not letting her go, could be he's an asshole. But I'll find out and deal with it. One or both of you and Vivica got access to her place?"

"Both," I whispered.

"Activate Vivica. Clothes, underwear, whatever the fuck bitches need. Get her ass there to get it and here for when I get Sandrine back. I don't know what she took so I don't know what we got on our hands. It could still get bumpy. You got that?"

I nodded.

"I gotta go," he told me.

I nodded again.

He leaned in quick to give me an even quicker kiss then he took off.

I sucked in breath as I lifted my phone to call Vivica.

Then I thought that day was turning out not so golden.

Then I thought, *Sandrine, she's gonna be the death of me.*

"Shit, fuck, stupid Sandrine. We get her sorted, I'm gonna kick her skinny white ass."

This was Vivica, pacing the landing between the kitchen and the sunken living room, ranting.

"Viv," I whispered, and she stopped and cut her eyes to me.

"Good news is, never been here. Sandrine said this crib was sweet. She didn't say it was *sah-fuckin'-weet*. Bad news is, you got a heart of pure gold. You're gonna be all Momma's-gonna-make-it-better when you should do that 'til it's better, *then* you need to back me up with you-do-this-again,-Momma's-gonna-kick-your-skinny-white-ass."

I pressed my lips together.

My phone in my hand rang.

I jumped, looked at it, saw the call was from Knight, took it and put it to my ear.

"Sweetheart," I whispered.

"Babe, got her. Heads up, she is fucked up. We're ten minutes out. When we get there, you're on duty. You get Vivica?"

"Viv's here."

"Good. Shower first. The one in the front hall."

"Okay, but should we take her to the hospital?"

"Bad high mixed with booze, but if she was gonna stop breathing, she would have done it hours ago."

"What did she take?"

"Better question, what didn't she take? Smoked meth. Got wired, he freaked, gave her shit to bring her down. She went down, gave her shit to take her back up. Motherfucker's got money so he's also got a pharmacy, and not all the legal kind. All that on top of her being absolutely hammered."

I sucked in breath.

Knight kept talking.

"Kurt's dealing with him."

Oh boy.

Knight went on, "Towels in the hall bathroom are clean. She's probably gonna crash soon. That's gonna happen in the TV room so sort that. And a bowl. Fuck knows, she might still puke, though the dude she was with said she's been doin' a lotta that, but he didn't need to tell me since I smelled it at

179

his place. That's likely why she's still breathing. If she has to do it again, I just fuckin' hope she waits until she's outta my ride."

I did too. Aston Martins and drunk/high vomiting did not go together.

Or *any* vomiting.

God, Sandrine.

"Okay, honey," I said softly.

"Be there soon. Later."

"Later."

I disconnected and my eyes went to Viv.

"They're close. We're up," I told her.

"Have I said today I love him?" she replied.

I smiled. It was freaked, it was happy, it was hopeful.

"No," I whispered, then sighed, "but yeah."

Then I put the phone on the counter and hustled to the hall bathroom.

I left a fuming, eyes-to-a-movie Vivica and the now-sleeping Sandrine in the TV room and walked down the hall to find Knight.

As I was going, Kurt crossed the mouth of the hall.

His eyes came to me, his chin went up, he grunted, "Yo," but he didn't break stride and thus disappeared.

As I got to the end of the hall I stopped and looked to the left to the front door to see it closing. Then I looked to the right and saw Knight outside smoking.

I walked there.

He was hips against the railing watching me even before I made it to the door.

Once I stepped through and closed it behind me, I said, "She's sleeping."

"Good. She wakes up, she'll feel like fuck, but you still do not hesitate to rip that bitch a new fuckin' asshole."

I stopped two feet away and pressed my lips together.

"You stopped too soon," he informed me and I moved the rest of the way.

He instantly wrapped an arm around my waist and pulled me so I was resting most of my weight on him. I lifted my hands and placed them light on his chest.

"I'm so sorry, Knight. She ruined our golden Sunday," I said quietly.

"Yeah, she did and I'm pissed about that. I'm pissed about the state I found her in. I'm pissed I had to deal with that shit. I'm pissed I had to fuck up Kurt's Sunday off callin' him in. I'm pissed your posse is here not havin' a nice dinner and some wine, but dealin' with that shit. And I'm pissed they're here at all because I have you all day. You wanted me to get inspired and I was lookin' forward to that." His arm gave me a squeeze. "But the gig is, Anya, you should be pissed about all this, too, and a fuckuva lot more than me. This bitch is *your* bitch, and she doesn't get smart fast, this budding tendency toward creating bad scenes that are gettin' worse is gonna get outta hand."

He was so right.

So I agreed quietly, "Yeah."

"Your *other* bitch looks fit to be tied and hangin' on from lettin' loose by the skin of her teeth. You should be, too," he told me.

"That's what Viv says."

"She's right, and so am I."

I pressed my lips together.

Knight watched and took a drag from his cigarette. He blew out the smoke in a thin, pissed-off stream and crushed it out on the ashtray on the railing. Then both his arms curved around me.

"Right," he started. "Kurt got the full story and the fuck of this is, this guy last night, he's loaded. Serious as shit. And somethin' else, he's had his eye on Sandrine a while. And not to fuck her up and play with her in ways she doesn't want. The stupid fuck actually *liked* her. He thought it was *him* needin' to prove somethin' to *her*. Partier. Player. Big man. High roller. Show her he's got connections. He's cool. Hip to the fuckin' scene. Do not know how this dude makes his money but he has fuck all confidence. He's never even *smoked* meth. Why the motherfucker had it is beyond me. Those two smokin' meth when neither of them knew what the fuck they were doin' is so fuckin' ridiculous I can't even begin to describe it. To have meth at all is jacked."

He was right about that too.

"That is not my problem," he continued. "My problem is, I got a woman who's got a girl who's got her head jammed so far up her ass, she cannot fuckin' see. This guy was her ticket. And instead of just bein' classy and beautiful and sweet, she put herself out there when this guy only wanted the classy, beautiful and sweet and to lay the world at her feet so she'd take his cock and, probably, take it long enough to get his ring on her finger, make babies and spoil her until she died. Now, he's got puke all over his house, he's had a visit from Kurt and me that was extreme and if she was even together enough to give him her number, he's probably erasing it from his phonebook right now if he hasn't already. So that's my problem, Anya, because you and Vivica don't pull her head outta her ass, this is gonna stay your problem, and through you mine, for a long time. And I'll give you this one heads up, a man fucks with her, which means through her *you* experience a crash and burn, and I'm talkin' he date rapes her or we're takin' a trip to the hospital for any fuckin' reason, by association, she gets my services. And that means, the guy who did it is breathin' through a tube, and that's only if I'm in a good enough mood to leave him breathing."

I held my breath and held his eyes.

Knight kept talking.

"I am not kidding. I'm also not exaggerating. So save me that hassle and pull her head outta her ass."

"Okay, Knight."

He stared at me.

Then, softer but still firm, he told me, "I had a man who saw and heard the entire fuckin' thing that went down with Nick. She put your ass out there, Anya, and I know it. I wasn't at the club that night, my man wasn't close, I do not like to think where Nick woulda taken that with you. You say Vivica is protective. You are too, and what you did to pull Sandrine outta that shit proves it. You made the wrong decision then, baby. Don't make the wrong decision today. In this situation, your protection needs to run the way Vivica's does. Don't buckle and be sweet. Don't swing your ass out there. Don't swing mine out there. Don't swing Vivica's out there. You get me?"

I nodded.

He pulled in a sharp breath through his nose then his eyes drifted over my shoulder.

I watched him get lost in thought then I slid my hands down his chest so I could wrap my arms around him. His chin dipped down and his eyes caught mine.

"Told you about my Dad," he stated apropos of nothing. "Didn't tell you he isn't my Dad. He's my stepdad. I have no fuckin' clue who my Dad is because my mother was a prostitute before she met him."

I blinked and my body went solid.

Oh my God.

"Oh, Knight. Honey," I whispered.

His hand slid up and curled around the back of my neck but his eyes never left mine.

"She was fucked up. All I ever knew until Carl came into our lives and sorted her shit out. Nick's his. He never made me feel I wasn't. He adopted me legally, gave me his name. I was a little kid, but I remember all that shit before Carl. Makes no sense, don't know how she did it, but even fucked up, she was a good Mom. She loved me, took care of me the best she could. They obviously never talk about it and I sure as fuck never asked, but my guess, he was a john, he was a regular and he fell in love with a streetwalker. Got her off the street. Got her clean. Gave her a good life. It's jacked but it worked."

"I'm pleased you're sharing with me, sweetheart," I told him softly and cautiously. "I wanna know about you. But I'm wondering why you're sharing this now."

"Why is because she had a good life, good parents, good schooling. She went off the rails doin' stupid shit for men. It got messier and messier until her whole life was mess. I don't know my grandparents, neither does Nick. They got shot of her and she made them do it in a way where they never looked back. Even for grandchildren. I am not clairvoyant. But I learned really fuckin' early a lotta bad shit can happen to women. A lot of it. And you might think I'm wrong, but I'm not. A lot of that happens because they do stupid shit and they're weak. Your girl is weak, and not because her Dad thinks she's beautiful and precious and told her so. Because she just is. It's time she sorts herself out before, one way or another, she's beyond anyone saving and protecting."

"Viv and I'll talk to her," I promised.

"Do it until you're blue in the face and break through. You don't, I'm gonna keep an eye on this and the time comes you need to scrape her off to protect yourself, I'll be leanin' on you to do that. She's your girl and that'll be your decision. But I won't let up. Get me?"

"Get you," I whispered.

His arms gave me a squeeze.

"Right," he muttered. "Now, I'm gonna make you and Vivica lunch. Is there anything she doesn't eat?"

God, God, *God,* this was a good, kind man, even if he calmly talked about making people breathe through a tube.

"Anything green and healthy on the weekends. She keeps to a strict, twelve hundred calorie, heavy on the veggies diet Mondays through Fridays so she can do whatever she wants on the weekend. So, don't make salad. Viv won't eat it."

I watched his lips twitch then he murmured, "I think I like this bitch."

"She's a submissive."

Oh God! Did I blurt that out?

I watched Knight do a slow blink.

Yep, I blurted that out.

I pressed deep and gave him a squeeze of my arms. "Don't tell her I told you," I begged on a whisper. "I don't even know *why* I told you."

"She out that before or after you told her I own you?" he asked, totally clued in.

Oh boy.

"After."

He grinned. "Built-in advisor. Lucky for you, babe."

I rolled my eyes.

I felt his body shake with his chuckle as his arms gave me a squeeze.

When I rolled them back he asked, "She owned?"

I shook my head and whispered like Viv, who was space and walls away, could hear if I didn't, "Looking."

"Won't look long," he muttered.

"She made it sound like it wasn't easy to find the right one."

His eyes held mine and he replied, "It fucking isn't."

Oh.

My.

His eyes got lazy, his head dipped, he kissed me lightly then he pulled back.

"Lunch," he declared. "No salad."

Yes, a good, kind man.

"Thanks, honey," I whispered.

"You're welcome, babe," he whispered back. I got another squeeze, he let me go and we walked in together.

Knight went to the kitchen.

I went to Vivica and Sandrine.

"Roll, baby."

My body sated, my wrists tied to the slats of the headboard with soft, strong, black silk scarves, I rolled to my belly, which meant I rolled close to Knight whose front was now pressed to my side.

It was much later. Viv had taken Sandrine home and it was finally just us.

"Pull yourself up, cock your elbows out. It'll be more comfortable," Knight said softly, his hand coming to rest on the small of my back.

Apparently, he wasn't going to untie me. And he'd just done me while I was tied to his bed and I'd come hard.

Twice.

But still, knowing that Knight wasn't going to untie me, I quivered.

I wrapped my hands around the scarf and shifted up, cocking my elbows out and found he was right.

"Rest your head on the pillow, keep your eyes to me," he ordered gently and I lay my head down and kept my eyes to his beauty.

His face dipped close to mine.

Then he went on softly, "Spread for Daddy."

I licked my lips as I quivered again, this time stronger, and I opened my legs.

"Wider, baby."

Oh God.

Another quiver.

I spread wider.

His hand slid down to my behind and his fingers dug in.

His voice was firm when he ordered, "Anya, *wider*."

I went as far as I could, my left leg having to push through his heavy ones and he hooked one around.

"That's it," he said softly, his hand now stroking my bottom. Then it was just his fingertips trailing light along the skin of my ass and the small of my back.

He pulled back and settled in with an elbow in the pillow, head in his hand, eyes and fingertips on me.

Then he asked conversationally, "Tell me, you get through to your girl?"

I didn't expect this, to be tied to the bed, naked, spread open and then have a chat.

God, weird.

And hot.

"She felt like shit, but she totally freaked when I laid it out. She expected that from Viv. Not from me. It freaked Viv out too, but Viv rolled with me and we tag teamed her."

His fingers kept at me, lazy.

"You think she took it in?"

"I don't know," I answered quietly. "There was a lot of crying and excuses. She was embarrassed. We went over the Nick situation. I told her what you told me about the guy being into her and her losing her chance at that. She was upset at that news and Vivica was pretty harsh. So I hope so."

"Good," he muttered, his eyes wandered to my behind as his fingers kept drifting.

I stayed still. Knight watched his hand move. This lasted a long time. Long enough for it to go from hot and sweet to hot and torture.

Then Knight whispered, "Love my baby's ass."

I loved it that he loved my ass.

His eyes came back to mine.

"And she gave me Sundays."

I smiled up at him. It was lazy and my eyes were hooded because I was getting way turned on, but I did it.

"What should I give her back?" he asked.

Another quiver.

I had a thousand ideas, but I bet he had more and his were better.

I didn't say that.

Instead I pointed out, "You've already been super generous to me, Knight. I just moved some clients. It's not a big deal."

His head tipped into his hand. "It is to me."

"Okay," I whispered. "But I also owe you for stepping up for Sandrine."

One side of his mouth went up and he agreed, "Yeah, you do."

I grinned back, but I used my whole mouth.

Suddenly, he leaned into me, his face to mine, his fingers slipped in a barely there touch between my legs and my hips jumped.

"So what're you gonna give me?" he asked.

"What do you want?" I whispered.

"To know what you'll give me."

"Whatever you want," I replied immediately and his fingers came back up in a barely there touch. Then they did it again, there but not there. I could feel the hint, the promise but they weren't really touching.

I squirmed.

"Whatever I want?" he asked.

"Yes," I breathed.

"Whatever I want," he murmured as if turning this concept over in his mind.

"Yes," I repeated on a breath, and squirmed again as his fingers kept giving without giving.

"Still, baby," he warned, and it took effort but I stilled.

His fingers moved, giving everything and nothing.

I closed my eyes.

His hand went away.

"You know I don't like your eyes closed, Anya."

I opened them.

His hand came back.

"You wanna know what I want?" he asked.

"Yes," I panted.

"I wanna know how long you can take this before you lose control."

Oh God.

"About two more seconds," I whispered.

"That would be disappointing," he replied.

God!

"You gonna try to hold on?"

"Yes," I breathed as his fingers kept at it.

"Good girl, holding on for Daddy."

God, just those words nearly made me lose control.

He watched my face, held my eyes as his fingers played. I held on. He kept doing it. I kept holding on.

I was holding tight with both hands to the end of the scarf tied around my wrists and panting, my legs and bottom tight and quivering and he whispered, "Fuck me, magnificent. How much more can you take, baby?"

"Keep giving it to me and we'll see," I gasped.

"Fuck, *magnificent*," he growled.

Then he kept giving it to me without giving it to me.

Finally, to keep control, my head went back an inch and my teeth sunk into my lip.

"Okay, Anya, you're done," he decided.

His finger grazed my clit, my neck arched, my hips bucked and I came instantly.

When I was coming down, his fingers were slipping through and his lips were at my ear.

"Saturated," he growled. "Roll to your back, you know how I like it. Offer that pussy to me. Daddy's gonna lick you clean."

He pulled away and I didn't hesitate. I rolled to my back, lifted my knees high and spread my legs wide.

Then my Daddy licked me clean and made me come again doing it.

Then he fucked me hard and he made me come doing that, too.

He didn't untie me after he turned out the lights and settled tight to my side. He made me fall asleep with his hand cupping me, two fingers inside.

I slept like a baby.

Not a single dream.

Chapter 12
Mr. Sebring

I wandered down the hall in my platinum high-heeled sandals, wearing my kickass, platinum satin dress that clung to all the right parts of me. It was super short, had some intriguing drapes and was held up at my shoulders by slim, oval metal links. My clutch was tucked under my arm and my neck was bent, head twisted, forearms raised because I was still putting in my earring.

I heard Knight on the phone and I knew he was somewhere in the kitchen-living room area.

It was Friday, three weeks from Sandrine Scene, the Sequel.

The good news was, as of Wednesday, I was officially a certified skin technician. Classes were done and three of my nights were free. The other good news was, Knight's employee, Kathleen, booked a weekly manicure on Monday nights. *Weekly!* Sixty extra dollars a month, and that didn't include tip. Crazy cool. Further good news was, Sandrine was laying low and licking her wounds that she messed it all up, and strange, somewhat loser-ish rich guy who was still into her slipped through her fingers. She hadn't been out since, which meant she might have learned her lesson (hopefully). More good news was that it was the end of April, the weather was warming up and summer, my favorite season, was around the corner.

And the last good news was all things Knight.

We didn't see each other often but we slept in the same bed every night (well, some of it, at least, since he was never home before two thirty). Sometimes, though rarely, he simply joined me and I didn't even know it until the alarm sounded and I woke up beside him. Most times, he woke me and did me bossy. A few times, he woke me and made gentle love to me.

I liked all three.

We talked on the phone at least once every day. Depending on when this was, it could last a few minutes to longer. If I was at work, he just checked in. If he was at work and I was at home, sometimes he'd have time, sometimes he wouldn't, sometimes he'd get called away.

He'd come to work to take me to lunch one day, though, and since I told him, and he thought it was uproariously funny (and I knew this because he laughed uproariously when I told him), he knew he was going to be given the once-over by the office girls.

He showed up in a suit, an electric blue tailored shirt and he still hadn't had a haircut.

It was reported to me that he also smiled at one of our receptionists, Rosie, when he asked for me. And since everyone was hanging out in reception, they all caught the smile.

Not surprisingly, he was given enthusiastic thumbs-up all around.

When I informed him of *this,* he again laughed uproariously.

We had our Sundays together and I knew these were sacrosanct because after the first one blown by Sandrine's antics, he didn't take a single call all day the last two. He was always in demand, having calls come in when I was on the phone with him or people wanting his attention. So I knew he laid down the law.

For me.

After the first Sunday when his phone didn't ring once, the second one, I turned mine off.

For Knight.

Now, even though it was nearing ten on a work night for him and he was usually long gone by then, he was taking me to Slade. I didn't know why, but I was going because it was an order.

"Pick a dress. When I look out the window of my office, I wanna see you," was all he said.

I didn't know what I'd do by myself, me and whatever security he assigned to me alone in a sea of people in his club. But I figured I could entertain myself.

And bottom line, if Knight wanted to see me out of his office window, I'd be there to be seen.

So I'd spent the last hour and a half after Knight made me dinner dolling up.

Now I was ready.

I'd turned the bend in the L and was wandering down the other hall not listening to him, mostly because I was concentrating on walking, holding my clutch, my bracelet I couldn't get clasped by myself dangling from my fist, and finding the hole in my ear all at the same time.

I hit the open area and the curved post of my earring slid in. I stopped to slide on the plastic doohickey to keep it from working its way out and I dropped my hands and looked to Knight.

He was in the kitchen by the bar staring at me, eyes moving over me and they were hungry.

My knees got weak.

"Anya's ready," he rumbled into his phone, his voice not smooth by a long shot. "We're done talking."

Then he hit a button and dropped his phone to the counter.

"Here," he growled. "Now."

I went there and I did it immediately.

When I got there, his hands came instantly to my waist. They slid up over the smooth fabric at my sides then slid down. I held onto his biceps as I watched his eyes watch his hands move. Then his hands slid back and I came closer as they hit my behind. They clenched in and he jerked the skirt of my dress up.

I drew in a sharp breath and my fingers tensed into the hard muscle under the expensive fabric of his suit.

His eyes held mine and one finger slid deeper then traced the fabric of my thong, pressing in and gliding down, down...

My lips parted.

"Just checkin'," he muttered, his hands retreating then smoothing my skirt over my bottom.

I swallowed.

Then, my voice low and slightly throaty, I asked softly, "Can you do my bracelet? I can't get the clasp."

"Give it to me," was Knight's answer, which I correctly took as a yes.

I did, gave him my wrist and dipped my head to watch him work the clasp.

"Your girl, Vivica," he said as he attached the bracelet. "She do only brothers or does she prefer other flavors?"

He finished with the clasp and my eyes went to his to see his on me.

"She prefers her own kind," I answered.

"She got any kink?" he went on and my head gave a slight jerk then tipped to the side.

"Kink?"

"Kink. She a freak?"

"Um…"

His hands came to my hips and gave them a squeeze.

"She into deep shit? Serious shit?"

"Well, we haven't gotten into specifics, but I think she just likes to give over control and I know she likes to be a bad girl occasionally. Though I did open the floodgates of that, she knows she can share with me and she didn't describe anything like that. I got the sense she was relieved she could talk about it at all so she would and didn't. So, my guess, no."

"Find out," he ordered and I blinked.

Then I asked quietly, "Why?"

"Heard the boys talkin'. There's a brother who's lookin' to own and his goal is to possess a woman properly, which means long-term. He's seen your girl and flat out said he wanted to bring her to heel. I asked a few questions. He's way into that shit, but like me. He wants all woman and sweet. He absolutely does not want kink. She's that woman, I'll give him the high sign."

I stared at him and I knew my eyes were big at the thought of Knight Sebring, matchmaking.

Then I breathed, "Really?"

One side of his lips curled up and his hands slid to the small of my back bringing me close as he muttered, "Really."

I arched back an inch and tipped my head to the side again. "Can you vouch for him?"

I watched and smiled a small smile as Knight burst out laughing.

He pulled me closer, one hand staying at the small of my back, one hand gliding up to between my shoulder blades, when he said, "Uh… what he does with his hands, mouth and dick, no. I cannot vouch for him and I'm not goin' there. They hook up, that's up to your girl to find out. If you mean is he a good guy? Absolutely."

I relaxed into him and murmured, "Okay." I slid my hand up to his neck and my fingertips drifted through the hair curling at his neck. "Do you guys talk about that, um… stuff a lot?"

"If you're askin' do I share how much I get off on bein' your Daddy, fuck no. No one knows shit about me and definitely not about you. Can they guess about me and us, probably. My desire for control is not a secret. That said, Rhashan's a man who knows who he is, doesn't give a fuck what anyone thinks of him, likes to get off like he likes it. So if he's recruiting, he asks around and he's choosy." He grinned. "The club's the club, babe. Boys know and get a lotta pussy. A bitch is that way, they'll know and throw her his way. And your girl is that way. Club pussy, usually not worth it. One-time deal. What I know of your girl, Rhash will think he hit the fuckin' mother lode."

I started giggling and Knight smiled as he watched me do it.

My fingers drifted back through the hair at his neck and my eyes dropped to watch before going back to his.

Then I said quietly, "You need a haircut, honey."

"Uh… no," he said quietly back. "Every time I let you use your hands, you get excited, you fist them in my hair. I like to feel you get excited any way, including that way. I start lookin' like a biker or a hippie, I'll go to the barber. Until then, my baby's got something to hold onto."

I melted into him and assured, "You don't look like a biker or a hippie."

"Then we're good," he muttered, his lips twitching.

"Though, when I have Jeans and Heavy Metal Tee Knight Sundays, you look a little like a biker, but it's hot."

Another lip twitch then, "So we're still good."

"Yeah," I said softly.

His brows went up. "Jeans and Heavy Metal Tee Knight Sundays?"

"Best day of the week," I whispered. His brows went down, his eyes dropped to my mouth, but not before I saw them get dark. Then his head dropped and he kissed me.

I had to fix my lip gloss and Knight had to go to the bathroom to wipe my old off before he put my ass in his awesome ride and took me to the club.

❧

I wandered in the club, my hand in Knight's, the lights flashing, the music loud, but my mind was on the sign on the wall in the alley.

Space Restricted—Mr. Sebring

Mr. Sebring.

I thought about my life two months ago.

I thought about it now.

I thought about my man, Mr. Sebring.

And I was looking to the floor, my lips curved, but inside I was smiling wide.

I saw the steps in front of me, Knight already up one, and I lifted my foot shod in a sandal that cost nearly nine hundred dollars when I heard:

"*Surprise!*"

My head jerked back and I saw the VIP podium filled with my friends and bright balloons that shouted, "Congratulations!" and "Graduate!"

Oh my fucking God.

My body froze except my eyes shot to Knight.

He was looking back at me grinning.

I'd received my skin technology certificate on Wednesday.

Oh.

My.

Fucking.

God.

I felt my face begin to crumble as emotions overwhelmed me, and luckily Knight moved fast or everyone would see me, face smushed, crying. But they didn't because I was in his arms with my face pressed into his neck.

"Baby," he whispered in my ear.

"She... she did... didn't... I was out of the house, on my own. I didn't get a gra... gra... graduation party in high school," I stammered into the skin of his neck and his arms gave me a squeeze.

"Well, you have one now," Knight told me.

"It's just... just..." my breath hitched then I heaved out, "*skin technology.*"

His arms squeezed again and stayed tight around me as he said in my ear, "It's an accomplishment. You worked for it. You earned it. Now, you fuckin' celebrate it."

I sucked in breath, pulled my head back and dashed my fingers on my cheeks, looking at him.

He was slightly watery.

He was still all kinds of beautiful.

"Thank you." My mouth moved with the words, but no sound came out.

I know he got it when his face dipped, his lips went to my ear and he whispered, "Anything for my baby."

I took in a stuttering breath.

My body was taking in needed oxygen.

But I knew as it got what it needed to breathe, still, I'd lost my heart.

Knight let me go but took my hand.

Then he led me up to my party.

Knight had stayed for half an hour, but then he had to get to work.

But I had no orders. This was my party.

I drank lemon drops.

For my man, I didn't go to the dance floor.

On lemon drop three, I cornered Viv in relative privacy.

"Right," I leaned in, semi-shouting in her ear, "don't get pissed and maybe later you'll thank me but right now, gotta know. Are you into kink?"

She jerked back and her brows were knit over narrow eyes as she shouted, "What?"

I leaned in again and semi-shouted, "Kink. Serious shit. Sexually."

Her head turned, she caught my eyes and semi-shouted back, "Why we talking about this now, girl? Knight do something to flip you out?"

"No," I semi-shouted in return. "He… uh, might have a live one for you."

She again jerked back, but her brows shot up this time.

I held my breath, hoping that she wouldn't be pissed at me for telling her secret.

Then she asked loudly but curiously, "Brother?"

I let out my breath and fought back a smile.

Vivica, God, I loved her.

I nodded.

"Hot?"

I shook my head. "No clue. Knight vouches for him though. Said he's absolutely a good guy, but he's not into, um… kink. Straight up, um… other stuff. And he's seen you around and said straight out he wants to," I leaned in and semi-shouting again said in her ear, "bring you to heel."

She leaned back, her eyes wide, her lips forming the words, "Oo lordy."

I grinned.

Her eyeballs rolled to the ceiling. "Please God, make him be hot. Please God, make the brother be hot."

"Is that the go-ahead for me to give the go-ahead to Knight to give the high sign?" I asked.

Her eyeballs rolled back to me and she yelled instantly, "Fuck yeah, bitch!"

I giggled as I unclasped my bag, pulled out my phone and typed in a text.

K, V not into kink. Give R high sign. She's nearly panting. xxoo A

I got no text back.

Fifteen minutes later, a six foot seven inch, broad, bulky, muscled, bald, glorious, midnight-skinned black man, in a suit like Knight's but with a black shirt, came walking up the steps, eyes glued to Viv.

My eyes first went to Viv to see her eyes glued to the brother and she was doing a bad job at pretending she wasn't hyperventilating.

Then my eyes went to Knight's window.

I smiled.

Huge.

✣

On lemon drop five, when I was bordering on tipsy, I felt a hand light on the small of my back.

It wasn't Knight. I would smell him.

I also knew this because the touch was light and it was quick then gone.

I twisted my neck and looked up at Hulk, aka Kurt.

"Yo!" I shouted. He blinked then the sides of his lips inched up a quarter of a millimeter.

Then he announced, "Knight wants you in his office."

Oh goodie.

"You're escorted," he finished.

"Lead the way, my man," I invited, still shouting.

He shook his head.

Then he led the way. I followed, and when we left the VIP section, he stayed close. Sometimes, his body skimmed mine. Sometimes, his hand skimmed my waist to guide me. Sometimes, he shifted in front of me, arm out, professionally pushing people aside so I could get through.

Mr. Sebring.

God, my boyfriend was hot and cool in such a myriad of ways, it was mind-boggling.

And he was all this and he didn't even have to be there.

The bouncer that stood beside the door to the stairs to Knight's office saw us coming and he had it opened before we got there.

I smiled at him and went through.

The door closed behind me.

Kurt didn't follow. I was alone on the stairs.

I walked up them, carrying my lemon drop, and when I got to the top, I knocked.

The answer was Knight calling, "Anya."

I turned the knob, pushed it open a couple of feet and stuck my head in, twisting it around the side of the door until I saw Knight standing at the chest against the wall that had all the booze.

"Okay if I come in?" I asked.

"Babe, Kurt was sent to fetch you to me. You don't even have to knock."

I smiled at him and came in fully, keeping my eyes on him and watching him shaking his head, lips twitching.

I closed the doors and went to him, belatedly noticing he was opening a bottle of champagne. One of those bottles that had the flowers painted on it.

Which meant an expensive bottle.

There were two sparkling clean champagne flutes sitting on the low chest.

Celebration.

For me.

Okay, all right.

Okay, right.

I licked my lips.

This was it. It had happened.

God.

I was in love.

God.

The cork popped.

I stopped close, put my clutch and lemon drop glass on the chest and leaned a thigh into it as I watched him pour.

"Um… already spoiled with the party, sweetheart," I said quietly.

"Not enough," he muttered, still pouring.

My belly dropped.

Yep.

In.

Love.

"Okay, then, further spoiled with you hooking up my girl."

His eyes came to me and he held the glass out to me.

"Not enough," he said firmly. I took the glass and he went for the other one.

I shut up.

He poured.

Then he set the bottle aside and ordered, "Here."

I was a foot and a half away.

I went there.

His arm curled around me. My free hand went to rest on his shoulder and he lifted his glass.

I did too.

He touched his to mine and caught my eyes. "Proud of you, baby, workin' your ass off, findin' ways to make life better."

I smiled into his eyes. "Thanks, sweetheart."

I noticed his glass going up, I brought mine up too, and we drank.

When Knight was done, he immediately put his to the chest then slid mine out of my hand and it joined it. He shoved his hand in the pocket of his trousers.

"Hand, babe, palm up," he muttered.

I lifted my hand, palm up.

His hand came out and he dropped a set of keys into my palm.

My breath left me as I stared. Then I stared harder.

I thought they'd be for a car which I couldn't accept. I loved him but he'd already done enough for me. But they weren't.

I already had the keys to his house.

I felt my brows inch together as my eyes went from the keys to him.

"What—?" I started and he turned fully into me. I had to close my hand around the keys and put it to the chest as he pulled me to him using both arms.

"Notice," he stated confusingly then went on, "Monday. The bossy bitch who likes to spend money is on stand-by. I'll give you her card, you call her, sit down with her, tell her your vision but if you don't want black, don't mention red."

I shook my head, still confused. "Pardon?"

"Once she does her gig," he continued, not answering me but still talking, "she'll inform me. The firm who does my marketing for the club will pull together a strategy. You want a one-woman show, it'll be small. You wanna hire staff, they'll do it up."

"Knight, what are you talking about?"

"Own most of this block, babe, had a shop close down. Opposite corner. Those keys open the front door. That's your new spa."

Oh my God.

Oh my *God*.

Oh my God.

My chest seized, I pulled out of his arms, hard, heart beating, harder.

"I can't accept that," I whispered then finished, "And I won't."

His brows snapped together.

"What?"

I shook my head. Overwhelmed. Happy he'd want to do that. For me.

But it was not going to happen.

"I'm sorry," I said louder. "That was rude, honey. What you've done is sweet. I appreciate it. But I can't accept."

His eyes narrowed.

"Why the fuck not?"

"I just…" I faltered. "I just can't."

He studied me then he crossed his arms on his chest.

"Why, Anya?"

"I… you wouldn't understand."

"Try me," he ordered.

I pulled in a breath and looked across the room.

Then I thought maybe he would understand.

I looked back at him.

"It has to be me. It has to be mine. I have to do it on my own."

"Love you, babe," he said, throwaway. My stomach clenched and dropped and my heart squeezed, because he meant it but said it in a way like I already knew it. "Love you," he repeated. "But that's fucked."

I powered through the fact that he loved me.

Loved me!

And I stuck with the current matter at hand.

"Knight, honey, you did this all on your own." I flicked a hand out to indicate the club. "Can't you get me?"

His head cocked to the side and he said, "I did not fuckin' do all this on my own."

I blinked.

Then I asked, "What?"

"Babe, do you have any clue how much it costs to set up a place like this?"

I totally didn't.

"No."

"A fuckin' lot," he told me. "I had a silent partner. He was the capital, I was the face. He existed to drive me up the fuckin' wall. I did all the work. He shoved his nose in, fucked things up. Repeatedly. He did not get the concept of 'silent', no matter how often or what tactics I used to explain. Couple of years in, I was done with him drivin' me up the wall. I made moves, took over, forced him out. Hostile. Though, I was thorough and he was half asshole, half idiot. Didn't put up much of a fight. Now I own the club outright and he lives in Costa Rica with three local women who, sources say, regularly get in catfights, not for his attention but for his generosity, 'cause he's still got more money than sense. One of his bright ideas for this place was female mud wrestling. He's havin' the time of his life."

I felt my lips quirk and I asked, "Female mud wrestling?"

"Like I said, the dude is half asshole, half idiot."

I started giggling.

Knight didn't find anything funny.

"I'm tired of you crawlin' out of bed three hours after I joined you in it. I'm tired of classes and client nights and Saturdays, which mean I cannot have dinner with my woman but once a week. And bottom line, I'm not gonna sit back and watch my woman work her ass off when I can do something about it. You need to lose the day job."

"Knight—"

"You can't not accept because that's unacceptable," he cut me off. "You put notice in, no more than two weeks, Anya. And you spend your time with that bossy bitch who likes to spend money and move your clients to days. And your nights, before I have to take off, are spent with me. You design the spa you want. You decide how you're gonna play it. We market it to get you clients. And I cover all that and your rent and living expenses until you get that show on the road."

"Knight—"

"This isn't a discussion."

"Knight!" I shouted.

"What?" he clipped.

"Okay, but I have twenty thousand dollars saved for when I was gonna start my spa, and I handle my rent and living expenses until I get that show on the road. And you keep track of what you spend, and when I start turning a profit, we'll set up a schedule for me paying you back."

This was the wrong thing to say, and I knew it by the hard look that settled on his face.

"You don't pay someone back for a gift, Anya."

"But this is too much," I replied carefully.

"When a gift is given, isn't that for the person who's giving it to say?"

Damn, he had a point.

"I—"

He interrupted me again to rap out, "You happy?"

"Yes," I whispered.

"In a way you know it's gonna last?"

He asked that because he was happy in a way he knew it was going to last.

My heart turned over and I stared at him. Then I looked over my shoulder at his window, not able to see my party but knowing it was there.

A party he gave to me.

Mr. Sebring.

I looked back at him.

"I'm in love with you, so yes."

He closed his eyes and he did it slowly, dropping his head.

That meant something to him.

I stared at him. Tall, broad, strong, scary, dude-you-don't-mess-with Knight Sebring, head bowed, overcome.

No, I was wrong.

It meant *everything* to him.

My nose began to sting.

He opened his eyes and looked up, catching mine.

"Come here, baby."

I moved back into his arms.

"Please let me give this to you," he whispered.

"I can't now nor will I ever be in the position to give you—"

Kristen Ashley

He squeezed me quiet and his face dipped close. "Toasted almond pancakes. Sweet soft 'okays'. Makin' me laugh more in a few weeks than I have in decades. 'Yes, Daddys' I feel in my dick. The first voicemail you left me, babe, I saved it and I listen to it once a day. If I lose focus, I see you on your back, knees high, legs wide, offering your sweet, wet pussy to me. You smile at me in bed every time you wander outta my bedroom in my shirts, my tees or your work clothes and honest to Christ, it sets me up for the day. And no matter what shit goes down, I get through it knowin' whichever bed I climb into at night, you're in it ready to snuggle into me or give me what I wanna take. Your girl, a headache. You, never. And in a life that's been full of headaches, babe, having that, there is no price tag. You gotta get it, and do it right fuckin' now, that there's a lotta different kinds of give and take. And you give as good as you get, baby, trust me."

"We haven't been together very long," I reminded him.

"You love me and I love you. How long does that need to be?"

Another excellent point.

"I don't want you ever to think I'm using you," I whispered.

"You ask for a Maserati?"

I shook my head. "No."

"You ask for anything?"

"No. But—"

"You start takin' what I don't offer, babe, or askin' for the moon, we got a problem. But I'm tellin' you right now, and mark it, Anya, I'm fuckin' thankful your cell phone was jacked. Because if it wasn't, you wouldn't have wandered into my bedroom that night and I wouldn't go to bed at night with the scent of your hair all I can smell, the taste of your pussy still in my mouth, and your sweet body close to me and know I'll sleep easy and wake up happy. And I wake up happy, baby, because I possess beauty and I own that beauty in all the forms it can take and the least important of those are physical."

Oh God.

"Knight—"

His arms gave me a squeeze. "Let me give this to you."

I fell silent, not that I was saying much of anything.

His face got closer. "Let... me... *give this to you.*"

I held his vivid blue eyes.

Then I whispered, "Okay."

202

It was then his vivid blue eyes held mine.

Then he whispered back, "Okay."

I closed my eyes tight then opened them and asked softly, "You love me?"

"Baby, you were made for me."

Oh God.

My face started scrunching up again and his hand wrapped around the back of my head and shoved it in his neck.

I held on but muttered a broken, "Thank you."

"Fuck, you're the hardest bitch I've ever met to give shit to," he grumbled.

My emotions careening all over the place, I pulled back and narrowed my eyes on him.

"Oh, so, you were also generous with your smorgasbord of pussy?"

He grinned. "Baby, don't ask me that, but I will say I never gave any of them a spa."

"Good," I snapped.

"Or a phone that cost a G," he went on.

"Excellent," I snapped again.

"Maybe a dress or shoes, but not both and definitely not three," he muttered then finished musingly, "Or even two."

"It might be a good idea to shut up now, Knight," I suggested.

He grinned again.

Then he noted, "Now who's bossy?"

"I'm allowed to be bossy. I'm about to be the owner of Denver's most kickass spa."

Knight's arms got tight around me and he burst out laughing.

I watched.

I did it smiling.

And I did it in love with Mr. Sebring.

Chapter 13
My World

On Knight's black, marble counter my phone rang while I was at the stove, boiling water for spaghetti and browning hamburger for sauce. I left the meat, grabbed the phone and saw on the display the call was from Viv. I took it while wandering back to the stove and put it to my ear.

"Hey, honey," I greeted.

"I was a bad girl."

I blinked at the hamburger.

Then I burst out laughing.

Through my giggles, I asked, "Were you now?"

"Very," she said through her own giggles. "Have I told you today I love Knight Sebring?"

I pushed the meat around, smiling at it and said, "Not today. Yesterday you did. Not today."

"Well, I do."

"I take it things with Rhashan are going good?" I asked softly.

It had been just over a month since my party. I was no longer a file clerk. All my nail clients, and I lost only one, were able to move to days. But losing the one was okay because two of my clients took on six-weekly facials. Kathleen added a monthly facial and so did Sandrine and Viv. Kathleen got her girlfriend Louise to bring her acrylics business to me. So I was actually ahead.

I spent part of my days talking to Mahleena, the bossy bitch who liked to spend money who actually didn't seem bossy to me, but she definitely liked to spend money. We were now implementing the plans to deal with my gonna-be kickass spa. I was also taking an online course in small business management that Knight suggested.

So even without the day job, I was still busy.

But my nights were at Knight's. In fact, the last two weeks since my last day at work, my apartment felt like my workplace since I'd go there to work and come home to Knight. We had dinner together then he left for work. I rambled around for a few hours, reading, watching television, talking on the phone, doing my coursework at his computer in his study, and I went to bed in satin sheets. I woke up in them, too. And without having to be at work at eight, I woke up later and got to sleep longer with Knight.

It was the bomb.

Life was good.

And now it seemed it was good for Vivica too.

"Hun… *nee,*" she whispered as an answer to my question and said no more.

Surprising both Viv and me, Rhashan had started things out with only dating and this had lasted three weeks. He was feeling Vivica out. She was my age, he was thirty-six. A nine year gap which concerned him, because as he told Viv, when he first saw her, he saw her clubbing. He was in settling in mode and looking for The One. And he wasn't fucking around, not even literally. It wasn't about getting off. It was about finding a partner for more than spanking.

Viv was impatient. She liked to get herself some, and like me before Knight, had hit a dry spell even for normal sex. But she was understanding as well as intrigued. As date wore into date, that understanding deepened and she got smitten and she was smitten with more than the fact he was seriously hot.

Last week, Viv reported, he broke the seal. "Vanilla sex" she said that was "out of this world".

The night after Rhashan broke the seal, he started breaking her in. Or, in Rhashan lingo, bringing her to heel.

Viv was on top of the world.

"After you were bad, was he good to you?" I asked.

"A powerhouse, six foot, seven inch brother doling out punishment?" she whispered. "Yes, Anya, my guy was good to me. He can wield a crop, and I mean that in more ways than one. At one point, I think I was in a different galaxy."

I put the spaghetti in water, thinking vaguely I should ask Knight to take us shopping and find some way to be naughty while smiling and murmuring, "Great, honey."

"He ties me to him while we sleep."

I blinked.

"What?"

"He ties our wrists together while we sleep so I won't go very far. He likes his woman close while he sleeps."

My belly melted.

I loved that for her.

I just hoped she did.

"You like that?"

"Cuddling a warm, hard mountain of muscle who wants me close? Girl," she drew it out softly. "Abso-fucking-lutely. Living the dream."

"Oh Viv," I whispered.

"Anya."

I jumped and turned to see Knight, who'd been in his study, standing at the edge of the bar, eyes on me, face weirdly unreadable.

"Hang on, Viv," I said into the phone and put it to my shoulder. "Yeah, sweetheart?"

"Let Viv go," he ordered, and his tone was as weird as his expressionless face.

I knew he could do impassive, but he didn't do that very often anymore. Not with me.

And his tone...

I held his eyes as I put the phone to my ear. "Viv, Knight needs to speak with me. Gotta go, honey."

"Right, babe. Been bad?"

I smiled a small smile still looking at Knight. "Not lately."

"Get on that. Report back. Later."

"Later."

I disconnected and the minute I did, Knight said, "Turn off the stove."

"But the spagh—"

"Baby, stove. Off."

I drew in breath.

Then I turned, set my cell aside and switched off the burners on the stove.

I turned back to Knight. "Everything okay?"

"You might or might not get a visit from the cops. I'm tellin' you now so you'll be prepared in case you do. And I'm tellin' you 'cause you got the right to know."

My body locked, but my lips whispered, "What?"

"David Watson was shanked today. Bled out before they got him to the infirmary."

My hand flew out, found counter and held tight.

David Watson killed my parents.

I stared at Knight.

Then I whispered, "How do you know?"

"I know because I looked into shit, found out who he was and where he was. Then I talked to some people who talked to some people and I made it clear I'd look on it favorably if David Watson wasn't enjoyin' his state-funded, lifetime vacation."

Oh my God.

Knight wasn't done.

"I did not call the hit. That said, I do not give a fuck that dirtbag is dead. Though, I would have preferred they played with him a while longer before he hit the yard in a pool of his own blood."

Oh my *God*.

"Why did you do that?" I asked quietly.

"Because he set my woman up for eleven years of misery. And I did it before I even knew the fullness of what that bitch of an aunt of yours took from you. I knew to carve a decent life for yourself you worked or went to school sixty hours a week. I also knew you had a cell phone that didn't work, which meant you were unsafe. And a woman with a father who gives a fuck about her, no matter her age, would not be unsafe. Not like that. And I knew you had no real family to speak of. He made that happen. I'm not down with that. Payback was not him not being here. Payback was making him pay. That's no longer an option. He's dead."

I didn't know what to do with this. I didn't know what to think about this. I didn't know what to think about *Knight* doing this.

Therefore I didn't speak.

Knight did, eyes pinned to me.

"It's time you learn something about me, Anya," he said gently. "I don't live in your world. I live in another world. It's my world. I took it over. I rebuilt it. I own it. I control it. I have a code. Anyone in my world lives by my code. And in my world, a man who shot a husband and father on the way to work then put a bullet in that man's wife's brain, my woman's mother's brain, does not breathe easy. I can see you strugglin' with this and I'll give you time. But you need to come to terms with it. The understanding of retribution is essential in my world. You do not fuck with what's mine."

"That was twenty years ago, Knight," I whispered.

"I don't give a fuck, Anya."

"You didn't even know me then, not even close."

"I don't give a fuck about that either."

"He was paying for his crime," I reminded him.

"Not hard enough," he stated firmly.

This, I could not deny, was absolutely true.

I held his eyes.

Then I said quietly and cautiously, "Don't you think that's a little crazy?"

"Not... even... close."

I held my breath.

Knight held my eyes.

I let out my breath and looked away.

"Eyes to me."

"I need time," I told the floor.

"Look... at... your... man," he growled, and, my heart beating wild in my chest, my eyes went to him. "You do not fuck with what's mine."

I was silent.

Knight was not.

"Carl Sebring came in my life when I was seven and that was the beginning of the end of a life that was pure shit. David Watson came into your life when you were seven and that motherfucker made your life shit. Only when *I* came into it twenty years later did it stop bein' shit. It is not lost on me we share that age when our lives rocked, but I lived seven of bad and I got twenty-eight years of good. You lived seven years of good and got twenty of shit. That is absolutely not acceptable to me. And when something is unacceptable, I do something about it."

I loved it that he felt that way.

I still could not process what he'd done for me.

So I remained silent.

Knight did not.

"He harmed you, irrevocably. He changed the path of your life. You mentioned my smoking once and then didn't say dick about it. Women bitch about shit like that. You do not. And it's not because you were used to it with your aunt. It's because it reminds you of your father. You loved him, you miss him. So you don't say dick. You dream more than any fuckin' person I know. You say they're all not good. You don't sleep all night by me, but you sleep by me, babe, and if you think for a second I don't feel you jerk awake at least once every fuckin' week because you had a bad dream, you're wrong. I feel it. Every fuckin' time. You said that started when you were seven. They died when you were seven. He gave you that. He did *all* that. And he paid. That's what happens in my world to someone who fucks with what's mine. Like I said, you need to find a way to come to terms with that. You want me to help guide the way, I'm here. You can find that path on your own, good. But you need to find that path, Anya. Because I own you. You live in my world. You need to find a way to live with that, baby. There's no other option."

I pressed my lips together and I ran them back and forth.

Then I nodded.

Knight studied me.

Then he asked quietly, "When's the spaghetti gonna be ready?"

"Maybe fifteen minutes. I'll call you," I answered softly.

"Right, baby," he whispered. Then he turned and walked away.

I watched him go. Then I stayed frozen in place watching where I last saw him.

I turned and finished the spaghetti.

I was awake when Knight opened the front door.

I rolled and looked through the dark at his alarm clock to see he was really early. It wasn't even two in the morning yet.

I rolled back.

My guess, he was worried about me. Or where my head was at. I barely spoke through spaghetti. As he was changing into his suit, I sat on his plush, gray suede couch in front of the TV, mindlessly watching it to the point where, when he came in and his fingers sifted in my hair and gave it a gentle tug back so he could lean in and kiss me, my kiss and farewell were distracted. I knew he felt it, noted it, because Knight noted everything. I also knew because his hand in my hair held my head back seconds longer than usual and his eyes roamed my face.

Then he let my hair go, but kissed the top of my head and left me.

After he was gone, I didn't zone out. I was Knight's and I'd been with him long enough to know what that means. He said he'd give me time, but in Knight's world, even with something this important, that didn't mean days or weeks. That meant on his schedule. He was decisive. He expected those around him to be the same.

So I tried to figure it out. How I felt about this, and it wasn't lost on me that I never really allowed myself to think about how I felt about the way Knight dealt with my Jerk Landlord Steve, or what Knight did with Dick.

He told me he didn't call the hit on David Watson. He told me he sent his boys to talk to Jerk Landlord Steve and they didn't like what he said. They didn't go in and bust him up. He was a jerk, *then* they made their point. And Dick quietly moved away. I didn't see him, but no one mentioned that he looked beat up or that there was any ruckus in the building. Dick gave notice, he moved, and from what I heard from neighbors I ran into, they were relieved.

Truth be told, I spent so much time burying the fact that David Watson still existed in the world, I honestly could not call up much emotion for the fact he no longer did.

He killed my parents. Knight was right, he altered the path of my life and he harmed me irrevocably. It was random. He didn't even know them, they'd done him no wrong. He was looking out for himself and jacking up lives along the way: his girlfriend, his baby dead, my parents dead, my life changed forever.

It wasn't Knight's responsibility he was dead. He didn't ask for that. And I didn't know what it said about me, but digging deep and thinking about it, I could also not call up much emotion about the fact that Knight took measures to make him pay. I wouldn't do it myself. I didn't condone it. But I didn't think less of Knight because he did it. He did it for me. He did it because that was the kind of man he was and that was the kind of world he lived in.

And I lived in that world now, too.

This was not lost on me, though I had been doing what Knight said I was doing. Burying my head. Not thinking about it. But right off the bat, Knight was always who he was, he did what he did, he never hid anything from me.

And I took his hand and walked right into his world.

I could not quibble now.

I had a choice.

Now that my head no longer was buried I could walk out of his world and never look back.

Or stay.

I also knew I didn't have all the information. Knight said he'd tell me about him when he was ready for me to know. He doled out information care-

Kristen Ashley

fully and unlike with everything else, he was not generous. I understood this. In his world, I was sensing, he needed to proceed with caution. Even with me. But from the little he told me of his early years, they would mark anybody. There were women—heck, not just women but people—I knew who would hear his mother was a prostitute, part of his growing up years he grew up in that life and didn't know who his father was, and they'd think things about Knight. That would make anyone wary, especially if they were falling in love. He undoubtedly faced those judgments more than once in his life. And he'd given me so much. I could give him time to share at his pace with me.

And that was just it. He'd given me so much. And I wasn't talking phones, shoes and spas.

I was safe. I was spoiled. I was adored.

I was loved.

I couldn't dictate how that came about.

Especially not to a man like Knight.

I heard and saw his shadowy frame walk into the bedroom and I watched, motionless, lying on my side in bed, my arms cocked, hands lying in front of me.

He moved around the bed to his side and even though my back was to him, I heard him disrobing, his expensive clothes falling to the floor.

The covers shifted, the bed moved, but I didn't.

Just like Knight, he didn't waste time. He slid in behind me, one hand trailing down my arm to find mine, his fingers laced through and he pulled both our hands close to my chest as he pressed into my back.

I felt his body, his warmth and smelled his cologne.

I closed my eyes.

His lips came to my ear. "You find the right path?"

He knew I was awake.

I was right. He came home early worried about me. Where I was. With him.

I had to decide.

Right now.

Walk out of his world and never look back.

Or stay.

My mouth decided for me.

I opened my eyes and whispered, "Yes."

212

His fingers tensed in mine and I listened to him draw in a deep breath, wondering what was next. What he'd do.

He let me go and rolled away.

I lay still.

"Up on your knees, Anya, facing me."

I felt a heady curl between my legs.

I'd made the right decision. Call me crazy, but I was the woman for him just as I was, and just as he was, Knight Sebring was the man for me.

I pushed up, the covers fell away and I turned, getting up on my knees, facing Knight.

"Closer, baby."

I shifted closer.

"Lose the cami."

My fingers went into my camisole. I lifted it up, pulled it off and tossed it aside.

His fingers trailed along the top of my thigh lightly then disappeared.

Through this and after, I trembled.

"Pull your shorts down and your panties."

Another heady curl that whirled up to my belly.

I pulled my shorts and panties down to my thighs.

"Drop to a hip, baby, get rid of them then back on your knees."

I fell to my hip, pulled my pajama shorts and panties free of my legs and tossed them aside. Then I regained my knees.

"Closer," he whispered, and I shifted close so my knees were against his side. "Anya," his whisper had changed, slight rebuke, "you know what I like."

For a second, I was confused.

Then I slid my knees out slightly wide.

I was rewarded as his hand slid up the inside of my thigh then started lightly playing between my legs.

"That's it, baby," he murmured.

The curl started to become an ache.

He was silent as his fingers moved and played oh so light between my legs.

"Give Daddy more," he muttered, and my legs slid wider. I did good and I knew it when his thumb flicked hard against my clit and I gasped. "That's good, baby."

I noticed movement and watched as his hand went to his cock and as he played with me, he idly stroked himself.

God, I loved to watch him do that.

I loved it, but watching it, I wanted to do it. I wanted him in my mouth. I wanted him in me.

I whimpered.

His thumb again flicked my clit and my hips jerked.

"Whose world do you live in, Anya?" he asked so softly I barely heard.

"Your world."

Another flick. Oh God, *God,* it scored through me.

"Who owns you, baby?"

"You do."

Another flick. My hips jerked again and I mew slid out of my throat.

Two of his fingers slid inside, deep, and I bit my lip.

"Who owns this cunt?" he whispered.

"You do."

"Who does?"

"You do, Daddy."

Another flick, another hip jerk, another mew.

God!

His fingers slid out and he went back to playing.

"Who possesses your beauty?"

"You do."

"You're right, Anya, I do."

I waited for the flick and didn't get it so I whimpered.

His hand went away and I whimpered again.

"Tonight, my baby feels greedy," he muttered.

I was always greedy.

"Bend to me," he ordered.

Instantly, I bent to him. Halfway down, his hand caught my hair.

"Stop."

I stopped. His hand gathered my hair and twisted it then he put pressure on and my face was heading to his cock that his hand was still stroking. He guided my mouth to it. My lips opened and I took the tip before his fist in my hair got tight.

"Just the tip, baby, hold onto Daddy's cock and roll me with your tongue."

Yes, I wanted this. I wanted more, but I'd take this.

My lips closed around tight and I rolled him with my tongue as he stroked. This was hot. I loved the taste of him, the silk of him on my tongue.

"Sweet cunt, sweet mouth, my sweet baby," he whispered.

Then his hand went away and his hips surged up, filling my mouth with his cock.

Heat flooded me and I took him.

His hand in my hair gave me my cues. He wanted me to stroke and suck.

I did. Fast, hard, working it, loving it, listening to him groan, feeling his hand in my hair, wanting my hand between my legs, or his hand, but getting more excited because I couldn't have either.

God, I could come just doing this.

His fist in my hair pulled me back and his voice growled, "On your back, knees up, legs spread, hands behind your knees opening you wide. Prepare to take me."

I rolled, lifted, positioned and he was right there, cock in his hand, guiding it in, his other hand in the bed beside me, arm straight.

He drove into me.

My neck arched, my back left the bed, my own hands jerked my legs even wider. Nothing better.

Nothing better than being connected to Knight.

"Eyes," he grunted, driving fast, deep, brutal, fucking me raw. My chin tipped down and my eyes went to him. "You can touch me."

Immediately, my hands went from behind my knees to him.

He dropped his forearms to the bed beside me, giving me some of his weight, still thrusting fast, hard, but my hands had more available to them so they moved over his skin, his muscle and they did this feverishly.

"You love me?" he growled in my ear.

My hand slid into his hair and fisted. "Yes, honey."

"Who do you love?"

"You, Daddy," I gasped, it was coming.

"No, baby," he whispered. "That's sweet and you know I love it, but say my name. Who do you love?"

I turned my head, shoving my face in his neck and breathed, "I love you, Knight."

His head came up. Mine went back, his eyes caught mine through the darkness and his cock slammed into me as he growled, "You love *me,* Anya. Don't forget that."

"I won't, honey," I breathed, holding on, my arm tightening around his back, my fist tight in his hair.

"Never, baby."

"Never, Knight," I gasped then came.

He fucked me harder.

Oh God.

"Give me your face," he grunted, slamming into me and I focused on him. "That's it, baby, give me that beauty."

Then his mouth crushed down on mine, one of his hands shafting up, fingers driving into my hair, fisting, his tongue thrust in, started plundering, his hips went wild and he groaned down my throat.

He kept plundering then he gentled the kiss and his cock started gliding then he planted himself to the root, his lips slid to my ear and his fist loosened in my hair but his fingers stayed tangled there.

"My mother named me Knight because she needed one."

Sated, still coasting, his unexpected, revealing words made my body still.

Then I wrapped my legs around him and held tight.

"Fuck me," he whispered, voice low, nearly hoarse, "so fuckin' sweet."

"Tell me," I whispered back, giving him a squeeze.

His head came up. He shifted slightly to the side but stayed connected to me. He did this so his hand could slide out of my hair to wrap around the side of my neck and his thumb started stroking my jaw.

"Her little man," he whispered, "her knight. I would protect her, she told me. She needed that. She was so fucked up, her life so jacked, her only hope was a fuckin' baby."

My body melted under his, but my limbs stayed tight as my hand in his hair drifted so my fingertips could brush through the curls at his neck.

"I hate that for you," I whispered back.

"It's what she raised me to be. It's all I know, Anya. Protection. I was born then I was raised to be a shield."

My hand slid to cup his jaw as tears filled my eyes and I whispered, "Honey."

"I loved her then, I love her now. It was not a hardship, Anya. It's who I am. It was what I was made to be."

"Okay, sweetheart."

"No one harms you," he told me.

"Okay," I whispered.

"I looked into your aunt."

I blinked in the dark.

"She's doin' a bang up job of makin' her own life a misery, she doesn't need any help. So I've left her to it. But I'll tell you right now, babe, if she was livin' even a little of the good life, I'd take that away."

"Knight, we don't—"

"No," he cut me off firmly, "bury your head tomorrow. Tonight, you get me. No one harms you, Anya, and like you do when I tell you to get on your knees beside me, when I take that sweet mouth with my cock when I want it, when I fuck that beautiful cunt as hard as I like, I do what I feel I gotta do and you yield to me."

"Okay," I whispered again.

"You chose your path and the path you chose, there's no turning back."

I started trembling.

"Anya, listen to me, mark this, there is no turning back."

My hand started to slide away from his face but he moved quickly, caught it and held it there.

"You had your chance tonight, babe. And you got to your knees beside me. There's no turning back. You can't give me that, *all* of that, and take it away. You need to get this, baby, and right now I need to know you do."

It was a test. Tonight wasn't the usual bossy. It was a test.

And as far as Knight was concerned, I passed.

I stared at the planes and angles of his shadowed face.

"Anya, do you get this?"

I licked my lips.

"Baby—"

"I get it, Knight," I whispered.

He held my eyes and even through the dark I could feel them burning into me.

Then he dropped his head, forehead to mine before he slid his nose along mine.

"I love you, Anya, you're the only woman who's had that from me and you're the only one who ever will."

He meant that. Every word. To his soul.

He meant it.

This rocked me so deeply I closed my eyes and my body tightened under him and all around him.

Call me crazy, but I liked that.

His lips came to mine and my eyes opened.

"Go. Clean up. I wanna eat you then fuck you again."

"Okay, Knight," I whispered and he slid out.

"Hurry," he ordered gently, then rolled off me.

I rolled out of bed.

And as my man told me to do, I hurried.

Chapter 14
Happy Birthday

The elevator doors opened, I took in a deep breath and walked out.

I was tipsy, not drunk.

Lemon drops.

But my legs were trembling. My stomach in knots. That tingle had spread up my spine, the back of my neck and over my scalp and also along my waist, my bottom and down my inner thighs, and it wasn't leaving.

And I knew I was already wet.

This was because I'd been naughty.

And this was because it was one thirty in the morning and thus for the last hour and a half, it had been Knight's birthday.

He didn't tell me.

After Kathleen's facial Wednesday, when we were gabbing, she'd asked in passing, "What are you getting Knight for his birthday on Sunday?"

I didn't know it was his birthday. And I was so thrown by this I didn't even remember what I said to her.

I was in a panic.

What did you get the man who had everything or could get it for himself?

I'd been to the mall twice since then; bought him things, and none of it was right. None of it was good enough. None of it would mean anything.

Then it came to me. Something I knew he would like.

It was August, two and half months after Knight claimed me for good because I let him. My spa was opening in a few weeks. My apartment was a full on mini-spa because that was all I did there. My stuff and some of my clothes were there, but I didn't need them since Knight had since totally spoiled me. New silky, lacy, satiny nighties. New jeans. Dresses to wear to Slade when we went. Shoes. Tops. He'd ordered me to, "throw all that shit away, babe. I catch you in any of it, you earn a red ass", meaning my underwear when I came home to bags and bags of seriously sexy undies.

And I had a new car. A two-seater Mercedes. Black. He said it was not flash, just class, but it certainly was flash to me. We had words. I refused to accept. Knight refused to accept my refusal. This went on a while. Then he got sweet and I couldn't keep refusing. Then he bitched about how hard it was to give me "fuckin' anything". We had more words because I informed him a car wasn't exactly "fuckin' anything" it was, "a fucking car, for fuck's sake, Knight!" (that was me yelling).

At this, he burst out laughing, which made me angrier. He shut me up and swept away my temper by kissing me, though that only worked because that led him to doing other things to me.

So now I had a sweet crib, a sweet ride, sweet kit and a sweet day job.

And a sweet life.

And Knight.

Knight just had me.

And I didn't know how to give him more.

Except this way.

So I'd planned. I texted him when he was already at work and told him Sandrine had called and we were going out. The truth was, I was out for drinks only with both Sandrine and Vivica. No dancing. No men. Just the girls in a back, corner booth, lemon drops (me), martinis (Viv) and cosmos (Sandrine). We'd cabbed it so we were safe.

Knight called four times which I didn't pick up, and left two texts.

So I didn't bite off more than I could chew, I texted him back twice too, telling him I couldn't hear the phone ring over the music but assuring him we were fine and I'd get a taxi.

Then he sent one last text.

Ass. Home. Now.

That was thirty minutes ago. I was pushing it, I knew.

But I was being bad.

And I was hoping that I'd succeeded in not biting off more than I could chew.

I pulled my key from my purse at the door, inserted it in Knight's lock, turned it and sucked in another calming breath, wishing I'd had one last lemon drop for courage before I pushed it in.

It barely clicked behind me before Knight, wearing dark gray suit pants, shoes and a tailored slim-fit shirt the color of the deepest, darkest raspberry, prowled out of his study.

I stopped dead when the vibrating heat hit me.

"You went out with Sandrine?" he whispered, and it was sinister.

I commenced, or I should say continued, the game.

I flipped my hand in front of me, starting to take a step and saying airily, "We were fine, honey."

"Stop... right... *there.*"

I stopped and focused more on him.

"You went out with Sandrine?" he repeated in his scary whisper.

"Honey, seriously, we were——"

He cut me off. "Without a man on you."

"Like I said, we were——"

Another interruption as he crossed his arms on his chest. "Did you get my messages?"

"I couldn't hear them over the music," I said softly then offered, "I got your texts."

"So you know I wanted your ass home three hours ago."

"Knight, we were——"

"Dress off, panties off, leave the shoes," he growled and my belly dropped.

"What?" I whispered.

"Right there, take your fuckin' dress off, your panties off and leave your shoes on. Then walk your ass into my study and position on my desk, ass to the door."

My legs trembled and my womb contracted.

"Knight——" His name trembled too.

"You do not," he clipped, "wanna make me say it again."

I held his eyes and he held mine.

I pushed it, for him.

Then his arms started to uncross as his body started to move and I dropped my purse and keys to the floor.

Eyes still on his, I lifted my skirt slowly and hooked my fingers into my panties. I pushed them down, they fell down my legs, the silk and lace flitting across my already sensitive skin as they dropped to my ankles. I stepped out of them and curled my fingers in the black silk of my dress, biting my lip and pulling it over my head.

When it fell from my fingers to the floor, Knight barked, "Study," turned and stalked away.

I walked on shaking legs to the study.

Okay, all right.

Okay, all right.

Evidence was suggesting I bit off more than I could chew.

I walked into the warm woods and golden tans of his office, straight to the desk, breathing heavily and hoping I knew what the heck I was doing.

Our safe word was giraffe. In all the time we'd been together, I'd never considered using it. And Knight frequently got inspired. I'd been gagged with a scarf and tied spread-eagled to his bed. I'd gone down on him in his steam room off the bathroom. He'd fucked my face and my pussy while I was strapped on all fours to his bed.

And I'd loved every minute.

This, he was so angry, that vibrating heat unrelenting, I was worried.

Maybe I should have let him in on the fact that Viv was with us. He liked her, trusted her and said she had a good head on her shoulders.

Shakily, I positioned and I did it carefully. Torso to his desk. Ass out. And I made sure my legs were as wide as I could get them comfortably. That was how Knight liked me, always. With training, I'd learned to do that automatically when asked. I didn't want to forget now.

I heard him come back and I pressed my lips together as I pressed my cheek to some papers on his desk. Then I rolled my lips.

I felt a light breeze and heard a soft whoosh as something hit the desk beside me but I didn't dare look.

Then nothing.

I waited, deep breathing, but failing to calm my escalating panic.

More nothing.

When I was about to say something, tell him Viv was with us, even tell him this was his birthday present, his hand suddenly was between my legs, pulling up rough yet gentle, like only Knight could do. I gasped. Then I felt something—I didn't know what it was—trailing across my bottom.

"You earned the strap tonight, baby." I heard him say softly.

Oh God.

Oh God!

Well, at least it wasn't the cane. I wasn't ready for that yet. Viv said it hurt like a mother.

The thing on my behind kept stroking as Knight cupped me between my legs and he went on. "This one's brand new. All for you. Break you in while you break it in," he muttered.

His hand went away and that thing, what I knew was the strap, glided between my legs.

My eyes closed because that felt nice.

"Let's get you ready," Knight whispered and my eyes opened.

Then the strap was gone and his hand was between my legs, two fingers thrusting up, tight and hard, and I cried out in shock and something else altogether.

"Drenched," he growled. "Fuck yourself on Daddy's fingers."

Oh God. I wanted that.

So I did it.

"Harder, Anya, you gotta be ready to take your strap."

I moved faster, harder, grinding into his fingers, and this went on a while; a scary, crazy, *hot* while until I was whimpering.

"Stop," he ordered, but continued to thrust into me. "Stay still," he kept ordering while finger fucking me. "You do not move unless it's to jump to the strap. You do not, under any circumstances, come. No matter what I do to you, baby. You whisper 'Daddy' if you think you're gonna come. Other than that, you do not speak unless I ask you something directly. Then you answer immediately. And you know how I want your answer, Anya. You get more if I have to remind you. Now do you get me?"

"Yes, Daddy."

His fingers stopped thrusting. They started rubbing hard at my clit.

I whimpered and he whispered, "Good, baby."

Then his hand went away and in short order I knew *exactly* what Viv was talking about.

This was good. Better than his hand spanking me. It was *awesome*.

The strap stung, no doubt about it. My ass jumped, I winced. And the sound of the crack against my flesh only made things better. But like when he used his hand, Knight never brought it down in the same place twice in quick or even close succession. And he also slapped it across my thighs.

Every blow the strap bit in, and the sting radiated out, the pain and sting traveling right between my legs until I was consistently whimpering with need.

But as sharp as the sting was, the pain was fleeting and since he didn't cover the same area repeatedly, it stayed fleeting.

He stopped and his hand thrust between my legs.

"Rub against that, hard. Take yourself close," he ordered, and I did what I was told and I did it until I was close, and then I moaned, "Daddy."

He stopped and the strap was back at me. More sting. More fire. My legs were quaking, my ass jumping.

Then his hand between my legs.

"Up, Anya, stay facing the desk. Fast, baby."

I pushed myself up and felt his body close behind me.

"You aren't done and you do not come until I give it to you. Yeah?"

"Yes, Daddy," I breathed.

Then he was moving, and I felt his hands working at the front and behind me. I felt something smooth curling around me between my legs from ass to belly, tight. Then it was rubbing back and forth, gentle, quick, the friction worked me, separating me until it was right there and my head fell back as I moaned.

Knight's lips came to my ear. "You like your strap?"

Oh yeah. I liked my strap. Fuck yeah.

"Yes, Daddy."

"Take the ends, back and front, rub yourself. Do not come. Stop if you think you will."

I nodded and found the ends of the strap, back and front.

"Hold them tight, baby," Knight ordered, I obeyed and he pressed his back to mine as his hands moved on me.

Oh God. This was good. This was unbelievably *good*.

I worked the strap as Knight's hands moved on me, all over me, and his mouth worked my neck.

I took myself close, mouth panting, and I stopped.

"My baby, bein' good," Knight murmured against my neck. "Give it time, come down and then keep going."

I gave it time, his hands moved over me. Then I kept going.

"That's it, bring yourself close again," he whispered, his hands moving up, then they were cupping my breasts. "Look at you. Fuck me, my baby, so fuckin' *sweet*."

Then his fingers were at my nipples, pinching, squeezing, rolling, pulling.

I stopped moving the strap.

"Keep rubbing," he growled on a sharp tug of my nipples.

"Daddy," I used the word as a warning. I was close.

He tugged again at my nipples and it shot through me, my head jerking back, hitting his shoulder.

"Do not come, Anya, and keep working yourself."

Oh God. I couldn't do this. I was going to come.

But I did what I was told.

"Fuck yeah," he groaned into my neck, grinding his crotch into my back.

"Daddy," I whimpered.

He squeezed my nipples.

"Do not come, baby."

"Daddy," I moaned, still rubbing.

"Do not... *come*."

I did as I was told and I was pressing my head in his shoulder, biting my lip, keening when he growled. "Drop it."

I dropped the strap instantly.

Then I was back to the desk, Knight's hands behind my knees shoving them high and wide. One of his hands went to his fly. It was back behind my knee and he was driving into me, brutal, savage, my eyes on him fucking me, his burning on my body jolting on his desk.

Stroke three, I came.

And I came.

And I came.

And I came.

And then I lost track of how many times I came.

Then with one last, violent thrust, Knight came.

Eyes still on me, hands still behind my knees, he went from thrusting to sliding.

He plunged deep and whispered, "Come here, baby."

I pushed up. His hands went to my ass, my legs wrapped around his hips and he lifted me up. My arms wrapped around his shoulders and he walked me across the room to his couch and took us down, me on my back, Knight on top, and he managed to do this entire maneuver connected to me.

He lifted some of his weight off me with a forearm in the couch and his other hand came to my face, his fingertips skimming my jaw, my cheek, his eyes on me and he asked gently, "You okay?"

"Happy birthday," I whispered and he blinked.

Then he whispered, "What?"

"Kathleen told me," I shared. "I wasn't at a club. I was with Sandrine, but I was with Vivica too. We were at a bar. Back booth. No one could even see us. No dancing. Nothing. Just us girls. We took a taxi so no one driving drunk. And Rhashan was in on the surprise, kinda, without a real share. He just knows it's a surprise birthday gig for you and he knew where we were the whole time."

He stared at me and he did this a long time, giving nothing away.

So I went on softly and now uncertainly, "I didn't know what to get you."

"Jesus, fuck," he finally muttered.

"Knight?"

"Jesus, fuck," he repeated.

"Did I... was that okay?"

He buried his face in my neck and groaned, "Jesus, fuck. Fuck me. Fuck me."

I didn't know what to make of this.

"Knight?" I called.

His head came up.

"Yes," he clipped. "Yes, Anya, baby, fuck me, baby. Yes, that was fuckin' okay. That was fuckin' beautiful what you gave me."

It was. He believed that. What I gave him meant something to him.

It meant a lot.

Tears filled my eyes.

"Knight," I whispered.

"Fuck me," he whispered back, staring at me, his eyes burning because his heart was beating there.

God.

Beautiful.

I smiled, lifted my head and lips to his. I whispered, "I'm kinda not done."

"Fuck me," he repeated and I smiled bigger.

"But you'll need to get off me."

I watched his eyes close slowly and then I watched as emotion washed over his features.

And I did this mesmerized.

God.

Beautiful.

He touched his mouth to mine, slid out and got off me, pulling me up with him. He held me close with an arm around my waist as I got steady on my feet.

When I shot him a grin, he muttered, "Nightie, babe. Desk."

So *that* was the soft whoosh.

My man, even pissed, he always remembered to take care of me.

My grin got bigger.

I went to the desk and pulled the red, silk and lace short nightie with the high slits up my sides that Knight bought for me over my head. I shot him another grin as I walked out to see he was still standing at the couch. He'd adjusted his trousers and his eyes were on me.

The minute I knew he lost sight of me, I moved fast.

I had it all planned and I put it in motion quickly. I cleaned up and took my shoes off. Then I grabbed the bag of wrapped presents. I went to where I'd hidden the store bought, fancy decorated cake with the candles and lighter. I shoved the candles in and lit them. Balancing the cake in both hands with the bag of presents dangling, I went back to his study.

Knight was sitting, ass to the desk where I'd spent a memorable amount of time, legs stretched out in front of him, eyes to his crossed feet, hands at his sides, fingers curled around the desk's edge but his head came up when I walked in carrying the cake.

His eyes went to the cake then to me and instantly his face got soft and his eyes warm but surprised and definitely pleased.

Totally beautiful.

"Jesus, baby," he whispered as I walked to him.

I stopped in front of him.

"Happy birthday, sweetheart."

His eyes stayed locked to mine.

"Anya."

I waited. He said no more.

"Make a wish and blow out your candles, honey," I whispered.

His body didn't move and neither did his eyes.

"Make a wish, Knight."

227

His eyes then moved, roaming my face, down my body, the cake, more of me then back to my eyes.

"Honey, the candles are gonna burn out," I prompted on a grin.

"Let 'em," he replied. "Got nothin' I want. Everything I want is standing right in front of me."

Oh.

My.

God.

My nose stung and my eyes filled with tears.

"Please," I begged softly, "blow out the candles, Knight."

He held my eyes. One tear slid out my left, followed by another on my right.

Then he bent forward and blew out the candles.

"Thank you," I whispered.

He grabbed the cake and plopped it on his desk. Then he pulled the bag out of my hand and tossed it on one of the two chairs angled at the front of it. He yanked me between his legs, in his arms, doing it roughly. Holding me tight, one arm around my waist, one hand in my hair, his mouth crushed down on mine and he plundered it.

I melted into him, my arms snaking around him and I let him.

He let my lips go. My head moved back an inch and his hand slid around to cup my jaw, his thumb moving through the wet left by the tear.

"Don't cry for me, Anya. Don't ever cry for me," he murmured.

"Is that an order?" I teased, and his eyes went from his thumb to mine.

"Yes."

My arms slid from around him so my hands could curl around his neck and I pressed up so I could touch my forehead to his.

"Lemon drops," he murmured and I smiled.

He remembered.

God, I loved this man.

"Praise God for faulty, cheap cell phones," I muttered. Knight's body gave a short jerk then both his arms closed around me hard as he burst out laughing.

"So which present do you like best?"

I was fishing for information, lying in bed in my red nightie next to and mostly on Knight, up on a forearm in his chest, smiling into his face.

"Uh... seriously? You askin' that shit?"

"Scary, crazy, hot punishment and resulting scary, crazy, hot, *hard* fucking not included." I amended my question and Knight's arm curled around my waist got tight as he chuckled.

Then he answered, "The Black Sabbath tee."

I tipped my head to the side and asked, "Not the biography on Beethoven?"

"Babe, got no time to read."

"But you like his music."

"What?"

"It was playing in your office when you, um... carried me in that first time."

He studied me, but I could tell he was harking back then his face got soft and he asked quietly, "You remember that?"

I felt my face get soft too, and I whispered, "I remember everything."

His hand slid up my side even as his arm got tight again. He murmured, "Baby." I dropped closer and he finished, "But that was Bach."

It was me who blinked then I giggled and asked, "Really?"

"Yeah."

"Well, whatever," I muttered then offered, "If you don't read, I will. Out loud. In bed. To you." I grinned. "Naked."

He grinned back and remarked, "Bet that'll make Beethoven interesting."

"I read the jacket cover. He's already interesting. Or he was."

"You can do it, babe, but you do it naked, I won't hear a fuckin' word, no matter how interesting."

"Then maybe I should put on a snowsuit," I suggested. His arms again closed around me as he burst out laughing and rolled me to my back.

Then he lifted up, his hand coming to my face to trail lightly along my skin but his eyes didn't leave mine.

"Best birthday ever," he murmured.

My belly melted, my arms snaked around him and I whispered, "Oh, honey."

His hand quit trailing, slid into my hair and he shared, "Even before Carl came into my life, Mom did her best, every year. Went all out. Got some of her girls to help. Carl was there, got even better. But this was the best."

Suddenly, my nose started stinging. This meant so much to me I whispered in a fierce whisper, "Good. I'm glad. That's what I wanted to give to you. That's what I wanted for you. And since I found out Wednesday that today was your birthday, I've been in a panic because I had no idea what to do to make it special for you. So I'm glad I figured it out and could give it to you."

"Jesus, fuck, fuck me," he whispered back, his eyes blazing into mine.

"I love you, Knight." I kept whispering then my lips quirked and went on, "And the good news is, it's barely even your birthday. You have birthday breakfast, birthday lunch and birthday dinner to look forward to. I have it all planned and I did a whopper of a grocery shop so the food's already here. And I'll be making you a homemade cake, not that store bought thing I brought into your study. I got that just so the presentation would be good. And since it's Sunday and I have you all day, you have me all day, wherever you want, whenever you want, whatever you want to do to me."

I was so busy laying it out, I didn't notice his reaction to it until his hand slid into my hair, fisted and his mouth came to mine.

"Shut up, Anya," he rumbled.

"Okay," I breathed, staring into his heated eyes.

"You need to sleep because I'm gonna eat your birthday breakfast, lunch, dinner and cake and I'm gonna do you in all the ways I can think of doin' you and you need to be prepared."

"Oh..." it was unsteady and remained unsteady when I finished, "kay."

His fist in my hair relaxed and he went back half an inch.

"Love you, babe."

"And I love you, honey."

"No," he stated firmly, his eyes locked to mine, "*love you*, babe."

Oh God.

Oh God.

I sucked in breath to make my nose stop stinging (again!) and then I slid a hand to his chest, up, feeling the hair abrasive, yet awesome, against my skin until it was up with fingers curled around his jaw.

Then I whispered, "And I... *love you*... honey."

He dropped his head and kissed me, wet and sweet. Then he lifted it up, reached across me to my nightstand to turn out my light. He rolled to his to turn that out. Then he rolled back to me and curved his body into mine, his arm wrapped tight around my belly, tucking me close.

I sighed, snuggled deeper and relaxed into him.

My eyelids were drooping when he called softly, "Babe?"

"Yeah?"

His hand slid up and curled tight around my breast. My eyelids drooped for a different reason.

"You go out again, don't care where or with who, without a man on you, it's the cane."

Oh my.

"Get me?" he asked.

"Got you," I whispered.

"No joke, babe."

"Okay, Knight."

His hand relaxed but didn't move.

My body relaxed, too.

Then I murmured, "'Night, honey. Happy birthday."

"Shut up and go to sleep, babe," was his reply.

I giggled.

About two minutes later, I did what I was told.

Chapter 15
Fuck Monster

It was a sunny day, but hazy. The bright green grass, fluttering insects, dripping willows and daisies dotting the lawn looked like they were seen through a filtered lens on a camera.

I lifted the delicate china cup and sipped my tea.

"You never pay attention."

My head jerked, and sitting with me at the table with an elaborate tea service on it, a tiered plate of perfectly decorated petit fours, was my aunt. Her lined, sneering face was topped with a huge, wide brimmed, heavily decorated, absurd hat.

"What?" I asked.

"You never pay attention, Anya," she snapped. "Look around. What do you see?"

I looked around then looked at her.

"Beauty," I answered.

"Trash, Anya. It's trash, you're trash," she leaned across the table, slamming her own tea cup down and hissed, "*He's trash.*"

Then everything melted and she was sitting in her preposterous hat and all around her was tall, steaming, reeking piles of hideous trash.

I jerked awake, my eyes opening, and I pulled in a breath thinking in that split second I hoped I didn't wake Knight. He seriously hated it when I had a bad dream.

Since I was pressed to his side, head resting on his chest and his arm was around me, this hope was dashed quickly and I knew it when his arm got tight.

"Anya," he growled, sleepy, sexy, rough and annoyed.

"I'm okay," I whispered.

Nothing.

Then, "I change my mind. I'm glad that motherfucker bled out in the yard."

Oh boy.

"What was this one about?" he asked.

The room was dark. I knew it was late since it was summer so dawn kissed Knight's apartment early. But Knight had told me weeks ago that he wanted me to talk out each dream, thinking if I let it go, they'd eventually let go of me.

So far, this wasn't working.

"It's still dark, let's go back to sleep," I whispered.

"I won't ask again."

I sighed then I told him quickly about tea, filtered lenses, my aunt, her hat and trash.

"That fuckin' cunt," he grumbled, "follows you in your dreams."

"I'm okay."

Nothing, but his arm was still tight.

"Honey, seriously. I'm used to this. I've been having them for years," I assured.

"We're gonna see about you stoppin' having them."

Finally I lifted my head and looked at his shadowed face. "I'm used to them, sweetheart. But it bugs me that I wake you. Maybe I should sleep—"

I didn't finish.

Knight's arm got super tight and he pulled me on him and up so my face was at his.

"Don't finish that. Not gonna happen."

"Okay," I whispered.

"We talk 'em out."

"Okay," I repeated on a whisper.

"You had trash. Her. Now you're livin' clean," he informed me.

"Okay."

"I had shit for a good while then I had good, Anya, and you're still the most beautiful thing that's touched my life. Mark that 'cause it's true. Ask Viv. Ask Sandrine. Ask Rhash. Ask Kurt. They all think the fuckin' world of you. Mark that. Take *that* into your dreams."

God, my boyfriend was *so* awesome.

"Okay, honey."

I felt his eyes on me through the dark.

"That fuckin' cunt, followin' you in your dreams," he muttered.

He still sounded pissed.

I needed to do something about that.

So I did.

My hand trailed down his chest, down to his abs and I nearly got to my destination before his fingers wrapped around my wrist.

"Where's that goin'?" he growled.

"Your voice is sexy, sleepy rough," I said softly. "I wanna hear you groan like that."

"Don't want your hand," he stated.

Damn.

"Want your mouth."

Yay!

"Get between my legs, baby."

Oh yeah.

"Okay," I whispered and his arm squeezed.

"Okay what?"

"Okay, Daddy."

His hand let me go as he muttered, "Good, baby, now position and take Daddy in your mouth."

I shifted and kissed his chest. I shifted again and kissed his tight abs. I shifted again and got between his legs. He cocked his knees and I saw he was stroking himself, preparing for me.

I took over and made my Daddy groan sexy, sleepy, *rough*.

I was walking from the coffeepot with my fresh mug of joe when Knight rounded the corner into the kitchen wearing an AC/DC tee and faded jeans.

I smiled at him.

One side of his lips tipped up then his eyes dropped immediately to my tee that was his tee. He was clearly headed to coffee and I was about to pass him, but stopped when his arm went out, hooking me around my belly.

He pulled me to his front and I adjusted my coffee so we didn't have spillage and second degree burns.

Then his hand dipped down and up so it was cupped on the bare skin of my bottom.

I stared into his eyes.

"Scary, crazy, hot punishment followed by fuckin' my baby hard notwithstanding, this is *definitely* my favorite birthday present."

It was a week and a half after his birthday and I was in his Black Sabbath tee.

"Cool," I whispered. His lips twitched, then his head dropped and he touched them to mine.

Then he let me go and went to coffee. I watched his ass move in his jeans then when he stopped and grabbed the pot, I moved out of the kitchen, skirted the sunken living room and out the opened glass door to sit on a cushy, streamlined gray cushion on his wrought iron furniture.

Plans were in high gear for the grand opening party of my spa that was two and a half weeks away. Mahleena was planning that, too. Knight's marketing firm was advertising it. I had hired staff. Manicures, pedicures, facials, body scrubs, massages and hair, the whole shebang. We even had a small steam sauna, a Jacuzzi and a shower. All low lighting (except the hair stations). Relaxing. Tranquil. The minute you entered, you got in the mood to let it all go and indulge.

I couldn't wait.

I was still riding the high of Knight's birthday. Not only was he moved by what I'd done for him, the next day he took a birthday call from his Mom and Dad and he talked about me with me right there. And all he said was good.

He was Knight so it wasn't flowery compliments, but he did tell his Dad, his eyes on me, "She's beautiful, Dad. You see her, you won't believe your eyes. You'll think you're dreamin'."

And I thought that was pretty flowery. Or at least it did a number on me.

He told them they had to come out to meet me, or we'd be going to Hawaii soon so I could meet them.

When he got off the phone, he said to me, "Mom says 'hi' and she's lookin' forward to meetin' you."

I stopped myself from twirling, giggling and shouting, "Squee!" and just grinned and kissed him.

Then he kissed me.

Life was good. Even if I expected things, I'd never expect it to be as good as this.

And Knight gave all of it to me.

He came out with his mug and did what he did every morning when we sat out on his balcony. Therefore my chair was already in position because I quit the hassle of moving it back, which also saved Knight the hassle of adjusting it when he made it to me.

He sat in a chair facing the Plexiglas-sided railing, hefted his long, muscled legs up to the top and crossed his ankles. My chair was angled to his so it was easy for him to hook an arm around both my legs, and that was what he did before tossing them over his thighs.

I held my coffee aloft in another effort to avoid spillage until he leaned back in his chair and sipped so I knew it was safe. Then I leaned back in mine and did the same.

"Decided what I want for my birthday," he stated and I blinked.

"Your birthday was over a week ago, Knight." I told him something he already knew and his neck twisted so his pure, vibrant blue eyes were on me.

I'd never get used to those eyes, ever. And I hoped I had eternity to prove that true.

"You kicked my birthday's ass so good, baby, I've decided to celebrate all month."

A smile curved big, but on the inside.

On the outside I gave him a false frown.

"I could barely walk for three days what with you 'doin' me all the ways you could do me', Knight. I'm still recovering."

His brows went up.

"I fuck you hard thirty minutes ago?" he asked.

"Yes," I answered.

"You suck me off in the middle of the night?" he pressed.

"Yes."

"That last one, babe, your idea." He looked back to the Front Range muttering, "You're good."

I so was.

"Whatever," I muttered back, loving our banter, not about to tell him that and bringing my coffee to my lips. "What do you want for your birthday?"

"You're movin' in."

I choked on coffee and his eyes came to me, brows drawn and he leaned toward me.

"You all right, baby?"

I patted my chest, swallowed and wheezed, "Yes," then, "You want me to move in?"

He stared at me.

Then he said, "Babe, your ass has been in my bed every night for three months. You got a whole dresser to yourself and more than half the fuckin' walk-in already. For a bitch who had no money, you got a fuckload of clothes."

This was true. All of it. Though the last was partially his fault.

"How much is the rent?" I asked.

"Nothin', considerin' I own the place."

"Okay, how much is the mortgage?" I amended.

"Why?" he asked.

"Because, if I move in, I need to know what my half is so I can budget," I answered and instantly his head tipped back and he looked at the bottom of the balcony above us.

Then he chanted, "Jesus, fuck, fuck me. Jesus, fuck, fuck me."

"Knight!" I snapped and his eyes sliced to me.

"You're not paying half the mortgage," he declared.

I opened my mouth but he moved quickly, his arm coming out, hand cupping my jaw, thumb pressing firm on my lips and I saw his eyes were deadly serious.

"This is not a discussion. On this you yield. You put in notice. You dump the shit from yard sales or that's got rips in it or anything you bought on fuckin' sale or anything anyone fuckin' gave you unless it has special meaning. The rest of the shit, we'll find places for it. You get me?"

He removed his thumb and I kept snapping, "That'll take a box to move since everything is from yard sales, got rips in it, I bought it on sale or someone gave it to me."

"Good, then it'll take about an hour to move you in. We'll do it today," he returned immediately.

That was when I looked at the bottom of the balcony and asked, "Please, deliver me."

"Anya, eyes," he ordered and I cut my eyes to him but they were squinty. He ignored that and growled, "Yield."

I didn't yield.

I announced, "I can't move in. The limited stuff I have that doesn't fit in one of those categories is girlie and it won't match your décor."

"Babe, I live in a fuckin' museum. Please, God, inject some personality in it."

I blinked.

"Not flowers or pink," he added then continued, "Or any of that white, chipped shit you got goin' on."

I stared at him.

Then I asked, "Anything else, Knight?"

He stared at me.

Then he answered, "Far's I'm concerned, you can lose it all. The only thing I give a shit that you move permanently is you."

That was a really good answer.

Still.

"You know, when you bring bossy into life and get so super generous I'll be wracking my brains for a millennium for ways to be bad to give payback and it pisses me off, it then pisses me off more when you get sweet so I can't be pissed anymore."

"You know that didn't make a fuckin' lick of sense," he told me.

I glared at him.

Then I turned my head and glared at the Front Range, muttering, "Whatever."

I sipped coffee.

Then I heard, "Notice in and move your shit, Anya."

"Okay, Knight."

"Jesus, fuck, fuck me," Knight muttered.

I took another sip of coffee. I did this calmly. But again, inside, I was twirling and screeching, "Squee!"

Then I announced to the mountains, "I feel a night out with Sandrine coming on."

"Christ, she sucked me off in the middle of the night, I ate her and fucked her half an hour ago and she's sittin' in my tee, no panties, drinkin' coffee, tryin' to get me hard," he griped.

My eyes went to him. "Your rule, honey. I can go put panties on."

His eyes came to me. "You do, I get the strap."

My legs shifted restlessly.

He stared at me.

Then he turned his head and muttered to the Range, "Fuck, I created a fuck monster."

I felt my eyes bug out.

Then I burst out laughing.

The thin, high heels of my awesome sandals clicked on the floor as I wandered through the apartment. I did it smiling to myself because while it was turned low, which might be a crime in some states, I could hear Black Sabbath.

I turned the corner into the living room and saw Knight outside on the balcony, heels up on the railing, drinking coffee and smoking a cigarette. I knew while I'd showered and got ready to face the day he'd probably moved to refresh his cup. Other than that, no.

It was one of the things I loved about him. Comfortable in his own company. He had very little downtime. What little he had he spent with me. But if there were moments like this, he didn't need to fill them with books or TV. Just music, coffee (or a beer or a vodka rocks), his smokes and himself.

Like everything about Knight, I thought it was hot.

His neck twisted and his eyes came to me when he heard my approach. His eyes to me, I watched him crush his cigarette in the ashtray.

I got close, his head went back. He moved his mug to his other hand so his hand closest to me could curl around my hip and I leaned in to touch my mouth to his.

I pulled back an inch and said softly, "Gonna check in at the spa."

"Right," he muttered.

"Can I ask you to think about something while I'm gone?" I requested.

"Anything," he told me and I lifted a hand to his neck as I felt my face get soft.

"Think of something I can do to contribute to our home. I get you wanna look out for me, but what you need to get is I need to do that. Groceries. Utilities. Paying the cleaners. Something. Until my spa becomes the whopping success I'm gonna make it be, I know with this place I can't afford to go halfsies and you'll never let me do that anyway. But I need to do something."

I knew he was stuck on the beginning of what I said when his eyes drifted to my mouth and he whispered, "Our home."

My fingers at his neck gave him a squeeze and I whispered back, "Honey."

His eyes came to mine and he told me quietly, "We'll talk about it tonight."

My man. He loved me and he'd give me anything.

I smiled at him and replied, "Okay."

His eyes dropped back to my mouth.

"Want that mouth again before you go."

I gave it to him. His fingers drove into my hair, holding me to him and he plundered it.

Then, after throwing him a smile over my shoulder as I walked away, I went.

❦

"See you later!" I called as I walked down the hall at the top level of my spa.

"Later!" one of the two dudes who were finishing up the steam room shouted back.

I grinned and wandered down the softly lit hall with its dark wood paneling.

Mahleena's plant people were coming that day. Plants. That meant we were close to opening. Live bamboo, mostly. The feel was clean, rich, warm, expensive with a hint of Oriental. Very little color as Mahleena liked it, with touches of warm reds at my demand. Mostly because they reminded me of Knight.

I wandered down the curving staircase and looked across the open area, its snug, paneled nail stations, pedicure lounges and open hair stations with the tall mirrors and lights dangling.

"Awesome," I whispered. I got to the bottom and wandered through to the high reception desk that was built out of thin panels of dark wood and set away from, but at an angle to, the front door.

I moved behind it. The phone had already been installed. The computer system was being installed the next day. If Mahleena or any of the workmen left me non-urgent notes, they put them there. I'd done a walkthrough when I arrived without going back there and had gotten caught up with talking to the boys so I was checking for notes before I left.

A trill shivered up my neck, and it wasn't the kind Knight gave me. Like they were guided by unseen forces, my head came up and my eyes moved out the huge, plate glass windows at the front of my place to the street and I sucked in breath.

Nick was walking down the street, looking over his shoulder at something; not me, but toward my spa. I didn't like this. This wasn't the coincidental scenario Knight threw out of me seeing Nick on the street. He was there for a reason. I knew it.

I shrugged my bag off my shoulder to the reception desk in order to grab my phone when the door to my spa opened. My back went straight and my eyes went to the door.

A heavyset man about an inch or two taller than me with a receding hairline, a deep tan and a gold chain tangling with the profuse amount of hair that grew up from his chest was walking in, eyes to me. I didn't like the look of him. Not at all.

Seedy.

No, *sleazy.*

"Sorry," I told him, "we're not open yet."

"Anya Gage?" he asked, not faltering a single step in walking to me.

Keeping my gaze on him, I opened the snap on my bag and dug in for my space age phone.

"Can I help you?" I asked.

"I'm Drake Nair."

I knew no Drake Nair, and by the look of him I knew I never wanted to.

I found the phone and pulled it out, lifting up my hand so he could see. His eyes dropped to it then came back to me when I spoke.

"And what can I do for you, Mr. Nair?"

He had stopped four feet away from the desk. "I'm Knight's ex-partner."

A surprise, and not the good kind.

I held it together and didn't even blink.

"Yes?" I prompted.

He studied me.

I informed him on a warning, "There are two men working upstairs, Mr. Nair."

"Not surprised," he muttered, still studying me, and not talking about not being surprised about men working in my place.

"Mr. Nair, I have things to do," I stated. "Would you like to tell me why you're here?"

He focused more fully on me and replied, "You asked me to guess ten years ago, I would say you're exactly what he wanted, but I wouldn't say you're what he could get."

I kept my back straight, my eyes on him and my hand curled on my phone. What I didn't do was speak.

He did.

"Still. Boy was a magnet for pussy. Fuck, they were all over him. You know, they wanted him to drive stock?"

"I assume you're referring to Knight and since I don't know you, I'd prefer not to discuss him with you."

He ignored me. "Girl, stock, that's the big time. He woulda owned it. Way he looks? He didn't even have to win. Big time investors and endorsements would be creamin' their jeans to have their logos on his car, his suit, his face in their magazine ads."

"Mr. Nair—"

"Live quiet," he whispered Knight's words and I shut up. "Minute it started heatin' up for him 'cause 'a the way he looked, the fact he won almost every fuckin' race he was in, fuckin' fearless, fuckin' *crazy*, he bailed and went into business with me."

"It would seem you're determined to say what you have to say, but it would be nice if you got down to saying it. Like I told you, I have things to do."

"Took it all from me," he said softly, and that unhappy trill slid up my neck again. "Turned tail, went to Costa Rica. Does somethin' to a man when another man makes a fool 'a him. Not a fuckin' dollar changed hands and he maneuvered it all right out from under me. Stole the whole fuckin' thing. The club. The girls."

My legs locked and my face must have changed because he smiled in a way I *did not like*.

"Oh yeah," he said, still talking softly, "Nick guessed it."

Oh God!

Nick!

Now that Sandrine had calmed her shit, *he* was going to be the death of me.

"Nick doesn't know anything," I snapped.

"Nick knows Knight sells pussy."

I stopped breathing.

"Yeah," he said, his tone eager, enjoying this and I knew I was giving it away. "You didn't know. Good girl. Just lookin' at you, I can see you're sweet, honey. And have no clue your man sells pussy."

Oh my God.

I didn't move. I wanted to. I wanted to run. But I couldn't.

Drake Nair wasn't done.

"Took my club, took my stable. Those were," he leaned in, lost it for a second and hissed, "*my girls.*"

He leaned back, pulling himself together as he kept his eyes locked to me.

Then, "Don't know, have no fuckin' clue how that boy's mind works, but I figure he got into all that business with me knowin' he was gonna steal my stable. He was always about the girls. So he took it all from me. You, his woman, a sweet, classy, good girl, what I 'spect he always wanted, but never, knowin' what that boy is, what he came from, who he'll always be, would get. You gotta know, it makes me all kinds 'a happy lookin' at your face right now, knowin' this struck deep, knowin' you know you can get anybody so you don't have to take a man who sells pussy."

"If you wouldn't mind," I said softly, "I'd like you to leave."

"Yeah, I bet you do. But I got one thing more to say."

I opened my mouth, but he walked swiftly to the desk and instead I took a step back, my fingers curling tight on my phone.

He put his hand on the desk and kept talking.

"You can get over that, I'll give you this. He doesn't only run pussy through *my* club, he runs drugs. You're in bed with filth, Anya Gage. You don't pull your shit together, like Knight Sebring was, is and always will be, that's all *you'll* ever be."

And with that, he turned and walked out of my spa.

I stared at the door and did this a long time, my heart racing, my breath coming short.

Then I turned my head and looked out the windows where I last saw Nick.

He was there, standing looking through the windows, eyes on me.

Smiling.

He set that up. He set me up. He set his brother up.

Douchebag *motherfucker.*

I jerked my head away and walked as calmly as I could muster into one of the cordoned-off nail stations and away from Nick Sebring's eyes.

Then I deep breathed.

"Hold the fuck on." I heard Vivica say in my head.

Okay, all right.

"You might hear fucked up shit about me from a variety of sources. But you talk to me before you react. I will confirm or deny, I will be honest and last, I will explain. If it's shit I don't want you to know yet, I'll explain that too and you'll wait until I'm ready. You feel you can't, then, babe, you still fuckin' talk... to... me before you leave me."

Okay, all right.

Right.

Right.

I lifted my phone, activated the screen and called Knight.

He answered on ring two.

"Babe."

"Drake Nair just left and he told me some things about you," I whispered and I did it quickly, my voice breathy.

Silence. Total. Complete. A whirling void of terrifying nothing.

Then, softly, "I'm at the club. Come to me right now, baby."

"Okay, Knight."

"Right now, Anya, babe."

"Okay," I agreed quietly.

I disconnected, walked swiftly to the foot of the stairs and shouted loudly but still shakily, "I'm going, guys!"

"Later, Anya!"

"Later!"

I turned and walked quickly to the desk. I shoved my phone in my purse, threw it on my shoulder and hustled out.

Then I hustled down the block to Slade. I'd been there during the day on occasion and it never failed to kind of freak me out. It was weird during the day.

I didn't notice it then.

I just opened the door and walked into the cool, vast interior that seemed eerie not jammed with bodies, flashing with lights or drowned with music.

Almost instantly I saw Knight striding swiftly toward me.

I moved to him.

When we met, he didn't say a word but grabbed my hand, changed directions, and I hurried to keep up with him.

On the stairs up to his office, making my heart leap in my throat, my belly knot and drop, he surprised me by stopping, turning and lifting me up in his arms. I didn't know if he was impatient with me having trouble keeping up or if he wanted me close.

I didn't ask.

But I hesitated before my arms slid around his shoulders to hold on.

Knight noticed everything. He noticed my hesitation.

I knew it when, his voice terse, tight, pained, he whispered, "Fuck me."

We got to the top. His torso dipped and he opened the door. He carried me into the office, the door closed behind us and he gently set me on my feet.

Quickly, I took three steps away.

My heart clenched because he let me.

"Do you sell pussy?" I whispered.

He closed his eyes slowly and my nose started stinging.

"Knight?" I prompted and his eyes opened.

"Got fifty-seven girls," he stated immediately.

Oh God. God!

"And drugs?" I was still whispering, but it was around a clogged throat and sounded croaky.

His head jerked and he asked, "What?"

I lost it and my voice pitched high and loud when I snapped, "Do you sell drugs?"

"Fuck no," he shot back.

I started breathing heavily.

Knight watched me do it.

Then I turned my head and looked to the window.

"Came home bleeding out the ass, from her pussy. Not sometimes, often." I heard him say and my startled gaze cut back to him. He kept talking and I knew it was about his mother. "Face busted up, lip torn open, eyes swollen shut. I cleaned that shit up. I was six."

Oh.

My.

God.

My body locked and Knight kept at me.

"Johns did that shit to her, but not only them. Her man did too. Her pimp. He got rough and his rough was ugly. And he availed himself often. Only thing could get him to go limp was a four year old in the room. He forgot and didn't lock the door or lock me in my room, I walked in and I did it as often as I could. Learned to pick my own lock and hers so I could get to her. See him on her. Get him to stop raping her. Be her shield. Pickin' locks. At *four*."

All my innards had seized and squeezed and the pain was excruciating.

"Knight—" I wheezed.

"I told you my life was shit, Anya, and it fuckin' was. Hers was worse. Her man, worst kinda human being there is. Kept his girls in blow, in smack, in crack, anything to keep them hooked to him. That's all he gave them and that was no fuckin' gift. No protection. He took his cut and it was a big one, babe. He got off usin' their bodies. He put them on the street, worked them hard. But they turned a bad trick, he didn't do shit. Johns learn. They know. They get a bitch they can't play with the way they like 'cause their man pays them a visit, they move on. So they knew which women to pick up. And my mother was one of them."

I pressed my lips together and rolled them.

Knight continued.

"I had no control. My first fuckin' memory in this life is walkin' into my Mom's bedroom, seein' her in bed bleeding from every orifice. Her slitted, swollen eyes came to me. She smiled a smile she had to force through pain, stupid and hopin' she was foolin' me, unable to move a muscle except her mouth and she whispered, 'Sweetie.' Blocked out the rest. Know, after that, not once but a lot of fuckin' times, I found that, I cleaned her up. She was so jacked, by the time I'm fuckin' six, she's lettin' me."

I swallowed the pain and hurt I felt for him, and it stuck in my gullet because it was a lot, and he kept talking.

"I had no control. None. I was a fuckin' kid. I could do what I could do and that was all I could do. She was good to me, Anya, she loved me. Not just because I was her shield, but because I was her boy. Only good thing she ever did, she told me, was make me. She thought the sun rose and set in me, and she still does. But I remembered that. As good as Carl gave it to her and me, I never fuckin' forgot that feeling of being out-of-control, livin' shit someone forced on me, and I became a man who never has to feel that shit again."

"Okay, honey," I whispered, but Knight wasn't finished explaining.

"Nair is an asshole. And yeah, I took his stable and I still got it. And I'm gonna keep it, Anya. He had a girl, she worked the drags."

He moved to the chest at the wall and ran a finger down the carved, female torso and turned back to me.

"She made that for me. Fuck, unbelievable what she could create outta a chunk of wood. An artist. A hooker. A junkie. She was Nair's. She led me to him. He thought I was a shit-for-brains racer hooked on speed. Thought he could play me. She OD'ed. All that talent," he jerked a finger at the torso, "vanished. The beauty she could bring into the world, lost. I let him think he could play me and I got in it to look after his girls. He was not like my mother's man, but he wasn't about protection. He was about pussy. Usin' it to get rich. Usin' it to get off. Made his girls service him, one, two, twenty. And I am not joking. Twenty bitches crawlin' all over him. Insane. Made 'em oil up and wrestle on his fuckin' bed so he could watch and jack off. He did not keep them clean. And it was hit or miss, depending on how lazy he was feelin', whether he'd send someone out to deliver a message, one of his girls got worked over. I spent a lotta time coverin' a lotta asses, which pissed him off. He wanted me not lookin' after his pussy, but bein' the face of this club. We clashed. I made moves. Got him out. Then rebuilt and grew his empire, such as it was. Girls that weren't clean, I got them clean. Girls who didn't wanna be in the life, I let them go. He had forty-two girls. I have more because *they* come to *me*. And they don't got track marks or habits, I take them on. I take their backs. They take clients they wanna fuck. Rhashan and Kathleen make arrangements, they do what they want, only what they want, and a man tries for more, we make certain he knows we're not down with that and that message is delivered crystal clear. That is our reputation. I made it that way so that shit does not happen often and my girls go out safe."

"Rhashan?" I whispered.

"Yeah, and if you're worried about your girl, don't be. She knows. He knows I don't like attention and asked me if he could tell her. Your girl Viv, she is far from stupid, so I agreed. He told her. She grew up in the 'hood. So did he. They both get it."

"She didn't tell me."

"She did, you or anyone, his ass would be out. And that came from me."

I felt a tremble glide through me as I asked, "So you were going to keep this from me?"

"Fuck yeah."

My voice was high and tight when I pushed, "Why?"

"Christ, Anya, 'cause of the way you are right now lookin' at me," he bit out. "I just told you how I grew up. Carl made that good for Mom and me. But I raced. You would not believe the skank pussy at races. I got even a hint of sweet, if I broke down, let them in, told them that shit about me, that sweet got sour. But not one of them, not one, Anya, was your kind of sweet. Never in my life did I expect I'd taste your kind of sweet so, yeah, fuck yeah, I was going to keep this from you to guarantee I'd keep your sweet."

"I thought you weren't hiding anything from me."

"I didn't. I didn't lie. I didn't adjust the man I am. I just didn't share."

"That's the same thing."

"You feel that way, nothin' I can do."

I held his eyes.

Then I whispered, "He said you ran drugs through the club."

"Well, he fuckin' lied," Knight shot back.

I didn't reply and he kept going.

"But cards on the table, babe, the Russians got this territory. I made that deal so I could control that shit. It's a fuckin' club. My boys could have eyes in the backs of their heads and not see all the deals that went down. Four years ago, five kids got hold of bad shit and cops traced it, sold by a dealer in my club."

He shook his head, clearly still dealing with this awful scenario even after five years, and he continued talking.

"First, I do not need that attention. Second, no fuckin' way am I cool with people dyin' because of shit they sourced in my club. We cracked down, we still could not stem the flow. It's was a fuckin' nightmare. Got to the point, I wanted to control that, I'd have to close my doors. The Russians approached me, made assurances they would not recruit buyers in my club, advertise outside the premises so anyone wanted that shit, they knew who to go to. They promised they'd see to the dealers that were workin' my club, sweep them clean. They got no problems doin' shit I won't do and won't allow my boys to do, to see that happen. They use them. I ask no questions but I get a clean club. They also promised their shit would be good shit, not laced, not bad. Some-

249

one fucked up, it would not be the shit they were takin' but them. And last, I allowed the connection in my club, but any deal goes down off the premises. I give them one. One fuckin' dealer. He does what he does, but only if people come to him. I keep an eye on that. The first guy they chose, he got ambitious. I went back to the Russians. They yanked him, put another boy in. He keeps a low profile. I got control of that. It sucks. Saw my Mom hooked to that shit, do not like it anywhere near me. And the Russian mob is fuckin' crazy. But they get me, they know my boundaries, they keep their shit on the other side and it's the only way that works for me. I do not get a cut of that because I don't want it. They do not sell to my girls. They do not sell to my staff. One of them approaches their dealer, they report it to me and that person is gone. The only thing I get from that is a club free of that bullshit except what I control."

Okay, all right.

Right.

"The girls come to you?" I asked cautiously.

"Yeah, believe it or not, some bitches get off on that shit. But not all of them, Anya. Most of them get in a situation where they need money. I am not a benefactor. Life leads them to that shit. I offer administration, vetting and protection. They gotta do it, they do it safe. That profession, babe, oldest in the world and it is never gonna die. You think it's right or wrong, life led me to my code. That business is not legal and it fuckin' should be. Women on the streets, they got nothin' unless they're really fuckin' lucky and they got a man who looks after them, keeps 'em safe and doesn't expect freebies. That is rare. The only one I have ever known is me."

"So you don't take freebies?" I whispered, and his face got hard. The room filled with his vibrating heat, and I again whispered, this time quickly, "You don't take freebies."

"Me or any of my boys. They got a taste, they pay. My girls do not give that for free. And I have never stuck my cock in one of them. Not one. They do not walk the streets. They did for Nair. They do not for me. Exclusively clients. And they do not get paid twenty dollars a blowjob. They get paid what they should for givin' that up to some asshole who gets off gettin' it. I get my cut for keepin' 'em safe and dealin' with hassle. Our first date, babe, the first day you spent with me, had a girl, too sweet for the fuckin' business, too weak. Took it up the ass. *Twice.* Two different visits from this guy. She did not want that shit. She did not get paid for that shit. *I* did not get paid for providin' that shit. And he did not say he wanted that shit. First time she took him, she didn't report it. Second time, she called Rhashan and Rhash called me. Dude got a visit. He's no longer on the client list and it was me, personally, who broke his cheekbone and his arm, so if he thinks he can go to another shop and pull that shit, he'll think again."

I held his eyes.

Then I asked quietly, "What did Nick do for you?"

"Nick was supposed to be my eyes and ears in the club. He watched the Russian dealer. He made certain no one but who I knew worked my club. No bitches not in my stable. No dealers. If he got a whiff that some outfit was casin', lookin' to take over territory, however they might do that, he reported it to me and we put a stop to it before they got any ideas or had enough time to assess my organization and find a weakness. He kept an eye on my staff. Bartenders skimmin' off the top, waitresses pullin' bullshit moves, he reported it or, if it was piddly shit, dealt with it. You know my problems with him. What you don't know is he did that shit and I paid him at the same time he played the big man. Sittin' in his VIP section, suckin' back Hennessy Paradis on me. That shit is not cheap. Took his eyes off the ball frequently in order to play big shot and get himself some pussy. And he was the Russian dealer's biggest client. Blow. Staff, unacceptable. Family, he made me eat that shit. The shit with you, babe, last straw. But even before that, had that shit in my life with my Mom a junkie. And the world as it is, I gotta deal with the Russians when I would definitely rather not deal with those fuckin' lunatics. I do not need my brother in that shit. And I didn't want it in my house. I talked to him, he didn't hear me. I told him that shit was not in my condo, he didn't listen to me. He fucked with you, I was done."

"Do your parents know that Nick——?"

Knight interrupted me.

"I shield them from Nick's bullshit, but other than that, my parents know everything, Anya. I told you I had a good life and except for daily headaches like everyone's got with work and shit, I do. And when I say everything, I mean everything. Way they met, Carl needin' to clean her shit up, they are not Ozzie and Harriet. They know I got girls. They know it's not only this club, the real estate I own, but also that business that set their asses up in their house in Hawaii and lets them live a good life. You might think it's whacked, but with my life, my family, it isn't. They're proud of me, they believe in what I do and they don't hesitate to say that shit to me."

I pulled in a deep breath and Knight watched me do it.

Then I shared, "I'm scared of buildings falling on me when I'm in underground parking lots."

At my words, the entirety of his powerful frame jerked.

Then he asked, "What?"

"I know it's irrational, but it's true. Shit happens. My parents got murdered during a carjacking. So I know. Some architect makes an error with his compass or... whatever, *crash*. The building collapses on top of me."

"Anya—" he whispered.

"And," I went on, cutting him off, "I'm scared of elevators. I get in them and unless I can focus on something else, all I can think is that they'll plummet me to my death. I never took the elevator in my building. You live on the fifteenth floor. I'm in okay shape but that, uh... no."

Knight was silent a moment then he asked softly, "Baby, why are you tellin' this shit to me?"

"Because you just told me all your secrets. I thought I should return the favor."

At my words, instantly, his head dropped to contemplate his boots, but I knew he wasn't seeing his boots because I saw his eyes close on the way down.

"Knight?"

His head shot up and he growled, "Here."

I went there and two feet away, his hands shot out, his fingers curled tight into my hips and he yanked me to him, his arms closing around me. One of his arms stayed super tight around my waist, plastering my body to his while the other hand drifted up and tangled in my hair.

His eyes holding mine captive, he whispered, "You cool with this shit?"

"It's a shock, I will admit. But you told me if I hear shit, I should come to you and you'd explain. You explained and you did it thoroughly. But bottom line, I'm the woman for you, Knight. I was made for you, just as I am. What you don't get is, you're the man for me just as you are. I get that, honey. And I got it a while ago."

I got out the "go" in "ago" but just barely before his hand in my hair tilted my head one way, his slanted the other and his mouth slammed down on mine.

Then he plundered and I held on, like usual, like *always,* enjoying the ride.

He tore his mouth from mine, but slid his lips along my cheek to my ear, holding me close, tight, in a way it felt he'd never let me go and he whispered, "Fuck, I love you."

"I know, sweetheart. I love you, too. And, while we're sharing secrets, you should know that I figured that out when you put the blanket on me."

His head came up and he caught my eyes.

"What?"

"Our first, very long, very weird, very intense date. I fell asleep and woke up and you'd put a blanket on me. Not since my parents died has anyone cared if I might get a chill. Until you. A man who would think about that and do something about it, I knew deep down in a place that made me smile, was the man for me. I didn't get it until, well... just now. But, you know... you should know."

He grinned at me but muttered, "Never throwin' that blanket away."

"You try, I'll wrestle you to the ground."

I felt his body shaking against mine and I smiled at him.

Then my smile faded and I whispered, "One other thing you gotta know, honey, and I'm sorry, but Nick set that up with Drake Nair. He was on the street outside my place. He watched it. He didn't get close to me, but Nair told me Nick spoke to him. And I know by the way Nick was watching me that he was the one to set that up."

I watched Knight pull in a sharp breath then blow out an annoyed sigh.

Then he muttered, "Sorry, baby."

"Me too, but it's done so whatever."

"Not whatever. Puntin' this shit to Carl."

My head tilted and Knight started to run his fingers through my hair as he replied, "Been dealin' with it. Not dealin' with it anymore. Carl knows Nick's fuckin' up this bad, he'll lose his mind. Brace, babe. He'll also strap his ass into a seat in an airliner about five minutes after I share and he'll come to Denver and rip his boy a new asshole."

I blinked.

Knight's lips twitched.

"Just so you know, Carl was muscle for a local big man. Only way he could pry my Mom from her pimp was bein' able to jack him up. Somethin' he did. Carl is a good man but that doesn't mean he's clean. What he is is big, built, and he did and still does take care of himself. Nick has not made a habit of fuckin' up exclusively with me. Carl has a way with gettin' him to get his shit in line. Nick doesn't take Carl's way, the least he'll do is make certain that shit no longer leaks to you and me. And Carl will probably be all kinds of pissed that I kept what I have from them and he'll be loud about it. You're around, don't take that shit in. He'll get in my face, but he'd never hurt a woman or freak her out directly. After he tears me a new one, you happen to be there, swear to Christ, babe, he'll turn to you and offer to get you a beer and give you a foot rub."

I started giggling.

"No joke," Knight told me.

I giggled harder.

Knight watched, smiled and his fingers ran through my hair.

I pressed closer.

His smile died and he said gently, "Okay, baby, you got it all. Now you got my word that's all there is, but it's also all you're gonna get. That shit, the girls, the Russians, it is my business, not my life. *You* are my life. That doesn't leak to it, except what I gotta do to maintain it that takes my time and energy. You are not new best friend to fifty-seven bitches. That does not exist for you. Rhash, he's tight and gettin' tighter with Vivica. He wanted no secrets, nothin' between them. But you should know, he laid down that law with her too. Business is business, home is home, life is life. The first, you and Viv don't have shit to do with, both of you are only the last two. You gotta share with her you know, so she knows she doesn't have to worry that she's keepin' somethin' important from her girl, you two talk. Once that's done and outside of that, babe, we live quiet. You with me?"

I nodded.

His eyes roamed my face.

Then he whispered, "You're with me."

"Always, Knight."

His gaze came to mine.

"Fuck me," he whispered. "Fuck me," he repeated, then warmth washed over his face and he said it again. "Fuck me."

He said that when I did something that moved him (and, of course, other times).

And that's when I got it. For Knight, my sweet never went sour.

And that meant everything to him.

So I knew then I was giving him everything, just the same as he was giving me.

And that meant everything to me.

So I pressed into him, my arms around him got tight, my head tilted back further and I smiled at my man.

Epilogue
The Real Ones

I felt Knight's hand slide lightly between my legs.

"Wake up, baby," he whispered in my ear and my eyes drifted open.

He'd called before I went to sleep and told me what he wanted me to wear to bed (my red nightie with the black lace and, as usual, nothing else) and not to pull the covers over me.

So I didn't.

I was lying mostly on my belly, my top leg hitched high, my bottom leg slightly crooked. Perfect access, and I knew this when my belly curled at what his hand was doing between my legs.

"I'm awake," I muttered sleepily.

"Good, baby," he whispered, lips still at my ear. "Get up. Position for Daddy. You know how I like it. Facing the headboard. Arms up in the air. Yeah?"

"Yeah, Daddy," I agreed softly and his finger trailed deeper through the wet gathering between my legs.

My eyes closed.

My reward.

His hand drifted away as did his heat at my back.

I shifted up. Getting on my knees, sliding them wide, I slowly lifted my arms up into the air.

I felt Knight move in behind me. His hands glided on the silk of my nightie, all over it, and that felt lovely. His lips came to my neck and worked there. That felt better. Then his fingers curled into the deep lace edge at the bottom of the nightie and he slowly pulled it up my body. His mouth left my neck, the nightie cleared my hands and was gone.

"Right, baby," his lips were back at my ear, "hold onto the headboard. Keep your hands there. Don't move them. And you can talk if you want. Okay?"

"Okay, Daddy."

"Okay," he whispered in my ear then his tongue trailed down my neck as I dropped my arms and grabbed onto the headboard.

His hands came back to me, moving, gliding, sliding, over my ribs, belly, hips, down the outside of my thighs, up the insides. A barely-there touch between my legs. Lips and tongue at my neck, my shoulder. Hands drifting up my sides, over the curve of my armpits, down my arms then back.

I trembled and held on as his light, loving touch melted through me.

More gliding, sliding then one hand went south, one hand curled around my breast.

Yes.

"Does my baby want her Daddy to play with her?"

"Yes," I breathed, quivering, waiting, wanting to strain against his hands that were cupping me warm but not giving me anything.

"You can move, Anya. I wanna feel you get excited," he whispered in my neck.

I was already excited.

But.

Goodie.

Knight played. I moved, moaned, whimpered, strained, rubbed, rolled.

Oh God. Fantastic.

When I could take no more, my head fell back, hitting his shoulder and my neck twisted.

Pressing my forehead into his neck, I begged, "I need you, honey."

"Arch your back, tip your ass and take me."

I obeyed immediately.

Knight's cock surged inside.

My head flew back and I moaned.

"Fuck, my baby likes my cock," he growled, one hand still at my breast, rolling and tugging my nipple. His other hand still between my legs, finger working my clit and he was right-*ish,* but I didn't like his cock. I *loved* it *and* all of him. "Move, Anya, meet me. Fuck me while I fuck my baby."

I did, hard. Slamming back into him as he thrust into me.

"My baby likes it rough. Love that, love it when she fucks herself hard," he grunted.

Oh yeah, I loved it, too.

"Christ, this cunt, *my* cunt, so fucking sweet."

Oh God. I loved *that* too.

I moved faster, harder.

His fingers at my nipple tugged sharper, his finger at my clit pressed and rolled deeper. My whimpers came faster, more desperate.

"Give that to me," he growled in my neck. My back arched further, my ass tipped up higher, my head pressed into his shoulder and I came on a low moan. "Fuck yeah. Keep givin' that to me, baby," he groaned, and his hands and cock kept at me so I had no choice but to comply.

When I was whimpering so much it was a keen, every inch of my skin oversensitive, Knight stopped manipulating my nipple and his hand cupped my breast. His finger at my clit stopped pressing and rolling and his hand slid deep, fingers separating around our connection, cupping me. He kept driving into me until both hands tensed, fingers digging deep and I felt and listened to him find it.

As he came down he took me gently, then slid in full and both his arms moved to wrap around me, one at my belly, one under my breasts.

"Love you, baby," he murmured against my skin.

"Love you too, Knight," I murmured back.

"Stay there, don't move. I'll be back. Gonna clean you up."

"Okay, sweetheart," I whispered.

Gently, he slid out, his hands drifting across my skin in a light caress as his arms left me. I felt the bed move as he got out of it. I saw dim light, heard the faucet in the bathroom. Then I felt the bed move as he came back. He wrapped an arm around my belly then glided a warm cloth between my legs and my hips jerked.

"Sensitive?" he whispered.

"Yeah," I answered.

"Like it like that," he muttered.

I did too.

He kissed my shoulder and the cloth went away. "Don't move."

"Okay."

He left the bed again to take the cloth back to the bathroom, but wasn't gone long before I felt him enter it again at his side.

Then he ordered, "Climb on me, Anya."

I shifted to him immediately. He had his back to the headboard, legs straight, so I threw one over his hips to straddle him. His arms closed around me, pulling me to him. His knees cocked and I felt his thighs against my bottom, his big, powerful, hard, warm body lightly and openly cocooning me.

Now *that*. *That* I loved.

I settled my weight into him, cheek to his collarbone, forehead to his neck. His hands drifted, sweet, light, beautiful on my skin. Fingers gliding through my hair making it slide along my back adding to the caress.

I melted into him, giving him more of my weight. We did this and we did it often. I totally loved it. It was supremely comfortable. It made me feel safe, precious, treasured. I could sleep like this, and I knew that as a fact since I'd fallen asleep against him when we did this more than once.

"You dream?" he muttered.

"No," I answered.

He drew in a slow breath then let it out.

They were gone, my dreams. The good ones, the bad. My sleep was dreamless, completely. It felt bizarre not having them, but I didn't miss them.

Knight had been right. It took some time, but talking them through, living our life, I let them go and they left me.

"Know it's late, Anya, but we got somethin' to talk about," he said quietly.

I pressed my lips together and tried not to tense.

We did. I just didn't know I'd given that away. I thought I'd been hiding it.

But Knight noticed everything.

One of his arms closing around me, he angled to the side, taking me with him, and the light came on. I blinked in the sudden bright and then focused on his hand at the nightstand, fingers curled around, his thumb flipping up the top of a small, square, expensive-looking box.

Then he pulled out what was inside as I held my breath. I stayed completely still and watched as his hand came back, lifted mine from his chest and somehow he managed to position and slide the ring on my finger.

It was a band, thick gold at top and bottom, the middle inlaid all around with sparkling, perfect, not-small-by-a-long-shot diamonds.

I stared.

His fingers curled around my hand then brought it back to his chest and pressed it flat.

Oh my God. Oh my *God*.

His arm that never left my back got super tight.

"Not what you're thinkin'," he said gently. "You know how I feel about that shit."

I blinked, rapidly, but my eyelids were the only thing that moved.

I knew. I did. He explained it to me ages ago.

We'd now been together, starting from when we met, closing on two years. We met in February. It was November the year following. After I (officially) moved in that August, he gave us a couple of months. Then, in bed, the first time we cuddled like this after he made love to me, he explained he was not only not into labels, but also not into traditional rituals. This included things like Thanksgiving and Christmas.

It also included things like marriage.

He told me he was committed to me but he'd never marry me. I was his, he was mine, we were together and we always would be, but "the government knows who I'm fuckin', everybody else can stay outta my fuckin' business."

I didn't agree with this. I was Catholic, though I didn't attend church very often (as in never since my parents died; my religious education something else my aunt never saw to). Still, I did when they were alive and I kept that part of them with me. I was lax with it in a variety of ways, but it didn't mean it wasn't important.

I was also a girl who wanted her day.

We discussed it and he didn't make me yield. We went to Vivica and Rhashan's for Thanksgiving dinner, though Knight left to go to work. He let me have a Christmas tree, but no Christmas music, cookies or other decorations. He did give me a gift, only one, but since it was a pair of ruby and diamond earrings that were exquisite, I didn't quibble. But he didn't stuff a stocking for me and made it clear he did not want me to give him one so I didn't. We spent time together that day. I made a nice dinner, we made love, we cuddled and watched movies, but we did none of the traditional things that day except exchange presents (I got him more than one, obviously, since it was my holiday and I liked to spoil my man as much as he liked to spoil me).

But this was as far as Knight was prepared to give in.

Marriage was not going to happen.

Although this was a disappointment, I knew it wasn't him preserving an out.

This was it, him and me. He loved me. He was committed to me. He wanted to spend the rest of his life with me and intended to do it.

I felt the same.

Kristen Ashley

So I gave in. It wasn't a hardship. I had Knight, and truthfully, I didn't need a piece of paper.

So, right then, I didn't get the ring.

Knight, as ever, explained.

On an arm squeeze and another one at my hand where he'd just slid what had to be a crazy expensive ring, he whispered, "You've been quiet."

Shit, I had. Damn.

"And I gave you that, baby, lettin' you work it out. I waited for you to talk to me. You didn't. But I know, Rhashan puttin' his ring on Viv's finger and her bein' all about her wedding plans, you're seein' what you're not getting."

He was wrong. I wasn't quiet because of that. I was quiet because of something else. I was over the moon that Rhashan asked Viv to marry him three months ago.

Knight kept talking.

"So, I gotta give you something. It's for you *and* for me. For me bein', that ring, no one will mistake it, you're mine. Wherever you go, with me or without me, they'll see. It makes that statement and I like that. For you, you get a little of what you want. With this," his thumb moved over the gold and diamonds now at the base of my left ring finger, "I'll give you a party. You wanna buy a beautiful dress, do it. You want it to be ivory, buy it. Sit down dinner, champagne, celebration, whoever you wanna invite. But I'm not cutting cake. No dancing. No fuckin' speeches. Just a celebration. You wanna have an anniversary, I'll spoil you, give you a gift that shows you what you mean to me, take you out to dinner and we'll do it every year on the night we met."

Oh. Wow. That wasn't everything, but it was unbelievably sweet.

And I'd take it. Definitely.

He wasn't done.

"It means somethin' to you, you get it for me, I'll wear your symbol. Whatever you want. Including a band on my finger so everyone can see I'm yours."

"I want that," I whispered immediately, his arm got tight and his body shook with a short chuckle.

His voice shook with it too when he muttered, "How did I know that?"

I stared at his hand around mine and my beautiful ring.

Then I told him, "I want the party, too."

He pulled me up. I lifted my head and his eyes came to mine, but he didn't move his hand pressing mine against the solid heat of his chest.

Then he said gently, "Plan it. Whatever you want, flowers, food. Wherever you want, I'll give it to you. No big dress that looks like a cake. This is just a party, but it's a party that celebrates you and me."

I stared into his vivid, blue eyes twisting my hand at his chest so my fingers curled around his.

Then I whispered, "Okay, Knight."

He stared into my eyes that were getting wet.

"You know I don't like tears, baby," he whispered.

I sucked in a breath through my nose and held his hand tightly. He watched me do this and waited until I got control.

When I did, he muttered, "Good." Then, "You like the ring?"

"It's the most beautiful thing I've ever seen outside of you."

His eyes flashed as his head gave a short jerk.

Then he whispered, "Fuck me."

I knew what that meant and felt my lips quirk.

Then I whispered back, "Thank you."

His arm slid up my back and got tight in a way my face had to move forward, even as his hand crushed mine in his.

"I love you, Anya," he growled fiercely, so low, deep and rumbling I felt it through my body. "You know that, babe."

"I do, honey," I whispered, clutching his hand, and I felt my nose sting again.

"No tears," he ordered.

I pressed my lips together, took another breath in through my nose and nodded.

His arm and hand relaxed.

"Now, sleep."

I nodded again.

He turned out the light and settled us, Knight on his back, me pressed to his side, his hand still holding mine against his chest.

Okay, that was beautiful.

Okay, that was *amazing*.

Okay, I loved this man.

But I had a secret. A secret I was worried would not please him. A secret that pleased me greatly but I was worried it would make him angry.

And he knew I had a secret. He sensed it. He'd guessed at what was bothering me.

But he was very, very wrong.

And after he gave that to me, with all that he'd given me, I had to find a way to share my secret.

I just didn't know how.

The thin, high heels of my ludicrously expensive sandals clicked on the floors of our apartment as I moved through the L-shaped hall toward the living room-kitchen area.

I had my phone to my ear.

"She's working my last nerve," Vivica declared. "Are you fuckin' coming?"

After a brief respite, Sandrine went on the prowl again. Then we had another brief respite after she hooked herself a handsome, built, wealthy jerk. They got engaged within a month and married two months later in an extravaganza that she threw together in a frightening display of "I'm a princess, all bow to me" that cost her father a fortune, and nearly Vivica's friendship. Against Knight's advice, I forged in and held my posse together by the skin of our teeth. But her behavior definitely lost her any of the dregs of what was left of the respect she had from Knight and Rhashan. They both put up with her for Viv and me and that was as far as it went.

Now they were getting a divorce and she was on the prowl again. Since she and her husband separated two months ago, she'd met and discarded two "loves of her life" both holding this title for less than a week.

She was looking for number three.

Her hunting ground wasn't normally Slade or other clubs. At twenty-nine, even Sandrine knew she was beyond that. She mostly hunted high-brow charity functions, dragging, on occasion, Vivica (who was now at a different hotel with no "assistant" in her manager title and a huge pay hike) or more frequently, me along with her.

But she wasn't averse to hitting the scene.

She also wasn't averse to getting her groove on, getting hammered and doing stupid stuff.

Like, obviously, she was doing now.

I moved into the kitchen.

"I'm about to leave. I'll be there in fifteen."

"Move your ass, girl, or Knight will be activating the cleanup crew to mop up blood after a very messy homicide," Viv replied and I grinned.

"Gotcha. There in fifteen."

"Later."

"Later."

I disconnected and shoved my phone in my red clutch. It was one of fifteen clutches I owned, seven of these being red. My dress was also red and it was one of about fifty that I owned, around thirty-five of those being red.

This wardrobe enhancement was because I liked to be around Knight, and our schedules, me at the spa during the day, him at the club at night, except for Sundays, meant we didn't have a lot of time together.

So I often went to Slade.

I did not know any of his "girls", but I did suspect, from some looks, some comments (not overt but thoughtful and respectful) that a number of them came to my spa. When I cottoned onto this, they shocked me. They weren't exactly what I would think of as professional, classy call girls. They also weren't skanks. They just looked like, well... women.

But I did know most of his waitresses and bartenders. There was a heavy turnover of both so there was always a new one, and all of his bouncers and security. Those didn't turn over. Knight was selective. He trained them carefully, treated them right. They respected him, he returned the favor, paid well and they stuck.

So I had Knight on occasion, his staff and often Vivica, Sandrine (unfortunately, these days) or one or several of my other friends would show and keep me company.

I also had my own, small VIP section. The last time Knight gutted the club, he'd had it built for me. It was higher than the others and could accommodate around ten people. It was fit for comfort, had some cool-as-heck screening that provided some privacy though you could shift to see whatever you wanted to see, but it was also positioned so, from his window, Knight could see me.

When at Slade, I hung in Knight's office or in my section with myself, his staff or my friends.

I was never bored.

I usually showed around ten, left around twelve thirty. I didn't see a lot of Knight, but I saw him and I knew he also saw me.

And I knew, even though he never told me, he liked to see me.

So I often went to Slade.

I was about to make a move to the front door when something caught my eye.

A flash of bright red.

I knew Viv needed me but still, I took a moment and surveyed the space.

Although there was nothing wrong with them, I got rid of Knight's counter appliances and replaced them with the same but in red. On the end of the bar delineating the kitchen from the living room there was a tall, slender, red vase that widened at the top that we paid a florist to come once a week and fill. She also filled the squat, magenta, cylindrical vase that sat on the chest at the upper landing by the wall in the living room. And, at Knight's demand, every week there were new flowers arranged in the two round, black vases in our bedroom, one on the coffee table in the seating area, a smaller one on my nightstand.

These were always, exclusively, perfect ivory roses.

Also Knight's demand.

I'd kept the rug in the sunken living room but got rid of the streamlined, leather couches that did not invite lounging or, well, *anything*. Now they were black, slouchy suede couches that practically begged you to kick your shoes off and relax. They were covered with different size toss pillows in magenta, aubergine and dark gray.

I'd also gotten rid of the print that didn't do anything for me. Getting what Knight called a "wild hair", I'd hired a professional photographer to come when Knight's parents were in town. I invited my posse, Knight invited nobody and we had a party while the photographer took photos. Now on that wall was a custom-made mess of interlocking, multi-shaped and sized black frames with ivory matting and black and white candid photos of family and friends.

Now *that* made me feel something.

And the black bowls on the chest were gone. Even though the wall above it was filled with photos, along the top off the vase of flowers, the chest was filled with more.

And those were just Knight, me or us together. Color and black and white, in Slade, at Thanksgiving at Rhashan and Vivica's, at my spa, at Sandrine's crazy wedding, in our apartment, dozens of silver framed photos sitting on the chest, jumbled. You had to get close really to see any of them. But I loved them. Mostly because Knight loved them, too. So much he got into it, and not often, but it happened, I'd be sitting on the balcony or at a stool at the bar, I'd turn my head and see he was taking a picture of me.

I returned the favor.

I loved the photos someone else took of us together.

The photos we took of each other were a close second.

It wasn't much (though it all cost a fortune), but it made Knight's apartment our home. It didn't look like a museum. It felt like a place where people lived happily. Something which was true.

Even though, it still was kickass.

I grinned to myself and walked out of the kitchen, switching off lights on my way. I went to the hall closet, got my sleek, black, to-the hip evening trench with the soft sheen and shrugged it on.

Then I walked to the door and stopped at the narrow table I'd put there that had a big, oval bowl on it where we tossed our keys. I grabbed my keys and looked up.

Then, as it always did when I saw it, pure joy slid through me.

Knight's only addition to making our house a home, outside my ivory roses in the bedroom, was what was mounted on the wall above that table. It was hanging there, I knew, though he did not say, so we would see it every time we came home and dumped our keys there and every time we left.

When I moved in, he'd found the faulty cell phone I never got around to throwing out, probably because it meant something to me. Then he'd had it mounted between two sheets of square glass framed in a black frame.

The frame and mounting was awesome.

The cell phone wasn't that attractive.

I adored it.

Adored it.

My eyes dropped to the sparkling band glittering on my finger that Knight slid there last night.

I smiled huge.

Then I walked out, took the elevator down to the garage, walked to my shiny Mercedes and got in. I buckled up, pulled out my phone, started my car and drove out.

When I hit the street, I grabbed my phone and found Knight.

Two rings then, "Babe."

"I'm in my car on the way."

"Right. See you soon."

"Okay, honey."

Disconnect.

I drove to the club and slid in behind Knight's Aston Martin.

The sign on the wall in the alley by my car said, *Space Restricted—Ms. Gage*

It hit me then that Knight was never going to give me his name. But, in doing so, I'd never lose the one my mother and father gave me. All I had left of them except memories would always be with me.

And when it hit me, it hit me sweet.

I bit my smiling lip, got out and Kurt was there.

"Hey, honey," I greeted, moving out of the door he moved toward to close.

"Yo," he grunted.

I again bit my smiling lip.

Kurt. Seriously. He said practically nothing. Still, I found him hilariously funny.

He put a hand light on the small of my back and guided me to the back-door.

We walked through and I headed to the door of the stairs leading to Knight's office. I felt Kurt's presence leave without a word. As was Kurt's way, the job was done, he moved on. He liked me, this I knew because Knight told me not because Kurt showed me.

Hernando, the security guy at Knight's door, smiled at me as he opened it.

"Hey, Anya."

"Hey, Hern," I muttered, rolled up on my toes and touched my lips to his cheek. I rolled back and caught his eye. "Is Knight up there?"

"Yup."

Goodie.

I grinned at Hern, walked through the door and started up the steps.

The club sounds muted as the door closed behind me and my happy mood suddenly slid clean out of me.

Knight was up there. His ring was on my finger. The wide, brushed gold band I'd gone out that day to buy him was in my bag.

And I had to tell him my secret. Time was sliding by. He'd done something beautiful for me and would expect me to snap out of the quiet, reflective mood I'd been in and if I didn't, he'd wonder. Then he'd get impatient when I didn't share.

I needed to share.

I stood outside his door with my hand on the knob, my eyes to my hand.

I had to do this now.

Face his anger, discuss and, God, *God,* maybe yield.

I turned the knob and walked in.

He was standing at his window wearing a dark suit and a wine red shirt. Both looked great on him as usual, and the instant I walked in, his eyes cut to me.

"Gotta do somethin' about that bitch."

Damn.

God, *Sandrine.*

I heard the door close behind me as I took a few steps in and stopped.

"What's she doing now?" I asked.

"Pissin' me off."

Oh boy.

"Knight—"

"Have words with her, Anya."

I drew in breath and nodded.

"When you go down, I'll call Kurt. You, Viv and Kurt get her ass in a taxi. It takes her home and she goes out again, that's on her. She comes back here, babe, she drinks easy and she doesn't piss me off. She's got one more shot. Then she's not in my club again."

"Okay," I agreed.

He studied me.

Kristen Ashley

"Been two hours, babe," he declared, this being the amount of time we'd been apart and I knew he was not happy I was standing across the room and not close, giving him a kiss.

"Do you remember the flu I had a few of months ago?" I blurted.

His head jerked and his eyes narrowed. I understood this. What I'd blurted made no sense. Also, he wanted me close and he wanted my kiss. I never denied this. Ever. Because I wanted both, too. And he also very rarely had to ask for it since I very usually just gave it to him.

"What?" he asked.

"Remember that flu that knocked me for a loop a few of months ago? You know, when I was in bed for forever and—?"

"I remember."

I pressed my lips together and rolled them.

"Anya—"

"I was so sick, I missed taking my birth control pills," I whispered.

His body went visibly solid.

Oh boy.

Okay, all right.

Right.

"I told you," I kept whispering. "And we used condoms for a while. One, um… must have broken or, uh… something…"

I trailed off.

Knight didn't move, his eyes burning into me, his face impassive.

Not a good sign.

I kept whispering, my eyes glued to him. "I'm pregnant."

He moved not a muscle and said not a word, and he did this for a long time.

Even I could barely hear my voice when I said quietly, "I want to keep it, Knight. And I want that badly."

Knight gave me nothing.

I wanted to close my eyes, cry, beg.

I wanted this baby. His baby. I wasn't expecting it. We'd never discussed children.

But I wanted it.

Like I said…

Badly.

"I think I've known for a while," I shared quietly and carefully. "But I took a home pregnancy test um… a bit ago. Then to confirm I went to the doctor Monday. I'm ten weeks."

Knight didn't move.

"Honey." My voice was shaking.

That was when he moved, but not to me. Nor did he say anything. He lifted his hand, shoved it inside his jacket and pulled out his phone, all the while his eyes on me.

My heart started beating as my stomach clenched. I didn't know what this meant, but it terrified me.

His eyes dropped to his phone as he hit buttons but they came back and pinned me to the spot when he put the phone to his ear.

I stood still, my eyes held captive by his and I waited.

"Hey, yeah, Knight," he said into the phone and I tried not to hyperventilate. "Got news. Anya's pregnant. Ten weeks."

I blinked and when I was done, his eyes were still on me.

"Fuck, Mom, I know it's great fuckin' news but stop screamin'." Pause then, "Fuck, give the phone to Dad."

My eyes filled with tears and there was no way I could control them. They spilled right over.

He didn't take his phone from his ear when he ordered low and slow, "Babe, get… over… *here*."

Tossing my clutch across the room to the couch, I flew to him, my body colliding with his, my arms wrapping around tight and his arm did the same, holding me close.

I felt his lips at the top of my hair and then, "Dad? Yeah. Yeah, she isn't lyin'. Anya's carrying my baby. Ten weeks." Pause then, "No. Unexpected. She got sick a while back, flu, missed some pills." Pause then on a squeeze of his arm in a gentle, soft voice, "No, Dad. It's good. We're happy."

It's good.

We're happy.

He talked more but I didn't hear much, mainly because my body was bucking against his due to my sobbing.

He said his good-byes, shifted me so he could pry me away from his frame and put his phone back in his pocket then both his arms wound tight around me.

271

"Babe, eyes," he ordered gently and I tipped back my head. His eyes moved over my face then caught mine. "You didn't want a ring. You wanted my baby," he whispered.

"Yes," I whispered back.

"Mom's fuckin' beside herself," he shared, something I guessed.

I'd met his parents, three times.

They'd been to Denver twice. The second time for a nice visit. The first time Carl came out with Knight's Mom to deal with Nick.

Nick now lived in Hawaii with Carl riding his ass. He was clean of blow, Carl's first order of business. But he was still "dicking around" (Knight's words). Though, "At least it gives Dad somethin' to do. He doesn't golf. He doesn't surf. He doesn't garden. He cracks heads. He was goin' crazy. Now he's got a head to crack," (also Knight's words).

We'd also gone out to see them. When we did, we saw Nick. To me, he'd changed. He was far less of an asshole and he'd actually found a quiet moment, just him and me, to apologize and, I thought, do it sincerely. Knight warned me not to be fooled. He explained Nick could get contrite then Nick could turn back into an asshole. Luckily, while we were there, he didn't slide back into the asshole.

And, it should be noted that although Nick took the time to apologize to me, he didn't take the time to apologize to his brother. Something I didn't like all that much. Something Knight took in stride. Therefore something that clearly had happened before, repeatedly. This an assumption I'd made that Knight had confirmed when I asked him.

I tried to smile through my tears and replied, "Good."

"Dad's pleased." He kept sharing.

"Good," I repeated on a hitched breath.

His arms left me so his hands could cup my jaw, his thumbs sliding through the wet on my cheeks and he ordered softly, "Baby, quit crying."

I drew in a shaky breath. This didn't work so I drew in another one.

On the fourth, I got it together.

"That's it," he muttered, his thumbs still moving through the wet.

I held onto him and held his eyes.

"You're carrying my baby," he whispered.

"Yeah," I confirmed.

"You're carrying my baby," he repeated, his voice lower, gruff, thick.

I felt my nostrils quiver, but I held it together and nodded.

His forehead dropped to mine. His nose slid along mine, but his hands never left my face and I held my breath as he whispered with feeling, "Fuck me, fuck me, fuck *me*."

Slowly, I closed my eyes.

He wanted this, my man. He wanted me to have his baby.

I opened my eyes.

"You're happy?" I guessed, my voice quiet, but the words were still pitched high with hope.

"Fuck, baby, yeah. Fuck yeah. You got my baby in you."

"I was worried you'd be angry," I admitted, and his face went away just an inch.

"I get that. We haven't discussed it. Though, sayin' that, been thinkin' for a while about talkin' to you about it. Puttin' that ring on your finger reminded me I needed to get to that. Fate jumped the gun. I'm not complaining."

God, God, *God*.

I loved this man.

"So you want kids?" I ventured, even though the answer was obvious.

Still, it was good I asked because he smiled, and I loved to watch Knight smile.

"Absolutely."

"How many?"

"Two," he said immediately.

"Boys or girls?"

"Boys," he said again immediately, and I blinked.

"Really?"

"Babe, my life, girls?" He shook his head and kept shaking it when he went on, "Your beauty, even a little of it, you give that to our baby?" He stopped shaking his head and his fingers gave me a gentle squeeze. "Fuck no. I'll need to buy more guns *and* hire more men."

I giggled.

"Make me boys," he ordered.

I giggled again.

Then I pointed out the obvious, "Not sure I can yield on that, sweetheart. Think that's up to destiny."

His mouth came to mine and he continued being bossy.

"Do the best you can do."

"Okay, Knight."

"All right, baby."

God, God, *God.*

I *loved* this man.

After having that joyous thought, I got serious but did it quietly.

"Honey, you need to quit smoking."

He held my eyes and instantly agreed, "Yeah."

I relaxed deeper into him.

"You're forgetting something," he whispered against my lips.

"What?" I whispered against his, looking in his beautiful eyes.

"Babe, kiss me."

I grinned against his mouth.

Then I pressed tight in a variety of places and I kissed him.

His hands left my jaw so his arms could cage me in close, tight, safe and warm, and then my Knight kissed me.

I stood with just my head out the door to the balcony that led from the nursery and, adjusting the telephoto lens, I took the shot. Then another. Then another.

I pulled back. Moving my thumbs over the buttons, I checked the screen at the back of the camera.

Then I smiled.

I got it.

I carefully closed the door without a sound, walked into the room, put the camera on the dresser and walked out.

Then I walked to the kitchen and retrieved my mug of herbal tea.

After that, I moved to the glass doors to the balcony, skirting the sunken living room.

Knight was out there. He was slouched in a chair, feet up on the railing, ankles crossed, mug of coffee on the table beside him.

I moved through the doors to the empty chair angled toward his and caught the glimmer of sun glinting on the gold band on his finger that was on his hand, which was resting on our baby girl's rounded, diaper-covered booty. She was curled, dimpled knees tucked under her, little fist resting beside her face, asleep on her daddy's Black Sabbath tee-covered chest.

I sat in my chair, holding my cup aloft as I lifted my own legs and carefully positioned them resting over my man's thighs.

Knight trailed a finger light along the skin on the outer side of one of my thighs and tingles radiated out from my skin even as they went up my spine, my neck to cover my scalp. Then he rested his hand curled around the top of my thigh, close to the apex of my legs, the pads of his fingers on my inner thigh.

"Get the shot?" he muttered, eyes to the Range.

Jeez. He noticed everything.

I lifted my mug to my lips.

"Yep."

"Babe, she's a couple weeks old. You keep fillin' the house with frames, we won't be able to move through it."

I took a sip, eyes to the Front Range and staying there, I swallowed and replied, "So, buy us a bigger house."

"That I can do," he murmured instantly.

Yes.

Oh yes.

God, God, *God*.

I loved this man.

I looked to him and got his profile, strong, aggressive, unbelievable male beauty.

I looked to my daughter, my little Ekateirna, baby Kat, and her eyes drifted open and closed. Then they opened, and I knew she probably couldn't, but it looked like she focused on me.

I reached out, stroked her super soft, chubby cheek and grinned into her clear, pure, Prussian blue eyes that I knew in my heart would stay that way.

Then her eyes drifted closed.

I dropped my hand over Knight's on my thigh. His twisted and curled around mine.

My eyes drifted to the Range and I sipped my tea, living a life I never expected, living a dream I never even tried to dream, living it now entirely dream free.

Except, of course, the real ones sitting in the sun, one holding my hand and one sleeping next to me.

The Unfinished Hero Series will continue with the story of **Creed**.

Printed in Great Britain
by Amazon.co.uk, Ltd.,
Marston Gate.